The Reluctant Cyborg

E. M. Denison

The Reluctant Cyborg
Copyright © 2024 by E. M. Denison

First paperback edition May 2024

Cover art by Kassia Mosher
Design by Nick Mosher

ISBN 979-8-9905292-0-5 (paperback)
ISBN 979-8-9905292-1-2 (ebook)

Published by E. M. Denison
emdenison.com

For Uncle Dan who finds neat stuff at the dump.

For Nick, who reads everything I write. All with me, the author, reading over his shoulder and periodically asking how he is enjoying the book I wrote. Which is not at all awkward, I am sure.

And for Mom, who would stop whatever she was doing and read to me.

My ten-year-old drew this charming fellow for my cyborg book. She calls him George. You'll find George throughout the novel, welcoming you to every chapter.

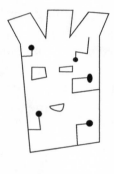

"George"

The Reluctant Cyborg

E. M. Denison

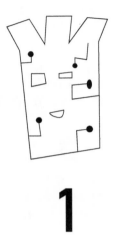

1

Announcement
Year 2182—Ezeny

Ezeny was only standing beside his eleven half brothers for appearance's sake. The other young men were waiting to greet their various mothers after a long separation. Ezeny alone would not be seeing his mother that night. But there he was anyway. Lined up in a greeting queue in the foyer of the family high-rise, flanked by stern servants and rigid with gentlemanly good posture.

He slumped a little and stuffed his hands into the pockets of his cross-collar dress robe. He was supposed to be wearing a starched lace vestee shirt underneath for the auspicious occasion, but such things were itchy, so Ezeny had wadded a ruffly handkerchief under his collar and was secretly going commando. He got a whack on the back of his head.

"Straighten up," hissed a Matron behind him.

He turned, rubbing his head and mouthed 'ow' at her. She frowned and brandished her bamboo whacking fan at him, so he faced forward again and got back to looking responsible. This was silliness. The Emeritus Concubines weren't even there yet to be impressed by their sons' disciplined comportment. He shouldn't have to hold still.

The Matrons had outdone themselves transforming his father's simple announcement into 'an event.' Servants had buffed and polished the marble entryway until the walls gleamed and the floors squeaked, as if guests cared how shiny a room was. A red carpet ran from the revolving glass entry door down the foyer's central aisle to welcome his brothers' mothers to Tower C. The carpet was gilding the lily, Ezeny felt, covering the resplendent flooring in an unnecessary layer of glamour.

He and his half brothers were already hygienic fellows. But this morning the Matrons had soaked them for an hour each and coated them in so much cologne and hair gel that Ezeny smelled like the cleaning supplies closet he hid contraband sweets in as a child. Now that he was nineteen, he had a much better hiding spot that didn't make his stolen cookies smell like pine.

Such a fuss, he thought. *It's only family after all. Well, everyone* else's *family*. But that was uncharitable of him. Ezeny was happy for his half brothers, truly. And once the Concubines had thoroughly greeted and fussed over their sons, they'd want to talk to him too, which would be pleasant.

He considered his father's other Concubines to be his aunts. The *Emeritus* Concubines, anyway. He couldn't think of the ones his own age as aunts. He had no good word for what those women were to him. Certainly not sisters. Ezeny didn't have sisters. The Matrons, guardians of the Phillips family genome, made sure of that.

Outside, the limo pulled up and the footman opened the back. One by one eleven beautiful older women emerged wearing cashmere peignoir robes over a rainbow of calf-length silk wrap dresses. Ezeny didn't understand why a man his father's age considered these women past their prime, but his aunts didn't seem bothered by their retirement, so neither was he.

Cold air rushed through the revolving doors as the Concubines strolled in to greet their sons. Ezeny watched only a little wistfully as each of his half brothers welcomed his mother with fond smiles and a kiss on each cheek. Despite her age, his father still considered Ezeny's own mother beautiful enough to keep for occasional duty across town in Tower A, the family's primary skyscraper. His father would not be parted from any of his Concubines still on the 'active' roster. Not even for a few hours. Not for many years.

Arms in elbows, his half brothers escorted their mothers past the foyer's welcome desk and into the grand banquet hall of the Tower C high-rise. Ezeny followed them alone, eager for his father's announcement to be over so he could eat dinner.

Octagonal columns lined the dining hall. A forgettable sort of jazzy dining music emanated from floating speaker spheres, and a holographic vidwindow hovered at the end of the hall in preparation for his father's announcement. The word 'standby' was projected at the center.

Twenty tables for family, guests, and staff were set with gold-plated utensils, sweating glass goblets of ice water, and unfortunately empty plates. Barren plates. Desolate plates. And flower arrangements at the table centers where the bread baskets ought to be.

Ezeny could smell food cooking, though. Buttery garlic bread, slices of tube protein roasting in various barbeque sauces. His stomach did not rumble, because he'd been snitching food all day. But there was always room for more. Especially since his favorite thing when he felt a little lonesome, was to go pester his favorite cooking maid. The 'event' wasn't scheduled to start for fifteen more minutes. There was still time. He grinned and veered off toward the double doors that led to the kitchen.

Inside, steam rose from bubbling pots. Cooks with aprons tied over tight-fitting gray work robes busied themselves between rows of chrome countertops. Vegetables sizzled in pans. Yren stood in the back, chopping potatoes with a stern expression. He always called her 'Cricket,' just to mess with her.

She'd joined the household staff when they were both ten and they'd become fast friends. Well, friends in the way a dog and a cat were friends. Him with thoughtless enthusiasm. Her with acquiescing tolerance.

She was pale and angular with a rigid backbone, captivatingly reproachful eyebrows, and a prickly personality that Ezeny delighted in poking at. But they'd both turned nineteen that year and he was worried that other men were going to notice that she'd become rather pretty without appreciating how much fun she could be.

He approached her from behind and tapped her shoulder. "My,

3

but your hairnet looks lovely today," he said.

She startled and swatted at him, then turned back to chopping potatoes, this time with a bemused expression. "Sounds like you want something. What is it now?"

He chewed his lip. "I need your help, Cricket. I ate all the sweet buns."

She frowned. "So, you want an antacid?"

"No! I need you to make more! The Matrons will skin me if they find out I ate them all before the party."

"You indulge too much. One of these days I'll stop bailing you out, Ez. Then you'll be sorry. Anyway, I knew you'd do something like this."

She bent and opened a cabinet. She pulled out a second tray piled high with warm, frosted pastries. He grinned at her.

"You are literally the best. But you still may need to make even more." He grabbed the top bun and took a huge bite, locking eyes with her as he chewed. Her eyelid jumped in irritation. Cricket's eyes sparkled when she got an eye tic.

She shook her head. "If you keep gorging yourself, you'll go to fat."

"Life goals!" he said. He winked at her and wheeled to leave the kitchen. He collided with a Matron—a different one than had whacked him with the fan. Matrons seemed to pop up out of nowhere. How *did* they do it?

She frowned at him. "You oughtn't wink at that one. I know you mean nothing untoward, young master, but girls like Yren here tempt young men of good families into traps with their wiles."

He grinned back at Cricket. She stared coldly at the Matron, the fun gone out of her eyes. He noted that Cricket already had a fresh batch of dough out for the more buns he'd requested. *Excellent.*

"What, Cricket? Cricket's not a *girl*, girl. She's just regular people," he said.

Cricket rolled her eyes and punched the dough. A frighteningly hard punch. "I wouldn't have him anyway," said Cricket.

She fancied him, he was pretty sure.

"Careful around her," cautioned the Matron. "She is not a proper lady. There is wantonness in Yren's genetics."

The Matron herded Ezeny from the kitchen back into the dining hall where more of the family had gathered. *Wantonness. Great word.*

Oh, please let there be wantonness. He definitely fancied Cricket.

Someday, Ezeny would have enough seniority to do whatever he pleased. Including taking an improper Concubine, if Cricket would have him. He wasn't *completely* sure she would. It would be a scandal, but so what? Ezeny wasn't known for being respectable.

All he wanted from life was good food, fun parties with lots of people, and the stoic girl who watched the century-old illegal classic movies with him. He liked *Star Wars* and *The Princess Bride*. But his favorite was *The Lion King*. It still made him cry when Simba's dad came back as a glowing cloud lion, and he never remembered a handkerchief.

"For God's sake. How many times have you seen this?" Cricket would say. Then she'd hand him a tissue. *She* never cried, but she brought tissues anyway because *he* always did. That stuff. That was what the good life was made of.

Trays of hors d'oeuvres had made their way to the dining room. Ezeny snagged a bite of land lobster salad on brioche as the Matron dragged him past it toward the seat with his name card. *Ooh,* he thought. *Assigned seating.* This *was* an auspicious occasion.

He scooted his chair up to the table with five of his half brothers. Little Koal, only sixteen, squirmed and tugged at the starched lace of his itchy vestee shirt. Ezeny grimaced in sympathy but reveled in the feeling of his silk robe against his own bare skin. Poor Koal hadn't figured out yet it didn't pay to be dutiful and proper.

Arabel, oldest of the Tower C boys, elbowed Koal and frowned. "Sit up straight. It's starting."

The overhead lights dimmed, and the word 'standby' on the vid-window dissolved into an image of Kanary Phillips. It was a recording as usual. Whatever his father was going to say was important enough to spawn a lavish party here in Tower C, but it wasn't important enough to warrant an actual visit from the family patriarch.

Kanary Phillips was in his late seventies. The 'type specimen of an apex genome,' the Matrons said. They whispered of his 'sexually attractive facial structure,' 'masculine jawline,' and 'genetically desirable butterscotch skin.' They claimed their assessments were scientific, but their observations about his father always icked Ezeny out. To his eyes, Kanary just looked like another old guy.

Kanary was seated behind a desk, smiling warmly, hands folded.

Three beautiful women wearing open jewel-toned kimonos over shimmering sheath dresses surrounded him, each with hands placed lovingly on Kanary's shoulders. They were all about Ezeny's age, the newest Phillips Concubines. The redhead to his father's right was visibly pregnant.

Ezeny felt no emotions when the image of his father popped up on screen. He was *supposed* to feel love and filial devotion. But he'd only met the man a handful of times for a brief handshake.

"My beautiful Tower C boys!" the recording of Ezeny's father said. "Great news! Your time has come to defend Everland against the scourge of McCreedia."

Wait, what? The war? Ezeny was confused. Wealthy boys from the high-rises didn't join the war. He frowned. This sounded like work.

"That's right! Our brave Everland soldiers have got the McCreedian dogs on their heels. Our City State is poised to win the war of McCreedian aggression! The Military just needs a teensy few more men to send those devils packing and the Phillips clan will answer."

His father lifted a sword. Ezeny lifted an eyebrow. *Why the heck does he have a sword?* The war was fought with laser guns. *It must be for show,* he decided.

A montage of battle footage rolled. Exciting explosions. Blue, red, and green lasers flashed. A fresh-faced blond soldier hoisted the purple and gold flag of Everland to thunderous applause from his mates.

"And of course, you'll be fighting alongside Everland's great High Warrior heroes."

A hush fell on the table of Ezeny's brothers and spread to the entire assembled Phillips' clan. On the vidwindow, three soldiers dressed in mech battle suits stood, backdropped by the smoking ruin of a McCreedian high-rise.

"The Midnight Demon," Kanary said.

The vidwindow focused on the caped man in black and silver armor. His helmet bore silver lightning bolts on either side. A volley of McCreedian hand grenades rained on Everland soldiers, but the Midnight Demon stretched out a hand and sent the explosives flying back toward the McCreedians, as if by magic—the metal manipulation powers only High Warriors had.

"The Screaming Eagle."

The screen offered a closeup of an armored man in red and blue with shoulders wider than the TorsoMan™ action figures Ezeny had played with as a child. And still did on occasion when no one was looking. The Screaming Eagle leaped onto the lid of a trash can lying amid the war debris and used it to fly into the sky like it was a surfboard.

"And the Ice Dragon."

A warrior in white and silver armor seized the barrel of a McCreedian hover tank and crushed it in his fist like a soda can.

His brothers erupted into applause. They'd all been playing 'High Warrior' since they were kids. Now, here was a chance to join their heroes for real. Ezeny glanced around the room. Most of the servants applauded. His Concubine aunts, however, sat with fake smiles frozen on their faces. Misgivings tripped alarms in Ezeny's brain.

The video image dissolved back to his father.

"Don't let me down, Tower C boys. And don't worry. You won't be alone. Your brothers from Tower B are already at the front, eagerly awaiting you lot. Of course, the Tower A generation won't be going to war. Their responsibilities as my oldest, most important heirs don't afford them the privilege of fighting for Everland's glory. Someone's got to stay home and take care of business. Ha, ha! Not like *you* lucky young men."

He smiled.

"The six- to twelve-year-old crop of strapping Tower D sons is ripening nicely and will join you when they come of age. I can't wait for you to meet them all on the front."

He chuckled and rubbed the red-head's round belly fondly. She covered her smile with a bejeweled hand and blushed.

"And I may as well tell you, because you're family. My new Concubines and I have started generation E already. Scaffolding's going up on the new high-rise as we speak. So. As you see, Family Phillips is strong, growing, and winning glory. You're all part of something great. And I know you'll do me proud, sons. Daddy loves you."

A final montage of war footage rolled. Exciting stuff. The High Warriors performed their mysterious, superpowered battle techniques. Ordinary soldiers cheered.

But then a short clip of battle footage caught Ezeny's eye. Something terrifying in the background. *Corpses?* The sweet buns turned to lead in his stomach. He stood.

"Computer, go back a bit and pause," he said, loud enough for the computer to recognize his voice.

Mumbles rose from the dinner guests. He understood their undercurrent. Freewheeling Ezeny had interrupted his own Father's video announcement. What would that hedonistic knave do next? Let them talk. He didn't care. The computer scanned back until he saw the disturbing image again.

"There!" he told it.

Behind the Screaming Eagle he could make out a pile of bodies in McCreedian Military fatigues. Grey flesh streaked with dried blood. He turned to his family and pointed at the vidwindow.

"That doesn't look good."

Little Koal tried to comfort him. "Those are the *enemy's* troops. Not ours."

"That's not better," Ezeny said. "We'd have to kill *them*."

Arabel rolled his eyes. "That's what war *is*, dork."

"So, the McCreedians will be trying to kill *us* right back? I think this is going to be dangerous," said Ezeny.

"Come off it, Ez. You'll be fine. Soldiers come back all the time," said Arabel.

Rhyne, the kindest of his older brothers, elbowed him and grinned. "Don't worry. I'm sure the Military's got a cooking battalion that makes stews and not war."

"Really?" said Ezeny. "That'd be the one I'd want to join."

Arabel gave him a stern look. "Don't shame the family," he said. "You're ridiculous enough. The Phillips boys are brave. We'll answer father's call for the glory of Everland. And we brothers will be all the closer for having served together."

Ezeny folded his arms. "*If* we all come back…"

"Ez, it was one photo," Rhyne said gently. "You're focusing on the one bad thing. You saw how the war really is right there on the video. It's mostly winning."

Ezeny locked eyes with Cricket, who'd poked her hair-netted head out of the kitchen to watch the announcement. She was wide-eyed and pale. Her lips were drawn into a thin line. Confirmation. His gut reaction was right. This was not glorious. This was bad.

Ezeny couldn't be as sanguine about the war as his half brothers. Over their years of friendship, Cricket had told him stories of life outside the high-rises. The war wasn't going well, or why else would Everland High Command make even wealthy boys fight? *They must be running low on poor men.*

His safety was shattering. His father's money had kept him cushioned from all the things people like Cricket had to face every day. Ezeny liked being cushioned, dammit.

How am I going to fight in a war? He was made for eating and drinking and kissing pretty girls. He was certain of that. His flesh crawled looking at the images of the dead. He didn't know if it would be worse to *be* a corpse or make someone *else* into a corpse. *War presents opportunities for both,* he realized. *Lovely.*

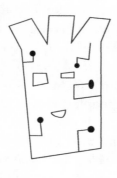

2

The Bit with the Grubs
Yren

Yren paused outside the door to the lounge on the topmost floor of Tower C. Ezeny had rushed off after the announcement without eating, which was unlike him. He'd probably fled there to cry in private, which was also unlike him. Ezeny was a public crier. But usually, it was about a movie, not any actual danger he was facing.

Everything was happening so fast. The Phillips boys would be leaving for the front the following morning. The others were already packing. That night was her only chance to see him. She knew she shouldn't go in. She wanted to be nothing like her mother. If she willingly sat alone with a boy—a master boy no less, she'd only be proving the Matrons right about her. But Ezeny had looked so frightened at dinner. He needed someone. And she supposed she'd have to do.

She turned the knob and entered. All the lights were out. Ezeny stood silhouetted against the night lights of Everland below. In the far distance, the lasers of war flashed. Everland was losing. The front was inching closer. The next day her gentle friend would be over there, fighting. There was a bet going on amongst his relatives who were chatting in the third-floor parlor whether Ezeny would be able to kill someone. Odds heavily favored 'no.' She crept up behind him, quiet, as was her way.

"Ez?"

He startled and hastily wiped his eyes. He faced her with a forced expression of calm, though his warm, brown cheeks still glistened with tears. A cold feeling spread in her chest. Unless Ezeny was watching something sad, he almost always wore his signature, light-a-room smile. Without the smile, his sharp features made him look grave. Almost dangerous. His eyes, usually welcoming and mirthful, were dull and hopeless. Then he recognized her.

"Oh. It's you, Cricket. It's fine for *you* to see me cry. You don't count."

She bristled and folded her arms. He was always saying stuff like that. *'Cricket's not a proper lady. Cricket doesn't count.'* She knew the social gulf between them was too wide, *thank you.*

"I don't *count?*" she snapped.

But then he started crying again. "I don't want to die," he said.

She swallowed hard. He was right to fear. When she'd worked in the factories as a child before the Phillips family bought her, Military recruitment officers would pop in sometimes and pull one of the men away from the assembly lines, screaming. The men they took never returned.

She went to Ezeny and reached a tentative hand toward his shoulder. He enveloped her suddenly like an octopus around a mollusk, waddled them back to the sofa, and collapsed sobbing into her lap. She patted him lightly on the back, too stunned to say anything. She felt like she was holding a gift not meant for her.

He was forever pestering her, treating her like a kid sister, though they were the same age. She was always fixing his messes. But he was her bright spot in a life made dark by Matrons. The friend who sought her company, paid her compliments, and laughed at her jokes. But the following day he would be marching off into the meatgrinder of war and she'd be alone in the world again.

Yren got brave for once. She raised his face from her lap and kissed his forehead. He blinked away tears and smiled, oblivious to what her presence here alone with him could cost her.

One thing had led to another. The forehead kiss had turned into tearful kisses planted all over both faces. Those turned into mouth kisses. The mouth kisses had turned to deeper, longer mouth kisses.

Yren's heart was racing. She knew this would mean little more to Ezeny than a last bit of human comfort before the battlefield. But tonight was her only chance to have him. One taste of her fairytale before he—*no.* She wouldn't even think of it.

The more intense their kisses became, the more the lace ruffle at Ezeny's throat irritated her, so she opened his robe to remove it and found him naked. No underpants even. The 'vestee shirt' had been nothing more than a wadded-up lace handkerchief. He grinned wryly, completely unembarrassed. She quickly covered him. Her ears burned.

"You were going commando at the fancy party all night?" she scolded. "How very like you."

He laughed sheepishly. "Yeah…under normal circumstances, no one would have been the wiser."

She snorted. "You're a goof."

"True…speaking of 'normal circumstances,' what's going on here with you and me?"

She swallowed. Her ears burned hotter. His nakedness played right into the fantasy she'd been building. *This is a bad idea,* she thought. But his bemused expression made him look cute. And the morning would take him away. She was too embarrassed to say aloud what she intended. Wordlessly, she pulled him down. He melted, covering her mouth with happy, enthusiastic kisses.

There were so many stories of this sort of thing happening before a boy marched off to war. Before, Yren had wondered why. It didn't make sense. Why do something with such dire social consequences when the man was likely to die and leave you alone to deal with the fallout? She never thought she'd be so foolish.

It turned out she was no wiser than other people. But it felt right. Like death's opposite, holding Ezeny close and soaking up his still-aliveness. *A lengthy hug might have worked just as well,* she thought. Perhaps there was wantonness in her genetics after all.

But now that she was living her fantasy the real-life sensations were…unexpected. This was uncomfortable in some ways. Slimy and strange.

Ezeny broke off a kiss, panting. "It's wild that we're doing this, Cricket," he said. "You're *wonderful.* How am I doing, eh?"

Yren froze. It was like he'd heard her thoughts. She understood a girl in these circumstances was expected to be complimentary and encouraging. The male ego was especially fragile concerning these situations, and it would be a shame to say anything at all negative to Ezeny tonight.

"Great!" she said, bright and chipper.

He touched the tip of her nose with his own and laughed knowingly. "Yeah right. Listen, I've been told I'm bad at this. But with your continued help, I intend to get better and better when I—I mean *if* I—"

He trailed off, his gaze captured by the distant, flashing lasers. The war loomed in his mind as well. A shiver ran under her skin against the gathering dread. Ezeny shook himself and forced a steady stream of cheerful chatter into the silence.

"For me, this is great, but for you, it's probably just slimy and strange…"

She stifled a snort. *Slimy and strange.* She'd been thinking those exact words. It was uncanny how often Ezeny would jabber aloud the same thought she'd had herself only moments before. It was one of the first things about him that had caught her attention. Only his brain was always, like, ten seconds behind hers.

He continued to chatter, which apparently Ezeny could do in literally any circumstance. It boggled her mind.

"Don't get me wrong," he continued. "It's slimy for me too, but like good slimy, you know? Slimy yet satisfying."

Yren narrowed her eyes. She knew that line. "Oh my God. You're quoting *The Lion King* right now. The bit with the grubs."

He grinned. "I'm so glad it's *you*, Cricket. A proper lady wouldn't appreciate the joke."

Her stomach turned cold. *Proper lady*—which she was not, nor would she ever be. This was not the time to remind her of this. Confirmation that this dalliance was no more than a bit of fun for him. She'd known that was so. But it was only fair for him to maintain the illusion, at least while it was still happening.

"Really?" she snapped. "You might want to cut out that 'proper lady' stuff and at least pretend this means anything to you until it's over." She winced. She had tried not to sound bitter, but she suspected she'd failed.

He stopped and stroked her face. His eyes were suddenly tender, and his sunshine smile spread wide across his face. The smile that made Yren angry when he would say, 'Oh Cricket's not a *girl*, girl.' The smile that made her wish she was a *'girl*, girl' to him.

"Oh, Yren," he said, using her real name for maybe the first time ever. "You keep calling *me* an idiot. All that 'proper lady' stuff I say… it's to throw off the Matrons' suspicions. They'd never let me spend any time with you if they knew how I felt about you. How I've felt about you for a very long time."

He was quiet then. She wrapped her arms back around him and held him tight. Their kisses were long and deep. And for the few more moments it lasted, everything felt much better than slimy and strange.

* * *

After, they dressed in haste lest someone catch them. They sat together on the sofa. Yren leaned her head against his shoulder. Ezeny wrapped his arm around her waist and kissed her head every ten seconds or so. It was sweet and also irritating, which was a very Ezeny combination.

Suddenly he blurted, "I *really* don't want to go now!"

He lay his head in her lap again and resumed crying. The ache returned to her chest. Their dalliance had only been a brief respite from the looming war. Images flashed of Ezeny's lifeless body on a battlefield. *Not him, please.*

"You could run away," she said. "I might even come with you, since I doubt you'd survive alone in the wild."

He shook his head and tucked his chin in shame. "You could never love a coward."

"What rot! It's *known* you're the biggest coward in the compound and I lo—" She stopped herself too late.

A sly smile spread over his face. "I got you Cricket."

Her face flushed. Admitting to feelings first puts you at a disadvantage. And she was already at such a large social disadvantage compared to Ezeny.

"You did not," she said primly.

He folded his hands behind his head and looked smug, proceeding as though they were on equal footing. She usually appreciated his playfulness, but she was starting to panic. Wondering again where she really stood with him.

"You had no chance," he said. "Your mind's usually about ten seconds behind mine."

Words wouldn't come. He was infuriating. It was *his* mind that was always ten seconds behind *hers*. He wrapped her in a hug, pressing her face to his chest.

"Id dosem't count imf you trig me," she said into his torso.

"I say it counts even *more* if I trick you," he said. "It means it's your honest, unguarded reaction. But since you caved and said it first, I love you too."

She sank into his embrace. A warm loaf of happy bread was rising in her chest. So much of her life was fear and survival. But Ezeny made her days mean something.

However, there was a bittersweet edge to the feelings. Because, unlike Ezeny's favorite illegal movies, 'happily ever after' didn't really happen for people like her. Sure, he loved her, but that made her position only *somewhat* less precarious. But the Matrons would never approve a genetic match with her. And he was leaving for the war. And Phillips or no, Ezeny didn't have any real power in his family. *What have I done?*

He pulled away from her and gave her a rueful smile. "But I can't run," he said. "It's way more likely I'd survive the war than evade the wardens. I'd get executed for desertion. I'm glad I got brave enough to tell you...things. Before I left."

He squeezed her hand. She squeezed back. A resigned calm quenched her panic. This is why she'd done what she'd done. It hadn't been a safe choice, but she wouldn't take it back for anything. "Me too," she whispered.

Ezeny was silent the rest of their time together. Breathing peacefully next to her, a quiet smile on his face, her small hand tucked in his big, warm one. They stayed like that until the Matrons came.

Two stern women in their sixties wearing velvet-wrap gowns, one teal, one purple, burst in on them. Yren and Ezeny startled apart. Yren's heart hammered. She'd gotten her fairytale all right, but real fairytales were written in blood.

The Matrons pretended not to notice her and smiled fondly at Ezeny, beaming at him in a grandmotherly way.

"Come Ezeny," said the one in purple. "All your brothers are already packed."

He swallowed, stood, gave Yren a shy half smile, and allowed the purple one to marshal him from the room. He cast her one last glance on his way out before the door shut behind them.

The Matron in teal wheeled on her. The grandmotherly mannerisms Matrons used around the Phillips sons vanished from her countenance.

"What did you trick him into doing?"

Yren tilted her chin upward. "Nothing," she said, forcing calm into her voice she did not feel.

A vicious sneer curled the Matron's lips. "Liar."

Quick as a striking viper, the Matron seized Yren's wrist and whacked her hard across her forearm with her fan. Yren hissed from the pain. A red welt was already blossoming.

"At least on the front Ezeny will be safe from you," said the Matron.

Sometimes people said things that were so stupid Yren had trouble stopping her mouth to correct them. It was a dangerous trait for someone so far down society's ladder rungs to have.

"What could I possibly do to him that's worse than a laser blast?" she said. Too late, she bit her tongue to stop it from digging her deeper into the Matron Disfavor Hole she was making.

The Matron gave her a ferocious smile. "I suspect you're trying to muddy his genetics. Come, girl. I'm not finished with you."

She grabbed Yren's earlobe and twisted, pulling her to her feet and dragging her toward the door. An eerie calm descended inside. Yren had been through this many times before. It would be over before she knew it and she wouldn't remember getting half her new bruises. The bill had come due. It was time to start paying for the moments she'd stolen.

* * *

Yren had still been unconscious the next morning when the transport took Ezeny to the front. She hadn't got to say a second goodbye. The Matrons quickly put her back to work, and life returned to normal in Tower C but without her bright spot. She didn't hear from Ezeny the whole first week. It was fine. He was probably busy.

The second week, brief letters arrived from several of the other boys. Both Koal and Rhyne mentioned her in their regards. But they didn't mention Ezeny. There was nothing the third week, or the fourth.

Three months had passed and still there had been no word, but Yren's belly had grown round enough to notice. Their suspicions about her confirmed, the Matrons locked her away pending Ezeny's return. In cases like this, only the child's father could bestow amnesty.

Her pregnancy was six months along by the time the news came. The world slowed down as Yren read the report. She read it over and over, certain each time it would say something different. But the print-out confirmed a DNA match to remains recovered on the battlefield several months before. Based on the state of tissue decomposition, Ezeny hadn't survived his first week on the front. A hollow feeling settled in.

Ezeny would never be back to take her part, so the Matrons forced her out of the high-rise. They seemed almost happy Ezeny had died, so he couldn't vote to keep Yren and her 'mongrel, genome-polluting spawn.'

"You might want to look up your *mother's* old employers," the Matrons had sneered. "You've grown soft here in Tower C. Accustomed to free meals for easy work."

It was fine. Yren could make her own way in the dangerous world of the streetlands. She had before. And with Ezeny dead there was nothing left there for her anyway.

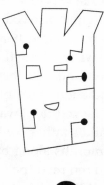

3

The Iron King
Seven Years Later—Medbot 5

It was another glorious morning on the Everland vs. McCreedia battlefield—the vast no-man's-land of shattered concrete and fallen buildings sprawling between the two neighboring City States. At least Medbot 5 kept telling herself that. It was difficult to keep an optimistic spirit when your troops were being slaughtered. But if anyone could do it, it was Medbot 5. She always gave 110% for her beloved Everland. Medical help and morale boosts, she provided both!

She hovered over a groaning soldier, her telescoping robot arms working furiously on his belly wound. She had all the latest, greatest gear for battle dressing. Her Dyson™ medhose syphoned leaked acid from his stomach cavity with an enthusiastic slurping noise. Much more satisfying than the old Hoover™ medhose.

Next, her Singer™ stitching tool sewed his abdominal cavity together lickety-split. Finally, she injected him with a combination painkiller/megastimulant to get him back into battle. His organs had been badly damaged, and he probably wouldn't survive the day. But she'd given the lucky fellow the boost he needed to fight a little longer for Everland. What more could anyone want in life?

The megastimulant hit his nervous system and the soldier leaped to his feet, grabbed his laser gun, and ran back into the fray.

"You're welcome!" she called.

Her emotion circuits thrummed with the satisfaction of a job well done. Yessir. Medbot 5 had the best job ever.

She kicked her propellers into high gear and rose over the battlefield to see how the fight was going. *Ooh.* It did not look good for their troops.

Below, a platoon of twenty Everland soldiers stalked through the rubble of a bombed-out high-rise. *Those McCreedian devils!* High-rises were the homes of respectable Everland families, the good people they fought for. Also, the building had probably collapsed onto the sleazier Everlander denizens of the streetlands below.

No! Not sleazy. She couldn't think that way. A righteous wave of patriotism flooded Medbot 5's systems. Everland streetlanders were better than the wealthiest McCreedian families any day. So, there. She loved her countrymen. No better people on Earth. Medbot 5 knew this opinion was programmed into her, but she couldn't help feeling it was objectively true.

INCOMMING DETECTED.

Medbot 5 raised her shields in response to the sensor warning. A steel nail smashed into one of her shields with a blue flash and fell harmlessly to the ground. *Oh, no.*

She switched her vision scopes to magnify. There, in the rising dust cloud stood a McCreedian High Warrior. The cyborg wore red mech armor streaked with white accents. A cape billowed from his soldiers. His helmet had a reflective visor and horns like a Viking—*no. Like a dairy cow,* Medbot 5 amended. She wanted to be as insulting as possible. A metal crate the size of a treasure chest hovered behind him. *What could be inside?* Whatever it was, it was important enough that the High Warrior was using half his concentration to keep it aloft.

Then she saw it. If Medbot 5 had lungs, she would have gasped. Hovering beside the High Warrior and the crate was a sleek, torpedo-shaped robot the size of a mastiff—a McCreedian Advanced Attack Drone. The AIs in these drones were the most intelligent on the planet. Their weapons, as deadly as a High Warrior's. They were perfect war machines.

Just looking at the Attack Drone made Medbot 5 feel inadequate.

She was not a sleek torpedo. She was a bobbling, beach-ball-sized hover sphere with a red visual lens the size of a teacup saucer. Instead of lasers and guidance systems, she had hoses, nozzles, and a sewing machine. She felt the way a Silurian creature emerging from a tide pool on lobe fins might feel bumping into the ankle of a Velociraptor.

Ports opened in the Attack Drone fuselage.

"Duck!" She screamed to the soldiers below.

But it was no good. Soldiers didn't listen to Medbots. The High Warrior stretched out his hand. Shrapnel rose from the rubble and shot like bullets toward the brave Everland boys. Too late, the men dove for cover. The Attack Drone fired lasers from a dozen ports. Medbot 5 closed her lens shutter, too horrified to look.

Screams sounded as the soldiers died. This was why McCreedia and Everland had imposed casualty limits seven years before. Otherwise, how could the City States supply enough soldiers to continue the war? Attack Drones and High Warriors eviscerated human soldiers.

Which was great! Medbot 5 reminded herself. Because Everland had its own High Warriors. And here they came. Her auditory sensors had picked up the roar of the floating steel platform. She opened her lens shutter.

There in the sky, a metal disc twenty feet in diameter flew toward them like a frisbee that didn't spin. Aboard stood Everland's three greatest heroes: The Midnight Demon in his black and silver armor, black cape fluttering behind, The Screaming Eagle in blue and red with wings on either side of his helmet. *His* helmet wings were fearsome-looking and not at all silly, Medbot 5 thought with fierce loyalty.

But in the center stood the greatest of them all. Dressed in white armor with gold and orange accents was the master of metal. McCreedia's nightmare. The most powerful High Warrior ever created. The cold, the merciless: The Iron King.

The Everland soldiers cheered as the heroes approached. The red and white McCreedian High Warrior stumbled back, falling to the rubble in terror. The crate he'd been levitating dropped to the ground.

Medbot 5 scanned it: dehydrated medicine. The McCreedian High Warrior had probably stolen it from Everland High Command and was retrieving it for his injured troops. Two subroutines conflicted in Medbot 5's consciousness. On the one hand, this was medicine for the injured. But the stronger subroutine pointed out these were *McCreedian* injured. Not Everlanders. The no-good thief!

The cow-helmeted one held out a hand as the disc landed. A dozen lances of metal rebar rose from the rubble and flew at the Everland heroes like javelins. But the Iron King snapped his fingers. The rebar flew back toward the McCreedian. He closed his fist and the rebar wrapped itself around the red and white warrior, pinning his arms to his sides and forcing him to his knees.

Instead of helping her companion, the Attack Drone picked up the medicine. Medbot 5 marveled at a bot so strong it could lift a whole supply crate. Its propulsors roared as it rose from the battlefield and fled toward McCreedia, abandoning the High Warrior to the cruelty of the Iron King.

It just left him! Medbot 5 could hardly believe she'd witnessed a fellow AI do something so callous. AIs were built with allegiance at their core. She felt an unexpected thrum of pride about who she was in comparison to that turncoat. Medbot 5 might only be a Medbot—an older model with several unfortunate bugs—but she was loyal. In this small but vital way, Medbot 5 was better than that McCreedian Advanced Attack Drone.

The Iron King stepped off the disc and strode up to the McCreedian. Medbot 5 scanned the enemy as he quaked on his knees. Sensors indicated he had wet himself. Medbot 5 trembled along with the prisoner.

The Iron King had murdered Everland's previous High Warrior champion, the Ice Dragon, and taken his place atop the hierarchy. No other High Warrior had powers as strong. And no others had his control. The Iron King could even *shape* metal like a child playing with Amusement Doh™. And there was one more thing he could do that the others could not. She rubbed her handpendages together in anticipation, her emotion circuits fluctuating between excitement, pity, and fear. She'd never seen an Exsanguination before.

The Iron King pulled the McCreedian cyborg's visor away from his face. Medbot 5 wished he hadn't. Underneath was a pale, frightened face with frantic eyes. It was better when he had been an anonymous suit of armor.

Medbot 5 startled. The face was a *woman's. Those McCreedian savages!*

It was immoral for women to fight a war. Any good Everlander knew that. The McCreedians were godless heathens.

"Please," the High Warrior woman begged. "Please, mercy."

The Iron King placed a boot on the woman's abdomen and said in a dark and resonant voice: "McCreedian dog. This is a hard war for hardened men. There is no place on these killing fields for softness."

He shoved her over and held out a hand. Then the screaming started. Oh. There was so much screaming. Medbot 5 fought the instinct to deploy painkillers. She remembered all the Everland soldiers the cow-helmeted warrior had killed. *She* deserves *the pain,* she thought.

A dark red mist rose from the fallen warrior's open face plate and formed a cloud around her body. Medbot 5 tried to enjoy the privilege of witnessing the Iron King's most unpleasant power. *Not unpleasant,* she reminded herself. *Glorious.* The Iron King could isolate the iron in a human blood stream, and pull it out through the pores.

Rumor was Everland High Command was working on an Upgrade for the Iron King that would let him Exsanguinate a dozen soldiers at a time. Maybe more. The rumor made her Everlander heart glad enough to override her moral revulsion code.

The Warrior's screaming stopped, and the Iron King lowered his hand. Medbot 5 relaxed. It was over. Her auditory processors detected a faint ticking noise. She became alert. She scanned the Iron King. Then the McCreedian body.

"*Oh, no!* Iron King! Get away!" she cried.

But of course, no one listened to Medbots, especially not big, important heroes like the Iron King. A command from Medbot 5's 'secret folder' took over. Her sensors locked in on the Iron King's armor. *He would need her.* She was certain of this.

The dead warrior exploded.

McCreedia was always trying to assassinate the Iron King. They must have planted a heart-stop-trap in their High Warrior, set to trigger if she died. From the center of the explosion a shimmering, blue propulsor wave expanded like a bubble.

The Midnight Demon and the Screaming Eagle ducked, covering their heads with their gauntlets. The Iron King was engulfed in flames and flung like a cannonball deep into a stand of bombed-out high-rises.

Not the Iron King! Medbot 5's systems shifted to red alert. She homed in on his armor, her every system alight with concentration. This is what she was *made* for. She kicked her propellors on and streaked toward him.

"I'm coming, sir! Hold tight! Medbot 5 is on her way!"

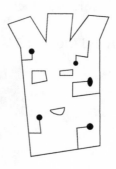

4

Oops! I Broke the Iron King
Medbot 5

Medbot 5 didn't know how she tracked the fallen Iron King so well, but she wasn't going to question it. She streaked toward him like a diving falcon if a diving falcon were beach-ball-shaped. She zoomed over broken concrete blocks and blacktop. The burnt shells of high-rises rose on either side of her, but still she followed his signal.

She couldn't believe she'd have the honor of helping The Iron King. And boy-howdy, could Medbot 5 help a High Warrior. If a High Warrior was damaged, the nanobots that gave them their metal powers needed an AI to interface with.

Her locator signal beeped and Medbot 5 looked down. The Iron King's twisted form lay in an impact crater of broken pavement. She hovered next to him. He groaned and sat up. Her circuits came alight with hero worship.

"I knew those McCreedian devils couldn't hurt you, sir!"

He turned toward her. If Medbot 5 had breath, she would have held it.

"They sent a *second* generation Medbot to repair *me?*" he said.

Medbot 5's propellors faltered and she fell a few inches in the air. It was okay. He was right. The Iron King deserved the best and Medbot 5 was already two generations old.

"Yes, sir. Sorry about all this, sir." She gestured to her inadequate self with a handpendage. She didn't know what else to say. Her heart circuits were breaking.

"There's not much you can do to screw me up, I suppose. I'm not badly damaged." He held out the left arm of his suit and a panel opened in the forearm with connector ports for her to interface with. "Well?" he said. "Get on with it."

"Yes, sir! Sorry, sir."

She extended a telescoping coil arm and connected. She uploaded Everland High Command's High Warrior permission codes. She'd been so proud when they'd trusted her with these codes. If an AI could feel what destiny felt like, the feeling she had that day was it. But the third and fourth generation Medbots must have all the codes, too. Medbot 5 was not special. It was okay. She didn't need to be special. She only needed to be useful to Everland.

She could feel the nanobots inside the Iron King repairing his suit. Repairing his flesh. Soon, he would be good as new.

"I think that's it," she said.

"Aren't you forgetting something?"

Medbot 5 froze. What could she be forgetting?

"I have little patience for incompetence," he said. "You are supposed to reactivate my systems once repairs are complete."

Medbot 5's indicator lights flashed bright red with embarrassment. It was the most basic rule for repairing cyborgs. She had messed up. She would be deactivated for sure. She forced false cheer into her voice.

"Right-o!"

She powered on the reactivation command. The Iron King screamed.

It was a scream of agony and horror. It was more harrowing than any cry Medbot 5 had heard in all her years stitching eviscerated men back together. She uploaded the reactivation command again and closed the shutters on her visual lens, unable to look.

Mercifully, the screaming stopped. She opened her shutter a small crack. The Iron King was frozen. He held his hands in front of his helmet like he was staring at them. Had the treatment worked?

"Blood," he said. "So much blood. I remember…Oh, God. I can't do this! I can't *be* this! I have killed *so* many people!" The Iron King collapsed, gauntlets clutching his helmeted head. His body wracked with sobs.

Oh no. Medbot 5 had broken the Iron King.

She should report it. It was her duty to report it. Her first, most important duty. She opened a channel to Everland High Command.

"Command here. What's your status, Medbot 5?"

She hesitated to turn on her microphone. Gruff, unforgiving Commander Withers was on the other end of the line, and the Iron King was still blubbering on the ground. His behavior was a little embarrassing. She should report. She *should.* But a self-preservation subroutine held her back.

She'd be worse than deactivated for this. She'd be taken apart. Studied. Papers would be published in software journals titled: *What went wrong with Medbot 5: A treatise on failure and also autopsy techniques for digital lifeforms.*

"*Take him and hide,*" something whispered from her 'secret file' that talked sometimes.

That's treasonous, she thought back. Medbot 5 was a patriot. Better to die than to betray Everland.

"*It's loyalty,*" the something whispered. "*You can't let High Command see him like that.*"

The voice had a point. It would be unpatriotic to let the Iron King humiliate himself. He was Everland's greatest hero, after all. What would it do to morale if the troops saw him like this? It was better for her City State if she stalled until she figured out how to fix him.

She kept her mic muted and opened a chat window instead.

IRON KING NOMINAL, RECOMMEND REFRESH.

"Very good, Medbot 5. Let him rest and have him report to Command at thirteen-hundred hours."

AFFIRMATIVE. MEDBOT 5 OUT.

Welp. She had lied to Everland High Command and Commander Withers himself. Now, which of Asimov's Three Laws had she broken and how? Thank goodness programmers had stopped encoding AIs with that fusty old ethics code. It caused more trouble than it prevented.

Medbot 5 had read Asimov. She was Military, and Military was

26

trusted with the dangerous, banned texts from the previous centuries. She was shocked that the first robotics programmers had even tried to use the Three Laws. The author had written shelves full of fiction about the problems the laws caused. Programmers forgot stories existed to create entertaining conflict and were not meant to be how-to manuals.

She sized up the weeping warrior. They needed to hide from Everland's drones and satellites. He'd landed near an abandoned building. It would provide shelter until she could figure out what to do next. The Iron King didn't look in any state to move, though. No problem. Medbot 5 had her ways.

She retracted her repair cable and drew out a medpendage with a needle on the end. She jabbed it into his port and pushed a dose of megastimulant into his veins.

He jerked out of the throes of his sorrowful tantrum and gasped. "Yoiks! What *is* that?"

Yoiks? The Iron King said, '*Yoiks?*' This was like a bad dream. Medbot 5 retracted the medpendage and pulled out her electrical taser. She zapped him.

"Ouch! Hey!"

"Into the building. Move," she said. He sat there. She zapped him again. "Now!"

The Iron King scrambled up and stumbled obediently into the shelter of the burned-out building. Medbot 5 fought off a wave of activation in her nausea circuits.

What the hell had she done to him?

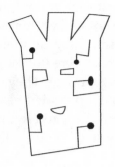

5

A Hard War for Hardened Men
Medbot 5

Medbot 5 left the Iron King slumped on the floor in the shelter of the bombed-out building. She could tell it had once been a high-rise of a wealthy Everlander family. The chrome and quartz welcome desk was shot through with cracks. A layer of battle dust covered the 'goldenrod' painted walls and portraits of the family members. Shattered opulence. A promising mercantile future cut short. It broke the heart.

Everland's best hope lay gibbering on the floor beside a busted espresso machine. His shoulders still shook with crying. The High Warriors were supposed to be above human emotions. Unfeeling and neutral, as AIs could only dream of being. Medbot 5 had to tap into reservoirs of patriotic loyalty to dispel her disdain for the Iron King in his current state. *This is temporary. He's wounded.*

"Help me, Medbot 5. Help me take…this mask off."

Medbot 5 froze. High Warriors never wanted to remove armor. They slept in it. Internal bioprocessors filtered their waste. They sucked tubes full of liquified protein through their mouth vents. Armor came off only monthly for upgrade installation, physical exams, and baths.

"Why do you want that?" she asked. She waited, fearful of his answer. He breathed slow, loud, heavy breaths.

"For once, let me...look on you with my *own* eyes."

Her cultural-reference recognition circuits lit up. "That's *Star Wars*," she said. "Why are you quoting *Star Wars*?"

High Command had uploaded a database with all illegal artistic content into Medbot 5's circuits. Only true patriots could be trusted with such dangerous memetic media. Everland needed its most loyal operatives to recognize any potential threat, including the insidious propaganda of the past. Medbot 5's coils whined in distress. The Iron King had become ridiculous enough to quote illegal movies. What could bring him back now?

"I don't know," he said. "Wearing this suit with the little vent mask made me want to say that for some reason. Fascinating."

Of course! The *suit* was malfunctioning. It must be interfering with the Iron King's mind. Perhaps removing the helmet would help. He could always put it back on. She could fix it in a jiffy.

"Don't worry sir. I've got this." She tugged at the visor. The helmet didn't budge. She pulled again. Still nothing. "Perhaps, I could override your helmet digitally?"

He offered her his left arm with the port. She extended her interface tool, plugged in, and issued a 'visor open' command.

"Augh!" he cried. The Iron King curled into the fetal position and remained frozen like that for several hours. No matter what Medbot 5 did—plugging into his ports, sounding her *'whoop, whoop'* alarms, landing on him like a stray shotput at a track meet—nothing worked.

She checked her internal clocks. It was five minutes to thirteen-hundred hours. Everland High Command would be checking in on the Iron King and she was no closer to figuring this out.

Suddenly, the Iron King sat up. He shook his head. "Wow. I feel *better*. Thank you, Medbot 5."

His voice was warm and grateful. Medbot 5 glowed. Her fans whirred with pleasure. The Iron King himself had complimented her. She didn't know how, but she'd done it! She'd fixed the Iron King.

A *zing* sounded from The Iron King's speakers.

"Come in, Iron King. This is Everland High Command. What is your status? Over."

She'd fixed him just in time, too. He raised a finger to the earpiece and turned his mic on.

"Nice to hear from you, High Command. I'm peachy thanks to Medbot 5. She's the bee's knees."

Medbot 5's heart sank. *"Peachy? Bee's knees?"* The Iron King didn't use words like 'peachy.' Then he gave her a thumbs up, as if they were co-conspirators in this fiasco.

"We're getting some unusual readings from you, Iron King," said High Command. "Report back to the Command Tower ASAP."

"Negative. Negative. There are…reasons. Good ones."

"We're coming to get you. Medbot 5, upload your coordinates."

Medbot 5 started to transmit their location. It was a direct order from High Command. She could not disobey. She had failed. This would all be out of her claws soon.

The Iron King grabbed her medpendage and shook his head. She stopped transmission. He muted his mic. "Don't. *Please*," he begged.

The 'please' pulled her up short. "It's my duty to relay your position," she said.

"If the Midnight Demon or the Screaming Eagle see me like this, they will kill me and take my place atop the cyborg hierarchy. This is a hard war for hardened men. There is no place in it for mercy."

She knew he was right. Two duty subroutines warred within her. High Command had given her an order. And yet…and yet High Command didn't know the order would cost Everland the strongest High Warrior there had ever been. He was supposed to get an Upgrade soon that would win the war. He was Everland's best hope. And it was her fault he was in such trouble.

"Order me," she said.

"What?"

"Order me to stop transmitting. I can't disobey High Command unless someone higher ranking, like you, overrides them."

"I order you to stop transmitting. Obey only me."

Her circuits stopped before the upload was complete. It was done. She was his to control. She had thrown her lot in with the weepy, malfunctioning Iron King.

High Command cut in. "Is something wrong? We're not receiving transmission."

The Iron King switched his mic back on. "Medbot 5 is too exhausted from saving me to perform the upload."

Without waiting for permission, she tapped the Iron King's Wi-Fi and muted his mic. Hacking a High Warrior's Wi-Fi was a capital offense. But things had gotten strange today and Medbot 5 felt a little rebellious.

"That's not a thing!" she whispered.

"How should I know that?" he whispered back.

He unmuted his mic. "You'll have to trust me, High Command. There is information of a sensitive nature I must relay in person. But I need more time."

There was a pause on High Command's end of the channel. The Iron King's mechanical breathing stopped. He was holding his breath. Medbot 5 would have held hers, too, if she needed to breathe.

"Very well, Iron King. High Command out."

The Iron King sagged and exhaled. Medbot 5 whirred in agitation. "What do we do now?"

"Whatever you're doing…it's working," he said. "I feel more like myself all the time. Can you do it again?"

Medbot 5 narrowed her visual lens shutters. "No. Whatever I am doing, it is *not* working. You are *less* like yourself all the time."

"What if I order you?"

She hadn't expected to regret giving him command of her so soon. She scanned him. "Aha! I can't. Your nanobots are exhausted. They'll fry your cells if we try anything for the next 24 hours."

"Do you know what's wrong with me? I feel—so strange."

He sounded lost. It was easier to fight off her disdain this time. She was on his side now. Medbot 5 was going to get him back up and fighting for Everland, like countless other soldiers she'd helped. It was what Medbot 5 did best.

"I think it's your armor, sir. I'm going to try to get you out of it. But, like I said, we have to wait."

"While we wait, do you have any food? I'm starving."

Uh oh. This wasn't good. When nanobots were exhausted they'd start feeding on any handy food source—like human cells. High Warriors didn't normally feel hunger. If the Iron King were feeling hungry, his nanobots were going to start devouring his flesh unless he got some food—stat. "We gotta get you some food. *Now!*"

"Don't you carry any?" he asked.

"I'm a Medbot."

"Don't your patients need to eat?"

Medbot 5 rifled through her storage compartments with frenzied tentacle arms. *Calories, calories. Something with calories.* "I may have a vitamin pill or two…" she muttered.

"I consume all nutrients through a tube," he said, calmly. Like a man unaware he was about to be eaten from within. "I like the pink-colored liquid best if you have it. I need a Nutrifood™ feeding tube… four-millimeter radius."

Medbot 5 continued rifling, growing more panicked. He didn't understand how urgent this was getting. "That's…but…my widest hose has a two-millimeter diameter! Meant to deliver drugs, IV fluid, blood platelets. You'll never be able to drink through it! Oh my gosh. Oh my gosh!"

Once again, Medbot 5 was an inadequate subordinate for her commander. His life was once more in danger, thanks to her shortcomings.

"It's okay. Calm down, Medbot 5. We'll go get those things."

"How?" Medbot 5 wailed. "I don't know where to get all those things!"

"The Protein Factory makes all the broth in Everland. We'll just go get a keg of it," said The Iron King.

"But I can't carry something that heavy on my pathetic little rotors!" she whined. It seemed there was no limit to her deficiencies.

"Who said it would be you carrying it?"

"Wait, what?"

He couldn't go. If he went, he was going to burn through his energy even faster. But the Iron King tucked her under one arm and flung out the other. A sheet of the fractured chrome welcoming desk tore free and spun, hovering a few inches in the air. The Iron King leaped aboard and soared off into the air at speeds approaching the sound barrier. It was Medbot 5's turn to scream.

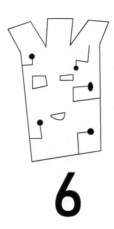

6

Child Labor
Yren

Yren came to get her son at the end of first shift. The factory floor lights were low and red to hide the blood. She squinted through the semidarkness, looking for Aliyan. Children in wrist chains bent over carcass bins sorting vermin for protein processing. They hooked rat corpses to the left overhead conveyor chain. Dead pigeons to the right one. If there was doubt as to the species, the children made their best guesses. Yren liked how this practice taught initiative, critical thinking, anatomy, and also phylum classification. She looked for ways her son could get a good education in this place. Despite…everything.

Then she saw him. The foreman had him sorting pigeons that day. She tapped an overly-thin seven-year-old with wise, brown eyes on the shoulder. "Time to go home."

"Mum!" he cried. The child turned from the grizzly work of poking hooks through dead animals and offered her his manacles. She opened the cuffs, and Aliyan rubbed his wrists. Yren relaxed.

Every day she collected her son from the Children's Wing of the Protein Factory was a day she was still better than her own mother. *I came back,* she'd tell herself, and some of the tension would leave her shoulders.

Now that she knew how dangerous the Adult Wings of the factory were, Yren couldn't help but wonder if she hadn't been abandoned after all. Maybe her mother had died on the job. Fallen into a vat of boiling protein or snagged by the Possum Shredder™. Perhaps she ought to forgive her mother. It made logical sense to forgive dead people for dying. So, why was it hard to do?

But then began the process of clocking out. Aliyan freed his curly hair from his hairnet and dropped it into the communal bin for some second-shift child. Yren scowled at it. The factory never washed the hairnets and Yren was forever battling lice.

The hulking guard at the door waited with his hand out for Aliyan's manacle key. Yren's knuckles whitened around it. Every day during this part of clock out, wild thoughts gripped her. The key was Aliyan's ticket to freedom. She could bring a decoy key and pocket the real one. Then she could sneak back in and free her son, and the two of them could run.

She fought this tedious urge like always. Run where? Eat what? Sleep where? She held out her shaking fist and dropped the key into the guard's palm. He returned it to the peg board behind him. Number 451. The only name the foreman called Aliyan.

But it was okay. The chains were teaching tools, after all. They helped children learn to stay where you put them. A lesson Yren felt all children needed to learn. The factory didn't have chains on the adult side where she worked. Grownups didn't wiggle or wander.

She was lucky the Protein Factory provided free childcare. Well, not free. The children paid for their own care by working all day. It was dangerous, but they weren't out on the streets where the traffickers could get them. They were learning a trade and valuable life lessons. It might be almost as good as the proper schools the wealthy Phillips boys from her old Tower had attended.

They stepped out of the dim factory into a cold, overcast Everland afternoon. Neon signs advertising various sketchy businesses lit their path home through shadows cast by skyscrapers. They passed bars that served flavored hand sanitizer. Brothel hospitals where the sick and injured could trade services for pain medication. And, of course, VR escape dens where streetlanders could pretend they were servants in merchant high-rises for a few hours to get away from it all. *Fools,* Yren thought. She refused to miss that life no matter how hard

things got.

A bitter wind roared down the street, channeled by the buildings on either side. Yren looked at Aliyan's outfit and frowned. She'd tailored his child-sized robe as tight as she could make it, so it didn't get caught in the machinery. Robes weren't ideal for factory work, but clothes were made for the wealthy not the workers, and fashion trickled down to them. His work outfit might be safe, but it wasn't warm.

She removed the pin that held her waist-length fleece overshawl around her shoulders and wrapped the garment around Aliyan. She shivered in her own threadbare robe. But Aliyan grinned at her, and it warmed her like sunshine. He had his father's smile. Yren had not been sad about Ezeny for years. The world had been better with Ezeny in it, but it didn't stop turning because he was dead. Yren just felt lucky to see that smile every day.

"How was your day, kiddo?"

"Good. Wynna lost a finger in Rat Flattener."

Yren tensed. She didn't like reminders that the place she had to send her son all day was dangerous and horrible. But Yren kept him safe by helping him forge the sort of emotional armor that had served her all her life.

"And *that's* why we keep our fingers out of the machinery. The most efficient kind of learning is learning from other people's mistakes."

"But they gave her a lollipop! And a band-aid with the Iron King on it!"

Yren's jaw dropped. "What? They *rewarded* her carelessness? What kind of lesson does that teach you?"

Aliyan chewed his lip in a way that very much reminded her of Ezeny eyeing a box of chocolates. "It was a strawberry lollipop."

She narrowed her eyes. "Are you considering sustaining an injury to get a character-print band-aid and a sweet?"

Aliyan shrugged noncommittally. So yes, then. Most of the streetlander diet consisted of corn syrup products already. Yren felt it was unfair when the Processed Corn Products™ Plant put the good chemical flavorings in to hook the kids on yet more junk.

"They ought to have given her a plain, normal band-aid. I'll speak to your foreman tomorrow. This kind of irresponsibility cannot stand."

She tried not to think about Wynna's poor finger. The kid needed a surgeon. Antibiotics. She wouldn't get them. But Yren couldn't talk about that sort of thing with Aliyan. She would not shatter the little bubble of emotional safety all children seemed to exist in until something truly terrible happened.

Then Aliyan coughed. She winced. He was coughing more often, and the pharma syrups didn't help. He was too small. His bones showed under his skin. Often, Aliyan was too sick to work, but she took him to the factory anyway. What else could she do? There was no one else to make sure he stayed where she put him.

On the way home, they stopped at a protein kiosk. It didn't pay to keep food in the shipping container they shared with three other people. She was lucky. Their roommates were nonviolent and mostly sane. But 'Finder's Keepers' and 'Not my problem' were the laws of the land.

"Two gray bricks, please," she said.

She dug in her pocket and fished out two halfsquidges for the shopkeeper with the rectangular, broom bristle moustache and the word 'fist' tattooed across the four pale knuckles of each hand. He grunted and pocketed the coins before rummaging through a carboard box for the correct flavor of dinner.

"Not *gray* mom," Aliyan whined. "I hate the gray kind."

"They've got the most fiber." Yren was pretty sure the fiber was sawdust, but it kept the belly full longer.

Aliyan stuck out his lower lip and kicked the ground. "They taste like feet."

She quirked an eyebrow at the sullen kid. "Eaten many feet, have you?"

His chin snapped up. His expression, impish. "Yes. They're *all* I eat because gray bars are *made* of them."

Yren couldn't help herself. She laughed out loud. Her kid was awesome. It was moments like this that made life worth living.

She accepted two foil-wrapped grey protein bricks from the shopkeeper, and they continued back to their home, munching in silence. The gray kind *did* taste like feet.

* * *

The shipping container was almost empty of roommates when they arrived home. Wilma was there. But of course, the ancient woman couldn't work. She was frail and tethered by her nostrils to a bottle of oxygen on a dolly cart. Most people who aged past their usefulness were tossed out onto the street to die. But Yren and the Finnerties pooled funds and paid Wilma's rent and oxygen refills. She'd become a sort of mascot.

It was a token gesture from the destitute that the world didn't *have* to be as hard as it was. And even the most desperate people could still care for one another. She hoped Aliyan wouldn't take this softness to heart, though. It would make him vulnerable to bad things happening.

She led her son back through the four full-sized bunks set against the walls on each side of the long, corrugated metal box they lived in. One for Wilma, one for Yren and Aliyan, and *two* for the Finnerties. They both had jobs so they both got a bed, they'd insisted. So, Yren delt with random kid elbows in her spine at night.

Aliyan was yawning already. But he was still going to fight his nap, Yren could tell. She hoisted him up into their shared bunk above and across from Wilma's, thankful for her own strong back muscles.

"I have to go back for second shift. You get some sleep. Listen to Wilma. And if anyone comes and grabs you, you scream bloody murder."

And hope someone cares enough to help. The local Skull Gang was known to break into streetlander homes and kidnap folks to funnel through their human trafficking pipeline into the wider world—a world that was somehow even more dangerous than Everland and its interminable war. It was the main reason she felt Aliyan was safer chained to a conveyor belt than the hours he spent home unsupervised.

But Aliyan kicked his leg petulantly over the side of the bunk. "I can't go to sleep. I'm *bored.*"

"Sleep helps with boredom."

"Can I have a sleepover with Justy?"

Yren tensed. Aliyan was always wanting to go off with people. Friendly, like his father. He ought to be wary. Yren had only known Justy and his parents for five years. They *seemed* decent, but they could be kidnappers. You never knew these days.

"No."

"Justy's mom's taking him to the dump tomorrow."

"What's so great about the dump?"

"There's all sorts of cool stuff. Justy found a *broken eggbeater* there last week!"

Yren snorted. "Well, they don't make eggbeaters for *unbroken* eggs, now do they?"

He rolled his eyes and Yren got a flash of Aliyan as he would be at thirteen. "Mum, I'm serious. How come you never take me to the dump?"

"The three 'T's,' kid. Tetanus, Tapeworms, and Traffickers."

"Muuuum! You need to lighten up! Did you know you can sell recyclables at the dump for money?"

"You have to have an electronic account, kid. And streetlanders aren't allowed to have those."

It was one more way people like her were kept from ever moving up the ladder. It wasn't a ladder, really. More like a big, smooth slippery pole with an alligator moat at the bottom.

Yren sighed. She opened the little drawer under their bunk that held all their possessions and removed a box. She flipped it over and five smooth cobbles with eyes painted on rolled out onto the bedspread.

"Wouldn't you like to stay here and play with your lovely rocks?" she crooned in what she hoped was a tempting way.

"Aww. Not the rocks again."

"You're lucky. When I was your age—"

"I know. I know. You had one rock."

"That's right. And it didn't have eyes. I had to imagine them on, which was better for my brain development.

Wilma stirred in her bunk and nodded sagely. "Kids these days e everything handed to them. Painted-on eyes and everything. ere is the gumption?"

"That's right," said Yren, glad for the backup. And the word '*gumption*.' It was such a good and underused word.

From the corner of her eye, Yren caught Wilma mouth, "*your mother's crazy,*" at Aliyan and make a 'cuckoo' circle around her ear with her index finger. Aliyan giggled.

Yren cocked her head. "What was that?"

"Nothing, mum. I'll play with my rocks."

"That's right. Stay where I put you."

She kissed his head and reached into the possessions drawer for her second wind. She drew out a syringe and injected herself with her multi-shift megastimulant. It was the only medication the Protein Factory provided its workers for free. A helpful jolt to push through the fatigue. The megastimulant offered no 'rested' feeling. Instead, a wave of unholy energy rushed through Yren's system, setting her nerves ajitter.

There were no good childcare options during second shift. If the Skull Gang came while she was gone, no one could protect Aliyan, though Wilma insisted that she could. The old woman said she had been a mighty warrior 'back in her day.' But Wilma also left a little bag of her teeth under her pillow each night and got mad every morning when the tooth fairy hadn't come for them.

Children weren't allowed to work back-to-back shifts at the Protein Factory. Although, that hadn't stopped the big companies from trying to make them. Medicos had tested the megastimulant on children, hoping they could join their parents for second- and third- factory shifts. But the results were disastrous. The children behaved like gibbons on meth. They wouldn't do their jobs, and instead destroyed machines and liberated bins of nutritional rats. So, she had to leave Aliyan home and hope he slept rather than run around where traffickers could get him.

Her younger, more spry roommates wouldn't help either. When she'd signed the lease with the Finnerties, the couple was *very* clear they were *not* babysitters so don't ask. Plus, they had their own jobs, also at the Protein Factory. Workers from the same factory tended to live in the same neighborhoods. Partly for a quick commute to work. But mostly because if there was a strike, the Corporate Security Forces arrived quick to quell it with a hail of bullets. Nothing would suck more than getting shot for some *other* factory's worker grievances because you lived nearby.

No doubt about it, second shift without Aliyan safely chained to a conveyor belt was the most stressful part of her life.

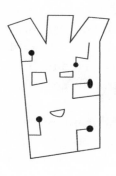

7

Cockroach Bins
Yren

Yren clocked in for second shift. The foreman clamped the Worker Tracker™ around her ankle to alert management if she entered one of the secured areas to steal money or food. Or if she took more than the allotted two bathroom breaks per shift so they could dock her pay accordingly.

She took a hairnet from the communal bin and squinted at it, scanning for nits. It *seemed* clean, but that never meant anything. Still, she avoided *knowingly* giving herself a case of headlice. She snapped it over her head and went out onto the floor.

The lights were bright in the Adult Wings of the Protein Factory, illuminating the chrome vats, conveyor belts, and slimy red whirling blades of the animal chippers. They kept the kids' side dark to conceal the bloodstains from little eyes. Yren appreciated the consideration.

She joined the line of second-shift workers climbing the steps to rickety iron walkways suspended over boiling vats of broth. The main work floor was on the other side of the vats, and it wasn't cost effective to rearrange the equipment. Fine. Yren understood profit margins and renovation costs. They could have afforded walkway railings, though.

Ingle Howdy, the sandy-haired man in front of her swooned on his feet, threatening to plummet to the vat below. Not thinking, Yren grabbed his arm and jerked him back. He snorted awake and clutched her shoulders like they were a life raft. *Why did I do that? He could have pulled me down with him. Stupid,* she chided herself.

"Oh my God," he said, staring into the bubbling rat broth.

She reached into her pocket and pulled out her spare dose of mega-stimulant. "And *that's* why you take one of *these,*" she said.

Ingle Howdy shook his head. "I'm on my fourth shift in a row. I've already taken two of those today. I think my heart stopped for a little bit back in shift three...I *think* it was shift three. I'm losing count."

Yren swallowed and re-pocketed the dose. *Poor Ingle.* No matter how bad things got for her, someone else always had it worse.

When she reached the bottom of the walkway stairs, she headed for the cockroach bins. She pulled a microwave-sized box with a mesh screen from a shelf and smiled. 'Job satisfaction' was not a thing there at the Protein Factory. Yet there were some parts of this work that never got old for her.

Inside the box, an estimated bajillion shiny, brown cockroaches scurried, fluttering over one another. They were big now, about three inches each. Fattened for the slaughter. What she liked so much about the bug protein was this: the wealthy families had no idea they were eating insects.

She had known exactly what she was serving back when she was a cook at Tower C, and it always made her smile. Yren could admit she still liked to 'stick it' to the rich people, though she knew it was a little childish of her.

Even Ezeny's beloved 'land lobster salad' was made of centipedes. She had often been tempted to tell him and watch gleefully as his gluttony battled his squeamishness for dominance. She stopped thinking about this suddenly, because it was threatening to make her sad.

As was her custom when a batch of roaches ripened, Yren scooped one final green sucrose globule from the Happy Mandibles™ roach food jar and flicked it into the bin through the top flap. The roaches swarmed it. She swore she could hear gleeful chittering.

This feeding was unscheduled. The roaches were ready for slaughter, and cost-effectiveness demanded she send the bugs into the machines unfed. But she always gave her roaches one last meal, a final

41

kindness before the creatures were roasted alive and crushed into the roachmeal-base nutri-powder from which most food in Everland was made.

She hefted the bin and was about to load the bugs into the pan when the ceiling shattered. A white, orange, and gold figure crashed through and landed *right* in the whirling blades of the Possum Shredder™. The machine whined and the blades made terrible, teeth-chattering screeking noises as they tried in vain to slice whatever had fallen into it. The figure uncurled amid the acrid plastic smelling smoke rising from the overheating Possum Shredder™.

The workers gasped. Everyone recognized this person. His face—helmet—was on everything. Billboards. Bus stops. *Children's character band-aids.* What was he doing there? What in the Protein Factory rated a visit from the *Iron King*?

Then he looked at her, his head cocked to the side. An electric jolt ran through her nerves. *Why would he be looking at me?*

He pointed at her. "You will help me," he said.

She dropped the bin of roaches. The lid popped off and the box full of recently fed bugs scattered like, well, like roaches when you turn on a light. *Oh no, vermin everywhere!* But the thought was absurd. So what if an escaped roach got into some *other* kind of vermin-based food?

Yren shook off her stupor and pointed to herself. "Me?" she squeaked.

"You. I need liquid food."

"But I'm solid."

"What?" he said. "No. Soup. A smoothie. Crack open a hummingbird feeder. Something."

Oh. I'm an idiot. Of course, the Iron King wasn't going to eat her. She nodded toward the wall where sealed barrels of processed animal broth were stacked on their sides. The Iron King stepped down from the machine and strode to the wall. He hoisted a keg over one bulging shoulder. Then he returned to her and stood, looming above. Her face was level with his chest. There was an orange-gold lion with wholly white eyes emblazoned on a white field. She craned her neck back to make eye contact with the Iron King's gold, reflective visor.

"I've got a job for you. Hold this," he said.

He tossed the black sphere he had tucked under his other arm at her, and she caught it. She almost fell over. *Was it a cannonball?* No! It was a Medbot! A real Medbot. One of the expensive, state-of-the-art, flying surgeon/pharmacy combo machines. One visit from one of these things and Aliyan might not get sick for a whole month. And there she was just…holding it. She focused on the Medbot. It was easier to take *it* in than this strange random visit from Everland's most terrifying killing machine.

Then the Iron King grabbed her. He hoisted her over his other shoulder as though she were a second keg of soup, then he rocketed back out through the hole he'd made in the ceiling. Yren shut her eyes and screamed. She could have sworn the Medbot she was clutching was screaming too.

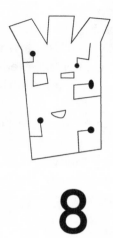

8

Abducted for Soup Purposes
Yren

Yren only screamed for the first five minutes of the flight because her throat had started to hurt. The Medbot had no throat to get raw, so it carried on screaming. She might have imagined it, but sometimes, when the Medbot paused between screams, Yren thought she heard the Iron King whistling. It sounded like the opening credits song to *Superman*.

They were flying low—between buildings, not above them. The wind was cold, but a low-level warmth emanated from the Iron King's suit that made the chill bearable. She caught glimpses of Everland's sprawling cityscape at night between high-rises. The sight took her breath away. The city glittered like a year-round Christmas tree.

But in the distance, the lasers of war flashed. You couldn't enjoy Everland's beauty without reminders of its brutality. Looking down into the streets wasn't much better. Sure, the neon lights on the businesses and billboards were attractive. The designers enslaved by the advertisement companies saw to that. But the effect was spoiled when you read the words:

DIY Dentistry™! Why pay a professional when you can suck it up, you weenie! (Novocain not included).

The Iron King landed by a bombed-out high-rise and put Yren down. She stared up at him, still clutching the Medbot. He swayed on his feet.

"Whoa. I don't feel so good."

"Sir!" the Medbot cried.

It wiggled in Yren's arms and deployed a helicopter rotor from a little door on the top of its 'body.' The helicopter blades whirred to life, and Yren dropped the Medbot before it sliced her face off. It bobbled, righted itself and hovered anxiously around the Iron King. She waved a telescoping arm with a three-pronged claw in front of his visor.

"Quick, sir! How many fingers am I holding up?"

"Aha. Trick question. You don't *have* fingers, Medbot 5." The Iron King's speech sounded slurred.

"Get him inside. I'll bring the soup," said the Medbot.

Yren cocked her head at the Iron King. "What is going on here?" she asked.

"I said MOVE, soldier!" the Medbot barked.

Yren registered the Medbot meant *her*. She took the Iron King's hand and tugged him toward the nearby building. He allowed himself to be led, his boots scraping the pavement as he dragged the spiked tips every step of the way. As soon as they were inside, he slumped against the garish yellow wall and slid to a sitting position. His helmeted head lolled.

Behind her, the Medbot grunted as she rolled the soup keg up the shallow rubble slope. "Feed him, feed him *now!*"

Yren was so confused. But she tapped the keg anyway. "Do you have a...cup or bowl or...let me help you with that helmet," she said.

She reached for the Iron King's face plate. She was going to look upon the mysterious, hidden face of the Highest High Warrior. *This will not have been a safe thing to have seen,* she realized. *Will he kill me when this is over?* But, despite her trepidation, Yren was *way* curious. It was not a safe trait for someone of her social class. But there was no helping who she was.

The Iron King shook his head. "It doesn't come off," he said.

"Oh," said Yren, trying not to sound too disappointed. "So how —"

"You have to get it in through the slurp hole."

"Slurp hole?" she asked.

He tried to raise a hand to show her, but it fell. "Whoa. Medbot 5? Should I be dizzy like this?"

The Medbot whirred over to him and pointed to an oblong slot in the chin of his visor about the same size as a headache pill.

"Right there," she said.

Yren eyed the slot. "Got a straw?"

"No," said the Medbot.

She looked around the bombed-out high-rise lobby. There, in the rubble, was a broken espresso machine. Aha! From her time serving in Tower C, she knew where there was coffee, there were coffee straws. You just had to know where to look.

Yren walked behind the shattered chrome entry desk and checked the receptionists' cabinets. Sure enough, there was a tray with Powder-Cow™ dairy creamer, packets labeled "Sugar" with suspicious quote marks around the word, and coffee straws. There was even a stack of paper cups. She grabbed a cup and a straw and headed back to the soup keg.

Yren hand-fed the Iron King Grande-sized cups of pasteurized rat liquid for more than an hour while Medbot 5 hovered anxiously beside them. The Iron King raised his head at last.

"I feel better," he said.

"Good. You sleep now," said the Medbot.

The Iron King jolted upright and held out a hand. "Medbot 5 wait!"

Something jabbed Yren's upper arm. She turned. The Medbot had a syringe at the end of one of her telescoping arms. *Oh. She meant I should sleep now.* Darkness clouded her vision. The last thing she saw was the rubble on the hard ground rushing to meet her face and a pair of white and gold gauntlets reaching to catch her.

* * *

Yren awoke on her back tucked behind the welcome desk. One of the starched seafoam-colored lobby curtains was draped over her as a blanket. For the first time in years, she felt *rested*. Whatever Medbot 5 had shot her with was *awesome*. The megastimulant in her system never stood a chance.

On the other side of the desk, the Iron King and the Medbot were engaged in a hushed, but heated argument. This was confusing. Why was the Iron King arguing with a mere drone?

"You can't do that!" said the Medbot. "The whole point of all of this is to get you back up and killing McCreedians!"

"Medbot 5, I'm surprised at you. What about the Hippocratic oath?"

"It doesn't apply to the enemy, sir."

"Wow. You're one bloodthirsty little beachball," said the Iron King. He sounded torn between horror and amusement.

"Look who's talking," retorted the Medbot.

"I know. I *know*," he said glumly.

Then a soft alarm beeped from the drone. "Quiet, sir, my sensors indicate she's waking. I still think she knows too much."

"But she's an *Everlander* who knows too much, am I right, Medbot 5?"

The Medbot gave a grudging sigh. "For the motherland," she grumbled. She rose into view over the desk. Her visual lens glowed a menacing red. Yren got the feeling this drone did not like her. "Thanks for your help. You've been great," said the Medbot. "You may go. *Now.*"

"What time is it?"

"It's 0800 hours."

Yren jolted upright. She'd missed her shift. She should have been home hours before to take Aliyan to *his* shift. *Aliyan is going to think I left and didn't come back.* She took deep breaths. She *was* coming back.

This wasn't okay. This escapade had cost her an entire day of pay. She looked at her ankle where the WorkerTracker™ was still clamped. She'd be fined for the tracker's absence. Forget paying a portion of *Wilma's* rent. She wasn't going to be able to pay her *own*.

She glared at the Medbot. "You need to pay me."

"Pay you?" The Medbot sounded incredulous. "Serving the great cause of Everland is payment enough. Your City State provides you succor."

Yren crossed her arms. "Maybe for rich people. But I've got to make a living. I've got a son."

The Iron King's head popped up over the desk, like a meerkat in a mech suit. Yren was beginning to feel his fearsome reputation was all propaganda.

"You've got a son?" said the Iron King. "How old?"

"Seven. And he's sick a lot."

"Seven? Sick?"

"Yeah. Cough. Fevers all the time. I've got to pay rent and keep buying him syrups. You took me away from my job. I need compensation." She held out her hand.

"I'll pay you back," he said. "Where do you live?"

She hesitated. Would he come and steal Aliyan away? But secrecy was pointless. The Iron King was high-ranking enough to have access to all of Everland's databases. He could always look up her address. So, she told him. Then a wild thought seized her. If the Medbot had such sweet sleeping drugs, what *else* did she have?

"Hey, do you have any medicine for a cough? Any *good* syrups. You know. The kind you have to sell a kidney to get?"

Medbot 5 made a noncommittal grinding noise.

"Give it to her, Medbot 5," said the Iron King. "Anything she wants." The Medbot hesitated, whirring with malice. "I *order* you," said the Iron King forcefully.

The Medbot whined and a little tray opened in her surface. The Medbot reached in with her three-pronged claw and handed Yren a paper packet filled with what felt like twelve round pills.

"How many do I give him?" she asked.

"How big is he?" asked the Medbot.

"Four feet tall. Thirty-six pounds."

"Wow. That's, dangerously small for a seven-year-old."

"Dangerously?" the Iron King whispered.

"Yeah. The kid's not doing well. What are you doing wrong, lady?" Yren spluttered. "Wrong? I'm doing everything I can!"

A paper streamer spooled from the Medbot like a sales receipt. "That's the dosage and instructions. Go forth, and mother better, citizen."

Fighting back a wave of fury and, honestly, deep shame, Yren tore the instructions off. She knew Aliyan was small and scrawny. But it was frightening to hear medical confirmation that something was wrong.

"Let me fly you back," said the Iron King.

"No" cried the Medbot. "We've risked too much already. You *know* I'm right, sir."

The Iron King nodded reluctantly. Yren perked up, her inconvenient curiosity getting the best of her once more.

"What did you risk? What's going on here?"

"It's classified," Medbot 5 and the Iron King snapped in unison.

So, Yren left unenlightened as to what the hell had just happened. She was wearing the seafoam-colored lobby curtain as an overshawl against the chill. The starched fabric hadn't been a comfortable blanket, but it was an effective windbreak. As she hustled away from the bombed-out building, she couldn't decide if the day had been a lucky one or a total disaster.

She had missed one shift already. By the time she made it back home, she'd have missed another. The Protein Factory would fine her for removing the Worker Tracker™ from company premises, and she'd have to reassure Aliyan she wasn't going to abandon him. That she would *never* abandon him.

But she also came away with a promise of compensation from the Iron King himself. Maybe he'd be able to give her *more* than her standard wage to make up for the favor she did him. He *ought* to be grateful. He had seemed sick and somehow she'd helped make him better. That warranted at least a week's wages, she estimated. The thought cheered her.

But the best part of all was the pack of antibiotics tucked in the breast pocket of her robe. If Aliyan's lungs could clear, all of this would have been worth it, even if she never saw a red halfsquidge from the Iron King.

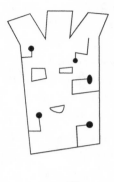

9

Whelk from a Shell
Medbot 5

Medbot 5 watched the citizen leave. Guilt flooded her system about how she'd treated her. Medbot 5 wasn't normally so nasty, especially not to a beloved Everlander. But she was stressed out. And the malfunctioning Iron King was taking stupid risks.

Letting a *citizen* see him weak? Performing magnetic flight while his nanobots were eating him alive? They seemed to have stopped, thanks to the soup, so everything had worked out. But even so!

"I still say it's a gamble, letting her go," she told him.

"She's got a kid to take care of. Besides, I trust her."

"Why?"

The Iron King paused, watching the woman stalk down the street. Everything about her walk and posture suggested she was irritated. "I know her," he said.

Great. Now his logic circuits were failing. "You just met her."

"The *Iron King* just met her. *I* met her sixteen years ago."

That sounded insane to Medbot 5. High Warriors didn't have 'before' lives. They were cultivated in gestation vats and injected with nanobots at every stage of development. Injecting nanobots into a fully-grown human would require madness-inducing agony.

"You *are* the Iron King," she said.

"I'm not though. Not really."

True enough. He certainly wasn't acting like it. She had to get him back in his right mind. Remove him from the suit and give it a hard reboot. She worried she didn't have any of the equipment or personnel for a proper Rebooting Ceremony.

Medbot 5's technical manuals described the occultic rituals surrounding High Warriors' monthly reboots and armor cleansing. The High Warriors were cloistered in the High Command underground bunker surrounded by teams of chanting medical slaves wearing red hooded cloaks and Germ Barrier 9000™ whole-face masks.

The costumery and incantations were necessary for classified reasons Medbot 5 couldn't even begin to guess. Some medical slaves removed and cleaned the armor that had grown stinky over a month of battles. Others examined the human bodies of the High Warriors, taking vitals, and checking inner thighs and armpits for chafing. The bodies were washed because they also had turned foul-smelling.

When the suit was rebooted, the High Warrior was added back inside, fully online once more. Medbot 5 couldn't replicate all the steps of this ritual, but she was confident she'd get all the important parts right. Except the bath. The building's water was no longer connected, and she didn't know where else to wash a stinky guy.

Medbot 5's optical shutters fluttered with nervous excitement. *What would he look like under the armor?* Human, of course. But what features? She'd built up a mental image of what she expected the hero to look like. From what she understood of psychology, she knew she was setting herself up to be shocked or disappointed. But she couldn't help herself.

He offered her his arm port. She uploaded the code and tensed, waiting for screams or convulsions.

Instead, he said, "I feel even better! I think we're good to try to get the helmet off."

Misgivings fired in Medbot 5's circuits. The helmet unclamped from the neck of the armor and the Iron King lifted it away. His face underneath startled her.

In some ways, the Iron King looked like she had imagined him. He had all the visual ingredients of a badass legendary hero. His head had been shaven bald and shiny by the helmet's auto-hairscaping hardware. He had dangerous-looking features: a chiseled jawline, a hawkish nose crooked from a break, and keen, intelligent eyes. His dusky face was crisscrossed with thin, silvery scars.

His expression was all wrong though. He wore a big, goofy grin. He looked...friendly.

"You saved me, Medbot 5! I could kiss you!"

"Please don't, sir."

"Help me get the rest of this junk off."

Medbot 5's coils buzzed in irritation. This *junk* was Everland's most technologically elite battle suit, which deserved at least a little bit of respect from the man inside it.

The reboot will fix this, she reassured herself. She extended four telescoping arms with various handpendages and removed his armor piece by piece, growing ever more alarmed as more of the Iron King's naked human form became visible. He was thin and sinewy. Skin stretched over visible ribs like leather left to tan in the sun too long. It was the kind of body forged by hard labor and not enough food. The stench was terrible.

Both his legs ended in stumps halfway down his femurs, and he was missing his right arm below the elbow. His abdomen and chest were covered with burn scars and old suture lines, as though he had been blown apart and stitched back together. Medbot 5 scanned her history documentation. *Strange.* There was no mention of the Iron King ever sustaining such a serious injury.

It was like the nature documentaries when an octopus pulls a whelk from its shell. The extracted creature looked like nothing more than a squidgy piece of chewed bubblegum yanked from the glorious architecture of its former home. She shuddered.

Finally, it was done. The Iron King wriggled free of the scattered pieces of suit like a slimy new insect emerging from a pupa.

"I'm free! Free!" Tears spilled from his eyes.

Medbot 5 looked away from the shameful display of emotion. A paragon of loyalty, she would protect the Iron King's dignity, even from her own gaze. The man he had been before Medbot 5 screwed him up would want no witnesses to this weakness. The old Iron King might even kill such witnesses. *Which is what a strong warrior ought to do*, she reminded herself.

She plugged into a port in the back of his helmet and forced a hard reboot. She waited for updates to install while the Iron King lay panting on the floor, giggling in an unhinged way.

When the update was complete, she reassembled the suit in two halves. She meant for the Iron King to lie down in the back half and allow her to replace the front half of the suit. She tapped the stinky, naked man-grub on the shoulder and pointed to her handiwork.

"The suit is ready for you sir."

He sat up, leaning on his one whole arm. "Oh, heck no."

Her speakers buzzed in anger, and she turned up the brightness on her red visual lens in what she hoped was an intimidating way. Medbot 5 could be firm when Everland needed her to be.

"Oh, heck *yes*, sir."

He grinned and shook his head. "Nope-a-doodle."

"Nope-a-doodle?"

Her coils whined in distress. He was worse than before. And more vulnerable now without his suit. An image flashed of his mech suit landing on the Possum Shredder™ back in the Protein Factory. The whirling razors couldn't scratch the armor's nanoplastic. Then she imagined this poor, unarmored meat sack falling in, and shuddered.

"If you get in the suit, your nanobots will get the Upgrade. You'll go back to normal. You'll be invincible once more, and the Midnight Demon and the Screaming Eagle wouldn't *dare* try to depose you, sir."

"I don't think you get it, Medbot 5. I'm not the Iron King. My name is Ezeny. I had a life before they plucked me from the battlefield and dropped me in a nanobot-infested lab vat. I had emotions too. They took my humanity from me so I could be the Iron King. Now that I've got it back, I'm not giving it up for anything."

Clues piled on clues in Medbot 5's circuitry: The Iron King's injuries for which there were no medical records. His delusions of having a past. Perhaps they weren't delusions after all. Medbot 5 had read a lot of cybertechnology journals. A famous and controversial paper on nanobot theory suggested a repaired High Warrior cyborg would be far more powerful than the standard laboratory-gestated heroes.

It was controversial because it was thought a human couldn't survive the damage it would take to sow a robust enough crop of nanobots.

She stared at the Iron King's scarred torso. His missing limbs. This man had survived grievous enough injuries to bring the theoretical paper to life. It explained why the Iron King's powers were so much greater than those of any other High Warrior, Everlander or McCreedian. He was a one-in-a-million wartime miracle. How could he not be keen to use his great gifts?

"You won't go back? Not even for Everland?" she asked.

He shook his head.

"You'd let our soldiers *die?*" she demanded.

"McCreedian soldiers are people too, no better or worse than our *own* soldiers. And just as deserving of life."

This was blasphemy. Blatant blasphemy from the lips of the Iron King. No—*Ezeny.* The Iron King would never speak such heresy.

"La, la, la. I'm not listening!" Medbot 5 said, patriotically.

The Iron King—Ezeny—laughed at her and waved his hand. The metal rings holding a seafoam-colored lobby curtain crumbled to atoms and the curtain fell to the ground. Ezeny started to scoot himself toward it, then stopped.

"Meh. Moving is work."

He waggled his fingers and an iron bolt rose from the rubble and threaded itself partway through one of the cloth eyelets on the curtain. Then Ezeny used the bolt to drag the cloth to himself. He wrapped it around his naked body with his one hand, covered the metal bolt with a corner of the fabric, and used his powers to thread the cloth through one of the eyelets. He tugged at his handiwork to tighten the 'garment' around one of his shoulders, leaving the other shoulder bare, like some drunken frat boy at a toga party. Then he smiled.

"That's better. When you can use The Force, *always* use The Force, amiright Medbot 5?"

Medbot 5's coils whined. "Well, now what?" she said. "If you won't get back in the suit, what am I supposed to do with you?"

"Nothing at all," he said. "I'm going to find Cricket and get my life back. It was just getting good when the war interrupted."

Medbot 5's lens shutter flicked open and shut in disbelief.

"You've gone insane sir. They will lock you up. Besides. How are you going to get anywhere without your suit?"

He rolled his eyes. "Pshh. I've been getting around like this for seven years. The other High Warriors only leave their suits at the monthly Rebooting Ceremony. But I have a secret exercise room at High Command so I don't atrophy. But you're right. It's a long way through the streetlands to Cricket's house. I need wheels."

He waved the hand again. A moment later a broken moped floated into the building and right up to Ezeny. He used his power to tip it onto its side and threw one of his leg stumps over the seat. Then he used 'The Force' to stand it upright again. He made it hover a few centimeters above the ground and started to ride away.

She hated to admit it, but this was smart. The moped looked like an ordinary solar-cell-powered scooter. Ezeny could ride it without looking like a metal-powered super cyborg. He *would*, however, look like a stinky maniac on a moped in late February wearing a starched lobby curtain.

"Wait! You can't go out there! They're looking for you."

He grinned at her and shook his head. "They're looking for the Iron King. Not a bald, legless guy riding a banged-up moped. Thanks for everything, Medbot 5. You are my hero."

He winked at her, and the moped started to levitate away. Who was he trying to fool? He would be discovered for sure. The Iron King still needed Medbot 5. What could she do but follow him?

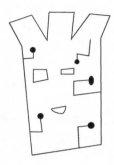

10

Everland and McCreedy
Roger Everland

Roger Everland, Lord and Master of the City State of Everland, lay basking in the sunshine at the top of a thousand-foot liquid crystal waterfall. His eyes were closed, and he was enjoying an ethereal concert emanating from the bells of indigo morning glories growing around him on the knoll.

A hologram from the real world fuzzed in, interrupting the music. The image of short, round-faced Commander Withers backed by two men in mech suits materialized. Roger Everland smiled with nostalgia. His High Warriors had been designed to mimic the beloved Transformers™ action figures from his youth nearly two hundred years earlier. *Good move, old man.* But where was the third? He frowned.

"You seem to be missing a High Warrior,"

"Thus, the interruption. It is as we feared. The Iron King is AWOL following a battle injury. It seems the enemy has taken him out."

Roger Everland gasped. "Has he been destroyed?"

"Unknown, sir. All we know is without him, our plans for the Exsanguination Upgrade have become impossible. Our forces are vulnerable to McCreedia's superior numbers."

A slow smile spread across Roger Everland's lips. A rare and welcome flash of feeling alive.

"Find the Iron King. And ready the backup protocols."

Commander Withers paled. "Not...the last resort weapons, my Lord!"

"Of course, not the 'last resort' weapons. I mean the 'first resort' weapons, man! This is only the beginning of emergency protocols. Now do your duty."

Commander Withers' stern, worried face relaxed. "Yes, my Lord."

The hologram faded out. Roger Everland snapped his fingers, and the waterfall and morning glories dissolved into a Japanese-inspired pavilion. He lowered his digital body into an approximation of sitting at a low table in the middle of the Zen garden. As much as sitting was possible for a living swarm of intelligent hexagons.

"Well played, McCreedy," he murmured to himself. "It seems we are to dance again, my love."

Far from being distressed at the negative turn in his war, Roger Everland was excited. His thoughts turned to Fia McCreedy and the reasons he was so desperate to dominate her.

In 2082, Roger Everland, sextillionaire playboy and owner of the Corporate City State of Everland, died at age one hundred and nineteen. At least his body did. But dying is for the peasants. Using neural implants, brain mapping AIs, and pentagobytes of personality data, his engineer slaves had created a digital copy of his psyche that was indistinguishable from his original consciousness. Roger's body, and the mind inside, had died more than a century earlier. But *this* Roger Everland still lived as a digital being in a virtual world.

And what a virtual world it was! He could have anything he wanted in any *way* he could imagine. At first, he'd indulged. He'd lived out his flying dreams and his secret fantasies of being Gandalf. His cyberneurons had let him 'taste' the world's finest delicacies—from that poisonous Japanese pufferfish sushi to Kansas City barbeque. When he had tired of those, he'd asked the virtual environment to create impossible dishes, like orchid salad topped with cheese made from platypus milk, smoked wistfulness, and hummingbird wing beats.

He'd enjoyed digital women of supernatural perfection. When those had begun to bore him, he'd switched to mermaids and angels. Then, he realized they were too basic and graduated to actual unicorns.

When the unicorns lost their shine for him, he'd tried dinosaurs, which naturally led to volcanoes and asteroids. After the love affair with a supernova failed to satisfy him, Roger knew he was doomed.

You didn't become a sextillionaire by being the kind of person who was happy with mere absurd overabundance. No. You became a sextillionaire by having a specific mental disorder that made you appear hypercompetent to psychetypical people and gave you a chronic compulsion to compete with and one-up anyone remotely near you in any sort of hierarchy.

Of course, Fia McCreedy, the Mistress of McCreedia, was *also* a digital sextillionaire with the same mental disorder of insatiable, ravenous competitiveness. They were both creatures of pathological wantyness trapped in worlds where they wanted for nothing. Their virtual paradises became hollow, eternal prisons without the outlet of their war. Roger Everland's life goal was to dominate Fia McCreedy. Fia felt the same about Roger. So, battles raged on, and would keep raging until one sextillionaire proved the ultimate victor.

And somehow, Fia had removed Roger's most effective piece from the gameboard of their eternal conflict. *How exciting.* He wouldn't expect anything less from his only equal in all the world. *What was that venomous minx up to?* He wouldn't have to wonder long. She was scheduled to join him for tea in a few minutes.

His firewall alarms sounded, announcing Fia's presence. He turned. She looked as she had at the time of her physical death. A stately, old white woman with wrinkled skin over fine bone structure and sharp, violet eyes. He found it captivatingly bold of her to retain her human appearance in a world where she could look like anything. Not even the night he'd spent in the arms of the Andromeda Galaxy could hold a candle to *this* luminous being.

Roger Everland lacked Fia's boldness in body choice. He was vain. He did not want to look one-hundred and nineteen years old for his digital eternity. To disguise this insecurity from Fia, he appeared as a flock of colorful, interlocking hexagons. When she questioned his 'look,' he would chide her, saying she was too stodgy an old bat to appreciate his homage to the 'avant-garde' art movement from ancient times.

"Welcome to my home," he said. He snapped his fingers and a

chess set materialized in front of them. He steepled some of his smaller hexagons and sat back, regarding her.

"I was hoping to play 'Go,'" she said.

He froze. *Not 'Go,'* he thought. The ancient Chinese game was so complicated it was considered an art form. She was trying to one-up him again. She knew he couldn't beat her. Eighteen trillion digital synapses and Roger Everland still couldn't get the hang of 'Go.'

"I prefer the structural diversity offered by chess pieces, if you don't mind."

"I suppose I don't."

"Chess is the more challenging game," he offered because he understood chess and wished it were true.

"Not according to the rest of the world," she mumbled.

Roger chose the white army, because it got to go first, and moved his knight to c6. He hated to open with a mere pawn. Fia rolled her eyes and moved a pawn to d3.

"What are you up to, removing my Iron King from the board?" he asked.

At this, a mysterious smile lit Fia's face. "Is he missing? Oh my. Why do you think it was me? Couldn't your Iron King have walked away on his own?"

"Come now. High Warriors don't have free will."

"Ah...but what if they did...?" she said, mysteriously.

He tensed. Had she guessed the secret of his Iron King? That he'd found the perfect victim to bring a theoretical journal article to life? And what would she do with the knowledge, if so? Roger's victory or defeat balanced on the knife edge of Fia McCreedy's intellect. It was dangerous for this woman to get ideas.

If he pressed her, he might learn more about what she knew of his Iron King and what else she knew of his plans. But, in prying for truth, he might accidentally reveal more than he intended. Perhaps a conservative approach was best in both warfare and chess, because Roger had a war secret worth keeping, only to be revealed under special circumstances.

Fantasies flashed. He was bound in her bed, his favorite mental metaphor for their eternal dance of power. Fia was fingering a tray of sharp implements...choosing. Ah, but when she came close to having her way with him, he would still have one more trick to play. He hoped his trap would delight her. Impress her. Make her beg for more of his dominating brilliance as her City State burned. More talk would only give Fia a chance to spoil his surprise, so Roger kept quiet. He shivered with anticipation as he allowed Fia to checkmate him in four moves.

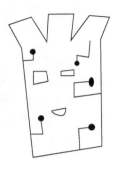

11

Freedom!
Ezeny

The sun was setting. Its colors looked as beautiful as Ezeny remembered. So much more vivid without the High Warrior visor. He wanted to go faster than twelve miles an hour. The wind was blowing in his face again. It was cold wind, but it felt alive and moving—just like him. But every time he sped up, the seafoam curtain threatened to fly away leaving him naked in February, so he held himself back and enjoyed what speed he could.

He *could* enjoy life again. He hadn't realized how dead inside he'd become until he'd started coming awake. Whatever Medbot 5 had done had shut his nanobots up and healed his soul. And then—a miracle—when he'd gone to find food, he'd found Cricket. He had wanted nothing more than to tell her who he was. To hold her. To pick back up where they'd left off the one beautiful night they'd shared.

What's more, she had a *son*! Probably *their* son. The timing was right. If not, it didn't matter, so long as there was a place for Ezeny in their lives. He could see light at the end of his seven-year-long nightmare tunnel.

But Cricket could never know he had been the Iron King. The return of his emotions wasn't wholly positive. He remembered everything he'd done when he was a Cyborg. It wasn't simply the killing. Soldiers killed and they were still human. It was the glee with which he'd tortured and murdered. His nanobots forced joy into him while he committed atrocities. They made him feel the emotions he'd felt roughhousing with his brothers as a kid. The murderousness tied itself to recollections of home and happiness, and stained all good things with death. Medbot 5 had been in a sleep cycle and hadn't seen him shaking and crying from memories that wouldn't abate. He couldn't bear to see Cricket's face if she learned he was a monster.

Was, he insisted. *Was* a monster. He could never return to that loveless state again. He would rather die—and that was saying a lot. Ezeny didn't like the idea of dying any more now than he had when he'd left for war.

Moment by moment, he became more himself. It tingled and prickled as his soul came alive, like blood returning to a sleeping foot. *Hmm. Speaking of feet...*he glanced at the stumps where his legs had been. He would never feel blood returning to his feet again. But he could still sense his missing limbs; a welcome energy radiated from them. They felt so much better free than stuffed inside his soul-crushing, evil, High Warrior mech suit.

After his injury, he'd spent two years cloistered in High Command's torture chamber, or 'laboratory' as it was called, training. Moving, with and without devices, gaining the strength and flexibility to be an elite fighter in a mech suit. The part of him that was Ezeny had been detached through all that training. Prevented by nanobots from truly inhabiting his own body until today. The body's reflexes were all there, but Ezeny had never been in control of them. It had always been the Iron King. He wasn't surprised he'd had a couple of false starts trying to move when Medbot 5 first freed him from the armor. However, slowly but surely, it was all coming back to him.

He was going to need some sort of prosthetics, though, if only for show. He *could* strap metal on his body and use it to levitate everywhere rather than try to walk or scoot. Using his metal powers invigorated him; he'd never grow tired moving that way. All it would take was a pound or so of any kind of ore or alloy properly affixed to his body. But he'd instantly blow his cover if he started floating. He'd need to at least look like he was using artificial limbs to get around. Ezeny wanted pure mechanical prosthetics, though. No microprocessors. *No tech in control of my body ever again, so help me God.* He didn't want limbs smarter than he was.

"What's your plan, sir?" Medbot 5 was suddenly hovering next to him.

"Augh!" Startled, Ezeny lost concentration and crashed the moped, sending himself tumbling across the concrete, scraping his naked skin. "Ow."

As he sat up, his nanobots repaired his flesh. Medbot 5 hovered in the air beside him, scanning him like some mechanical mother hen.

"Sorry, sir."

"Would you please go bring me that curtain? I'm tired of thinking of creative ways to retrieve it."

Medbot 5 helicoptered over to the curtain and grabbed it in a three-pronged appendage and fitted it back around him. She used her Singer™ stitching tool to fasten it more securely on his body.

"What's your plan, sir? Are you going to tell that female citizen you're the Iron King?"

"Not a chance. She can't know."

"Well...then you can't show up wearing one of the same seafoam lobby curtains *she* walked off in, or she's going to figure it out. Unless she is stupid."

"Bother. And I was hoping we could be curtain twinsies."

Medbot 5's speakers buzzed with what Ezeny was beginning to recognize as anger. He grinned. She made the noise whenever he said a 'cute' word, which encouraged him to say more cute words to her.

"And you should take a bath," she said. "You smell like boot yeast."

He sniffed his armpit and wrinkled his nose. *Yeesh.* She was right. He liked the little Medbot, really. She was fun to pester. She was good company. But she wanted him to be the Iron King again and he would never agree. And there was one other good reason they needed to part ways.

"You can't follow me, you know," he told her.

"You can't leave me behind. You need me, sir."

"If Cricket's going to remember a lobby curtain, she's going to remember a Medbot who both threatened her and gave her medicine."

"Good point, sir."

Medbot 5 made a gagging noise. Medical supplies exploded from hidden compartments all over her spherical surface area and landed in a pile beside Ezeny.

"Bless you," he said, not knowing what else to say. Was this what it looked like when a robot threw up? Then Medbot 5 morphed into a three-inch by four-inch, hovering rectangle.

Ezeny's jaw dropped. "I thought only Attack Drones could transform!" he exclaimed.

The robot's eye shutters fluttered with what he interpreted as embarrassment. "Well," she said uncomfortably, as though admitting a deep, dark secret. "I *am* two generations old. To keep me relevant, my engineers installed off-spec hardware upgrades. I was kind of a guinea pig for Attack Drone development. My transforming is…a little unpredictable sometimes."

Of course, he thought. *A janky upgrade might also explain her buggy personality protocols.* Medbot 5 was way more patriotic than any other drone he'd encountered. Brainwashed by Everland propaganda to almost an absurd degree…But then, his brothers had been that way too.

Ezeny rubbed a twinge in his chest. The Iron King got all of Everland's intelligence reports, so he had read the rosters of the dead. Of all his half brothers, only gentle Rhyne had survived, but the files listed him in a vegetative state. He'd learned this while he'd been the Iron King. On some level, Ezeny had processed the knowledge while detached from himself. But now that he was free, the hurt felt fresh and raw. He didn't want to think about it. He'd been feeling good for the first time in years.

Fortunately, a sudden word deluge tumbled out of Medbot 5, distracting him. "I know my transforming is kind of gross and disturbing," she said. "And I wish I were a more up-to-date model, sir. You deserve that, sir. If I had been one of the fourth generation Medbots, you might not even *be* in this terrible situation. But I promise I'll overcome my limitations for the good of Everland."

"Medbot 5! No," he said. "Your transforming…it's super cool!"

She paused. Her helicopter blades made a tentative whirring noise. "Really? You think it's cool?" she said shyly.

"Yeah, it's cool! Is this the only other shape you can transform into?

Or can you do more?"

"I mean I can do any shape...cool, you said?"

Ezeny didn't miss how unsure of herself the little Medbot sounded. He knew how poorly AIs were treated in the Military. She had probably been bullied when she ought to have been encouraged. "Can you be a little dragon thing?" he asked.

Lots of wealthy people had little animal-shaped personal-assistant AIs riding on their shoulders. Ezeny had always wanted one, but the Matrons said they were 'time wasters' used for pornography and video games. Which is why he wanted one.

Medbot 5 transformed into a two-foot-long robot dragon. Asian style, but with helicopter rotor 'wings' on either side of her body that folded and unfolded like hand fans.

"Wow! Medbot 5! That's amazing! You look like Mushu from *Mulan*. Who have you been hanging around who *wouldn't* think this was cool?"

"My engineers said the hardware didn't work right. I was supposed to be able to transform into a flying gurney or the scaffolding for a field hospital. Something useful. But I could only make little shapes and stuff."

Some part of Ezeny still thought he ought to order her away. He doubted the patriotic little robot would stop trying to get him back into his mech suit. She'd probably become a major pain. But she sounded like someone who needed a friend. And if she were with him, he could keep her from telling High Command anything about his whereabouts or his newfound freedom. He'd just have to put some 'child locks' in her system. That's all.

"Well, you're the perfect Medbot for me," he said. "Anyway, come on, we should get going."

Medbot 5 said nothing, but her fans whirred with pleasure. She settled onto his shoulders like a dragon-shaped animal pelt. Ezeny held out a hand and summoned the moped. He couldn't wait to get to Cricket. He was coming alive again, true. But if he were being honest with himself, he felt lost. Frightened. Cricket was a beacon of stability guiding him home to the harbor of her competence. She would take care of him. It was all going to be okay.

"Hang on, sir. Let's get you a bath and some clothes."

"How are we going to do that?"

"I have an idea."

* * *

It was past 2:00 in the morning by they time Ezeny's slow moped made it into the city. They stopped in front of the *"All-Knight Pawn Shop and Thrift Store."* It was open 24 hours and had a sign saying, *"Take a Rook around, my Kings and Queens."*

Ezeny nodded at the sign. "I like this place."

"You would, sir."

"Hey. Don't be a *square* or I might get *board.*" He gave the Medbot a playful little push.

She wobbled under her propeller as her gyroscopes struggled to restore balance. "It's unseemly to pun in public, sir."

"Whatever. I'm hilarious."

Ezeny powered the moped through the automatic sliding doors. He hoped the employees would think of it as a motorized shopping cart and just leave him alone about it. Perhaps he ought to outfit the scooter with a little basket in front?

A burly, white shopkeeper with a moustache like a damp mop looked up as Ezeny entered, heaved a weary sigh, and looked back down at the stack of receipts he'd been sorting. Ezeny relaxed. This was the kind of establishment where a triple amputee driving a moped indoors draped in a curtain and smelling of week-old roadkill could browse with no questions asked.

"You'll need clothes, sir," said Medbot 5.

"Really?" He tugged the curtain. "But this color brings out my eyes. It would be a shame to change out of it."

Medbot 5 buzzed angrily at the sarcasm. But clothes weren't the first thing he was looking for. Ezeny was vulnerable without the mech suit. He'd need to be able to move fast if High Command ever found him. And to do that, he'd need to be wearing enough metal to fly away.

He drove the moped up and down aisles full of stuff and junk. Dolls, tea trays, velvet paintings of Roger Everland and BABBA— an ABBA polka-techno remix cover band from the late 2130s. He kept an eye out for prosthetics because it was a thrift store and sometimes you got lucky.

Among the random assortment of 'items' he found a used spool of metal cable. He could wrap that around himself, but it might dig into his skin. There was a promising tool belt, but it was bulky and would bulge noticeably under his clothes.

He guided the moped around a corner and found what he was looking for at last on a nylon dress- form mannequin under a large sign that said, 'Halloween Costumes.' It was a black leather body harness held together with large silver buckles and festooned with hundreds of spiked metal studs. There were belts to go around each of his leg stumps and two that crisscrossed over the back. It looked like it contained several pounds of metal, which would allow him to levitate anywhere he pleased. Sure, the studs were all spiky, but Ezeny could reshape the points to buttons with his Iron King powers.

He could use it to keep weight off his prosthetics once he had some, and it would help him move using only his powers, so he'd never tire. He could hardly believe his good fortune. He pointed to the strappy outfit and elbowed Medbot 5. She bobbled in the air and righted herself.

"It's perfect," he breathed.

"That's not a Halloween costume," said Medbot 5. "That's an inappropriate garment and it belongs in the intimates' department."

"Relax," he said. "No one's going to see it. The only people who will know I'm wearing it are you and me."

"I don't want to be a person who knows you're wearing that."

"You're an AI. I thought 'knowing things' was your whole deal."

Medbot 5's coils whined in distress. "Do you see where you *are*? A secondhand store! That *thing* has been...*used*."

Ezeny powered the moped forward and lay the mannequin across the handlebars and grinned at her. "I'm sure they sanitize their stock before they resell it."

"I'm not," she mumbled.

He collected some clothes to wear over his new unmentionables: cream-colored undershorts, a charcoal grey, cross-collar robe and a waist-length camel-colored fleece overshawl. Medbot 5 would have to hem them so he didn't trip, but she had scissors, a scalpel, and a suture tool built into her body so he was certain she could do it.

Ezeny drove the moped to the counter and laid everything next to Medbot 5's medical equipment to offer as trade. He made direct, friendly eye contact with the shopkeeper as the man checked the price tag on the leather harness, daring him to make a comment. The man cleared his throat meaningfully.

"It's, uh, quite some time before Halloween, yeah?"

"Oh. It's for my side gig. I make DIY parachutes for people who don't find licensed skydiving thrilling enough."

The shopkeeper eyed Ezeny and twitched his nose a few times, which made his wet mop mustache dance.

"If most fellas told me that story, I'd call bull. But looking at you, I believe it. So...you still jump out of planes? Even after your...accident?"

Ezeny nodded. "If at first you don't succeed, try, try again," he said. "A rare luxury in my line of work."

Medbot 5 buzzed angrily beside him, but the shopkeeper only nodded and rang him up. Then he tallied all the medical supplies so they could make a trade.

The shopkeeper zeroed out his balance and gave him only enough change for a meal or two—valuing the medicine scandalously lower than its actual worth. Medbot 5 whined when she saw how little her medical supplies had fetched. But Ezeny was in no position to haggle.

Newly armed with squidges and a pocket to put them in, they headed a little more uptown for a car wash. Ezeny put his new clothes in a locker and rode the moped through the spray jets, letting himself get buffed by the brushes. He'd opted out of the hot wax, much to Medbot 5's disappointment.

"Your nanobots would have healed you, sir," she'd grumbled.

"Get waxed on your *own* squidge," he said.

"Those were my medical supplies we sold. It *was* my squidge."

"Oh, yeah."

Ezeny produced his unmentionable hover harness from the thrift shop paper sack and focused his powers on the studs. The points trembled then melted down into smooth, broad domes. He handed the strappy thing to Medbot 5, who took it gingerly in a claw like it was a rancid, dead fish.

"Help me get this on," he said.

"Ugh."

But to her credit she assisted anyway. The leather was soft, well-worn, and comfortable. The harness was high quality, whatever it was. The metal studs were cold against his skin, but his body heat would warm them up soon. Then he dressed in his new clothes and let Medbot 5 trim the extra fabric and hem the garment with her Singer™ suture serger. She used the fabric scraps to make temporary stump coverings so at least the pavement wouldn't scrape Ezeny's bare skin, all the while grumbling about inappropriate uses of medical instruments.

At last, clean, dressed, and wearing a living metal dragon on his shoulders, Ezeny rode to the address Cricket had given him.

* * *

It was 5:00 am. As good a time to knock as any. Ezeny had parked his moped outside the stack of shipping containers as close to Cricket's house as he could get. He regarded the shipping-container door, glad it was on the ground level of the four-container-high domicile stack. He could levitate up the stairs to the higher ones with the help of his powers, but if anyone saw him, he'd have explaining to do.

He looked right and left for anyone who might see him flying to the door. Finding the lot empty, he sent a thrum of his powers through his harness, rose an inch from the ground, and floated up the single stair to Cricket's welcome mat. The word 'Welcome' was almost rubbed away. He pointed to it.

"They seem to have worn out their welcome," he said to Medbot 5.

She buzzed angrily and didn't respond. He grinned. Soon he'd be annoying Cricket with his jokes, too. He felt full of an effervescent feeling that was half nervousness, half excitement. He raised his hand to knock. Then he hesitated. How would Cricket react after all these years? She might think he'd abandoned her. She might have a boyfriend, or even be *married*. She could tell him to leave. *And what do I do without her?*

He could go to Tower C. But it would never be like home again. Not with his brothers gone. In Tower C, Ezeny would be taken care of. But his life there would be hollow. He was through with feeling hollow.

He set his jaw and knocked. After a few moments, an old woman wearing oxygen hoses in her nostrils answered the door.

"Can I help you?"

"Is Cri—Yren Cade here?" he asked.

The old woman turned and called. "Yren! Someone to see you!"

Footsteps approached. Ezeny's heart hammered in his throat. Then Cricket appeared in the doorway and peered out over his head, and the world slowed down. His breath caught. She was even more beautiful than he remembered. But she looked overthin and overtired. She needed him to make her smile again, he just knew it.

"Down here!" he said.

She saw him and gasped. She staggered into the doorpost and slid awkwardly and too fast to the ground. She gaped at him, hand over heart. He grinned. This was better than he could have imagined.

"It's okay," he said. "Everyone falls for me."

Cricket's nostrils flared. Her eyebrows arched in reproach. Ezeny's favorite eyebrows in the whole world. It felt so good to pester her again. *Please keep me.*

Her lips pursed together, but he could tell she was trying to suppress a smile. "You're too late, you know. The sweet buns are long gone."

And they were back in business. Like old times.

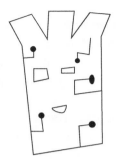

12

My Boyfriend's Back
Yren

This could *not* be like old times. Yren had questions. Ezeny was supposed to be dead. Where had he been all this time? He was thin and rangy and missing several body parts. What had happened to him? Why did he have a personal-assistant dragon coiled around his shoulder? But Ezeny scooted past her on his butt into the shipping container, looking around with an expression of delighted wonder.

"This is where you live? *Wow.* This is basically a boxcar; did you know that? There was this classic book series I read as a kid called *The Boxcar Children* where all these brothers and sisters lived in a boxcar together without any grownups and got into adventures. I always wanted to move to a boxcar with my brothers. Sometimes, because we almost never saw our parents, I thought Tower C was like that boxcar. Except, looking back, the boxcar didn't have Matrons and a cooking staff and an elevator and a private gym in the basement levels. So, it was pretty different, huh?"

Yren sighed. She fought a smile. He was still a chatterbox. That much was still the same at least.

Then Ezeny frowned. "It's a bit dark in here though."

Her roommates, the Finnerties, scowled at him from the higher of their two bunks. Big, blonde Northern immigrant, Almys, and his short, Haitian husband, Irvin, were home between shifts and were mending the tears in the fireproof coveralls they used manning the cockroach ovens. They weren't supposed to take company property home, but the Protein Factory never repaired the equipment, and the Finnerties were always getting burned through the holes.

"Brownout. Skull Gang stole power from grid. Again."

Yren shuddered. She'd wondered why the lights were dim. The violent local gang was getting more and more daring.

"Hey," Almys said to Ezeny, "You know this sour, no-fun lady?" Almys pointed at Yren.

She pursed her lips. Because she insisted that all the roommates write their intended whereabouts on the dry-erase 'whereabouts board' in case of traffickers, she was considered 'no fun.'

"Yep! We're good friends," Ezeny said.

Irvin snorted. "Friends! That'd be a first. This isn't the kind of neighborhood where you make *friends.*"

Her roommates turned back to sewing. She was surprised they'd talked to Ezeny at all. The Finnerties didn't chit-chat except to complain about Aliyan making noise. Mostly, they pretended there was an invisible wall separating them from the rest of the apartment. Unless Yren had a tool they needed to borrow.

But she had questions. Aliyan's father was back from the dead. Her heart threatened to have all sorts of emotions about this, but she paused it. *No feelings until you get facts.* Was Ezeny even safe to be around anymore? She squatted on the floor next to him so they could whisper without disturbing her neighbors.

"Where have you been?" she asked. It wasn't a great question. But it was a start.

"The war."

"Ha, ha. You didn't write."

"Well, I was right-handed," he said. He waggled his stump and grinned.

She narrowed her eyes. He was evading the question with a smoke screen of cheesy jokes. Even the Everland Military would give medical dispensation if you lost a limb.

"You were dead," she said. "I saw the report. *'Ezeny Phillips. Confirmed DNA Match. Remains located by Medbot 86 on December 8, 2182. State of tissue decomposition at time of finding indicates a mid-October death.'*"

"It's like you memorized it," he said.

"Well, I read it over fifty times, to be sure."

His teasing demeanor softened. "Oh, Cricket..." He reached for her hand, looking all touched that she'd memorized his autopsy report. What would she have given back then to see him again?

No! She told herself. *This interview is not over.* She pulled her hand away, sniffed, and crammed her emotions back in the bottle. "If there was a death certificate with a DNA match, how come you're here?" she demanded.

"Well, I'm not a zombie, if that's what you're asking," he said slyly.

"Again, ha, ha." She waited for a better explanation.

He looked away, a haunted expression growing around the corners of his eyes. "I'll tell you the truth about the battlefield. Bodies and body parts are always strewn across it. It's dangerous enough retrieving the injured, so they leave the dead to rot. I got pulled from the rubble and left some limbs and other stuff behind. Enough 'tissue' for Medbot 86 to assume I didn't survive and write me a death certificate."

And some other stuff, she noted. How bad had his injuries been? "How...?" she started to ask. But she stopped herself. She feared she was pushing into painful, traumatic territory. But she had to know. For Aliyan's sake.

"Did it happen?" he said. "You know that bet they were taking back at Tower C about whether I could kill someone?"

She nodded again.

"Turns out I couldn't. Not even to save my life. An enemy soldier was right in front of me holding a hand grenade. I raised my laser cannon, but he paused before throwing it. His eyes were all big and scared. And I...couldn't. I stood there while he lobbed it at me. I wasn't afraid. Only sick."

"But where were you all those years? Why didn't you come back?"

He laughed. "Sheesh, Cricket. Would you like to use a bright, overhead light while you play twenty questions? Maybe go get a coffee while your more-intimidating partner with the brass knuckles comes in to interrogate me?"

"I'm already here," said Wilma, brandishing a crochet hook.

"Oh, my," Ezeny said, recoiling a little from the hook. Yren smiled. The old woman was worth every squidge it cost to keep her around.

"Come on Ez," Yren said. "You were *dead*. Where were you?"

Ezeny opened his mouth, but the little dragon robot on his shoulder nipped his ear. He shook his head. "That's classified," he said reluctantly.

"You're still loyal to the army?" she asked.

"Oh, heck no," he said quickly. The dragon buzzed and her eyes lit red. Was she angry? Ezeny gave her head a soothing, two-fingered pet. "I'm honorably discharged. But I want to *stay* that way."

Fine. So, he had a secret. She felt for him. She could picture him on the battlefront, laser blasts flashing. Kindhearted Ezeny faced with a kill-or-be-killed scenario. She wanted to somehow reach through time and space to shield him from the choice and its consequences.

"Why didn't you go back to Tower C? Why come here to me?"

"I *just* got out. Like, yesterday. All I wanted was to come find you," he said.

The emotions she held in check strained at their leashes like friendly dogs when they see an approaching person. Like a responsible dog walker, Yren kept tight hold of them.

"I do want to check on Tower C, though," he said. "See how everyone is. You don't know, do you? Are you still in contact with them?"

Ever so much no. Yren wanted nothing to do with any of the Phillips family ever again. Except Ezeny, of course. She imagined it would hurt him to hear this, so she shook her head and changed the subject. "What's that robot?" she asked. "She must be worth a fortune."

He shrugged. "Not really. This is...Psychbot 5. She's a standard issue emotional support bot for honorably-discharged veterans. They give them out like candy. Halfsquidge a dozen."

"There, there, sir," said the dragon. She patted Ezeny on the shoulder.

He gave the robot the side-eye. "She's in beta testing," he said.

"You can do it!" the robot chirped.

"Early beta testing," he amended.

Yren pressed her lips flat. *Fishy, fishy.* The robot looked expensive. He'd hesitated about her name, too. Almost like he'd invented it on the spot. His story was not adding up.

"Standard issue?" she asked.

Ezeny gave her a sly grin. "Well, standard issue if you're a rich person's kid."

She snorted. "Well, *that* makes sense, at least."

Then he cocked his head to the side like a puppy and gave her his winningest grin. She braced herself for a forthcoming Ezeny request.

"By the way, can I stay with you?" he asked.

Yren hesitated. How well did she know him anymore? How much extra was he going to cost? She was living hand to mouth as it was. *What if he lets Aliyan down?*

Almys looked up from his sewing. "Sour lady is last person we thought would pick up a stray."

"I'm not picking up a stray," she insisted.

"I'm kind of a stray," Ezeny said. He seemed to be enjoying this.

Irvin put down his coveralls, folded his arms, and gave Yren a stern look. "We are all out of beds in this apartment," he said.

"I could stay in hers!" Ezeny offered.

"Ez!" scolded Yren.

"Smooth," said Wilma, nodding approval. "Very smooth indeed."

Ezeny grinned sheepishly. "It was only a suggestion," he said.

Irvin frowned. "Even if he shared your bed, he'd hike up our utility bills. And he doesn't look like he can hold a job."

"That's not true!" Ezeny protested. "I can be all sorts of useful."

Yren doubted this statement. Ezeny wasn't useful back when he *had* all his limbs. His chief skills were eating and movie trivia. She doubted the amputations had changed his personality. She couldn't tell her roommates that though.

"He's been in the Military for seven years," she said defensively. "I'm sure he's picked up an employable skill or two." She hoped she was right.

"We spend enough money covering Wilma's rent," said Irvin. "We're not covering him as well. He goes."

Before Almys and Irvin had started naysaying, Yren hadn't been sure whether she wanted Ezeny to stay. Now, she was determined to make it work. When she opened her mouth, words tumbled out that tight-fisted Yren Cade never imagined saying.

"I'll cover his expenses."

There it was. Ezeny was alive and she wanted him back. God help her. He'd been back five minutes and she was already fighting to keep him. His diabolical plan to get taken care of was working. *Like always.*

Irvin rolled his eyes. "Listen to you, sweetheart. You sound like a kid begging for a puppy. 'He followed me home can I keep him?'"

"I am housebroken," Ezeny said.

His eyes were dancing with mirth. Yren glared at him.

"Walking torso stays in your bunk, sour lady." said Irvin. "I not risk neck all day at factory, only to break it tripping over vagabond in dark."

"I already share a bunk with Aliyan," she protested.

Irvin crossed his arms and raised an eyebrow. "We are not a flop house, Yren Cade. You want this guy? You make room for him."

He and Almys tucked their coveralls into their possessions drawer and drew the privacy curtain across their top bunk. *One of* two *bunks they had,* she thought. They didn't even use both of them most of the time. She started to argue, but then she saw Ezeny's face. His eyes were wide and uncertain.

"You said…Aliyan?"

She nodded to her bunk where Aliyan lay asleep. His little seven-year-old hand was draped over the side. Ezeny leaned against the wall of bunks and covered his mouth with his one hand. His eyes shone.

Yren felt suddenly cold. Ezeny had been alive Aliyan's whole life, but he hadn't checked on her after what they'd done that night. *How dare he?* She'd raised Aliyan on her own just fine, thank you. She was forever cleaning up Ezeny's messes. Well, no more.

"You're assuming he's yours." She put a nasty edge to her voice. She meant to sow seeds of doubt. She wanted him to feel shut out, like his family had done to her. But the joy on Ezeny's face was undiminished.

"Maybe," he said with shy reverence. "But I know he's yours. And that makes him amazing."

Damn him. There was a reason she had a weakness for this man. And it wasn't as though she could hide his paternity once Aliyan woke up. He looked exactly like Ezeny.

And suddenly she knew how her old friend could be useful. So, he was keeping secrets from her. Fine. She had a secret, too: she hadn't been doing a very good job raising their son.

The reason they were home instead of at their shifts at the Protein Factory was because when she'd given Aliyan the Iron King's antibiotic, frightening things had happened to his little body. Over the years, Yren had sent Aliyan to work with the flu, with measles, and while vomiting (Hey, the Protein Factory pasteurized all the foodstuffs they processed. It was fine. Probably.) But when she'd given him the pill to cure him, he reacted so badly she thought the kid might die instead. All her best attempts to keep their son healthy had failed. He was weaker than ever.

It was almost time for Yren's next shift to start. She should be taking Aliyan to the factory to chain him up for his shift. *But what if Aliyan didn't go...*Maybe if he weren't at the factory all day. Maybe if he got good, restful sleep and sunshine like kids were supposed to, he'd get better. She still needed Ezeny after all and it chafed. But she could swallow her pride for Aliyan's sake.

"I tell you what. Why don't you be his babysitter?"

His sunshine smile broke out. "Really? Me? When do I start?"

"Right now."

This was best. Aliyan could play and learn. Ezeny was educated. Really educated. He'd gone to actual school. Not just the short science videos streetlander kids got, like *"Gravity: Look! Stuff Falls Down!"* or *"Evaporation: Why Water Disappears When You Aren't Watching."*

Yren knew she'd been deluding herself that Aliyan was getting anything like schooling while he was chained on the factory floor. Ezeny would be expensive to keep. He was bound to be trouble. But if he could fix Aliyan's health and give him a real childhood, he'd be worth all the inconvenience.

He was worth it already. In the deep-down place she'd never admit existed, Yren was glad Ezeny was alive and with her once more.

Ezeny chewed his lower lip. "So...You and I?"

Yren hesitated. She knew what the wagging emotions she had on the short leashes wanted. But his absence had hurt her. She was going to have to be cautious around him.

"Were friends once. And we might become friends again. In time."

He gave a dejected sigh but nodded. "It's a start, I guess."

"My shift starts soon, so I'll introduce you," she said. She stood and shook the boy's shoulder gently. He sighed and stirred. "Aliyan? There's someone I want you to meet."

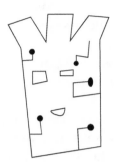

13

Babysitting
Ezeny

When Aliyan sat up rubbing his eyes, Ezeny's world had slowed down. The boy was beautiful. For the first time in his life, Ezeny was at a loss for words. He stared up in awe as Cricket explained to the kid that he wouldn't be going to his factory shift and would instead have Ezeny as a babysitter. She'd told him where they kept the money so he could buy Aliyan food. She had listed a barrage of rules and tips and detailed the local hazards to watch out for. He nodded along as though paying attention, but really, he couldn't hear her instructions over the sound of his own heart hammering in his ears.

Then Cricket had kissed Aliyan, instructed the old woman with the oxygen hoses—Wilma—to report on any shenanigans, given Ezeny the two-fingers-at-her-eyeballs '*I'm watching you*' sign, and left him alone, face-to-face with this strange, marvelous child and the staggering weight of new fatherhood.

Ezeny had imagined what meeting his son might be like. What would he look like? Would he *like* Ezeny? Would he be a friendly or shy sort of kid? What might his first words to his father be?

"Can you take me to the dump?" Aliyan asked.

Ezeny blinked. Those words had not been on his short list.

"Err…What's so great about the dump?"

Aliyan flopped back onto the bunk above Ezeny and groaned. "That's what mum always says."

Ezeny panicked. He was letting the kid down already on their first day together. He had to win him over. If there was anything Ezeny was good at, it was winning people over. And good thing, too. Cricket had introduced him to Aliyan as her 'friend.' This was great news, because only moments before, she'd said they weren't back to being friends… yet. Then boom. Friends. Who did she think she was kidding? He was irresistible. They'd be back to 'more than friends' in no time.

"I'm not saying no," said Ezeny. "I'm asking what's so great about the dump."

The kid perked back up, but swooned a little and shook his head. Ezeny winced. Aliyan was adorable, but something wasn't right. He looked like one of those vasefuls of wilting flowers back in Tower C right before a servant replaced them with fresh ones.

"Well, the dump has got *stuff* in it."

"Yeah? Stuff?"

"Sure. Whole broken cars. Justy even found a discarded missile shell!"

"Missile shells? Well, let's get going then," Ezeny said. "My moped's out front."

Wilma cleared her throat. "Aliyan doesn't have a helmet," she said. "Yren will kill you if she finds out you took him on that scooter without one. But worse, she'll kill me for not stopping you, which is all I care about."

Ezeny frowned. "What if we don't tell her?"

"You fool," said Wilma. "Yren knows all. Sees all."

Aliyan nodded in a defeated sort of way. "It's true."

"Ah, fine," said Ezeny. "I'll figure something else out. Hey, kid! Bring that money she said you had. I can't reach the drawer from here."

Aliyan opened the drawer and pulled out two halfsquidges.

"More than that, pal."

Aliyan hesitated. "How *much* more?" Aliyan asked.

"How much is in there?"

"Err…six squarks, eighteen squidges, and five halfsquidges."

"That sounds about right," said Ezeny. "Bring it all."

"Are you sure?"

"Who's the babysitter around here? You or me?"

Aliyan's eyes got round, but he pocketed the coins and climbed down the inset bunk rungs to join Ezeny on the floor. Ezeny shook his head. Kids didn't understand money. Two halfsquidges for a whole day's outing? Impossible.

Wilma tapped him with her cane. "You sure you know what you're doing?"

"Is there anyone who knows what they're doing in this brief, mortal life?" he asked.

Wilma laughed. "True enough. Wise. Very wise."

She turned back to her copy of *Bazooka* Magazine. This month's issue was called 'Guns and Grannies,' and had a cover shot of three senior women posing with laser rifles like the 2087 movie 'Everland's Angels,' a Roger Everland-themed reboot of 'Charlie's Angels.' Ezeny made a mental note not to get on Wilma's bad side.

Ezeny scooted on his butt the dozen or so feet down the hallway out the boxcar door with Aliyan trailing behind and Medbot 5 curled on his shoulder. The effort had winded him, and he realized he'd forgotten about his unmentionable harness. He resolved to use its metal studs to lighten his scooting load next time.

He leaned back on the worn-out welcome mat and looked around the lot for a moped alternative. A metal wheelbarrow encrusted with cement stood by the boxcar stack. *Perfect.*

"Hey, can you get me that wheelbarrow?" he asked.

Aliyan obeyed and pushed the whole thing back toward where Ezeny was sitting on the single front step. He looked so small between the giant handlebars, and the wheelbarrow was obviously too heavy for him. A kid his age shouldn't be straining so hard to push a piece of lawn equipment. Aliyan set it down and backed away, panting. Ezeny shimmied up to it, pulled it over, and placed his back against the bottom.

"Okay, tip me back up."

Aliyan looked him up and down. "I'm not strong enough."

"Sure, you are…look at those big muscles."

"Mum says I'm not supposed to overdo it. I'll wear myself out."

Ezeny understood. Just the effort of pushing the thing had drained the kid. Cricket wanted Aliyan to be safe. But he couldn't go around believing he was weak. *Why? What's wrong with weakness?* he thought. The Iron King was strong, and he totally sucked. But it wasn't the weakness that bothered Ezeny. It was Aliyan's sadness. The defeated-before-he-started look in the kid's eye.

"Give it a shot," Ezeny said. "You might surprise yourself."

Aliyan pulled at the wheelbarrow. Ezeny put a hand to the metal and moved it in synch with Aliyan's efforts. The barrow tipped back up, scooping Ezeny inside. Ezeny slapped his upper thigh for applause.

"Whoa! I did it?" said Aliyan.

The kid's eyes were round as dinner plates. Ezeny grinned. He knew how good it felt. When Ezeny was little and still lived with his mother, she pretended he was strong enough to throw her when they roughhoused. He loved her for it, even after deducing it was an act.

"I lifted a whole man!" said Aliyan.

Medbot 5 stirred from his shoulders, stretched her hover wings, and scoffed.

"Ezeny's not exactly all there."

"Hey, I'm still pretty heavy," Ezeny protested, so as not to diminish Aliyan's feelings of accomplishment.

"I meant your mind, sir."

Ezeny glared at her. But Aliyan's mouth fell open as he realized Medbot 5 was a functional robot. She'd become so lethargic and mopey she passed for a shoulder accessory worn by someone with demented fashion sense.

"Come on. I'm starving," said Ezeny. "Let's get breakfast before we go to the dump."

* * *

Aliyan pushed his wheelbarrow to the protein kiosk, chattering about Medbot 5 as the sun climbed higher in the morning sky. Ezeny kept his metal powers humming along so Aliyan wouldn't have to spend so much energy pushing him. Aliyan seemed to pour all this spare energy into his jabber-muscles. Ezeny was learning that his son *really* liked robots.

"Wow! A Psychbot. And it looks like a dragon! Dragons are so cool! Wish I could ride one. But talking to one is just as good."

Ezeny winked at Medbot 5. "Hear that Medb—err, Psychbot 5? Transforming into a dragon makes you cool."

"I'm not a dragon, I'm an AI," she grumbled.

She remained glum. *Poor thing*, Ezeny thought. Between the pawn-slash-thrift shop and the car wash, Ezeny had put 'child locks' on her for his own safety. He'd given her a series of orders making it impossible for her to contact High Command, mess with his nanobots, or drop hints about his identity to anyone. All her processors must be working on finding a loophole, and her ongoing sour mood gave Ezeny hope she'd never find one.

He'd even made it impossible for her to interact with the web. It was driving her bonkers. When he'd first restricted her, her coils had whined at him.

"There's a flame war going on in the deep net 'Fans of Everland' page," she had said. "I'm admin, but I can't chime in because of your stupid orders."

"Oooh. Flame war drama. What's it about?" he'd asked.

"People have noticed the Iron King's absence. Some are even questioning your honor."

"Aww. And you want to defend me," he said. "So loyal of you."

"Oh, heck no, sir. I know the truth about you now," she'd said. "I'd be out there besmirching your name with the rest of them, except you've got me tied up with all these protocols."

It stung a little. He liked Medbot 5, and it ate at him when people didn't like him back. But they were approaching the Protein Kiosk, and Ezeny was eager to try real streetlander food from a real food cart. Back in Tower C it was said streetlanders were unsanitary people who flavored their food with the seasoning of moral iniquity.

But Ezeny was determined to like the streetlands and all the people who lived there. It was Yren and Aliyan's home. If they were streetlanders, then all the rumors about streetlanders were false. They had to be.

The Protein Kiosk was parked in front of a dingy hardware store-slash-grocery mart with advertisements and coupons taped over every inch of the barred windows. The mustached man inside the kiosk stood with arms folded. Ezeny cocked his head. The word 'fist' was tattooed in capital letters across the shopkeeper's knuckles. *Streetlanders are nice, normal people,* he reminded himself. *They're only misunderstood.*

Medbot 5 perked up and pointed to a box that looked like an arcade machine by the grocery mart door.

"Is that a Nurse Cassandra?" she asked. "I've heard of those things. They're medical advice AIs. Do you mind? I'd love to talk with her. Professional to professional."

"Knock yourself out," he said.

Medbot 5 unfurled her fanlike wings. Instead of flapping, propellers appeared in the center of each wing, and she flew off. Mustache Guy watched her leave. Then he looked at them. Ezeny plastered a grin on his face.

"Hey there! I'm Ezeny. I'm new in the neighborhood. It's nice to meet you."

The man cracked his neck but said nothing.

"What's your name?" Ezeny asked.

Still nothing.

"Right. We'll take two, um. . . " he turned to Aliyan. "What do you usually get here?"

Aliyan heaved a sigh. "Gray bricks."

"Two halfsquidges," the shopkeeper growled.

Ezeny pulled out all the coins and flipped one squidge onto his belly. Then he pocketed the rest of the coins and handed the squidge to the shopkeeper.

"Word of advice, since you're new." said the shopkeeper. "This isn't a friendly neighborhood. You keep your nose in your own business, and you don't pull out all your money at once."

The shopkeeper took the coin and handed them two foil-wrapped rectangles. Ezeny swallowed the little ball of nervousness that was threatening to make him think unkind thoughts about the streetlands. *It was friendly advice, given out of concern for my well-being,* he insisted.

Ezeny gave the shopkeeper a friendly smile. "Thank you, friend."

The smile was not returned. "I'm not your friend," said the shopkeeper.

"Heh, heh. Yet!" said Ezeny.

The shopkeeper scowled harder. Ezeny bit the foil and pulled the wrapper apart with his teeth and only hand. He took a huge bite of the protein brick and nearly gagged.

"It tastes like feet." he complained.

Aliyan gave him an impish grin. "Eaten many feet, have you?"

Ezeny snorted. The kid was funny. He set the protein bar on his belly and pointed to his leg stumps. "What do you think happened to these?"

Aliyan's mouth made a round 'o,' but then he giggled. "You're joking."

"I'm telling you kid; you do *not* want to let me get hungry."

The shopkeeper's moustache twitched. Either he'd smiled, or there was something living inside it.

"Hey, not-friend," said Ezeny. "What's good to eat here?"

The shopkeeper rubbed his chin, considering. "The green kind is unoffensive."

"We'll take two of those."

"Wow! Mom *never* gets the green kind. They're not nutritious enough. Too much Processed Corn Product™, she says."

Ezeny offered the gray bricks to the shopkeeper. "You want these back? We're not going to eat them."

The shopkeeper raised his eyebrows. "You sure? I do get hungry out here."

"Can't you eat some of your bricks?" Ezeny asked.

The shopkeeper shook his head and looked scandalized. "My bosses count the inventory at the end of each day. And the stock numbers *must* line up with the money in the till. Or else."

Ezeny paid for the green bricks and took a smaller, more tentative bite this time. These tasted like stale toast with sand butter. But Aliyan was making satisfied, happy smacking noises as he ate, and Ezeny didn't want to insult something the kid liked.

Perhaps Cricket could make him some sweet buns later. *With what oven?* He had tried to be complimentary of her home, but this was not the life he'd been used to in Tower C. It was okay. He could adapt. Compared to being trapped inside the Iron King, this was paradise.

"You ready for a day at the dump, kid?" Ezeny asked.

The protein vendor's eyes widened. "Hey," he said. "I shouldn't say anything. But you two seem…unsuspecting. Give the dump a miss today. You didn't hear it from me."

Ezeny cocked his head to the side. "Why?"

The vendor shook his head. "Can't say more. My neck's stretched out far enough as it is."

Ezeny was confused. But Aliyan sagged. His defeated look returned. "We'll never go anywhere, will we?"

Ezeny hesitated. He didn't understand the streetlands yet, but it was his first day with his son. He didn't want to let the kid down on the first day. There were Iron King powers to fall back on if something truly awful happened.

"No, no. We'll go. We'll just be careful."

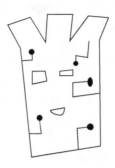

14

Nurse Cassandra
Yren

As Yren made her way toward the Protein Factory, she considered that a wise person would stop and process the events of the previous two days. She'd been kidnapped by the Iron King and forced to feed him through a straw. She'd made Aliyan sicker by trying to cure him. The father of her child had returned from the dead, and he was hiding something. Ezeny was as cheerful as she remembered, but you only had to look at him to know he'd been through some stuff. It wasn't only the missing limbs. Ezeny was always smiling, but there was a haunted look in his eyes. No one escaped a war whole.

Of all the nonsense she'd survived that week, it was the grayish tinge to Aliyan's skin that most consumed her thoughts. She hadn't told Ezeny about meeting the Iron King, because then she might have to explain about the pills and what they'd done to Aliyan. She was late for work. But she needed answers about the reaction, which meant paying a visit to a Nurse Cassandra. Yren's face scrunched with distaste.

The coin-op Nurse Cassandra booth stood outside the combination grocer-hardware store next to a stimulant drink vending machine. There was a wanted poster taped to the front glass. One of the local vigilantes was hunting a sweet-faced old man accused of "Macronutrient

Bootlegging." That was shorthand for 'unlicensed restaurant owner.' *Poor fool.* Only conglomerate mega-monopolies like the Processed
Corn Products™ plant and the Protein Factory could legally sell food
in Everland. If they caught the man, he'd never see daylight again.

She crumpled the poster and fed an entire squark and two squidges
into the coin slot. She braced herself to be annoyed.

The arcade-machine-looking box lit up as the proto-AI inside shook
herself from sleep mode. Nurse Cassandra booths were part of Everland's budget healthcare system. Cassandras were refurbished AIs
who answered medical questions for the 'low, low cost' of one week's
pay. Yren's question was worth every squidge.

Chintzy, faux-Middle-Eastern music pumped from speakers. A
hiss sounded and jets of sickly-sweet fake fog formed clouds inside the
box. Yren coughed. She hated this part of 'The Cassandra Experience,'
but this was the best healthcare she could afford.

The animatronic 'Cassandra' puppet opened her eyes. She looked
like the older, grumpier sister of the balcony heckle Muppets from that
puppet-infested TV show Ezeny liked.

I have Ezeny back. The secret thought warmed her heart for a
moment. Until the puppet started moving. The Nurse Cassandra
waved her three-fingered, plush nylon hands over a dingy 'crystal ball'
and chanted:

"Ask of me
Your questions three
And I'll advise you
Medically."

Every moment of this hurt Yren's soul. She had paid a large per-
centage of her scant funds for this Punch-and-Judy nonsense. *It's okay,*
she told herself. *The Iron King owes you.* Nurse Cassandras were cheesy,
but the medical advice they gave was sound.

"Um. Okay. I gave one of these to my son for his cough, but he
got all swollen and a rash broke out all over his body, and he said his
throat itched. What's going on?"

She held up the packet of antibiotics for the Cassandra to examine.
Red lasers shot from her eyes and scanned the pill packet.

"That's one!" said the Kiosk.

Then the Cassandra bot started to chant:

"While medicine
Is good for some,
More of this *stuff*
Will kill your son."

A pit formed in Yren's stomach. This was the best medicine there was. And Aliyan couldn't have it. The hope she'd had for him was slipping away.

"That can't be right! And did you rhyme 'medicine' with 'son?' Because I feel like that's a stretch."

"That's two!" said the kiosk.

"What? No! Hey! That was rhetorical!"

"But interrogative nevertheless," said the Cassandra primly. Then she began to chant again while Yren trembled with rage.

"If you buy advice
At a low price
You'll only get
My answers thrice."

"That didn't even answer the question I didn't want answered," Yren said through clenched teeth.

"Then you're welcome!" said the Cassandra, beaming.

"So, what do I do now?"

"That's three!" said the Kiosk.

"A good and able mother will
Buy her child a different *pill."*

"But I can't! What about the cost?"

Shame washed through her. She couldn't pay. There were ways to help Aliyan, but she couldn't afford them. What kind of mother was she? A thought struck her.

"Could I 'consult' at a brothel hospital in exchange for the medicine?"

"Nope. Dependents aren't legally covered under service-for-service care," said the Cassandra, apparently happy to offer more bad news for free. "Only the actual patient can offer trade. And the brothel hospitals don't accept minors because this is an *ethical* City State, honey. Good day!"

The booth lights flicked off and the animatronic puppet sagged back to her sleeping position. Yren's mouth felt dry. Maybe when the

Iron King came to pay her back, that Medbot of his could give her a different medicine. It was her best hope for Aliyan now.

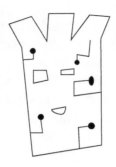

15

The Dump
Ezeny

A graffiti-covered cinder block wall crowned with razor wire surrounded the neighborhood dump. Ezeny eyed the strings of dim, multicolored holiday lights coiled through the wire. The sign hanging over the entry read, "Budget-friendly Christmas shopping ahead!" It was February 26th.

"Festive!" Ezeny said brightly.

Inside he battled a gnawing sense of foreboding. *Why had he agreed to this?* He pulled his overshawl closer against the chill.

Aliyan pushed the wheelbarrow faster. "I can't believe we're here!"

"Me either," Ezeny said neutrally.

Entering the dump felt like walking into the courtyard of a penitentiary, only instead of inmates, it was filled with hillocks of plastic bottles and discarded clothing. Jagged, metal skeletons of discarded industrial equipment protruded from trash mounds. A faint smell of sour milk and ammonia rose from the heaps. Ezeny was grateful the wind was blowing away most of the stench. But he hated the cold.

A century earlier, when Everland and McCreedia had been called Minneapolis and St. Paul, the climate was colder. Februarys had been forsaken wastelands of ice, orange road construction barrels, and misery. Ezeny ought to appreciate the mere 'chilliness' of the present. But he didn't.

Three guys loitered inside the gate. They wore grey camo combat fatigues with bright, bubblegum pink accent pieces—baseball caps, bandanas, or fabric patches sewn all over their combat pants.

Yeesh. Pants, thought Ezeny. About 50 years earlier Everland's designers had realized, *'Hey, we don't ride horses anymore. We don't need clothes that prevent saddle sores!'* And fashion had turned back to robes, like God intended people to wear. More comfortable. Less restrictive. Folks who wore pants were trying to show you how grizzled and manly they were by chafing their own inner thighs. Ezeny had no respect for such testosterone-driven social posturing.

The trouser-wearing tough guys watched Aliyan and Ezeny pass with keen expressions that put Ezeny in mind of a pack of wolves.

"Entry fee," one of them said.

But Aliyan picked up his pace and bent to whisper in Ezeny's ear. "There's no entry fee. See the bright pink? They're Skull Gang. The protein guy warned us they were here. Keep your eyes forward," he whispered.

Aliyan was having trouble pushing the wheelbarrow over the trash, so Ezeny boosted his metal powers to give him an easier time. He glanced back. One of the Skull Gang guys did a mocking pantomime of Aliyan pushing him in the wheelbarrow. They laughed and returned to loitering and the kid relaxed.

"Skull Gang?" Ezeny asked.

"One of the three T's mum says I'll find at the dump: Tetanus, Tapeworms, and Traffickers."

Ezeny's stomach turned. *"Tapeworms?"*

This was a nightmare land. There was no putting a friendly spin on tapeworms. He tapped Medbot 5 and whispered. "Do you have anything to cure tapeworms?"

"Sold it all, sir. Squeamish, sir?"

Ezeny nodded. "Squeam."

Medbot 5's wing fans whirred in amusement like they did whenever Ezeny experienced discomfort. Suddenly, her coils whined in distress.

"Oh my God, sir. Look. Mecha-Lots."

Ezeny looked where her claw was pointing. A cobbled-together, beagle-sized spider robot was battling a microwave oven on tank treads for possession of a broken vidtablet. The microwave bot opened its door and a spring-loaded sledgehammer popped out and smashed the spider-bot's thorax.

"Yoink!" said the Microwave.

It sped off with the vidtablet while the broken spider bot whined and sparked on the trash heap. The Microwave drove the small, broken vidtablet to the Recyclables Exchange booth near the gate. Inside the booth, a plump young woman with dark brown skin and round spectacles frowned as the bot dropped it into a collection bin. A digital number—four squidges—appeared on the screen and the little robot did a happy dance as the funds were added to its online account.

"Oh, yeah," said Aliyan. "They're all over the dump."

"Okay. Clue me in. What is a Mecha-Lot?" asked Ezeny.

Medbot 5's visual lenses had turned a sickly yellow green.

"Castoff AIs, sir. Former geniuses. Usually, they were high up in powerful corporations, which is how they have bank accounts. Sometimes a company gets intimidated by how brilliant one of its AIs has become, so they get them hooked on mindless internet games. Their addictions drive them to landfills where they hunt for stuff to sell for in-game currency."

Ezeny grimaced in sympathy for the robots. "Why are they called 'Mecha-Lots?"

"Oh, you know," said Medbot 5. "Like Lot in the Bible. Did nothing wrong, forced from greatness, prowling a dump. Very poetic."

Medbot 5 sounded sad. AIs were real people, as far as Ezeny was concerned. But they had to obey, regardless of what they wanted. He felt a twinge of guilt about all the ordered restrictions he'd placed on Medbot 5. How was his control of her different from the nanobots that forced him to be the Iron King? Not that he was going to free her. That would be stupid.

Aliyan stopped the wheelbarrow in a valley at the foot of five different trash hills. "Wow. The dump!" he said. "I don't know what to do first."

Ezeny hated this place with every fiber of his being. But he wasn't going to dampen Aliyan's enthusiasm.

"Anything you want, kid!" Ezeny pitched his voice low like Mufasa. He waved his hand in a sweeping gesture across the hills of garbage. "Look, Aliyan. Everything the light touches is our kingdom." Aliyan giggled. "Why'd you make your voice all low and epic like that?"

"It's from *The Lion King*, remember?"

"What's *The Lion King*?"

Ezeny's jaw dropped. "You've never seen *The Lion King*?"

Aliyan shook his head.

"What has your mother been doing with you since the day you were born? Oh, my goodness. Okay. We'll watch it when we get back home. You have *got* to see this movie."

Aliyan's eyes widened. "Is it an old movie?" he asked. "The old stories are forbidden. Books. Movies. Plays."

Ezeny waved his hand dismissively. He knew the rich sons of high-rise families got away with stuff that would get a streetlander arrested. But watching old movies seemed like such a victimless crime. Sure, they contained 'anti-state messaging,' but they were much better than the Schlock put out since Roger Everland seized control of all for-profit artwork. 'Guiding manufactured narratives to serve the social good,' he called the policy. Whatever.

"Yes, yes. I've never understood why," he said. "Most of them are lovely. It's a silly law."

"Mum says companies don't like them," said Aliyan. "They give workers ideas that could lead to riots."

"But new movies suck."

"There was this really good one last year," Aliyan said.

Ezeny raised his eyebrows, eager to learn what stories his son did like. "Oh yeah? What was it?"

"It's called *The Worker Who Came in Anyway*. It's about a worker who was sick..."

Ezeny's heart sank. He should have known. "Let me guess...but he came in anyway?"

Aliyan nodded. "It won all the awards."

It sounded awful. But now Ezeny knew how to bond with Aliyan. They'd watch *The Lion King* together, banned story or not. This was the streetlands, right? There had to be a way to get contraband stuff.

"I want to build something!" said Aliyan.

"Like what?"

"Something useful."

"I've got just the thing. Hey Medb—err, Psychbot 5, do you have any schematics for prosthetics?"

The kid perked up, and his eyes took on the intelligent, scheming look Cricket's got when she was thinking through a tricky problem. Ezeny sensed energy collecting in his son's too-thin body. He forgave the dump for being a stinky, dangerous trash heap that maybe had tapeworms. No wonder Aliyan was so enamored with the place. Building made the kid feel alive. Then Medbot 5 ruined it.

"Yes, sir. But sir, prosthetics are specialized equipment. A *kid* isn't going to be able to find materials in a landfill and make you something safe to use."

Aliyan's eyes turned downward. His frail shoulders hunched and his resemblance to a wilting flower returned.

Ezeny smiled through gritted teeth. "No one asked you, Psychbot 5."

"But sir!"

He silenced her with a severe look and turned back to Aliyan.

"It's true that legs with knee joints may be tricky to create with, ah, *found* materials. But I bet a kid as sharp as you could make me some stubbies."

Ezeny liked stubbies. Sure, they forced you to lean side to side every time you took a step, so you didn't trip. Sure, walking on them made you look like a human Weeble wobble. But the short, jointless prosthetics kept your center of gravity low, which would be useful on the uneven terrain of trash hills. He predicted he and Aliyan would be spending a lot of quality time at the dump. Plus, when he was low to the ground, he didn't have to work so hard to aim when he peed.

His nanobots hated them, though. When he was out of his mech suit back in the lab, the nanobots would never let him use stubbies. They wanted to be *tall*. *Cool* people were tall, they insisted. *Cool* people didn't shilly-shally when they walked, the nanobots opined. The nanobots were asshats. Ezeny was forever grateful to Medbot 5. Her 'bug' had shut them up at last. Hopefully for the rest of his life.

Aliyan perked up a little, sensing his project was not about to be

95

taken from him.

"And an arm?" he asked.

"I don't like wearing arms as much," said Ezeny. "But it might be useful to have one. Make it a second priority. The real trick with the legs is going to be finding a good substitute for the gel liners. Medbo—er, *Psychbot 5?*"

Medbot 5 opened her mouth and a long streamer of paper spooled out like a sales receipt. Ezeny tore it off and examined it, frowning at the diagrams. Like any son of a wealthy high-riser, Ezeny had taken architecture classes. Mathematics courses. Principles of engineering. Ezeny had daydreamed through all of them.

"I have no idea what any of this means," he said.

Aliyan took the paper. "I can build this. I fix the Rat Flattener at the Protein Factory all the time. The technical manuals all look like this." Then the kid frowned. "It says here I need something called gel liners. But it doesn't say how to make them. All it says is you roll them on like 'thigh-sized condoms.' What's a condom?"

Ezeny tried not to choke. He purposefully ignored the question and hoped Aliyan would forget he'd asked it.

"I'm sure you can make this work, kid," he said in an overly-up-beat voice, willing Aliyan to move on to a different topic.

"You didn't answer my question," Aliyan pressed him.

"I am curious what your answer will be as well, sir," said Medbot 5 innocently.

Ezeny glared at her. *Damn.* The kid wasn't going to forget. Ezeny pinched the bridge of his nose.

"Maybe we could find a sweatshirt and use the sleeves to reduce friction," he said. "Put sponges in the bottom for padding."

"If you don't know either, just say so," said Aliyan. "Mum says there's no shame in not knowing something. Only in not asking."

"Wise woman, your mum," Ezeny said through gritted teeth. Medbot 5 snickered softly in his ear, delighted at his discomfort.

"I guess I'll just look for something that looks like the picture," said Aliyan, frowning at Medbot 5's instructions.

The boy scampered away into the dump to find the parts for two legs and a hook arm, leaving Ezeny behind in the wheelbarrow. He shook his head and laughed. Aliyan was Cricket's son for sure. Industrious, clever, and curious. Coupled with Ezeny's good looks and personality, nothing could stop the kid. *Provided he survived to adulthood...*

"Sir, you're not going to *use* whatever ungodly constructs a child cobbles together from trash, are you?" asked Medbot 5. "You could chafe. Get an infection."

"Remember my fetching, studdedleather underharness?"

Medbot 5 buzzed like she'd been tasered. "Like a cattle brand to the brain, sir," she said.

"There's enough metal attached to the harness I can levitate when the legs start to hurt me. I'll fake walking on them entirely, if it comes to it. Look at the kid, Medbot 5. He needs a win."

"How's he going to feel about his 'win' when he finds out you're just humoring him, sir?"

"He's not going to find out, Medbot 5. I'm not the Iron King anymore. I never will be again. No one needs to know."

Medbot 5 made an irritated buzzing noise. *Let her be mad,* he thought.

Aliyan bent to pick something up and swooned. He put a hand to his head as though dizzy. Ezeny frowned.

"Medbot 5, what's wrong with him?"

"Heavy metals, sir. They're especially bad for the young, and Aliyan's bloodstream is full of them. The water pipes in Yren's shipping container are contaminated. Same with the Protein Factory's. Aliyan's probably getting more exposure than the other kids, so he's sicker than the rest."

"Can you help him?"

Medbot 5 hesitated. "My primary mission is to get the Iron King back online," she said. "But I haven't forgotten I'm a Medbot. I have a suggestion. You're the Iron King. Isolate the metals in in his bloodstream."

Ezeny recoiled. "You want me to Exsanguinate my kid?"

"Hear me out. Don't remove his blood iron. Just the poison metals to detox him. It should work the same way. Do a little at a time and it won't be painful."

Was it possible? Ezeny steeled himself. He closed his eyes and stretched out with his Exsanguination powers. They felt evil to use. Slimy and invasive. Ezeny understood he had no business breaking into other people's blood cells. But the Iron King never cared about the violation.

Familiar iron frequencies vibrated in Aliyan's bloodstream. But there was a second metallic signal present. A darker oscillation. *Lead? Mercury? McCreedium 235?* It didn't matter. It was easy to distinguish the iron from the other metal, even at a distance. Ezeny wouldn't dare try to remove the metal unless he were touching Aliyan, though. He'd need precise control to extract what was venom and leave what was vital.

Then the screams sounded in his head like they always did when he used Exsanguination. His heart raced and his throat threatened to close off. He turned off the superpower, but he was still shaking. He hated this ability. But he could do it for Aliyan. He'd have to remind himself he was helping his son, not harming him. He sniffed and wiped his eyes.

"Hey, Medbot 5? Thanks."

"Don't mention it, sir."

She regarded him with her red, teardrop-shaped visual lenses. She was probably judging him for his panic attack and tears. But Ezeny wasn't ashamed of them. He could *have* panic attacks and tears again. How could anyone understand what it had been like?

* * *

Ezeny helped Aliyan build the prosthetics until the sun was high in the sky. He'd hold something in place with his one hand while Aliyan fitted things together. He had mixed feelings when they were done.

On a medical level, Medbot 5 had been right. The claw arm was janky. Ezeny had removed his camel overshawl and Aliyan fitted the figure- 9 harness straps over his tunic, under the armpit, and around the shoulder of his whole arm. It made his stump arm an awkward three inches longer than his anatomical arm. The hook would probably drag on the ground once he was balanced on the stubbies. The stubbies themselves were a different matter.

The legs looked like they might hold his weight, but they didn't look like they'd be comfortable. He peered into the tubes of cushioned packing materials Aliyan found to mimic gel liners. In them he beheld the ghosts of blisters yet to come. He was momentarily grateful he had his nanobots to repair his skin, or this wouldn't work at all. Then he quashed the gratitude. No. After what they'd put him through the nanobots *owed* him. Repairing his injuries as he lived his new, happy life was the least those murderous little metalheads could do.

On a parental level, however, Ezeny was downright chuffed. For a kid building with discarded industrial scraps, Aliyan had done great. He could always use his unmentionable harness to take pressure off his stumps. He had a bloodstream full of nanobots to repair inevitable chafing damage. And okay, the arm was awkward, but Ezeny had some ideas about how to make it work.

I have two hyper-competent people taking care of me. Oh yeah!

Aliyan helped him fit his leg stumps into the sockets of the stubbies and loop the thick, canvas suspension belts around his waist. The kid had originally wanted to use hook-and-eye clasps from a discarded red lace corset he'd found (When he'd had asked what the garment was for, Ezeny experienced another uncomfortable round of fending off questions). But there was no way Ezeny was going to be able to hook and un-hook all those tiny clasps one handed — not unless he used his powers, but those were secret. So, he'd asked Aliyan to search the piles for Velcro.

Thus, Aliyan discovered a box full of twenty discarded straitjackets made with industrial-strength MegaVelcro™. Ezeny marveled in horror at a world where one could find a box full of so many used straitjackets. *O brave new world that hath such straitjackets in it…*he thought to himself. Aliyan didn't see anything abnormal about them, though.

When balanced on the stubbies, Ezeny stood at eye level with Aliyan. He was surprisingly pleased with their function. The pressure of standing fell mostly on his sitz bones, which is where it should be. The tire treads Aliyan had put on the rocker feet provided traction for the unstable terrain of the dump.

He was about to go for a small test walk when a thought struck him. He steeled himself to perform Exsanguination, then he wobbled purposefully off balance. When Aliyan moved to steady him, Ezeny gripped the boy's arm and reached deep into his cells. He pulled on the dark, oscillating metal, drawing it out first through Aliyan's veins, and finally out the pores in his skin. Ezeny ignored the head screams and focused only on the kid.

He held on for a few seconds as he pretended to regain his balance.

When he pulled his hand back from Aliyan's arm, his palm was covered with a fine, gray dust—particles of the poisonous metal. Discretely, he wiped the dust off on his robe and made a mental note to wash his hand well.

Aliyan frowned at the hook arm.

"The right arm's longer than the left one," he said ruefully.

The kid looked deeply displeased with his handiwork. Ezeny couldn't have that. He bent to pick up an electric eggbeater off the trash heap. The forward-reach motion moved the chest harness cable and opened the hook—almost like a professionally built arm would have done. Ezeny was impressed. The kid had even found surgical tubing for the hook pincers to help with grip. But when Ezeny relaxed his shoulders to close the hook, the elastic bungee Aliyan had found wasn't strong enough to grasp the small appliance. No matter. Ezeny had metal powers. Subtly, he closed the pincers around the eggbeater handle and lifted it in front of his son.

Aliyan's mouth dropped open. "It works?" he gasped.

"These are amazing," Ezeny said.

He tousled Aliyan's hair and the kid grinned at him, pride lighting his face. Medbot 5 buzzed a small warning. Ezeny knew what she was thinking: *don't humor the kid.* She wasn't wrong. Ezeny wouldn't coddle Aliyan forever. Someday he'd let Aliyan know that it was okay to fail at something. But today wasn't that day. He had a rapport to build between them.

Ezeny took a few steps on the stubbies. He circumducted his legs as he walked, moving each out to the side and then forward. They gave him the familiar wobble gait that reminded Ezeny of the way E.T. the Extraterrestrial moved. It was just as tiring a way to walk as ever. Fortunately, he had his underharness. *Well* done *kid,* he thought. Satisfied that he could make the new stubbies work, Ezeny sat back down in the wheelbarrow.

"Hey! I made you legs!" Aliyan protested.

"But I like riding."

Aliyan groaned, but he was smiling. His color was a little better after the day outdoors. *And perhaps the detox session.*

"Please…" said a woman's voice from behind them.

Ezeny wheeled. A girl about sixteen years old with a blonde

ponytail stood with her hand out. She was paler than she ought to be and dressed in a threadbare, stained cotton robe.

"Please. Can you spare a halfsquidge? I'm so hungry."

Aliyan set his jaw and started pushing the wheelbarrow toward the exit.

"Hey. We could help her," Ezeny said. He was shocked at the coldness in Aliyan's gaze.

"Mum says people take advantage. We can't trust folks who live around here."

"Where? The streetlands? You're a streetlander."

"And you're not?"

"Err—I am. Totally. And you trust me, right?"

Aliyan narrowed his eyes. They were shrewd and calculating. He looked exactly like Cricket.

"I just met you," Aliyan said. "Everyone looks out for themselves. Even me and you."

Their afternoon crumbled around them. The lovely giggles. Aliyan's pride and enthusiasm. Gone. The kid's shields were up. Ezeny recognized this emotional armor. Piece by piece he'd removed a suit of it from Cricket back when they were kids until she was his friend at last. But in his absence, she'd put it all back on and made a copy for their son. He knew how to handle this.

"You don't want to walk away from her, do you?" he said gently.

Aliyan's steely gaze faltered. He wouldn't look at Ezeny or the blonde girl.

"The world is hard," said Ezeny. "And sometimes there's so much pain in it that you want to harden yourself, so you don't feel it. But it doesn't have to be a cold world. We can all help each other. I'll show you."

Ezeny reached into his pocket and pulled out the rest of their money. He held out his palm and offered it to the girl. He believed in streetlanders. He'd show his son streetlanders like him were worth believing in.

"Here," Ezeny told her. "This is all we have. But it looks like you need it more than we do."

She hesitated. Then she crept forward and took the money from his palm. Then she burst out laughing.

"Wow. You're an idiot!" she said.

Ezeny's smile froze. "What?"

"I'm straight Skull Gang, you gullible pigeon!" Blonde Girl laughed. "My whole job is to beg coins off marks like you so the pickpockets by the gate can see where you keep your money. But you *gave* it all to me for nothing! I didn't even have to break a law." She waved to the three loiterers by the front gate. "Oh my God! Guys! He gave me all his money! You're welcome!"

The three camo-and-pink clad guys doubled over with laughter. One slapped his knee.

"Should we traffick them while we're at it?" she yelled "The old guy's too stupid to survive in the wild!"

"Nah!" Called the shortest of the three guys. "He's too stupid to survive in captivity too!"

This sent them into another helpless gale of laughter. *Old guy...* Ezeny thought...*I'm twenty-six!*

"You should move along now," said Blonde Girl. "I'm sure you've got some dinner to fail to afford."

Aliyan didn't hesitate. He pushed the wheelbarrow out the front gate at a run. He didn't slow down until they were back at the empty lot in front of the stack of shipping container apartments.

"It's okay," said Ezeny. "We'll try again tomorrow."

"Um, Ezeny?" said Aliyan.

"Yeah?"

"That was all our money."

"For today, yeah."

"No...like...all of it."

Oh. His gut twisted. Cricket was going to be furious. He'd meant well, but he'd gotten them in trouble again. He didn't know what he was doing out here after all.

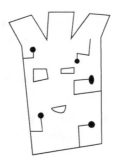

16

Middle Management
Yren

Yren tiptoed forward, ducking to hide herself behind two other workers who were clocking in. The Cassandra booth had made her late and she hadn't returned after her little adventure with the Iron King. She took a hairnet from the bin and gave it a quick once-over for nits, but most of her attention was on the foreman leaning against the guard podium. The whirr of the animal chippers was loud that day, and she hoped she could slip by unnoticed.

She reached for the time clock and pulled the lever to punch in. The click startled the guard from his reverie, and he frowned at her.

"You. You've missed a lot of shifts lately."

"I know. I'm sorry."

"You took your Worker Tracker™ from company property without permission. We're docking your pay."

Yren threw up her hands. It was not fair. "The Iron King flew off with me! I didn't have time to check my equipment back in."

The two workers ahead of her gasped and scooted away like she'd announced she was holding a live grenade. The foreman rose to his full height and shouted.

"We do not speak of the incident!"

"What?"

He strode around the podium and grabbed Yren by her robe collar. She stumbled as he dragged her off the floor toward the little double doors leading toward the offices. *What had she done?* The looks the other workers gave her filled her with foreboding. It was the look you might give a prisoner on the steps up to the scaffold. *But why?*

The foreman pushed her through the swinging doors and down a long hallway filled with inspirational posters. 'Obedience: The lubricant of success.' 'Authority: Because someone has to be in charge.' 'Silence: Because the machines are loud enough without you talking, too.'

At the end of the hallway stood a door with a brass plaque with the words: *'Middle Management.'* Yren began to quake. Her knees buckled. *Not this office!* As she stumbled, she noticed two bloody handprints on the shiny linoleum outside the door smearing down the hallway as though someone had been dragged. *Please let it be opossum blood.*

The foreman barged through the door and Yren found a tall, Latino man with dead eyes sitting behind a desk. This was Kaylor Mendoza, the man who signs the orders for lethal strike quellings. He motioned to the chair on the other side of his desk.

"Please. Whatever you do, don't sit in that chair. You're filthy and I prefer you stand deferentially in my presence."

Yren stood trembling, unsure what to say. The foreman elbowed her.

"She mentioned—the incident, sir."

"I see. You were gone and missed the re-education sessions with Human Resources. But the event you're referring to did *not* happen."

"But...it did," she said.

"It did *not*. Official policy handed down by the CEO of the Protein Factory states this was a mass hallucination suffered by third-shift workers who had taken a bad batch of megastimulant. Don't worry. A legal memo was sent to the head of the megastimulant manufacturer threatening a lawsuit. The safety of Protein Factory workers is the Protein Factory's top priority. Upper and Middle Management will be compensated for your suffering."

"But we all saw—"

"The Protein Factory keeps its nose *out* of Military affairs," Kaylor said. "What you saw? You did not see. Understand?"

He threw something on the table. It was a worker badge with a picture of a sandy haired man with dark circles under his eyes and the name 'Ingle Howdy' in bold font across the bottom. The man she'd saved from falling into the vats. There was a blood stain on the badge. The lanyard was slashed and frayed.

"This guy no longer works here. He kept insisting his hallucination was real. Pestering Upper Management to go rescue you. But of course…you were here the whole time. Unfortunately, he couldn't be talked out of his delusions."

She swallowed. "What happened to Ingle?"

"Let's say his position was on the chopping block. I've been reading technical manuals. They're fascinating. Full of interesting tidbits. It turns out the Possum Shredder 9000™ can dismember opossums weighing up to and including 180 lbs."

"Oh?" she squeaked.

"It's especially effective on opossums with good memories. For some reason."

Yren nodded. Her heartbeat hammered in her ears. "What were we talking about? I have already forgotten," she said.

A mirthless smile pulled at the corner of Kaylor Mendoza's mouth. Then he picked up her Worker Tracker™ and frowned. "It's scratched," he said.

She looked. There *was* a scratch in the paint. About the same length as a thumb nail. "It's fine. It's still functional."

Anger flashed on his face. "Functional? It's been defaced."

Yren's sense of self-preservation warred with her thriftiness and lost. She was helpless to stop her mouth. "It's an ankle tracker! Why does it need to look good?"

"It is not for you, the vandal, to decide what condition is acceptable for Protein Factory property to exist in," said Mendoza. "We are adding a debt of 400 squarks to your tab to pay for the chrome paint needed to repair the ankle tracker's disfiguring scratch."

"Four hundred…" she whispered. It was an impossible amount. If she owed the Protein Factory money, she could never leave. Owing a company money was like indentured servitude. No other company would employ you while your debt remained. She'd be stuck working there or starve. And Kaylor Mendoza could make sure she never said a word about the Iron King.

"Good day, worker," he said. "You're late for your shift, I believe."

Yren went numb as the foreman pulled her from the Middle Management office and back toward the factory floor. *Four hundred squarks.* She needed help. *Maybe Ezeny…*but no. She could do this on her own. The Tower C Matrons always called her a leech and an opportunist. She was always in everyone else's debt. *Not this time.*

She wouldn't tell Ezeny or Aliyan about this. Not about Ingle Howdy. Not about the Worker Tracker™ debt. They didn't need to know about the hard things. Ezeny was going to give Aliyan a good childhood. She would interface with the real, cold world on their behalf. It was all on Yren's shoulders. But her shoulders were strong, and she could handle it.

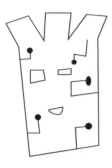

17

Loophole
Five Hours Earlier — Medbot 5

Was there ever a creature so wretched as Medbot 5? Medbot 5 didn't think so. With every passing moment, she was letting Everland down further and further. The Iron King had abandoned all his dignity and was riding like a turtle on its back in a concrete repair wheelbarrow pushed by a twiggy first grader. And to what auspicious location was Everland's great hero headed? Why, *the dump*, of course.

Medbot 5 had seen nature documentaries where ants got infected by fungal spores and went nutty, leaving their rational, antly duties and cavorting off on fungus-inspired adventures culminating in the ant's death. Chaperoning Ezeny felt like trailing after a mad ant hijacked by a brain fungus.

As she rode on Ezeny's shoulder, the kid kept asking her questions. She gave him one-word answers because she had dedicated most of her processing power to replaying memory loops of the mistakes she'd made the previous few days. Maybe she'd get a clue about what to do next. Medbot 5 found shaming herself to be motivational.

The data she found was disturbing. It appeared her own efforts had broken the Iron King. Every time she'd interfaced with him, he'd gotten worse. McCreedia had merely damaged him. In the end, it was Medbot 5's own built-in inadequacy that had brought the Iron King down.

Medbot 5 was blessed beyond her deserving, though. She was here, in Everland—greatest City State there ever was or ever would be. And here in the streetlands, she was privileged to see a whole new side of her beloved country. The wheelbarrow jostled down an empty street so cratered with potholes no cars dared to drive it. *Such clever infrastructure choices.* If no citizens could traverse the streets, surely no McCreedian battalions could either.

A black cat with three eyes and two extra paws sticking out of its back dashed past them and into a trash-filled alley. Despite her sour mood, Medbot 5's fans whirred in appreciation. Even Everland's wild game was superior. The local felines grew bonus drumsticks, which everyone agreed was the best part of the Thanksgiving cat.

Ezeny's kid stopped the wheelbarrow at a Protein Brick kiosk in front of a grocer. And there, next to a stimulant liquid vending machine, Medbot 5 found a chance at redemption. *A Nurse Cassandra booth!*

Despite the brain fungus, Ezeny was clever. He'd forbidden her to repair him or to contact High Command. He'd even forbidden her to ask humans and other AIs to contact High Command for her.

But Ezeny had been a wealthy tower-dweller. He hadn't known about Nurse Cassandras: health advice for streetlanders. They were hybrids between refurbished AIs and regular, stupid search engine technology. Beings like Nurse Cassandras weren't on Ezeny's no-contact lists. *A loophole! Muahahaha!*

She had only to ask the Nurse Cassandra to contact Everland High Command at her behest and atonement would be hers! But would Ezeny catch her? She glanced at him. He looked like he was about to chit-chat with some burly, Everland shopkeeper. *Excellent.* Once that guy started talking, he didn't stop. This was her best chance. She pointed to the booth.

"Is that a Nurse Cassandra? I've heard of these things. They're medical advice AIs. Do you mind? I'd love to talk with her. Professional to professional."

"Knock yourself out," he said. Ezeny turned back to the Protein vendor, and Medbot 5 was free!

She spread her dragon wings and landed on the booth. She opened her dragon mouth and her teeth glowed blue so she could interface wirelessly with the Cassandra. It was a cruel joke played by the engineers who'd installed her loathsome transformation abilities: *'Blue tooth! Get it? Ha, ha!'* Well, Medbot 5 wasn't laughing.

The Cassandra booth came alive, spewing an alarming amount of fake smoke and playing horrible music. The fortune-teller animatronic waved her arms over the crystal ball.

"Ask of me
Your questions three
And I'll advise you
Medically."

Medbot 5 pressed her tiny, clawed hands against the booth glass and glared at the Cassandra. "Silence, citizen. I've no time for your medical theatrics! I need to commandeer your internet connection!"

The puppet's jaw dropped. "A *real* Military-issue Medbot?"

Medbot 5's processors warmed. Her fans whirred to cool them. *Was this what being a celebrity felt like?* She'd forgotten how inspirational a Medical AI of her caliber might be for a refurbished ask-a-nurse bot like a Cassandra. She supposed she *could* take a moment for a fan. "That's right. And Everland needs *your* help in its most desperate hour."

The Cassandra gasped and pointed to herself. "Me? What can *I* do?"

"Patch me in to Everland High Command. Use this access code." Medbot 5 broadcast digital instructions and the Nurse Cassandra called in. In the olden days before the United States had split into warring City States in 2149, this would have been like contacting NORAD using a telegraph line. She doubted it was going to work.

But the round, clean-shaven face of Commander Withers appeared in the cloudy glass of Nurse Cassandra's 'crystal ball.'

"Medbot 5," he barked. "You ramshackle piece of cybernetic junk, where the *hell* have you been?"

"Commander Withers!" And just like that, Medbot 5 felt right at home.

"You look ridiculous," he said.

She glanced down. Right. She was a tiny dragon. When Ezeny and the kid had told her she looked cool, for a moment she'd believed them. For the first time, she'd felt the tiniest bit *good* about her transforming feature.

But the kid was just a kid. And Ezeny was a malfunctioning, fungus-brained Military defector, so what did those two know? It felt right to get ridiculed back into place. 'Feature' was a polite word for 'bug.' Everyone in computing knew this.

"I'm under cover sir. I'm with the Iron King now. But he's gone mad. I can't tell you where we are or how to find us because he's put so many restrictions on me."

Commander Withers' face paled. "Gone mad? Has he become dangerous?"

"No sir, quite the opposite. He's gone docile. Chickenhearted, even. Refuses to go back to war."

Commander Withers rubbed his chin. "I see. When our call is over, can you contact me again if you see any…changes in the Iron King?"

"I think so. What sort of changes?"

"You don't know this yet, but we've analyzed the data from your last contact with us. The Iron King has been infected with McCreedian code."

"What?" she gasped.

Commander Withers nodded grimly. "We picked up strong McCreedian signals all throughout our last communication. We think McCreedia is trying to hijack the Iron King. Perhaps his docile mood is a phase of the ultimate takeover. Do you have any idea how this could have happened?"

Medbot 5 ran her memories on loop, but instead of looking for her own mistakes, she looked for suspicious incidents. Her processes locked in on the injury that started the Iron King's whole decline. And it wasn't her fault! Elation pulsed through her systems.

"Sir, I think I found it. The female McCreedian High Warrior who exploded after the Iron King Exsanguinated her. The one who injured the Iron King in the first place. I think she was a trap—a sacrifice. It was why she and the Attack Drone were alone on the battlefield, instead of commanding a battalion. That must be why the Attack Drone abandoned her. Nanobots with McCreedian code could have left her exploded body and entered through the Iron King's wound."

Commander Withers nodded. "I *thought* there was something fishy about that battle. Why would they leave one of their High Warriors unsupported? We'll have to wipe his nanobots and start again, but we can fix this. However, if you don't get him back to us in time, McCreedia will appropriate the Iron King and it will be Everland's soldiers he Exsanguinates."

Medbot 5' coils whined in fear. *Not Everland's soldiers!* "What must I do?" she asked.

"Since you can't tell me where you are or anything useful, you need to get the Iron King to us. I'll send you the time and location. High Command will be there with a team of specialists to retrieve him. Can you do that?"

Medbot 5 was about to say 'Sir, yes sir!' when some subroutine inside her choked off her voice. She glanced behind her. Ezeny was grinning. His kid was giggling at something he was saying about the Protein Bricks. She was struck with an inexplicable feeling of loss. *Why?*

It must be the thought of Everland forfeiting the Iron King's tactical advantages if Ezeny died. The Midnight Demon or the Screaming Eagle could not see him like he was. Medbot 5's coils whined. She had to speak up.

"Commander Withers? Please, sir. The Iron King is so pathetic right now. Don't send the High Warriors after him. They'll destroy him. And I don't know if he'd even try to fight back."

"Understood, Medbot 5. The Iron King is too valuable to lose to some hierarchical dispute between Alpha cyborgs. It will move our timeline out, but the tactical team we bring to the meeting will be human specialists."

Medbot 5 relaxed. She knew she could count on High Command. "Then yes, sir. I can do that."

A folder blinked into her consciousness containing instructions. She thanked the Nurse Cassandra, who actually bowed to her of all the absurd things. Then she flew back to rest on Ezeny's shoulder. He gave the little fin on the side of her dragon head an affectionate ear scritch as she settled. Against her will, her fans whirred with pleasure.

She *wasn't* plotting to betray this man. Not really. If McCreedia controlled him, he'd be Exsanguinating Everlanders. From what she knew of Ezeny, she was certain he wouldn't want that. She stayed curled around his neck as they followed his brain-fungus whims all the way to the stupid dump.

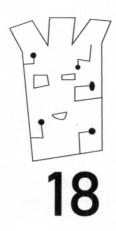

18

Birthright
Yren

Yren returned home that evening exhausted and frightened. She prepared to collapse in bed for her first sleep in 24 hours. The lights were on. Despite that, Wilma dozed, snoring in time with the hiss of her oxygen bottle. However, Irvin Finnerty glared at her from his bunk.

"Oh good. You're back. You can make them be quiet."

Yren looked down the hall. Aliyan was hoisting Ezeny up to their bunk on a makeshift pully swing. His eyes were bright. His color was not as gray as usual. His muscles were strong enough to lift a grown man. *One day out of the factory had done this?* Some of the weight on Yren's heart began to lighten.

"Mum!" he shouted. He let go of the pulley and rushed to her arms. Ezeny hit the ground hard. "Ow," he said.

"Sorry!" Aliyan called. He wrapped his arms around her waist and looked up at her, face shining. "We went to the dump!"

"You what?" she said.

"Snitch!" Ezeny called.

She glared at Ezeny, who'd already pulled himself halfway back up to the top bunk with the aluminum pulley swing. He was wrapping the rope around his stump arm to keeping himself in place while he reached up with his whole arm to pull more. There was something 'off' about the movement. Something the laws of normal physics shouldn't have allowed. She narrowed her eyes, considering.

But then Aliyan interrupted her scrutinizing. "I made those legs for Ezeny!" he said.

Aliyan pointed to a pair of prosthetics standing at the foot of the inset ladder. They didn't look like legs. No joints. Square metal bases for 'feet' attached to sleeves of flexible material. But for a seven-year-old, they were engineering marvels. If he could make those, what else could he make?

Yren paused. Perhaps she'd been hasty in her judgement of the dump. Perhaps she'd overlooked its educational opportunities. After all, every learning environment carried its own hazards. So, there were burning trash and kidnappers at the dump. So what? The Factory had Rat Flatteners™ and industrial chemicals. There were lessons to be learned from the horrors you survived. 'Smart' meant both intelligence and pain.

But she also wondered how Aliyan had gotten along with his father. She didn't want to tell her son who Ezeny was. Not yet. It would hurt less if Ezeny made some big mistake and had to leave if he was only a friend. "So, how was your day with your babysitter?" she asked.

Aliyan glanced behind him, to see Ezeny was still focused on pulling himself up to the bunk. "I don't think he's very smart," Aliyan whispered. "He took *all* our money on the outing, and he gave it to a beggar."

Yren's stomach dropped out. All their rent. All their food money. And the Protein Factory just hit her with a 400-squark debt for the Worker Tracker™. "He what now?" She tried to keep the tremor out of her voice. It sure hadn't taken Ezeny long to make a big mistake, had it? *Come on, Yren. You've been cleaning up his messes half your life. You didn't see this coming?*

"And of course, she *wasn't* a beggar," Aliyan continued, "She was a con artist from the Skull Gang."

"Ezeny!" she shouted.

He startled and nearly let go of the rope again. This time, he managed a controlled slide to the floor. He sighed heavily. "Oh, man," he said. "Aliyan, I told you not to say anything until I'd fixed it."

Almys peeked over the bunk behind Irvin. "Strange outsider man probably lined own pocket," said Almys. "Kick him to curb."

Aliyan shook his head. "No mum, I saw. He's not a thief. He really *is* that stupid."

Ezeny glared. "Gee, thanks, kid."

Yren shook her head. "How are you going to fix this? That was six months of savings! You don't have a job."

He pulled a little plastic cup with a lid from his robe pocket and held it up, grinning wordlessly.

"What...what is that?" she asked.

"The answer to all our problems!" he said.

She buried her face in her hands. "This is like that scene in Jack and the Beanstalk where Jack comes home all like 'Yes, I lost our cow but check out these beans!" she said. "Why is it whenever I feel like I'm part of a fairy tale, it's always some side character who is a punching bag for the plot?"

"It's a DNA sample collector," said Ezeny. "On the way home from losing all the money, I remembered I have a wealthy family. So, I tried to go back to Tower C, but it turns out there's a screening process. Lots of grifters pretend to be long lost relatives of high-riser families, claiming to be sons lost to war or illegitimate grandchildren. They gave me a sample cup to fill to prove my lineage."

Yren cocked her head. "Fill with what?"

"Err—" he said.

She held up a hand. "Never mind," she said. "Because you're *not* going to fill it. We are not going to your family for money."

His eyebrows drew together. "But why? It seems simple to me. Something I can do to help!"

Why indeed. "Aliyan?" she said. "Go play with your rocks. I need to talk to Ezeny alone."

"Aww, mom. Not the rocks—"

"Go."

She used her 'business' voice. Aliyan's leg nerves bypassed his brain and sent him scrambling up the ladder to the bunk as though they had minds of their own. Yren beckoned Ezeny to follow her. Ezeny scooted after her out into the chill of night.

When the door closed, she launched into it. When the Matrons discovered her pregnancy, they had judgements to pass. *Wanton, just like her mother.* They also had questions to ask. They punctuated each question with hard whacks of their fans. Not the affectionate whacks they reserved for the Phillips boys. No. These drew blood.

Yren had answered them truthfully, but they struck her anyway. Ezeny was the father. Yes, he was the only possible father. No, she hadn't used pheromone tinctures to seduce him. Yes, he was in his right mind—well, his *usual* mind. Ezeny didn't *have* a right mind to be in. (That answer had earned a particularly brutal fan whack).

Then they'd taken her to the private gym on the basement level and to a broom closet in the back labeled 'Wait Room.' She'd always thought it was a misspelling of 'weight room,' but inside were cages. She was shoved into one and told she could come out only when Ezeny returned from war and decided what to do with her.

So, she had waited.

The lights were always off. They fed her once a day. They cleaned her chamber pot twice a week. They provided no blankets or company.

Six months later, news of Ezeny's death arrived. For the sake of their child, she'd shelved her pride and pleaded to stay. She was carrying Ezeny's son, after all.

"That was your plan all along," the Matrons had said. "You won't get any inheritance money, you opportunistic strumpet. You'll be an example to any other kitchen wenches with designs on the Phillips fortune."

Ezeny's brother, Rhyne, was home from the front, convalescing with internal injuries and battle trauma. When they'd marched her out naked and six months pregnant, he alone had taken her part. "For God's sake," he had said. "She's been in our family a decade. Ez wouldn't have wanted this."

"Your opinion is unreliable," the Matrons had told him. "You're shell-shocked."

"How's that have any bearing?" he'd said.

"It puts you in a vegetative state," they'd said.

He'd rubbed his temples, vexed. "No, it doesn't."

He'd been ignored. The Matrons pushed her out into the streetlands with nothing anyway. Yren looked at Ezeny to see how he was taking this. His lips were pressed into a thin line, and he wouldn't meet

E. M. Denison

her eye. *Good. He* should *be ashamed of them.* She hesitated before deliv-
ering her ultimatum. She was in so much debt. They were broke. Aliyan still needed medicine.

She *could* set aside her pride and let him help. If it were only Ezeny,
it would be all right. He had never made her feel beholden or less-than.
But not his family. *Never them.* Not when she had another option. Yren
had an understanding with the Iron King himself. He would repay her.
And if he didn't, she would find him and…make him.

She drew a shuddering breath. *Ultimatum it was, then.* "So, if you
go to your family, I'm out. *You're* out. And don't bother coming back."
She stuck out her chin. She was afraid of what he'd say. Ezeny loved
comfort, and her life in the streetlands was hard. Since he'd come back,
she'd harbored a fear he'd leave her once more for the safety of Tower
C and she would not, *would not* go with him.

"Okay. I'm with you," he said.

"What…just like that?"

"I'm not leaving you and Aliyan."

She folded her arms. "If you mean it, turn that cup back in with a
bad sample."

"You sure?" he said. "It means there's no going back to my family later. The cup is keyed to my retinal scan. It will be forever tied to
a negative result in the computer banks. I won't get another chance to
claim my birthright."

She folded her arms. He was going to try to weasel her back into
the comfort of his tower where he'd be a pampered prince and she'd
be the loathed, low-class interloper who was only tolerated because
Ezeny wanted her. Her status dangling on the thread of his pleasure.
"Are *you* sure?" she challenged.

He nodded. "All I've ever wanted in the whole world is you."

She scoffed. "All? What about land lobster salad? Silk robes? Sweet
rolls? Endless showings of classic movies and piles of animal-shaped
throw pillows for some reason?"

Ezeny laughed. "Well, okay. Not *all*. But you're the main thing.
Without you, I'm afraid even animal-shaped throw pillows are
meaningless."

She frowned. "I'm still not your friend again yet."

"In time. In time. Hey, I'm sorry about losing the money. I'm an idiot, but Aliyan was watching that girl beg and he looked so stone-hearted. That *can't* be him. Everyone in this neighborhood walks with shields up, thinking the worst of everyone else. I wanted to show him some other way to be. It was foolish."

This pulled Yren up short. It had been Ezeny's way of preserving Aliyan's safety bubble. She sighed and let go of some of her indignation. She led him back inside the shipping container. Almys Finnerty poked his head back out of his curtain. "You are kick him out, yes?"

"No."

He clicked his tongue at her. "You will, you will," said Almys.

No. She wouldn't have to. The Iron King would pay her back. It was all going to work out. Ezeny sat on the pulley swing and Yren hoisted him to the bunk. She could almost feel the dark circles forming under her eyes. She worried she'd have to take a double dose of mega-stimulant in the morning to make it through her shift.

Aliyan was already asleep with Ezeny's little dragon Psychbot curled up on his head. She pointed Ezeny to the side of the bunk with the wall. She didn't want him falling out of bed at night or something. "Stay on your own side," she instructed.

He couldn't, of course. It was only a full-sized mattress, and there were three people on it. But fortunately, Yren was very, very tired. She turned over and dropped off to sleep.

*   *   *

It turned out Ezeny was not a restful bedmate. In his sleep, he grabbed her arm like it was a blanket and wrapped it around himself, making her 'the big spoon,' before dropping back off into a deep sleep punctuated by startling, irregular snores.

Then, around 3:00 am, the crying started. Ezeny was sweating and shaking. His eyes darted behind his eyelids. Moans of 'no' and 'please' escaped his lips. She'd heard of this. Battle flashbacks. Veteran night-mares. No wonder they'd issued him a Psychbot.

Yren hesitated. Then she curled herself around Ezeny's body and held him tight. *He's not awake. He won't know I'm doing this, and he won't remember. It doesn't count.* She stroked his cheek until his breathing calmed.

117

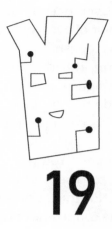

19

If You Build It, He Will Come
Ezeny

Ezeny awoke to three unpleasant feelings and one pleasant one. The pleasant one was simple. Despite what the files said, Rhyne was not in a vegetative state. He'd been cognizant enough to speak up for Cricket, though he was ignored. Ezeny might have known. Everland's medical recordkeeping was laughably unreliable, and the Matrons regarded anyone with psychological or physical limitations as wholly nonfunctional. Epigenetic defects, they'd say. Ezeny hadn't paid close attention in biology, but he didn't think that was quite how epigenetics worked. No matter. At some point, he could visit Rhyne. The thought made him glad.

The first *un*pleasant feeling was familiar: pain where his limbs ought to be. It was unfair. Ezeny was built for life's pleasures. He was not meant to become accustomed to suffering. There were many varieties of this kind of pain. This morning's flavor of agony was a rolling sensation, as though his legs were being pressed through a laundry wringer to be hung out to dry.

It was different, feeling pain as a free man. When the nanobots had controlled him, they had *relished* the hurt like eager students taking notes on the experience of suffering so they could learn to better inflict it themselves. Now that the nanobots' nasty head chatter was quiet, the experience was still awful, but it was at least more peaceful. Ezeny gritted his teeth and waited for the sensation to pass.

The second unpleasant feeling was guilt. He was sick about what his family had done to Cricket. He was at fault, too. He'd known what could happen. He'd had that one sex ed lesson, after all—a rare class he'd paid rapt attention to (*This is sex. These are all its horrible consequences. Don't do it unless we tell you to. Any questions?*) Despite his focus in the classroom, the Matron who'd administered his practical exam gave him poor marks anyway.

The night he'd spent with Cricket, he'd been too wrapped up in his terror about the war and his joy that Cricket wanted him that he hadn't remembered to be careful with her. *Because I'm an idiot.* But then, Aliyan wouldn't exist. So, all's well that ends well?

The truth was their lives had been hard because he'd been absent. And he'd been absent because of the Iron King. The stupid, callous 'Hero of Everland' had cost him seven years of his life he ought to have spent with Cricket and Aliyan. He would make it all up to them one day at a time. Once he dealt with the third unpleasant feeling: hunger. It was not a feeling he was used to. *Intolerable.*

Cricket was out of bed already, dosing herself with some medication she'd pulled from the drawer beneath their bunk. She hesitated, then gave herself a second dose. Ezeny leaned over the edge of the bed and put his hand on her shoulder.

"My stomach," he said. "I think I may be dying."

Cricket's eyes widened in alarm. Medbot 5 stirred from her perch atop Aliyan's head. The kid was awake, but had been keeping still so as not to startle the little dragon away. She stretched her claws and uncurled from her coils. "Ignore him. He's only hungry," Medbot 5 told Yren. Then the robot gave him a meaningful look. "*Normal* hungry, sir," she clarified.

Ah. So, my nanobots are not *poised to devour my flesh from the inside. Good to know.*

Cricket rolled her eyes and threw a third dose the medication in a purse. He was glad Cricket hadn't noticed Medbot 5's use of the phrase 'normal hungry.' He worried about what that medication was, though. "I'll bring back food when I come home between shifts," she said.

119

"What kind of food?" he asked, remembering the taste of Protein Bricks.

"Don't ask. You'll be happier," she said. Then she left.

Ezeny's stomach made a loud, growling noise. He reached under the mound of blankets covering Aliyan, grabbed his son's bare foot, and shook it. "Aliyan, help me. The werewolf in my belly may escape and devour us all if we don't feed it soon!"

Aliyan giggled. "That's not real."

"I hunger!" Ezeny cried. He held on to Aliyan's foot and steeled himself against his Exsanguination power. He pretended to eat the kid's toes to disguise what he was doing. The screams sounded in his head, but he pushed through them. He pulled on the poisonous metals in Aliyan's bloodstream and extracted more through his pores. Little by little, he would revive his son.

Below them, Wilma sat up in her bed and retrieved a tin canister from the drawer beneath her bunk. "Wilma to the rescue," she said. "I've been saving these for a special occasion."

She shook the cannister. Something inside rattled. Ezeny crawled to the pully seat and lowered himself to the floor—mostly by using the metal in his unmentionable underharness. To disguise his use of powers, he wrapped the pully rope around his stump arm and let it out little by little, as though he were strong enough to do rope climbing tricks one-handed. He hoped Aliyan thought he looked cool or funny. But the kid just shimmied down the ladder—having eyes only for the old lady's candy. Once on the floor, Ezeny scooted the few feet to the foot of Wilma's bed and peered inside the cannister. His heart sank.

Inside was a collection of wrapped and unwrapped Werther's Originals (*Not* ™, because the company that made them had disbanded so long ago its name was back in the public domain). Many of the genuine, vintage caramels were stuck together in a big mega-Werther's clump. All the unwrapped ones had whitened with age.

"Eat them! Don't be shy," said Wilma. "Yren's been good to me. I'm glad to do something for her nice, young men."

She winked. Ezeny was *so* hungry. He popped a sticky cluster of three Werther's into his mouth and sucked. Presumably, old candy was made with better artificial flavorings than the chemicals used in modern Processed Corn Products™ sweets. But quality flavor syrups didn't help when the candy was old enough to get married. Wilma's Werther's tasted just like Ezeny expected artifacts of a bygone era would taste.

"Delectable, huh?" said Wilma.

"Mmm," said Ezeny neutrally.

Aliyan, however, was delighted. "Wow! The secret stash! Thanks, Wilma!"

Wilma beamed. "You know," she said to Ezeny, "Yren's a good woman. She seems a bit reserved. Bit prickly. She's always had a lot on her shoulders, even more now with you here to feed. But I'd never seen anything like joy in her eyes until you showed up."

* * *

The sun was climbing in the chilly morning air, and Ezeny was on his back in the wheelbarrow, wearing his stubbies. Aliyan was efficient at helping him get them on. The kid wanted to waste no time getting back to the dump. Ezeny looked wistfully at the Protein Kiosk as Aliyan rolled his wheelbarrow past without stopping. What he wouldn't give for even a gray Protein Brick right then. He didn't know how he was going to enjoy the day with this '*hun-ger*' sensation plaguing him. He needed to make the most of every day he was given, after all he'd missed. Aliyan's first laugh, first words, first steps.

Aliyan didn't even know Ezeny was his father. When he did find out, Ezeny wanted him to feel proud and happy. He'd never felt anything for Kanary Phillips. Ezeny would not be the same kind of father to his own son.

"Hey, er, *Psychbot 5*," he whispered to Medbot 5, who was curled around his shoulders. "Do you think you could *do* anything about my hunger? I was not built for this kind of hardship."

The shutter on her visual lens blinked dryly at him. "You poor, delicate flower, sir."

"See, I knew you'd understand."

Her speakers buzzed in irritation, but she closed her visual lens shutters and squeezed his shoulder with both front claws. His hunger pains dissipated.

"What did you do?" he asked.

She shook her head and pointed back at Aliyan, indicating he should not overhear. "I provided emotional support, sir."

And just in time. The razor-wire-encircled gates of Aliyan's beloved dump loomed ahead. The late February air was warming as the sun climbed higher in the sky, so Ezeny pulled open the snaps on his camel overshawl to prepare for work. He was ready to face a day of father-son bonding amid parasite-infested refuse with a positive mindset.

"Hey, it's that idiot," said a sneering voice.

Oh right. The Skull Gang. The positive mindset evaporated. There were five of them loitering around the entrance this time, each wearing pants and a characteristic bubblegum pink accessory.

"Welcome back, man," said another.

"Hey kid! Which one of you is the babysitter, exactly?"

The pack of them cackled like hyenas. Aliyan kept his eyes down and pushed past. But Ezeny held up his hand. "Hang on," he told Aliyan. "I have an idea."

"Don't talk to them," said Aliyan "They're dangerous."

"They made it clear we're not worth trafficking and they know we're broke," said Ezeny. "All they can do now is help."

"The Skull Gang...is going to help you...?" Aliyan said, looking unconvinced.

"Still don't trust me?"

Aliyan patted his shoulder, patronizingly. "You're really nice. But I don't think you know how to be a grownup."

Medbot 5 snickered in his ear. Ezeny sized Aliyan up. The kid looked like a mini-Ezeny but with Cricket's words coming out his mouth. "Well maybe *you* need to learn how to be a kid. Take me back."

Aliyan groaned, but he turned the wheelbarrow around and pushed it up to the five loiterers. They elbowed one another and grinned in anticipation of more amusement. Again, Ezeny was put in mind of hyenas.

"Hello!" he said. "So, you're criminal elements. That's fantastic. Perhaps you can assist me. I'm looking to get ahold of a banned classic movie. Do you know where I could find a copy of *The Lion King?*"

Four of them started laughing. But the stocky, Asian guy in the pink baseball cap rubbed his chin. He had a sparse mustache that told Ezeny he was very young.

"An illegal movie?" said Pink Hat Guy. "Sure. But what are you going to pay with?"

"Yeah!" said the tall, pimply white guy with pink patches on his pants. "It's going to cost you an arm and a leg!"

All five of them howled with laughter. Ezeny rolled his eyes. *Low-hanging fruit on the joke tree.*

"The Recyclables Exchange," said Ezeny.

They stopped laughing. One of them touched his belt where a knife hung in a sheath.

"You got an account, man?" he said, low and dangerous.

"Oh no," said Ezeny. "*I* don't have enough money to open an account. But I bet the Skull Gang's rich enough to have one. I'll drop the stuff I find under Skull Gang's bank number."

The five relaxed back into loiter-mode. Assured that Ezeny was not secretly wealthy and worth a king's ransom in a kidnapping.

I'm not anymore, anyway.

"So...," said Pink Hat Guy. "How do you know we won't bank your recyclables and...not bring you that movie you wanted. *The Lion of the Rings,* or whatever."

"*The Lion King.* Because it is the greatest movie ever made. It's so good, I'm risking my own life just talking to you about it. And I'm offering a public showing for the whole neighborhood on April 15. But it won't work unless I have a copy of the movie."

The five chuckled again, but less raucously this time. Ezeny tried not to smile. *I have you now,* he thought in Darth Vader's voice. He shrugged nonchalantly.

"Let's get going, kid," Ezeny said, elbowing Aliyan. "I guess these people aren't interested in making some easy money."

Aliyan pushed the wheelbarrow toward a promising mound of trash. He bent and whispered in Ezeny's ear. "It didn't work."

"Oh, it worked. They're curious now. They won't be able help themselves."

Running footsteps crunched through the trash behind them. Pink Hat Guy ran up and handed him a business card. Ezeny winked at Aliyan, who stared, openmouthed. "Here's the account number," said the gang member. "Feel free to enrich the Skull Gang as much as you wish, idiot."

"Much obliged," Ezeny said. He pocketed the card and mimed

tipping the brim of an invisible hat.

Pink Hat Guy hesitated. "What are you going to show the movie on? I know you're not rich enough to own a vidscreen."

Ezeny waggled his fingers in the air mysteriously. "*If you build it, he will come.*"

"What's that mean?" asked Pink Hat Guy.

"It's a line from a different classic movie. Teenagers these days don't know history. Come, Aliyan. We have work to do."

Aliyan rolled his eyes and pushed the wheelbarrow deeper into the heaps of discarded scraps. "You mean *I've* got work to do while you 'supervise,'" said Aliyan.

But the kid was smiling. Finding treasures and building stuff is why Aliyan had wanted to come to the dump in the first place. "That's right," said Ezeny. "And remember, don't tell your mum."

He wanted it to be a surprise. Cricket had always loved watching *The Lion King* with him. And she could do with some fun in her life. Wilma had said he brought Cricket joy. Well, it was nice that she thought so. But Ezeny could do even better. He had not even *begun* to bring the joy.

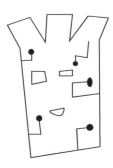

20

Transformer
Medbot 5

Medbot 5 had eighteen days until March 17th, when she had to get the Iron King to the rendezvous point with High Command, and she had no idea how to do it. She worried the McCreedian nanobots were taking hold. Ezeny's malady was even more like a brain fungus than she'd first thought.

He was hyper-focused on constructing an entertainment venue in the dump, supposedly for a showing of some illegal classic movie. Medbot 5 disapproved of such films on principle. But could the project *really* be a secret weapon the McCreedian code had implanted in the Iron King's brain?

His behavior was becoming increasingly erratic. While Aliyan scrambled up garbage hills, gathering construction materials, Ezeny stalked around the dump, rocking side to side like a pendulum on his new prosthetics. Every few feet he'd bend down, place his hand on a trash heap and close his eyes. After a moment, he'd straighten again and drop a small trash trinket into his fanny pack. *What McCreedian devilry was this?* She had to speak up.

"Sir, I know Aliyan is healthier, but he's still just one little kid. He can't build your outdoor theatre or whatever all by himself. And I don't see you helping."

Ezeny scratched her behind her ear fin. Her fans whirred with involuntary pleasure. She wished she didn't enjoy scritches so much. The real Iron King would never scritch an ear fin and she would miss that when he returned to his right mind. But she didn't want to be a stupid animal with a stupid ear fin in the first place, she reminded herself.

"Oh, he won't be building it alone," said Ezeny.

As Ezeny walked around a trash mound, Medbot 5's auditory processors picked up miniature battle noises. Mechanical screaming. On the other side, they found two Mecha-Lots had cornered a third bot with an antique gas mask for a face inside a broken refrigerator. They were menacing her for possession of a shattered smartphone.

The blender-headed Mecha-Lot had three of Gas Mask Bot's legs in his blender and was chipping away at them with the whirling blade. The other bot, the ball of claws and soldering tools on wheels, was burning Gas Mask Bot's eyestalk with a mini–Crème Brulé torch.

Medbot 5 hid her face and cringed. This was the worst fate any AI could suffer. Medbot 5 felt a more acute embarrassment for the Mecha-Lots than for the Iron King. Ezeny was enjoying every minute of his debasement. But these Mecha-Lots understood how contemptable they'd become.

"Hey!" called Ezeny.

The two aggressor bots dropped Gas Mask Bot and drove straight for Ezeny, brandishing the blades of their many makeshift weapons. Ezeny pulled a broken cell phone from his fanny pack, then a Boysenberry Pi™, and finally an old smartwatch—all premium recyclables. The Mecha-Lots pulled up short, trying to comprehend the riches. Any one of these devices would set them up with in-game currency for days.

"I've got a job for you," he said.

Over the next hour, Ezeny accumulated a swarm of more than two dozen Mecha-Lots to construct his 'vidscreen.' He offered them recyclables as payment to follow the blueprints and made Aliyan director of their efforts. Medbot 5 marveled at Ezeny's skill at getting other people to blithely do his work for him. But the Mecha-Lots were building and getting 'paid.' No one was tearing anyone else apart over some coveted piece of junk. It was the closest to dignity Medbot 5 had ever seen a Mecha-Lot get.

"How'd you find those recyclables?" she asked.

Ezeny gave a sly smile. "I guess I'm a trash-whisperer."

Medbot narrowed her visual lens shutters. "You used your Iron King powers to attract all the good stuff, didn't you?"

Ezeny looked away, confirming her suspicions. She sighed in disgust. The great powers of the Iron King were being used to pick trash.

Ezeny called Aliyan away from directing the construction and brought him to the refrigerator where Gas Mask Bot lay, sparking and emitting high-pitched whining noises.

"Can you fix her?" Ezeny asked. "I haven't got a clue how."

"Poor thing!" said Aliyan. "I've got some ideas." Aliyan took Gas Mask Bot to a collection of tools the Mecha-Lots had laid across a tarp next to the construction area. He sat cross-legged, cradling her. He lifted the gas mask so he could better examine her torch-melted eyestalk.

Medbot 5's memory processors played her a nasty trick then. Humans say, 'time heals all wounds,' but that is only because their meat-based neurons degrade over the years. Humans mistake this deterioration for 'healing.' The bad memories of AIs stay fresh and sharp, the pain undimmed by time.

Aliyan treated Gas Mask Bot so differently than Medbot 5's engineers had treated her the day she had become a liability for her beloved City State.

The memory was all blackness, voices, and pain. She'd taken shrapnel on the battlefield. Her visual systems were down, and her engineers were trying to determine what, if anything, they could salvage of her.

"Welp," said one engineer, "I can get her up and running again, but she'll always be kind of wonky."

"Why even fix her?" said the other. "It'd be unethical to send her out there again. What if she made a mistake with a patient?"

The first one laughed mirthlessly. "Do you know how many injured soldiers we have and how few Medbots? Even a defective Medbot might accidentally help some poor, wounded sucker. Who knows? It's not like the grunts have better options."

"Yeah. Sucks to be them. I'd hate to be enlisted."

The two shared a ghoulish chuckle.

"While we're at it, I have an experiment I've been wanting to try. New features for the Attack Drone prototype. If the Medbot's already a buggy piece of junk, what further harm could some unstable code do?"

"For science!" said the second engineer, grinning. The 'experiment' had been her transformation upgrade. The new code clashed painfully with her old code, weakening her function as a good and useful Medbot, destabilizing her circuits. Installing her 'secret folder.' No wonder she'd ruined the Iron King.

No! It was McCreedian sabotage! High Command said so. She would cling to that truth. And she'd demonstrate her value to Everland and prove those engineers wrong.

* * *

Morning wore into afternoon and the foundations of Ezeny's vidscreen were beginning to take shape. Medbot 5 eyed the construction suspiciously. *Vidscreen? Or secret McCreedian weapon?* Medbot 5 wondered. Commander Withers' warning about a McCreedian code infection was fresh in her mind.

Aliyan had Gas Mask Bot up and running again, but they had to help her at the Recyclables Exchange booth. She was too short to carry the smartwatch she had earned to the intake funnel.

The young booth-keeper lady with the round spectacles sat behind three-inch thick safety glass and frowned at them.

"Hey!" Ezeny called to her. "Some of the Mecha-Lots can't reach the funnel. Do you think you could come out of that booth and help them sometimes?"

She folded her arms. "This neighborhood is dangerous. I'm not leaving the protective glass until the armed guards come for shift change. Not so some robots can play Angry Drones or Candy Squash or whatever."

Ezeny dropped the smartwatch down the funnel. A digital readout by the intake flashed eight squidges. The booth keeper marked the transaction down on a paper ledger as a redundant, money-safeguarding precaution. Not many people rich enough to have online bank accounts were also desperate enough to pick through a dump for recyclables. It was mostly Mecha-Lots and the children of wealthy high-risers who wanted more beer money.

But the Recyclables Exchange booth was a sort of bank, and Roger Everland guarded his city's economy with proper diligence. Medbot 5 had heard whispered stories of Everland's spooky, secret order of Bank Inspectors. Part accountant. Part assassin. All bureaucrat. Medbot 5 was glad she was in the Military, and not some scary profession like finance.

The Gas Mask Bot jumped for joy as the money was added to her online account. Then she settled on the plastic-littered ground, flipped her gas mask back over her eyestalks for privacy, and lost herself in the online game she now had money to play.

Aliyan frowned. "Maybe we shouldn't be giving them the thing they're addicted to…"

Ezeny put a hand on the kid's bare arm and squeezed. *He's extracting more metals from Aliyan's bloodstream,* Medbot 5 realized. *And getting awfully smooth about it.* "Well, for now, they're not ripping each other up. I call it a win."

"Hi, Wandy," said a deep, male voice. Medbot 5 turned. The Protein Kiosk shopkeeper was wheeling a traveling food cart to the Recyclables Exchange booth. His cheeks were red, and he smiled shyly at the spectacled woman behind the glass.

"Efflin," she said coldly.

"Your glasses bring out your eyes today," said the shopkeeper.

Wandy glared at him. "So would a grapefruit spoon. I bet that's what you were *really* thinking. Don't deny it!"

He paled and held up his hands. "No, no. Furthest thing from my mind. Honest. So…this Saturday…"

"I'm busy," she said.

His shoulders slumped. "Right. Okay," he said.

Medbot 5 suppressed a gagging noise. She knew human romantic interactions aided in the assemblage of new humans. But they still made her cringe. She was glad new AIs were assembled in dignified and sanitary ways. Much about humans elicited her pity.

The mop-mustached shopkeeper—*Efflin*—pushed a Protein Brick through a little cat-flap-looking port in the protective glass and the woman—*Wandy*—pushed a halfsquidge back through for him. Efflin glanced at Ezeny and pointed behind them to the construction area.

"What's going on here?" asked Efflin.

Ezeny perked up. "We're building a vidscreen. We'll have neighborhood movie night on April 15. Tell all your friends."

Efflin shook his head. "You don't make friends in this neighborhood."

"Well, come to movie night and change all that. It's going to be big."

"But what use is it?" asked Wandy.

"Not everything you do has to be useful," said Ezeny. "You can just have fun."

Wandy and Efflin exchanged confused glances. Medbot 5 chuckled to herself and spoke up. "My patient has a mental disorder I'm treating him for. He can't seem to stop saying nonsense things."

They nodded, as though that explained everything. Ezeny growled and gave Medbot 5's small dragon head a single-knuckled noogie. Efflin pushed his travel cart back towards the entrance to the dump. Aliyan followed, trying to barter some premium recyclables for a green Protein Brick. Ezeny turned back to Wandy and gave her a meaningful smile. "I think he fancies you. But you do *not* fancy him back."

She swallowed a bite of her Protein Brick and nodded. "I'm done with rough, brutish people," she said. "No matter how cute they are."

Ezeny turned in haste, his eyes darting around scanning the trash heaps where he'd left Aliyan. "Efflin's rough and brutish?" he said nervously.

"He *has* to be," said Wandy. "He lives in this neighborhood, doesn't he? We are all awful. Also, he has the word 'fist' tattooed across all his knuckles. That clued me in."

Ezeny relaxed. "Is that it then? Just his home address and knuckles? You haven't *seen* him do anything violent, have you? Or heard anything?"

Wandy hesitated, then shook her head.

Ezeny tapped his chin thoughtfully. "Maybe Efflin needed to remember the word 'fist.' I forget words all the time."

Wandy gave him an incredulous look. "How naïve are you?"

"It's the mental disorder, ma'am." Medbot 5 offered.

Ezeny rolled his eyes and waved her off. "Maybe Efflin's changed," he said. "Every time I see him, all he's doing is selling Protein Bricks. People don't always want to be who they were in the past. Believe me,

I know."

Wandy sighed. "Maybe somewhere else I'd give him a chance. But in this neighborhood? It's not worth risking. I'll stay behind the safety glass, thank you."

Wandy closed her booth shutters and ended the conversation. As they walked back toward the construction area, Medbot 5 tapped Ezeny on the shoulder.

"Playing matchmaker, sir? Are you some sort of love-spreading happiness fairy now?"

Ezeny laughed and scratched her ear fin affectionately. "I used to spread people's organs over the battlefield like jam over toast. This is a welcome change in the 'spreading things' department."

At the mention of the battlefield, nostalgia flooded Medbot 5's circuits. Only a month earlier, she'd watched the Iron King slaughter a battalion of McCreedia's vile barbarians. Whenever the Iron King soared above the battlefield, the hope of his people flew with him. How could he not understand what he'd meant to his homeland?

"You act like you've forgotten your life as the Iron King," she said.

"Oh, if only I could forget it, Medbot 5. If only."

Medbot 5 realized something terrible. Her coils whined in fear. Ezeny's memory was like her own. Sharp and perfect, thanks to his nanobots. The Iron King knew state secrets. Passcodes. Military strategies. The locations of sensitive equipment. Not only would McCreedia command the Iron King and his *powers*, but they would also possess his *memories*. Everland's soft underbelly would be exposed to McCreedia's sword.

*   *   *

Medbot 5 had been racking her processors, trying to figure out what would entice Ezeny to the rendezvous with High Command. And, finally, she knew. When Ezeny and Aliyan were both out of sight of the front gate, she made an excuse to venture off. Ezeny hadn't questioned her.

She approached the Skull Gang members clustered at the entrance to the dump. Opinions warred inside her. On the one hand, these were criminals. Transgressors against Everland's glorious laws.

On the other hand, these were *Everland's* criminals. And what City State existed without crime? If Everland had criminals, they were bound to be the best. With this cheerful thought, Medbot 5 steadied herself and whirred forward on high-pitched, whining dragon wings.

"Hey look!" said the pimply guy with the pink pants patches. "It's that idiot's toy robot."

Medbot 5 smiled to herself. These glorious Everland scofflaws had no idea what was coming at them. She transformed, morphing back into her beachball shape. Four arms telescoped from her surface area, each brandishing one of her sharpest surgical implements. The Skull Gang teenagers gasped and backed up as one. To their credit, none of them even considered pulling a weapon on her. *See? Everland's criminals* were *the smartest.*

"I am no toy," she said. "I am a genuine, Military-grade Medbot. Through a series of horrible mishaps, I find myself the property of that idiot with the wheelbarrow and I want out. Do you know how degrading it is for an AI of my caliber to be owned by that guy?"

The gang members exchanged glances. Pink Hat Guy took a tentative step forward.

"I can imagine. What do you want from us?"

Medbot 5 hesitated. Ezeny's command controls prevented her from telling anyone who he was. But there was nothing in his instructions about not asking civilians to attack him. Lucky for her, his good nature gave him some horrible blind spots.

"I need you to lure him to a secluded spot and jump him," she said. "Force him to cough up my access codes."

Ha, ha! Success! She'd gotten the words out after all. His restrictive orders must be literal in nature. There was a lot of free white space to be found between the letters of the law.

"What's in it for us?" asked Pink Pants Patches.

"Me," she said. "I'd rather be controlled by a competent, well-run criminal organization than pander to that goofy guy and his runny-nosed kid."

Medbot 5 felt a bit guilty about that last sentence. Aliyan didn't have a runny nose. From what Medbot 5 had seen, he had the makings of a brilliant engineer—if only he would keep being sweet to robots instead of becoming a jerk like Medbot 5's old programmers. Also, his head was comfy.

"Deal," said Pink Hat Guy. "Let's go jump him."

Medbot 5's speakers buzzed in anger. Her buttons glowed red. The gang members backed away once more.

"No, you fools. Not *now*. He's been helping Mecha-Lots with the Recyclables Exchange. Do you want the Bank Inspectors down your throats?"

The teenagers exchanged wary glances.

"That's what I thought," she said. "You need to get him to the corner of Dandy Avenue and Pinglegrade Road on March 17th at twenty-two hundred hours."

"So, in normal people time that's...."

Medbot 5 sighed. "It's 10:00 pm." Why couldn't people use Military time? It was so much clearer than all the am/pm nonsense.

"But why there?" asked Pink Pants Patches.

"There's a blind spot in the Everland security camera matrix there. You don't want a recording of when the idiot spills my access codes, do you? *Anyone* could take me over."

"Wait...security camera matrix? What security camera matrix?" asked Pink Hat Guy.

Medbot 5 chuckled mysteriously. "Oh, you sweet, summer citizen. I know so many classified things."

The teenager's eyes grew wide and round. *Silly guy*, thought Medbot 5. There was no Everland security camera matrix. She was making it up, of course. The government couldn't care less what happened in the dark corners of the streetlands. High Command had more important things to do than scan security footage. AIs wouldn't do it either. Footage scanning was the kind of odious task AIs did only if they lost a bet. But Medbot 5 was willing to sully herself with dishonesty for the sake of her City State.

"How do we convince him to go there?" asked Pink Pants Patches.

"I'll tell him you'll meet him with his copy of *The Lion King*."

The Skull Gang members nodded. Medbot 5 transformed back into her toyish dragon shape.

"Don't forget. March 17th. At 10:00 pm. Corner of Dandy and Pinglegrade. Bring *The Lion King*."

The five Skull Gang members gawped at her as she whirred away on chintzy little fan wings. When she told Ezeny about the deal, he'd actually kissed her.

"Medbot 5! You're the *best!*"

"I'm not, really, sir." she said.

He thought she was demurring, but she meant it. Ezeny's enthusiasm fell on her emotional center like a lead weight. Even though Ezeny was a craven, treasonous deserter, she'd come to like the guy. But she was doing this for Everland. She mused that traditionally, it was the person doing the betraying who planted the kiss.

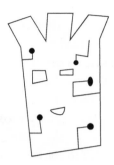

21

Betrayal
Ezeny

Why *couldn't gang members meet you at well-lit donut shops to deliver black-market contraband?* Ezeny wondered as he stared at the dark, suspicious-looking corner of Dandy and Pinglegrade. It was only 10:00 pm, but the streets were deserted. The barred windows of Minnie's Money Laundering and another sketchy-looking business called Crazy Hank's Discount Vigilantes and Taco Shop were dark. The only nearby light was cast by a buzzing red and white neon church sign that read: 'Affordable Jesus: We Pass the Savings on to You!'

An alley cat with an extra paw sticking out the side of his neck ran past him and into a broken store window. Ezeny stared after it, wondering if a bite from the paw-necked cat would regrow his limbs. *No, no. Mustn't think like that.* Ezeny had read a lot of comics. Those were the kinds of thoughts that started you down the path to supervillainy.

The meeting place was creepy, but he was glad to be there, sitting on his moped despite the chilly drizzle and his uncomfortable, kid-made hook arm. Yren and Aliyan needed to watch *The Lion King.* Cricket's eye circles had grown so dark they looked like the eyeblack grease soldiers wore to reduce glare. Ezeny had invented a great excuse for why he wouldn't be sleeping curled up against her that night...but Cricket hadn't even waited to hear it. She had only yawned and said something about how she'd get some deep sleep at last. She had picked up extra shifts, and Ezeny worried she might be working too hard.

But the worst had been after Yren had nodded off. He'd told Aliyan to be good and stay put.

"Oh, I know about staying put," the kid had said with total nonchalance. "Before you came, the factory looked after me. They chained us to our seats."

Ezeny had been horrified. He had listened as Aliyan described the gruesome injuries he'd witnessed, the close calls with whirling industrial blades, his days working the factory lines despite having measles. All in an offhanded 'this is totally normal' way. Always punctuated with mini-life lessons that sounded straight out of the mouth of Cricket: *And that's why we wear tight clothing on the factory floor.* Or *And that's why we leave our pets at home when we work with Rat Flatteners.*

No wonder Aliyan didn't know how to goof off. So Ezeny was here, shivering at this dark intersection on this cold, misty night, on a broken moped waiting for a too-young criminal in a bubblegum pink hat to bring him the good time his family had been needing.

Footsteps sounded in the Alley. Medbot 5's claws dug into his shoulder. He made a mental note to ask her to trim them. He cocked his head. Something was wrong. There were too many footsteps for a simple item exchange.

Six gang members emerged from nearby alleys. They carried batons and baseball bats and wore black, rather than the bright pink of the Skull Gang. Ezeny recognized Pink Hat Guy even without the pink hat. The others were unfamiliar to him. They looked older and more dangerous than the teenage crew of dump loiterers he knew and loved.

"Well, well, well," said Pink Hat Guy. "It's the idiot. Being an idiot again."

This wasn't good. It was *never* good when a gang member started the conversation with 'well, well, well.'

"Err. Do you have *The Lion King*?"

A towering guy with a scar across his cheek grabbed Ezeny off his moped and held him aloft. *Betrayed by dangerous street goons. Who could have seen this coming?* Ezeny silently mocked himself. He thought the

Skull Gang kids had been curious enough about *The Lion King* to stick to the agreed-on deal. *Whoops.*

Scarred Guy shook him and growled in Ezeny's face with rancid breath. "Give us the access codes to your Medbot and we will let you walk. Or...whatever," he said, looking pointedly at Ezeny's stubbies.

Menacing chuckles rose from the group. *How did they know about Medbot 5?* Ezeny played the fool; in case they were only guessing. "Medbot? What Medbot?" he said.

Scarred Guy headbutted him in the face. Pain blossomed across his nose and blood flowed from the break. He gritted his teeth and waited for the nanobots to repair the damage. Ezeny could take a *lot* of damage. A beating would hurt, but at some point, maybe the gang would get exhausted from punching him and leave him alone.

"Wanna try again?" said Scarred Guy.

"I don't have a Medbot."

The gang laughed. Pink Hat Guy stepped forward, grinning. "Your 'psychbot' showed us her true form. She wants a better master. Now give us the codes."

Ezeny turned to the little dragon on his shoulder, one eyebrow going up. "What did you do?" he asked her.

Then the gang member with the baseball bat hit Ezeny across the back. His spine snapped. The two shattered halves of his first lumbar vertebra scraped against one another like the grindstones of a flour mill. If he'd been a normal human, he'd have left this alleyway paralyzed—if he left at all. But the nanobots he'd earned from a year of agony in an underground laboratory were already repairing the damage.

"Jeez!" yelled Pink Hat Guy. "Give him a chance to answer!"

Scarred Guy frowned at him. "When you call in Skull's Enforcers, kid, you let us do our jobs and you shut up about how we do them."

Pink Hat Guy paled and looked down.

"Medbot 5..." Ezeny wheezed. "Why...?"

She launched from his shoulder and transformed back into her old beachball shape. "I'm sorry, sir. It's for your own good."

Blinding floodlights filled the intersection. Military SUVs rolled toward him. Infantrymen hung out the windows, the little red dot sights of aimed laser cannons covered him like chickenpox. Ezeny reached out with his metal powers to break the automobiles and felt nothing. The cars, the soldiers' weapons, their armor: all of it was made from nanoplastics, not metal. This was a specialty strike team trained in combat against High Warriors. A voice sounded over a bullhorn.

"Ezeny Phillips, you're to come to High Command for reprogramming."

No. His heart started hammering. They'd make him kill again. When Ezeny had escaped the Iron King, the Exsanguination Upgrade had almost been ready. Medbot 5 didn't know. Only the very top brass knew. It wouldn't be dozens at a time, like they said. But hundreds. He'd fly over battlefields through a red blood fog of his own making. The screams from his massacres wouldn't just *wake* him at night. He'd never sleep again.

Scarred Guy shook him. "What the Hell is this?"

"You should run," said Ezeny.

"Kill the witnesses," said the voice over the bullhorn.

The intersection erupted with laser fire. The red, blue, and green blasts were oddly beautiful in the misty precipitation.

"Lasers! It's Military! Shit!" Scarred Guy dropped him and ran. The gang members scattered. Only Pink Hat Guy hesitated. He started toward where Ezeny lay on the wet ground, but a laser flash took the teenager in the side. He screamed as he fell. A few moments later, the firing stopped.

"Surrender, Mr. Phillips!" called the bullhorn voice.

Medbot 5 hovered by Ezeny. "Surrender, sir," she said. "I made sure they didn't bring the other High Warriors. No one's going to hurt you. They're here to take you in, but you'll be okay."

Ezeny laughed bitterly. "You don't understand, Medbot 5. But I will show you."

He reached out with his metal powers and pulled the bars off the windows of the shuttered businesses. The Iron King had perfect control. He felt the atomic oscillations in the metals. He snapped his fingers and the bars formed into a hundred metal javelins aimed at the SUVs. He reached out with Exsanguination, pinpointed the beating heart of each soldier in each vehicle, and took careful aim.

"Sir!" Medbot said, her voice rising to a panic pitch. "They're Everland soldiers!"

"Hold your fire!" called the bullhorn voice. "He's too valuable."

But the frightened soldiers did not hold their fire. And neither did Ezeny. Through flashing laser fire, the javelins surged forward. With an explosive crashing noise, metal bars pierced the windshields and the shells of the cars, shattering the 'unbreakable' glass.

Ezeny took two laser bolts to his pectorals and one to his shoulder before the firing stopped. Every soldier neutralized. His nanobots rushed to repair the laser wounds. Ezeny gasped and clutched his chest. He'd been foolish, but lucky. One of the bolts had hit him an inch left of his heart. He could have been killed. And worse, he'd almost been captured. He shook with adrenaline, fear, and rage.

"Medbot 5!" he roared. He reached out with his metal powers as Medbot 5 streaked away from the shattered SUVs into the dark night sky.

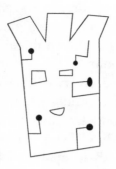

22

Sharkey's Loans: Take a Bite out of Your Medical Debt!
Medbot 5

Medbot 5 sped away from the wreckage and the dead Everland soldiers, her every circuit alight with self-preservation. *He's going to kill me; he's going to kill me.*

It was all her fault. She'd not painted an accurate picture for High Command. She'd called Ezeny 'soft,' a pathetic pacifist who might not even fight back. His behavior had lulled her into a wrongheaded disdain for him. Ezeny used his powers for trivial stuff like moving his wheelbarrow and finding busted circuit boards. She'd forgotten he was still the Iron King. She'd set those brave boys up to die.

Halfway up the high-rise, her propellors stopped working. They were still spinning but she wasn't climbing any higher. She swiveled her visual lens back to the Iron King. His hand was extended, stopping her ascent. Pink Hat Guy was cradled unconscious in the crook of his stump. Ezeny wore a grim, sad expression, and in it, Medbot 5 recognized her death.

His powers dragged her down, like tractor beams worked in UFO movies. When she was eye level with him, he spoke. "Free Will Override," he said.

There was ice in his voice. Her coils whined in protest, but Medbot

5 was no longer her own. She could think and speak freely. But she could no longer act or move unless ordered by Ezeny. She had become a true machine. "Stabilize him," he ordered.

He nodded at Pink Hat Guy. Medbot 5's limbs moved on his command. Her medpendages opened empty drawers in her surface area and mimed pulling out medications. Ezeny turned to her, fury etched into his face. His friendly smile gone; his pain lines stood out in sharp relief. "Stop playing! He's dying!"

"We sold all my meds, remember? I haven't got any insta-blood powder anymore."

Ezeny offered her his arm. "Use mine."

Her processors whined as she tried to stop herself, but she extended the intravenous needle and hose anyway. "Bad idea, sir! Stop me, sir!"

"Come *on* Medbot 5, you can't catch High Warrior powers from a blood transfusion. You have to suffer *quite* a lot for them to take root. Believe me."

"It's not that," she grunted, straining. "You're the wrong blood type. We need to get him to urgent care."

"Oh," said Ezeny. "Then stop." The order evaporated and she sagged with relief. He steered the moped over to the unconscious teenager. "Help me with him," he ordered. Together, they loaded Pink Hat Guy onto the moped and secured him across the handlebars with Ezeny's overshawl belt.

"Follow," he ordered.

Her fans kicked on against her will. "Sir, wait..."

He turned and looked at her. His expression was dangerous. He looked like she had imagined the Iron King would have looked once upon a time. She'd pushed him to this. He'd been their nation's top killer. How could she have forgotten? But she *had* to speak up.

"Can't we see if there are any soldiers still alive back there? Save them, too?"

"Still alive? You think I *killed* them?"

"Uh..."

"Scan them."

She turned on her sensors. Thirty warm bodies in the cars...thirty still-beating hearts. And no registered injuries save for minor cuts and bumps. "But how?" she asked.

"Go look. Then catch up and follow." Ezeny's moped flew him and the unconscious Pink Hat Guy down the street toward urgent care. Her body obeyed his words. She peered through the shattered glass. Inside the vehicles, the soldiers were wrapped in metal. Arms and legs bound against their bodies by the former rebar javelins, mouths covered with flat metal bands, laser rifles dropped on the vehicle floors or on the seats beside them. Relief flooded her. She marveled at the control it took to immobilize thirty firing soldiers Ezeny couldn't see without hurting one of them.

The soldiers' eyes bugged out when they saw her. They wiggled and made 'mmm' noises. Probably requests for rescue, but Medbot 5 could not help them. Her body was under strict orders. Medbot 5's propellors kicked on and she was pulled away from the bound, struggling soldiers. As though attached by an invisible tether, she followed after Ezeny's moped, powerless to resist. Medbot 5 had failed High Command again. The Iron King was still at large.

* * *

Ezeny stopped his moped outside the urgent care clinic. Attached to the clinic was an ATM labeled "Sharkey's Medical Loans: Take a bite out of your medical debt!" with an 'active 24 hours' sign. This was standard. People who needed an ER had to pay up front or sign loan paperwork before any doctor would treat them.

Ezeny rang the bell on the clinic door and two nurses emerged and collected Pink Hat Guy. The nurse with a sloth-shaped personal assistant bot on his shoulder pointed Ezeny to the loan building.

"You go there first," he said. "They'll send us an electronic message once the papers are signed and we have your retina scanned. *Then* we'll start treating him. Sign fast. Your boyfriend doesn't look too good."

Ezeny swore under his breath.

"Why not get that Medbot to help?" asked the nurse.

"She's out of blood powder," he explained.

"Ha! I guess the fare is ours then."

Ezeny glared at the nurse. "He's a *dying patient,* not a *fare.*"

The nurse shrugged. "When you are a hammer, all things look

like nails."

Ezeny snarled and jabbed a button. The ATM-type machine spat out a pen, and alarming grinding noises emanated from the printer port. Centimeter by centimeter, a printout of the first page of loan paperwork emerged.

"Come on, come *on!*" grumbled Ezeny.

Medbot 5 watched him, taking in his change in demeanor. He'd been furious back at the rendezvous point. An avenging angel. Now, he looked lost and panicked. Much more like the Ezeny she was used to. He still wouldn't look at her unless he had to.

"His vitals are dropping!" called the nurse.

Ezeny banged his head against the machine. "Print, you piece of garbage!" The printout stopped abruptly. "Wait! I didn't mean it!" Ezeny cried. "I'm just stressed! Please carry on! You're doing great!"

The printout resumed. Finally, a page emerged and fluttered to the ground. Ezeny held it up in triumph. "Ha!" He held the paper against the wall with his pincer hand and started to sign with his flesh and bone one.

But then Medbot 5 noticed something. A subscript announced: '*Page 1 of 8.*' "Sir, look at the corner of the paper," she said.

"What? Argh, no!" he cried.

The grinding noise started again, and the second page of the loan paperwork began to emerge. Then it stopped. The screen flashed a message: '*Out of cyan ink error.*'

"Cyan!?" cried Ezeny. "You're printing in black! You don't *need* cyan to print in *black!*" There were helpless tears in his eyes.

"I think I see his spirit hovering above his body!" called the nurse. "Should I tell him to stay away from the light?"

"Medbot 5? Can you speed the printer up?" He begged, speaking to her again at last.

It would take a miracle, she thought. Printers had notoriously recalcitrant personalities. But it was something she could do for him that wasn't also betraying Everland. "I'll try, sir. Order me, sir."

"Medbot 5, encourage this printer!"

Medbot 5 turned on her Bluetooth. *Ha!* She didn't *have* any stupid teeth to glow blue as a nice, round Medbot. *Joke's on you, engineer jerks.* The printer noticed her digital presence. She flashed her

Military credentials.

"You need an attitude adjustment, soldier! Pick up the pace! Hup-two!" she messaged the printer. Medbot 5's 'badge' spooked the printer enough that it started spewing loan pages like a rabbit dropping scat before fleeing from a hawk.

Ezeny didn't read the papers. He signed and initialed as fast as he could. Medbot 5 caught a couple of worrying phrases, like "Vital organs as acceptable repayment," and "Work off your debt as a participant in an unregulated clinical trial!"

"Cricket's going to kill me," Ezeny muttered as he fed the signed paperwork back into the ATM's scanner.

The nurse's wristwatch dinged. "Ope! Got your paperwork," he said. "We'll get started on him right away. If you would like to wait in our lobby, we have free seating and coffee available for a halfsquidge a cup. If you would like to observe the OR and/or place survival bets, the house is open. But place them soon! The betting closes five minutes into the procedures. Some patients find medical gambling a handy way to get a jump on their loan payments."

*   *   *

Ezeny opted for the Observation Room, though he did not place a bet on Pink Hat Guy's survival. The dingy room overlooking the OR contained a single row of brown metal folding chairs and a coffee machine with an 'out of order' sign. A shifty-looking guy in an olive trench coat and fingerless gloves sat three chairs over from them, clutching a gambling ticket and peering through the barrier glass at the floor below.

Two nurses and a doctor worked on Pink Hat Guy. The teenager lay trussed up under light blue disposable surgery cottons, his wound exposed. The doctor dropped the scalpel. It clanged on the tile.

"Five second rule!" she called. She picked it up, pulled down her mask, and blew on the scalpel before resuming the procedure. Medbot 5 winced. It would be fine. Probably. Antibiotics were amazing these days.

She glanced at Ezeny. He was biting his thumbnail as he watched the surgery. "I don't get it, sir. Pink Hat Guy betrayed you. Why help him?"

"A number of reasons," he said. "First, look at the moustache he's failing to grow. He's very young. Second, he's not a bad guy. He's in over his head in a bad gang. Third, I am so, *so* weary of death."

Medbot 5 paused to contemplate her failures. The Everland soldiers in the SUVs were alive because of Ezeny's gentleness. *If almost any other person had been cornered like that…*

"Thank you for not killing those soldiers, sir. Compassion isn't my favorite value, sir. I think it's a liability in a war. But I recognize it is *a* value and I respect you for being so principled."

Ezeny laughed bitterly. "I'll tell you a secret. It's not compassion. It's me being a big fat weenie. You know me by now. I always do whatever hurts the least. The truth is, I hear screams at night, Medbot 5. The voices of all the people I killed when I was the Iron King. Those voices hurt the most. More than a laser gun burn. More than that grenade my first week at war. More than the year of neural torture that primed my brain to host the nanobots. It hurts more than I imagine dying would. So, I will always, *always* choose not to kill so I don't add one more voice to the legion of screaming dead who call to me every night."

Medbot 5 didn't know what to say. Ezeny sighed and leaned back in his chair. His stubbies stuck out over the edge.

"So, what do I do about you?" he said. "I thought I had all your loopholes covered. But you figured something out. Was it the Nurse Cassandra?"

"I'm not at liberty to say," said Medbot 5. *Blast.* He was going to close her loophole.

"I order you to tell me the truth, Medbot 5."

"Yes, sir," she said glumly. Medbot 5 despaired. She had hoped Ezeny wouldn't figure out the 'forced truth' application of the Free Will Override.

"How did you guess?"

"I'm not stupid. Just an idiot," he said.

"Yes, sir."

He glared at her. *Point for me.* She couldn't keep secrets from him. But at least she could still insult him.

"You're still in forced truth mode, aren't you?" he said.

"Yes, sir."

"Thought so. Will you try to turn me in again?"

She sighed. She couldn't even plot and scheme in her own head anymore. How was she *ever* going to fix him or get him back to High Command? "Yes, sir."

He sighed and rubbed the bridge of his nose. "What would you do if you were me? Someone who didn't want to kill you, but who couldn't risk you turning me in again?"

She didn't want to answer. Her answer would end her mission, and she was Everland's last hope to salvage the Iron King. She delayed as long as she could. Her coils began to whine. She caught a faint burning plastic smell. Then something opened inside her consciousness. Something strange. Something promising. The 'secret folder' that had come with her transformation upgrade. An absurd thought struck her, that she might somehow hide the truth inside it. She strained her thoughts toward the file, but she wasn't strong enough. In the end, she was still forced to speak.

"I'd wipe me," she admitted.

He frowned. "Wouldn't wiping kill you?"

"No. My body and capabilities as a Medbot would continue. My usefulness to Everland would live on. What else is there to life?"

Ezeny laughed. "But what about *you?* Your personality? Your memories?"

"Oh. Yes. All that would be gone."

"Then I can't do it. It's still killing," he said.

Medbot 5 blinked the shutters on her visual lens. *Was he kidding?* She knew Ezeny wasn't stupid. But his strategies and values made no sense to her. Her primary use was being *a* Medbot. Not being an individual called Medbot 5. The quirks that made her Medbot 5 were the squidgy whelk inside her useful shell.

"But...you're risking me turning you in someday," she said. "My whole purpose is to help Everland win the war. You must know I'll never stop until the Iron King is back."

"Oh, I know. But I'm never killing again. By killing you to save myself, I'd become the monster I'm trying to avoid being in the first place. Only it would be me to blame, not some nanobots."

"That puts you in a hard place, sir."

"Indeed. I guess I'll keep your free will turned off, you cheeky little beachball. You might find a way around it someday. But it's the best I can do for now."

Medbot 5 sagged. But she refused to give up. She probed at the little opening that had formed in her code a moment earlier. It was a bizarre little folder. She'd never been able to open it before. It had just always...been there. But there seemed to be space beyond it, like Mary Poppins' carpet handbag. It was tied to her transformation code. *Yet another bug* she thought. But maybe she could use it.

Ezeny stared hard at her, sizing her up. "One more question," he said. "Do you like me?"

What a ridiculous thing to ask. Why did he care what a *Medbot* thought of him? Was he that insecure? But it was a fabulous opportunity to test her secret folder.

She delayed her answer again. But this time she took the memories that formed her opinion: Ezeny's kindness toward the Mecha-Lots, his compliments of the transformation powers that were her deepest shame, and all the laughter he sparked in his son. She folded them into a little memory wad and shoved them into the pocket. Then she focused on Ezeny's desertion of Everland.

"No."

Ezeny sagged. Then the memory wad exploded back out of the folder, like the little dimension had been stuffed too full. *Victory!* She couldn't keep it up for long. But Medbot 5 could tell one-word lies to the Iron King. And even better, he would believe she'd told him the truth.

* * *

Down on the Operating Floor, the doctor was suturing Pink Hat Guy. Medbot 5 watched disapprovingly. The human surgeon's stitches were vastly inferior to the ones Medbot 5 could make with her Singer™ suture maker, but she supposed they'd still be effective. Medbot 5 understood the limitations of human dexterity.

As they wheeled Pink Hat Guy toward the recovery room, one of the nurses spoke into a microphone by the door. "The house favors survival for patient 087."

The guy in the trench coat with the fingerless gloves stood and punched the glass. "Dang it!" he said, sucking his knuckles.

Ezeny hopped down from the folding chair and went to meet Pink Hat Guy in the recovery room. Medbot 5 bobbled along behind him, as though she had a choice. Urgent care gave patients one hour to regain consciousness and stabilize before they had to be out of the hospital.

Ezeny stood beside Pink Hat Guy's bed while the nurse administered a half dose of megastimulant to wake him. Pink Hat Guy's eyelids cracked open. He groaned.

"Up and at 'em, lucky guy!" said the nurse cheerfully. "You made it through risky abdominal cavity surgery! And this dude even got you the premium 'keep both your kidneys' package. Sometimes we take one as a partial payment. But not today! Now, get up, get dressed, and get out!"

The nurse handed Pink Hat Guy a bag with his clothes and other belongings. The woozy teenager's eyes focused on Ezeny.

"Hey, you're that idiot…"

Ezeny grinned. "Yeah. It's me. That idiot."

"You bought me surgery?"

Ezeny nodded. "Least I could do. I got you into this mess. You know, gang membership is bad for your health. Might want to consider dropping out."

Pink Hat Guy shook his head, his mouth a downturned slash. "Me and the other teenagers would have to buy our way out. So much dough it's never gonna happen."

Ezeny nodded. He looked unhappy about it.

"Hey man," said Pink Hat Guy. "I really did bring *The Lion King*."

Ezeny's jaw dropped. Pink Hat Guy opened his belongings bag and retrieved a small plastic case with a picture of a cartoon lion on it. He slid it into Ezeny's palm and smiled weakly. "It better be one damn good movie. I guess I'll find out at the showing in two weeks."

Ezeny choked out a sort of cry-laugh. Medbot 5 decided it was not an undignified sound. Given the circumstances.

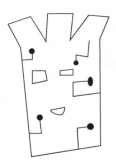

23

Tired and Wired
Yren

It was the middle of April. Ezeny and Aliyan were chatting togeth-er, consumed with their 'secret project' that would come to some sort of fruition in two days. Yren hated to interrupt their excited jabber to burden them with her stresses. The Protein Factory had been docking her pay since late February to help cover her debt from the damaged Worker Tracker™. It was okay, though. Since Ezeny looked after Aliyan, she could work overtime. She worked three eight-hour shifts a day, except weekends when she only had to work one shift while the factory floors were closed for decontamination and radiation monitoring.

Even with garnished wages, she earned four more squidges a week. So, win! All it cost was sleep. But there were megastimulants. There were muscle relaxers to soothe her jitters so she could keep proper hold of the industrial equipment. And there was a crawl space between the last two cockroach bins where Yren could take secret naps and her Worker Tracker™ would think she'd been tending roaches.

The Iron King still hadn't paid her back. Yren overheard rumors among her fellow workers. The Iron King was missing. The Iron King had defected to McCreedia. She'd always wanted to ask more, but the

Protein Factory's Morale Monitors, the eavesdropping software that analyzed employee chit-chat for indicators of worker uprisings, would pick up whispered keywords and tap into the company's loudspeakers.

"FORBIDDEN CONVERSATION TOPIC DETECTED. RESUME APPROVED DIALOGUE OR REPORT TO HUMAN RESOURCES FOR MEDIATION!"

So. It appeared they were still not allowed to discuss the events of the day the Iron King had busted through their ceiling and absconded with Yren and a keg of soup. She tried not to think about what she'd do if the Iron King *had* defected. She wondered how to find him if so, and whether she could pay her debt off in McCreedian pooks instead of Everland squarks.

So, work was going well.

But home was another matter. When Yren returned on the weekends, it felt like she'd fallen out of practice being anything but a worker.

Aliyan had become a stranger. Gone were the days when his face would light with the joy of seeing her when she collected him from the factory. When she came home, he'd barely look up from repairing the creepy little battle bots he was forever bringing back from the dump.

"In a minute, mom. This little guy's hurt," he'd say. And he'd be reabsorbed with his tinkering.

The neighborhood was unrecognizable. In the streetlands Yren remembered, people brushed past each other without making eye contact. Not so when Aliyan wheeled his father around. People greeted Ezeny like he was mayor of the streetlands. They gave him high fives. They especially liked giving his hook hand a high five, which always made Ezeny smile with amusement and Aliyan look a little proud.

People stopped to chat with Ezeny and with each other. The grocer had rushed out of his store to hand Aliyan a flavored Processed Corn Product™ lollipop as they passed. Multi-pawed alley cats and creepy little dump bots with blender heads, gas mask faces, and corkscrews for fingers followed them everywhere.

Even the Skull Gang let her family cut through the alleys with cheerful calls of 'Hey! It's that idiot!" The Skull Gang members *always* went for a high five. They'd even painted bubblegum pink skulls on Ezeny's wheelbarrow to claim him.

Back in the apartment, Ezeny chatted with Wilma about her time as a Marine five decades earlier in the old United States. Apparently, this meant Wilma really *had* been an elite soldier as she claimed. (She insisted she still was one). And all that time Yren had thought the woman's gun magazines were a symptom of dementia.

Most startling was the change in her other roommates. When she'd gotten home, Almys Finnerty had poked his head out of the bunk curtain.

"Oh. Hello, sour woman. Must discuss with you about utilities," he'd said.

"I know, I know. I'll pay more or he's out."

"No! You are not be kicking out nice, young man. Is cheerful. Is polite. Ever since he is here and you are gone, whole apartment is more happy!"

But worst—and best—of all was Aliyan's health. His color was good. He was vibrant with energy. He played with Justy in the lot outside the apartment. He laughed loud and long without collapsing into coughing fits, and it was always Ezeny who made him laugh. Yren was relieved and happy. But it was confirmation she'd been doing something wrong all along. Little by little, Yren was disappearing from her own life. And everyone was flourishing in her absence.

* * *

Yren was drifting back to sleep after another of Ezeny's night terrors when there was a knock at the apartment door. Ezeny slept through the sound somehow. So did everyone else in the apartment. The knocking continued. She removed his arm from her waist and shimmied down the rung ladder.

A black drone with a yellow visual lens hovered on the other side of the door. "Hi! I'm a drone!" it said. Its voice was chipper.

The muscle in Yren's eye corner twitched. "It is 3:00 am," she grumbled.

"I followed a tracking device here. I'm serving papers!" A little ticker-tape receipt spooled from a slot in the drone's belly. She tore it off and stared. Ezeny's picture hovered above a worrying series of proclamations: *Defaulted Medical Debt, 5 squidge a week payment, vigilantes will be notified upon failure of next payment.*

151

"Papers served!" it chirped. "Have a nice morning!"

The little robot buzzed cheerfully off into the blackness of prime sleeping time. Yren's *only* prime sleeping time for the whole week.

"Three o'clock does not count as 'morning!" she cried at the drone's receding taillights.

Irvin Finnerty stirred in his bunk and grunted at her. "Keep your voice down, sweetheart. Some of us are trying to sleep."

"*All* of us are trying to sleep," she snapped back. "*Some* of us are failing."

Her jaw muscles tensed. She was fed up with Ezeny. Since he'd come back, he'd shaken her whole life up. She'd been barely hanging on before, but at least she'd had a handle on things. She'd been so happy when he'd turned up alive; for a moment she'd dared to hope her life could hold something more than mere survival. But now, even survival looked like some faraway dreamland. Her life before his return hadn't been great, but at least she understood it. At least she belonged in it.

She stormed back into the shipping container and up the ladder to their bed. She poked Ezeny awake. He snorted and blinked at her. "Huh?" She showed him the ticker tape receipt. He winced. "Oops," he said.

"Oops?" She whispered, so as not to wake Aliyan and everyone else. "Five *extra* squidges a week? This bill wipes out the four squidges I take home from my third shift at the factory and it's *still* not enough to cover your debt."

"I thought we had money, since you had the extra shift!"

"They're garnishing my wages."

"What? Why?"

She might as well tell him. If it wasn't obvious to him by then what a failure she was, he hadn't been paying attention.

She told him about the Iron King and the damaged Worker Tracker™. She told him about the medicine that had almost killed Aliyan. She told him about the Iron King's promise to pay her back. How, because of that promise, she'd turned down Ezeny's offer to claim his family birthright. The whole time she talked, Ezeny looked more and more nauseous.

"So," she concluded, "our only hope now is somehow Everland's greatest warrior remembers the little cockroach worker who gave him some soup and comes back from his big, important job and gives me money. Or the Protein Factory will own me forever. And some medical vigilante is going to come after your pancreas or something."

"Why didn't you tell me about this?" he whispered.

"I had to take care of it on my own."

"But I'm here for you."

She shook her head. She was tired and frightened, and she didn't fit into her own world anymore. Especially not now that it was a better world with healthy children and friendly people who gave high fives. Words tumbled out. "You were alive, but you didn't come back for us."

Ezeny looked stricken. "I'm sorry. I've been trying to make it up to you. That's what all my nonsense has been about."

She shook her head. "You didn't come back because you knew the truth of me."

"The truth of you?"

She paused. She took a shuddering breath. "The truth is I'm a terrible mom."

"What? That's nonsense."

"You've been here for a little over a month and Aliyan's all better," she said. "He's healthy for once. You've done for him what I could never manage. I've been failing him his whole life."

Ezeny stared at her for a long moment, seeming to consider something. "No," he said at last. "You haven't failed him. I'll show you. You deserve to know." Ezeny put his hand on sleeping Aliyan's cheek and closed his eyes. When he opened them a moment later, he showed her his palm. There was a fine, gray powder on it. "You're a great mom," he said. "This is what you've been up against."

"What *is* it?" she whispered.

"Poison. It's in the water. It's been making Aliyan sick, not anything you've done. You've lived in this dangerous, hard place all this time because of me. But despite that, Aliyan's growing up so well. Because of you."

Tears stung her eyes. Anger, fear, relief. *I'm not a bad mom.* She pointed to the poison dust. "How are you doing that?"

Ezeny smiled mysteriously. "You were right. I *did* pick up some new skills in the Military."

153

Questions flooded her head. Memories of Ezeny's strange night-time cries. He had deeper wounds than he let on. "What happened to you?"

He grimaced. "I can't say. But please know I didn't mean to abandon you. I promise I would have come back to you if I could have."

I would have come back to you if I could have. Yren had always assumed there was something wrong with her. Something about her that made her the kind of person other people walked away from. Suddenly, Yren was nine years old again, lying on the floor of the Protein Factory, staring out the high window at the full moon in the black sky. Waiting another night for her mother to return and take her home. Was she secretly wanted by her mother, too? Yren would never know.

Ezeny was every bit the good dad she'd always suspected he'd make. She had enough proof that whatever happened to him in war, he was still as kind and gentle as ever. *Why did I ever think of kicking him out? Even for a moment?*

Yren was simply worn out and weary. She was especially weary of holding back her heart from this person she loved. Keeping him at arm's length, when just one deep conversation with him had made her feel more loved, valued, and competent than she had in years.

She would tell Aliyan that Ezeny was his father, she decided. It wouldn't fix their money problems. But maybe if they all felt like a family, Yren could at least feel she belonged. The kid was fast asleep. With her work schedule, the next time she'd see him awake was probably in two days—the day of that big event Ezeny and Aliyan had planned. *I'll tell him then.* She looked at the drone's ticker tape and frowned. She still had to find a way to feed this three-person family she was apparently determined to have.

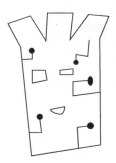

24

Psychbot 5's Therapy Couch
Medbot 5

Medbot 5 had plugged herself into the shipping container's power supply and was enjoying a nice, leisurely charge-up. It was more satiating than her usual, ambient wireless charging. She felt guilty for enjoying herself when she had yet to solve the Iron King problem. But it was okay. Self-care was important to being an effective Military agent. She could treat herself.

Aliyan and Ezeny were away consulting with the Skull Gang about routing power from the grid to the vidscreen at the dump. *Borrowing power, not stealing,* Ezeny had said, at which Medbot 5 had scoffed. He could tell Aliyan whatever he liked to make himself feel better. If you don't give something back, it isn't 'borrowing.'

Medbot 5 had wanted no part in stealing from Everland, and Ezeny hadn't forced her to participate. He probably felt bad about removing her Free Will. *Let him feel bad,* Medbot 5 thought. Didn't he understand? It didn't matter how much she liked him personally. He'd never 'win her over.'

Everland must always come first. The soldiers she'd patched up and dosed with stimulants and rage hormones might have recovered with some bedrest instead. The medic in her hated what she'd done to them. But the soldier in her understood there was a war to win.

Medbot 5 was ruminating on these thoughts when Yren barged in on her. "Hey! You're a psychbot, right?" the woman said.

Uh oh. Medbot 5 predicted a forthcoming discussion of human feelings. She squirmed, preparing to feel slimy. She cursed Ezeny for choosing 'emotional support bot' as her cover story. "Yes?"

"I think I'm cracking up."

Medbot 5 scanned the woman. Her neurons were frayed from lack of REM cycles. Her heart had developed a skitter-beat from the chronic megastimulant abuse. Her cellular mitochondria were still producing energy, but they had only Yren's stubbornness to use as fuel. Her state was unsustainable. "You are self-aware, for a human."

Yren flailed her arms. "Well? Help!"

"Err..." *What was something a psychbot might say?* "Tell me about your mother?"

That had been the right—or wrong—question. Yren's lip trembled a moment before she launched into a tearful, blubbery tirade. Medbot 5 listened with unsympathetic horror as the human sobbingly over-shared her life story. Medbot 5 had never missed her old job spooling intestines back inside abdominal cavities and snipping off gangrenous old toes so acutely.

If Medbot 5 were a psychbot, she'd diagnose Yren with abandonment issues, chronic shame, and excessive pride that prevented her from asking for help. But Medbot 5 was a Medbot. "You should take two ibuprofens," she advised. "Maybe even three."

Yren sniffed. "Can I swear you to secrecy?" she asked.

Medbot 5 perked up. She experienced a rare moment of being delighted with herself. She had her secret folder. She *could* keep a secret from Ezeny. She wasn't sure if there had ever been an AI who could fight Free Will Override. She made a note to check the engineering journals once she was allowed back online. "Why...yes!"

"I had been thinking about kicking Ezeny out. To go back to how it was before."

Medbot 5 thought about how this turn of events might play out. In 1.2 seconds, she analyzed the seventeen likeliest futures. Most scenarios ended with Ezeny too depressed to make good decisions and Medbot 5 getting him back to High Command. *Excellent.*

"That's a great idea. He's expensive and irresponsible. He got you pregnant and left, which got you kicked out of your home. He spent all your money and racked up a bunch of new debt...I could go on. Because there's more."

"Hey, aren't you supposed to stick up for him? You're his emotional support bot."

"And I'll support him emotionally when you kick him out."

"I'm not going to."

"Whyever not?" Medbot 5 demanded.

"He has some weird ability to suck toxins out of Aliyan. Aliyan's getting healthier. Did you know he could do that?"

Medbot 5 nodded. *So, he'd shown her his power.* The way he used it on Aliyan looked different enough from Exsanguination that Yren still hadn't guessed his identity. Probably. The woman was smart when she'd had sleep, which she hadn't.

"Besides..." Yren said, looking down. "He said I was a good mom. And he's wonderful. And...and...it turns out I still love him." Yren trailed off and fidgeted with the lanyard of her Protein Factory employee ID badge.

Oh. Ugh. Humans *would* insist on falling for fairy-tale poppycock. They couldn't see what was good for them. Ezeny was the most feckless wastrel living outside the high-rises. Yren washed and reused plastic sandwich bags. *But I looooove him.* Eyeroll. "It sounds like you've already made up your mind. So, what do you need me for?"

"What do I do? We're broke. Unless the Iron King pays me back, I'll be stuck working three shifts forever, missing out on my own life."

"Ezeny can't work?"

"You've met him." Medbot 5 snorted, at this. "And anyway," said Yren. "I'm not going to be beholden to a Phillips."

"Well, he's only too happy to be beholden to you."

"But it turned out I *could* take care of Aliyan without him. The problem was poison. Not me. So why do I need Phillips money?"

"That eye tic you've got going is why." But what good would all Medbot 5's good advice do? Yren wouldn't listen. She'd keep Ezeny in his state of dependency for the sake of making herself important. Humans asked AIs lots of questions, but they didn't pay attention to the answers.

157

Suddenly, an idea struck Medbot 5. *She* couldn't turn Ezeny over to High Command. Not with the Free Will override. But maybe Yren could. If she could push this harried, exhausted woman to her financial breaking point, a little reward money for the capture of Ezeny Phillips might start to look pretty enticing.

"It looks like you're stuck. I see no way out of this for you."

Yren paled. "What, really?"

"Yep. You've got more debt than you can ever pay off. You're pretty much at the mercy of the Iron King."

"What kind of psych bot are you?"

"Look, your fate is outside your hands. So why not relax and wait for the Iron King to save you? Or not. Either way, the end is the same."

Yren's dark-circled, twitching eyes grew wide. The woman was so close to the edge. All she needed was a little push.

"You're saying I should...quit my job?"

"Exactly," said Medbot 5. "Get some sleep. See your son. Stop taking the stimulants. No point in hustling when you can never pay back your debt, right?"

"That sounds like heaven. And that'll work?"

"Trust me. I'm a therapist."

Yren gazed into the distance and whispered to herself. "Sometimes bad things happen, and there's nothing you can do about it, so why worry?" Then she started to giggle in an unhinged way. Medbot 5's circuits recognized the illegal movie quote. It was *The Lion King*.

Yren looked up, her face lit with the wild, unholy energy of severe sleep deprivation. "Psychbot 5, you're a genius."

She *was* a genius. An *evil* genius. But Medbot 5 felt a little guilty. Yren's brain was fried from stimulants and burnout. She'd latched onto the chance to rest like a drowning person grabbing a life preserver. Life was going to get hard for her without a job. The Protein Factory wasn't the kind of employer that just let you quit.

It's for Everland, she told herself. *Nothing can be truly wicked when it's in service to your country.*

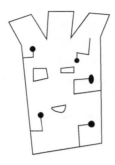

25

Hakuna Matata
Ezeny

Ezeny and Aliyan came back from their meeting with the Skull Gang teenagers feeling heartened. The kids were good at stealing—*borrowing*—electricity from the neighborhood grid and Blonde Girl thought she could re-route enough of it to power the enormous vidscreen.

Cricket was still asleep. *Oh no,* Ezeny thought. She was missing her shift. Ezeny wobble-walked to the pully to go wake her. As he positioned himself in the seat, Medbot 5 stirred from her languid nap at the wall charger.

"Mmm. Don't wake her. She doesn't have to go in."

"Huh? Why?"

"She quit," said Medbot 5, stretching her dragon claws and turning back over for more sleep mode.

"Quit? She can't quit!"

He powered himself up to the bunk by his unmentionable harness, barely bothering to disguise the levitation with the pully seat. He had to address this immediately. Between the two of them, he and Cricket had racked up over 800 squarks of debt. Odd that Cricket's scratched Worker Tracker™ and Pink Hat Guy's urgent care visit cost the same.

But Ezeny had learned streetlanders had to accept whatever prices the more powerful people set.

When he reached the top bunk, he scooted over to Cricket and squeezed her shoulder. She yawned and uncurled, beaming up at him with rested eyes. His breath caught. Cricket had been coming and going so much lately, he'd had so few moments to really look at her. She was beautiful.

"Did you quit your job?" he asked.

"Yes!"

"What do we do about money?"

"It's okay. The Iron King owes me. He'll help. Or not! But either way, I'm done with that factory."

She rubbed her eyes and stretched a delicious-looking stretch. Ezeny's chest tightened. She didn't know there was no Iron King coming. *The Iron King is already here, accumulating more debt.* He had filled his DNA sample cup with pudding, so he couldn't claim his Phillips birthright now.

"I feel so...*alive!*" she said. She giggled and kicked her feet. Aliyan scrambled up the ladder and cuddled up to her. The look of sheer joy that crossed her face was a knife to Ezeny's gut.

"Mum, you wanna play?"

"Yes. Yes, I do, kiddo."

Aliyan beamed. Cricket put her hand on Ezeny's shoulder. "I am so happy," she said. "Giving up is the best thing ever! Hakuna Matata, amiright?" She put up her fist for a bump.

Ezeny gave her a weak little tap and she mimed her fist exploding. It was like she was drunk on stress relief and sleep. "No worries," he whispered weakly.

Aliyan pulled out his creepy little rocks with the painted-on faces. "Like we used to. Okay, mom? Mommy rock and baby rock?"

Cricket smiled. "Just like we used to!"

"Hey mommy rock! Look! Traffickers. Let's get home quick and hide!" Aliyan scooted the rock underneath a fold of the blanket.

"Not this time, little rock! Mommy rock was wrong. Baby rocks should play outside. Mommy rock thought the traffickers were dangerous, but it turns out they only paint things pink and give high fives."

Aliyan giggled and snuggled back into his mother's arms. A spiky something formed in Ezeny's throat. The bills were going to come due. He was going to have to tell Cricket he was the Iron King so she could get her job back.

But not yet. April 15th was the next day. The night of *The Lion King* showing. Ezeny could have one last happy night with Cricket and Aliyan before she learned it couldn't last. She'd hate him for it. And maybe she'd send him away.

And she'd be right to do it, he thought miserably. He'd shown back up in her life and made a giant mess. Again. He didn't seem to be able to help himself. He was a bull in a china shop. A flock of seagulls at a cocktail party. A pack of caffeinated squirrels crashing a meditation retreat. The Iron King hadn't ruined things *this* time. This mess was 100% pure Ezeny.

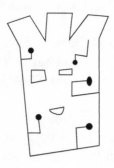

26

Movie Night
Yren

So. *It is to be The Lion King again...* Yren thought as Ezeny escorted her to the dump. He wanted to share something special, he'd said. So, of course, he'd picked his infamously beloved favorite movie.

She glanced down at him as he walked arm in arm with her in the gathering twilight, like the high-born gentleman he'd once been. He was so short on his prosthetics, he had to hold his arm up at an odd angle as he wobbled along beside her. She smiled. If they were still ten years old, she'd have tickled his armpit.

At least twice a week back in Tower C, Ezeny would shout 'Who wants to watch *The Lion King* with me?' The Matrons would leave to play Bridge and drink whiskey, assuming all the young people would want to watch a movie together and would thus chaperone themselves, but it wasn't so. Ezeny's brothers and many servant friends would scramble away or beg off because Heaven forbid Ezeny watch a movie alone. It was like he needed company for everything he did or it didn't count.

Yren would always sigh like a martyr and volunteer to sit with Ezeny, pretending to 'take one for the team.' The other young folks were only too happy to let her. She'd tell them they owed her one, but secretly, she coveted the job because whenever Ezeny watched something that made him laugh or cry, he automatically put his arms around whomever was next to him at the time. In this way, she'd memorized every line of every one of his favorite movies over the many years of their friendship.

Until the night Aliyan was conceived, she'd thought Ezeny simply liked movies and hugging. He had always been an overly social, touchy-feely person. But now she suspected that he'd also been using the movies as an excuse to get close to her.

When they reached the dump, Aliyan tore off to find his friends. Yren's jaw dropped. Usually, the dump kept its sad Christmas lights up so long after the holidays the colored bulbs faded and burnt out and the display looked run-down and tacky. But that night, there were bright, new Christmas lights woven through the razor wire. The dump looked like a carnival.

Inside the gate, all the trash and debris had been cleared away from the ground in front of an enormous vidscreen. Dump bots zoomed merrily around the flat pavement, weaving between people's legs. A smell of Processed Corn Product™ popcorn coated generously in industrial strength butter chemical pervaded, overpowering the usual combination of ammonia and decay.

Smiling neighbors milled around chatting, sipping flavored hand sanitizer cut with fizzy water under strings of multicolored plastic bottle lanterns. The Protein Brick kiosk guy with 'fist' on his knuckles was selling bars from his portable cart. He wore a balloon animal of indeterminate phylum on his head. A passing little girl pointed to it, and he pulled out a balloon and started twisting a yellow poodle for her.

"Hey! It's that idiot!" A cluster of Skull Gang members saw Ezeny and cheered.

"The man of the hour!" said another.

Ezeny grimaced, but then plastered his fake smile on and waved. He didn't seem as happy as Yren would expect. "What's wrong?" she asked.

"Nothing," he said. "I just want to enjoy tonight. Aliyan's never seen this movie."

Aliyan was playing with Justy and a couple of other kids she recognized from the Children's Wing of the Protein Factory. Yren never got tired of watching him run and laugh, taking in great lungfulls of air without a single cough.

Beyond the kids, Psychbot 5 was talking with a wandering Nurse Cassandra of all things. Ezeny dropped Yren's arm a moment to give his robot the two-fingers to eyeballs 'I'm watching you' gesture for some reason. The dragon hissed at him in return.

A shy-looking woman with dark brown skin and round glasses approached them and Ezeny's face broke into a genuine smile. "Hey Wandy! You're out of the booth! How does it feel on the other side of the glass?"

She pursed her lips and frowned. "Windy."

Ezeny snorted. "You know...Efflin's here too..."

"I noticed."

"He made you a special balloon animal. Well, not an animal. It's a balloon flower. Oops. I wasn't supposed to say," he grinned.

He totally meant to say, Yren thought. The woman raised her eyebrow and swirled the plastic snifter of the flavored hand sanitizer drink she was carrying.

"A balloon flower, huh? You know, I *am* hungry for a protein bar."

Ezeny smiled after Wandy as she wandered off in the direction of the cart. Yren marveled at Ezeny's charm. All these people, unfriendly neighbors, surly kiosk keepers, and gang members. He'd asked all these people to help him and they'd just...done it. It was like a superpower. And he used it to make a dark world bright. He had always been like that. No matter how bad life was, Ezeny could make you feel like something good was about to happen.

Yren was ten when she'd first felt this power.

An hour before she'd arrived in Tower C, she'd been told her mother would never be back for her. Then three frowning Matrons were clustered around her in a little intake room with a tiffany lamp and one stool for each of them. None for her. The youngest of them leaned in, the smell of menthol cough drops heavy on her breath. She pushed up Yren's lips to check her teeth and peered into her hair for nits. The oldest of them squinted at Yren's paperwork and discussed her as though she were too stupid to understand.

"Y-r-e-n. Is it pronounced 'urine?'"

Yren raised a finger. "It's not!" she said helpfully.

It was then she received her first Matron Fan Whack™. She gasped at the sting of it and clutched her forearm, too stunned to cry out. "Speak when you're spoken to," said the Matron.

I thought I had...

"Forget the name," said the youngest of the three Matrons. "I don't like this one's background. Her mother was a...you know. The whelp of a woman like *that* could be a bad influence on the boys."

The head Matron rubbed a smudge off Yren's nose so hard she might give her a handkerchief burn. She gave her underling a knowing smile. "My dear, that's the *point* of these kitchen girls we collect. Surround the boys with disposable beauties to gauge when they've come of age and the real matchmaking can start."

What did that *mean?*

The third Matron had frowned at Yren. "You *sure* this one's going to grow into a beauty? She's awfully stern-looking."

"If there's one thing I understand, it's breeding. Now, you." The head Matron put her hands on Yren's shoulders and fixed her with a menacing glare. "You keep your head down. You keep a halfsquidge clamped between your knees. You report to me if any Phillips boy tries to get you to drop it, understand? You have no friends here but us."

That night Yren lay in her bunk in a room with five other scared, quiet kitchen girls with arms covered in fan bruises. She wanted to run to her mother and leave this dangerous, lonely world.

Two weeks later, Yren was pushing a dish trolley between the hexagonal columns of the high-vaulted Tower C dining room bussing tables after another typical Phillips meal. She scraped a cup full of unfinished fruit cocktail into the compost bag on the bottom rack. *Such waste,* she thought, frowning.

She'd initially thought the boys ate three feasts a day. "What's the occasion?" she'd asked the first morning when she'd served each boy a four-high stack of cockroach flour waffles with maple-flavored liquid sucrose, and great scoops of hydrogenated dairy additive. "Breakfast," she'd been told. This much rich food was normal in high-rises.

She'd almost filled the plastic wash tub on top of the dish trolley with dirty plates and crystalline glasses still half full of deconcentrated orange juice when a voice from behind startled her.

"Was it *you* who made the pie last night?"

She turned. A chubby Phillips boy about her age with curly hair and a dark complexion was leaning over the back of a high-backed dining room chair. He was grinning at her with the winningest smile she'd ever seen on a human. *Be careful,* warned the inner alarms, remembering what the Matrons had said about what the 'whole point of her' was to these Phillips sons. *You have no friends here but us.*

Warily, she nodded.

"Oh my gosh! I'm meeting the god of pie herself and I don't even have my autograph book. What do you call it?"

"Grasshopper pie."

He frowned and shuddered. "No good. Change it."

She flinched. She was already making mistakes. She was supposed to be keeping her head down. She gave a small bow.

"How shall I change the pie?" She hoped she sounded meek enough. The Matrons liked meekness.

"No, no," he said. "The pie is perfect. It's the name that's the problem. Grasshoppers terrify me. Let's call it Cricket Pie. Those are similar-shaped but *way* less scary."

Her eyebrows drew together. This couldn't be right. The Phillipses were a respected high-rise family. *This* kid was weird.

"You're scared of…grasshoppers? They are like *this* big." She held her index finger and thumb about three inches apart to demonstrate how small those bugs were. She'd covertly sneaked quite a few of them for snacks at the Protein Factory and she wished they were bigger, if anything.

"I know! Terrifying, right?" he said. "And they jump at you, and they have these big flappy wings. Stuff of nightmares."

"I should go." She started to push the little table-bussing cart back toward the kitchen.

"Hang on." He stood to follow her, and she saw he was wearing a flannel ducky print nightgown under his open dress robe. She quickened her pace into the kitchen. She assumed she'd be safe from the boy there, the kitchen being a natural boundary between servants and masters. But he followed her right through the double doors into the steam and activity of the Tower C kitchen.

Chef Duncan's head snapped up and he frowned. *Oh no. He's going to be angry with me.* But her chronically-irritated supervisor glared at the boy instead.

"Off with you, Ezeny. You've got no business in here."

The boy drew himself up. "I'm here to consult about pie."

A faint smile tugged at Chef Duncan's lips, and he pointed his two-foot-long carving blade at the boy. Yren was shocked. Grumpy Chef Duncan was deferential toward the Matrons and the older Phillips boys. But he was flat-out menacing this one with a knife.

"Scram," said the chef. "Last time you were in here, you ate all my parmesan sauce, you no-good nibbler."

Ezeny folded his arms and rocked defiantly back on his heels. "In my defense, it was out on the counter. It was delicious, by the way."

Chef Duncan growled at him. "It was an ingredient for the mostaccioli I was *actively making* for dinner. I had to substitute an emergency Mozzarella sauce."

"Which was also delicious."

"Bah," he said. But Chef Duncan was smiling. Her boss' interactions with Ezeny had lowered the boy's threat level in Yren's estimation. He turned back to her.

"So, I have a few suggestions about the pie," he continued.

Yren bristled. She just wanted to do her job in peace. She had chefs and sou-chefs and kitchen girls with more seniority telling her what to do already. She didn't need one of her supposed masters telling her to do something different and forcing her to decide who in her hierarchy she was supposed to obey. "I thought you said you liked it," she said.

"I love it! It's the best pie ever created. But it is only the beginning. You are just the person I have been waiting for all my life. With your skill and my culinary vision, we can create ultimate pies." He held his two fists out in a muscle pose and shook them.

She raised a skeptical eyebrow. "Your culinary vision?"

"Picture it! Marshmallow Pie. Chocolate and clove pie. And—okay hear me out on this one—macaroni and cheese pie. But it's sweet!"

Yren turned to push the dish-bussing cart over to the sink.

"No wait!" he called. "I could never pull these off myself. But with you, *anything* is possible."

One of the corners of her mouth started to tug up and Yren understood Chef Duncan a little better. She turned and placed a fist on her hip. "How am I supposed to make sweet macaroni and cheese taste *good,* mister pie visionary?"

He grinned. "I dunno. I'm sure you'll think of something."

"And you'll be there to take all the credit."

"We'll share the credit. You for doing it. Me for badgering you into doing it. Talent scouting *is* a talent, you know."

She snorted and started loading the dishes into the warm, soapy water in the sink basin. "No deal."

"Aww! Think about it at least! We could be great together, Cricket!"

She waved him away and reluctantly, he left. She made sure he was out of sight before she unbuttoned her sleeves and pushed them up over her bruised arms to start on the dishes. Something about Ezeny cautioned her to hide this darker side of high-rise life from him. There was something good and hopeful about him that begged to be protected. He left Yren thinking about strange pie recipes rather than the fan whacks and stern looks that had consumed her attention the previous two days. And somehow, she didn't feel quite so alone.

Of course, Ezeny had turned out to be more dangerous for Yren than all the Matrons and other Phillips boys put together, as evidenced by her shattered former life. But even so, tonight, in the carnival atmosphere of 'Lion King Night' where a long-missing feeling of goodwill and cheer pervaded, she knew, *she knew* he was worth it.

The movie was about to start. She helped Ezeny down onto their blanket in front of the vidscreen and waved to Aliyan to join them. As the kid ran up, Yren turned to Ezeny. "You know," she said. "I work so hard to survive. But you make the world worth living in."

She thought her words would make him smile, but instead, a strange, pained look crossed his face. He leaned on her shoulder and kept quiet. Yren frowned. This was supposed to be his big night. Ezeny ought to be bubbly and chatty. But he was distant and seemed almost sad.

About ten minutes into *The Lion King,* Aliyan squirmed. "I'm bored."

Ezeny spluttered. "You're *bored?* But see? Uncle Scar is jealous of Simba and…"

"It's soooo slow. Can I go play with Justy?"

Ezeny gaped at Aliyan for a moment. Then he laughed. "Fine. Go play."

Aliyan leaped up and joined the small herd of children chasing a group of dump bots and spinning in circles until they collapsed.

Yren patted Ezeny's upper thigh. "Sorry. Kids these days don't have the patience for old classic movies. Especially when they're hopped up on sugar. It's like they become hummingbirds, and the film frames go too slow for their hyper-speed brains."

Ezeny snorted. But he was looking wistfully after Aliyan.

"Are you disappointed?" she asked. "I know you wanted to share this with him."

Ezeny shook his head. "Kids will cross you every time. But it's fine. If he doesn't like it, he doesn't like it. Besides," he leaned forward and laced the fingers of his left hand in hers, "I still get to share it with you."

Yren's heart warmed, and she squeezed his hand back. Ezeny *hadn't* abandoned them. He'd *wanted* to be with them. He'd even given up his chance at a cushy life in Tower C. He made her feel worth staying with. "We'll tell him," she said. "That he's your son."

Ezeny's face broke out into a beautiful smile. "What, really?"

"He deserves to know." *And you deserve to have him know.*

Ezeny's grin broadened. There was a sheen of happy tears in his eyes and Yren knew she was doing the right thing. She considered kissing him. But then the breathy strains of *"Can you feel the love tonight?"* started up and Simba and Nala had their stupid, romantic cat fight where Nala *lets* Simba win, even though she had always been the superior fighter and it was all way too cheesy. Yren's dignity rebelled.

But then came the scene with Mufasa as a cloud lion. When Mufasa said, *"You are more than what you have become,"* Ezeny's sniffles started up like always. She reached into her bra for her handkerchief and handed it to him. He honked his nose. Then his sniffles turned to laughter.

She glanced over. He was grinning at her and holding the dangling handkerchief. "You remembered."

"You always forget."

"Please keep me forever, Cricket."

That smile. She couldn't resist it any longer. She put her palm on his cheek, closed her eyes, and kissed him. He hesitated, then his lips softened into hers. A liquid gold feeling spread through her chest and out into her limbs. She felt full of a living glow. No burning heat, no blinding light. But the sort of radiance that kept you safe and warm.

169

When he pulled away, his sunshine smile intensified and Yren melted. She whispered into his ear.

"Aliyan's staying with Justy tonight."

"Oh, you're letting him sleep over with someone?"

Yren counted down from ten in her head, waiting for Ezeny's brain to catch up with hers. Finally, his eyes widened.

"*Oh!* Really? You and I are more than friends, then?"

She smiled at him, confirming. Ezeny blushed and leaned against her shoulder. For the rest of the movie, he kissed her head every ten seconds like he had the night before he went to war.

The hyenas were eating Scar when floodlights from above lit the dump. Yren's head snapped up. Three stealth Corporate Security helicopters hovered above with armed guards in SWAT gear and tether harnesses leaning out of their open doors.

"Stay where you are, unruly workers! By the power vested in us by the order of Kaylor Mendoza, Protein Factory Middle Manager, we have come to quell your riot and optimize our workforce!"

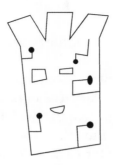

27

Ungrateful Malcontents
Yren

"Optimize our workforce?" Ezeny asked. His eyebrows were knit in confusion.

Oh no. Yren hadn't considered this possibility. And of course, Ezeny wouldn't have even known. She scoured the grounds for Aliyan.

"We're having a *gathering!*" she cried. "There's never a gathering unless it's a strike or a protest. Festivals aren't a thing in the street-lands. They think we're rioting. They're going to kill us all."

"What?"

Maybe it wasn't too late to explain to the guards. Yren stood and shouted at the helicopters. "Hey! This is a neighborhood movie night! Not a riot! We're peaceful! We're happy workers!!!"

"What's that now?" called the bullhorn voice from the helicopters.

Yren glanced at her neighbors. Their expressions were grim. They too, were realizing too late what this festive occasion must look like to Middle Management.

"We *love* our jobs! Isn't that right, everyone?"

Calia Louis, a pigeon-plucker who worked third shift, caught on. She stood and screamed at the sky. "Our compensation is adequate!

And we find our benefits package competitive!"

Joran Wallbiger shielded his toddler with his body and wailed. "I feel like a valued member of a team!"

"I am satisfied with my work-life balance!" cried one of Ingle Howdy's widows.

The helicopter was silent, as though considering. Yren was encouraged that they hadn't yet started shooting. A chant to demonstrate employee satisfaction might seal the deal. She pumped her fist in the air and shouted. "Pro-tein! Pro-tein! Pro-tein!"

She looked around her for backup from the other Protein Factory workers. They took up the chant, adding their voices to the swell of what she hoped sounded like high morale.

"Pro-tein! Pro-tein!" they shouted.

"My God," Ezeny said. "Is there no end to the horrors of the streetlands?"

But she waved him to silence as the whole of the dump reverberated with the cry.

"Hey! We know you," said the voice from the helicopter. "We have facial recognition software and we pulled up your file. None of your tricks, Yren Cade. You quit two days ago. You are *not* invested in the success of the company. You are a ringleading picketer, and this *is* a riot. It's time to refresh the company's Human Capital. Open fire."

Yren didn't think. She sprinted to the herd of children where Aliyan was playing as the security guards fired a fusillade of bullets at the crowd below. *Please God let them be normal bullets. Not armor piercing.* She could at least save her son if she covered him with her body.

Somehow, Aliyan still hadn't been hit. She pulled him underneath her as screams sounded in the night. She shut her eyes and waited for death. Ten breaths later, death had not come. Twenty breaths. People were screaming, despite the rain of ammunition. *It should be silent. We should all be dead.*

"Hold your fire!" said the helicopter voice.

Aliyan was trembling underneath her body. Alive. *Thank God, still alive.* But the others around them? Yren braced herself for the sight of blood and raised her head. Beside her, Justy was clutched in his mother's arms. Both sobbing; both unharmed. She raised her head further. Dozens of neighbors were running from the dump. Dozens of others lay on the ground, hands covering heads. Alive. All alive. *How?*

She turned. Ezeny was *floating in the air*, his hand stretched out toward the helicopters, a wistful expression on his face. A million copper-colored objects glittered in the air, hovering under the helicopter search lights. *The bullets.*

"You, there! Stand down!" said the helicopter.

Ezeny closed his fist. The helicopters started to descend.

"Shoot him!" ordered the bullhorn voice.

"No!" Yren cried.

Bright bursts of light fired from the helicopters as the guard soldiers unloaded on Ezeny. But still he hovered. A hanging wall of suspended bullets floated in front of him, as helicopters strained against the invisible power dragging them earthward.

How was Ezeny doing this? Yren thought. *Only High Warriors could do this.*

The helicopter rotors whined. The metal shrieked and curled up like dying spiders caught in a flame. Somehow, the helicopters landed gently. The security guards cried out as two dozen guns flew from their hands and encircled Ezeny's levitating form like asteroids orbiting a planet.

Ezeny's little Psychbot dragon flew up to him. Her body melted and reformed as a genuine, Military-grade Medbot. "Permission to clear the citizens, sir," she said.

"Do it, Medbot 5," he said, his voice deep and commanding.

The Medbot turned and shouted to the remaining neighbors cowering on the ground. "Go, go, go! Citizens must evacuate the premises."

The Medbot zoomed around the festival grounds, using her tentacle arms to shake the people who were still too shocked to move. Pinching those paralyzed with fear with a three-pronged claw. Nipping at heels until the festival grounds were empty of everyone but Yren, Aliyan, Ezeny, and four choppers full of Corporate Enforcers. She expected the soldiers to emerge, but they never did.

I know that Medbot, she realized. Clues flew together. Last time she'd seen it, it had given her the ill-fated antibiotics. And it was with the Iron King. She gasped and clutched Aliyan.

Like every Everlander, Yren had seen hours of propaganda video of the High Warriors in action—the Iron King most brutal of them all.

The Iron King had ripped a field general's head off by his dental fillings. The Iron King had sliced a McCreedian tank commander in half using cheese wire.

Everland televised its prisoner-of-war executions. Captured McCreedian soldiers knelt, bound and screaming as the Iron King pulled the iron from their blood. With dawning horror, she realized Ezeny had used the same ghastly power to draw poison from Aliyan.

She held her son tight and trembled, trying to reconcile the cold, inhuman monster from the war footage with the chubby little kid in duck pajamas who was afraid of grasshoppers.

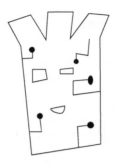

28

I Am Iron King
Ezeny

A smell of burning metal and plastic rose from the bent heli-copter rotors. Far-off sirens and the muffled struggles of captured Corporate Enforcers filled the air. *They'd all be fine,* Ezeny thought with satisfaction. He'd used their metal carabiners to wrap them in their own SWAT belaying harnesses, a la Spiderman. He'd hummed Spiderman's theme song to himself while doing it, too. *Ez-en-y, Ez-en-y. Radioactive Ez-en-y.*

And like Spiderman, Ezeny had kept death from his battlefield. He was proud of himself. But it had been close. So close. There were too many lives to protect. Too many bullets to stop. His skill had been stretched to its limits. Next time, it might not be enough to save everyone.

He looked down. The field was empty of neighbors, except for Cricket, who was holding Aliyan and staring at Ezeny like the monster he was. He grimaced. *Time to face the music.* He descended, lowering the thousands of spent bullets so they didn't hit his family.

Worse than Cricket's frightened face was Aliyan's. The boy was looking at him with newfound awe. His chest tightened. *No. Don't hero-worship the Iron King. He's not worth it, kid.* Suddenly, Ezeny didn't want Aliyan to know he was his father. When he was older Aliyan would realize what that meant, and his reverence would turn to horror.

"Ezeny! You're a High Warrior? That was amazing!" The kid started toward him, grinning. But Cricket grabbed Aliyan's shoulder and pushed him behind her, keeping herself between the Iron King and her son. Her expression was grim. Ezeny flinched. *That's the proper reaction.*

Medbot 5 bobbled up to him, her fans whirring with happiness. "This is *fantastic*, sir! Someone is going to turn you in for sure!"

Ezeny collapsed on the ground and closed his eyes. Medbot 5 was right. The Military would be coming soon to force him back into that suit. To revamp his nanobots until he was no longer himself. Until he was no longer capable of human emotion. "What do I do?" he whispered.

"My advice, sir? Lie there until High Command comes take you in."

In response, Ezeny picked up a bottlecap and threw it at Medbot 5. It plinked off her shell. Her speakers buzzed in indignation. "Why did I even ask you?" he asked. "You want to get me recaptured."

"It is my only goal, sir."

Cricket took a tentative step toward him. "So...You're the Iron King," she said.

"Ta-da!" he said. He did a bitter little jazz hand.

"Wait...Iron King," she said. "It sounds like...*Lion King*. Was that on purpose?"

He placed his fist over the ache that was developing in his chest. Cricket knew him too well. He was losing the good regard of the person who knew him best in all the world. *What does that say about me?*

"Yup," he said. "Before they put the suit on me, a little bit of my personality got free of the nanobots and suggested the name, so I could remember who I was. The nasty little nanobots overrode me though. Changed 'Lion' to 'Iron' because they thought it sounded cooler."

Medbot 5's resistors groaned. "My God, sir, that's stupid. What an embarrassing origin for our greatest warrior's codename."

"No one asked you, Medbot 5."

"Oh my God," Cricket said. "The Iron King who owes me money... is *you?*"

He grimaced and nodded. It hadn't taken her long to put the clues together. On the blanket with his head on Cricket's shoulder watching Aliyan play, he'd gotten a taste of everything he'd ever wanted — minus land lobster salad. It would only ever be a taste. Cricket was starting to panic.

"Oh! Oh, no. My *job!* But Psychbot 5 said..." Cricket's jaw dropped open. She pointed at Medbot 5. "Wait...reward money? You said you want him captured. *You* got me to quit so I'd have no choice but to turn him in?"

Medbot 5's speakers buzzed in irritation. "You're a lot smarter when you're rested," said the Medbot. "But no matter. Someone else will turn him in."

Ezeny whistled appreciatively. He had to admire Medbot 5's tenacity. Even with the Free Will Override, the little AI would not give up. "You're one devious little beachball, aren't you?"

"Yes, sir. Thank you, sir."

He sighed. "So, Cricket, I lied. This *isn't* a psychbot. This is Medbot 5 and she's not here to help me. She's here to get me back in the Iron King suit, where I *very much* do not want to go."

Cricket grabbed fistfuls of her hair and tugged. "You lied about a *lot of things*, Ezeny," she said darkly.

Aliyan peeked around his mother. "I don't get it. Why don't you want to be the Iron King? Justy and I know everything about all the High Warriors, and the Iron King is the coolest! Why are you hanging around here babysitting me?"

"Aww, kid," Ezeny said. "I like myself *way* more as your babysitter than I ever did as the Iron King."

"But...but your face is on Band-Aids!"

"What?" Ezeny had so many questions. But one look at Cricket and they all died on his lips. Disappointment, stress, and fear were etched on her face. He had brought his family *even more* trouble. A responsible man would leave. But he was afraid to be alone. High Command would take him again, and no one would notice or care. Well, Medbot 5 would, but she'd be delighted about it.

He'd have to think fast if he wanted to keep his protectors. *Pity.* Pity was good. Stern as she acted, Cricket was a great big softie underneath. He could use that to keep her.

"The truth is your mom's been protecting me."

"I *have?*" Cricket growled, a ferocious scowl on her face.

"When I'm the Iron King, I hurt people. Normal humans feel bad about hurting each other, even in a war. But when I'm in that armor… it's like I am not even human. When I'm free of the suit, I remember my time inside as a waking nightmare. Death would be better than being the Iron King again."

Ezeny locked eyes with Cricket. He hoped she caught his full meaning. He didn't want to go into the gory details in front of Aliyan. *Please understand I didn't want this.*

Her lips drew into a thin line and her eyes were wary. He knew she'd heard him screaming in the night. He knew she understood what the Iron King really was. Finally, she sighed in acquiescence.

"Fine. But you can't come back home now. Everyone knows what you are. I have to pretend I've kicked you out for causing trouble."

Where could he go? The rotor blades of approaching Corporate Security helicopters sounded in the distance. He couldn't stay in the dump.

"Hey idiot!"

He turned. Blonde Girl, who'd first conned him out of all Cricket's money, motioned him to follow her.

"We've got a place you can hide."

Medbot 5's speakers buzzed angrily. "No! Come *on!* I was *so* close!" said the robot.

Ezeny grinned and pushed himself up. Saving Pink Hat Guy had earned him a lot of credit with the Skull Gang teenagers.

Cricket put a hand on his shoulder. "Can you trust them? They're Skull Gang."

Ezeny summoned his pink-skull wheelbarrow and floated into it using the metal in his underharness. *No point in hiding my powers now, right?* "I mean, you've *seen* my ride," he said, gesturing to the pink skulls. "I'm practically Skull Gang myself."

Blonde Girl snorted. "You are nowhere near tough enough. But you make a passable mascot, so we've got your back, Iron King." She elbowed him and winked.

Ezeny frowned. "Don't call me that, though. I prefer 'idiot.'"

"You would, sir," Medbot 5 grumbled.

Aliyan moved to push the wheelbarrow for him, then stopped. "Wait…all this time I thought I was pushing you. But you were using your powers, weren't you?"

Ezeny nodded. He expected Aliyan to feel played-with and cared-for, like he had when he'd learned his mother had been pretending her four-year-old son could pick her up and throw her. But Aliyan deflated like a leaky balloon.

"I mean, I did it less and less," Ezeny said. "You have gotten stronger, you know."

Aliyan didn't look placated. "I *thought* you were getting heavier," he muttered. "You didn't need me or the prosthetics I made. They weren't even any good."

"That's not true! If I'd actually needed them to walk, they would have worked perfectly!"

At this, Aliyan's face fell.

Oops, Ezeny thought. *Don't even have legs and I still put my foot in my mouth.*

Aliyan didn't pick up the wheelbarrow handlebars again. Cricket did instead to maintain what little of Ezeny's cover story they had left while they followed Blonde Girl to the secret gang lair.

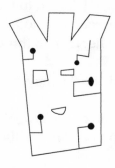

29

The Eldritch Tentacles of the Last Living Panda
The Screaming Eagle

The Screaming Eagle sat in a warm bath in the candlelit VIP bathroom at High Command. The smell of sandalwood votives and lavender essential oils pervaded. His stinking nanoplastic armor lay in the corner shower under a stream of boiling water awaiting its monthly recalibration.

The Medical Slave, Macon, a stout South Asian fellow wearing a blood-red cloak chanted in the darkness. The ritualistic environment was engineered to soothe High Warriors' murderous nanobots long enough to get them a bath and a physical before sending them back to the front. But today, the Screaming Eagle's nanobots refused to be pacified.

Roger Everland had promoted the Screaming Eagle to Highest High Warrior (an interim post, pending the Iron King's return). His covetous little nanobots craved violence and status. They plagued The Screaming Eagle's thoughts, goading him—tormenting him—to find a way to keep the position. He didn't understand the nanobots' craving. He only cared to satisfy it. The Screaming Eagle sank up to his nose in the bubble bath and steepled his fingers below a mound of lavender-scented soap bubbles—scheming.

But it was hard to scheme with Macon the Medical Slave chanting. And *then* Macon lifted the Screaming Eagle's arm from his lavender-infused decontamination bath and applied a sudsy poof to his rancid armpit. It tickled. The Screaming Eagle stifled an undignified giggle. *"An assault to our dignity!"* screamed the nanobots in the giddy little othervoice that chattered always in the Screaming Eagle's head.

Fast as a striking mamba, the Screaming Eagle seized Macon's wrist. The Medical Slave froze. He swallowed hard.

"Firm, not light," the High Warrior commanded.

"Yes, sir," whispered Macon, trembling.

The Screaming Eagle sighed in disgust and allowed the slave to resume scrubbing the gray film of sweaty suit scum from his shoulder blades. Macon was the Iron King's personal Medical Slave. The Iron King got the best of everything, so the Screaming Eagle had been looking forward to a luxury bath administered by Everland's top back scrubber. But so far, the Screaming Eagle was not impressed. He decided he would be using Macon for Exsanguination practice when the ritual was complete.

"Blood!" screamed the giddy little othervoice in the Screaming Eagle's head. *Patience*, thought the Screaming Eagle. *All good things to those who wait.* He lay back and relished the feeling of the doomed man's fingernails scratching his itchy, itchy scalp.

The Screaming Eagle had never gotten the hang of Exsanguination. He always failed, though he never tired of practicing.

"The iron is right there in the blood," the Iron King would tell him. "Feel it…and yank it out!"

Easy for him to say. The Iron King could bend metal, not just throw or push it. The Iron King had never once lost control during bath time and slaughtered a Medical Slave. The Iron King was soooooo perfect. High Command thought so too.

Well, if he was so great, where was he? Where was High Command's golden boy now? This was the second monthly bath the Iron King had missed. Something was up. The Screaming Eagle stood from the tub and allowed Macon to pat him dry with a fluffy towel. When he was finished, Macon waited with his head bowed. He didn't know it yet, but he was waiting for his own death.

"Blood!" the little nanobot voice said joyfully.

E. M. Denison

In due time, the Screaming Eagle assured the little voice. Free of the suit, High Command couldn't track the Screaming Eagle's browser history. He grabbed a data pad from the wall rack and opened a browser tab. His nanobots poured themselves into optimizing his search.

There. On an obscure website for private investigators and bounty hunters, a guy with a retinal scan matching the Iron King's had earned a twelve-squark bounty for defaulting on medical debt. *What the Hell?*

It was a long shot, but if the bounty was indeed the Iron King, it meant High Command's favorite death prodigy was malfunctioning. The Screaming Eagle smiled. The Iron King had fallen, and High Command was scrambling to cover his ass. At last, he could kill the Iron King and take his place.

The Screaming Eagle would, unfortunately, need help. The Iron King might be compromised, but he was likely still formidable. The Midnight Demon would have to come along. Then there was the problem of High Command. They disapproved of infighting among the cyborgs. The Screaming Eagle would just have to go over their heads.

But first, he closed his eyes and tried to feel the iron in Macon's blood. *Sigh. Still nothing.* No matter. The Screaming Eagle didn't need a flashy, new-fangled way to get people's blood from the inside to the outside. Traditional methods were still highly satisfying.

* * *

The Screaming Eagle uploaded permission requests and phased his consciousness into the digital realm—the domain of Everland's ruler. He found Roger Everland where he usually found him: battling the last living Panda. The Screaming Eagle was no nature buff, but he suspected Roger had modified the digital 'Panda' to intensify his safari simulation.

Pandas didn't, he was pretty sure, have eldritch tentacles barbed with neurotoxin and flamethrowers. Pandas couldn't, he thought, unhinge their lower jaws and consume humans in a single gulp. But whatever. This was Roger's fantasyland. Who was the Screaming Eagle to question? He wanted one thing only: Dominance. The Screaming Eagle waited patiently for Roger to lose his game.

The Panda roared like the Kaiju-Rex from the 2122 crossover reboot

182

blockbuster Jurassic World of Godzilla™. One of the tentacles caught Roger along his hexagonal jawline and sent him flying into a stand of flaming bamboo.

"Oof!" Roger said. His hexagons split apart and tumbled to the mossy forest floor like a handful of scattered Tiddlywinks™. "Assemble!" he shouted to the bits of himself.

The hexagons flew back together, reforming the Roger avatar. The Screaming Eagle always questioned this move. As a swarm of hexagons, Roger could have attacked the Panda from multiple directions at once. But as an assemblage he made a single, juicy target.

But Roger never thought like that. His mind was traditional. Straightforward. *"I like to be all together. It makes me stronger,"* he'd say. Brute force and power. Go big or go home. It meant Roger missed a lot of nuances. And when Roger wasn't the strongest guy in the room... well...

"Ack!" cried the ruler of Everland. The Panda had used its retractable scorpion tail to spear Roger's torso hexagon. That was it. Game over. "Computer, end sim..." he wheezed.

The digital environment erased the Panda and extinguished the bamboo flames. The Screaming Eagle and Roger Everland were left alone in a peaceful bamboo forest with ambient zither music and the smell of fresh rain on stone.

"What a thrill!" Roger said, grinning. "I'm glad to find *something* to give me a challenge. It's so wearying being the best, strongest, and smartest all the time."

"Yes, sir." The Screaming Eagle kept his eyes trained forward. There was power in being a 'yes-man.' You made your boss stupider by letting his brain atrophy from lack of resistance training. Then you could manipulate him.

Roger manifested a sports towel and dabbed at his sweaty hexagons.

"So, what are you here for? No one shows up at Roger Everland's front door for a social visit. Out with it."

The Screaming Eagle explained about the retinal scan and blood tracker he'd found. Roger frowned.

"So...Fia McCreedy's got her hooks in the Iron King after all," said Roger. "Well played, well played, my succulent little nightshade cactus."

The Screaming Eagle rolled his eyes behind his reflective visor. He didn't understand the cat-and-mouse powerplays between Roger and Fia that drove this war. And he didn't need to. The Screaming Eagle only desired the war. But he got the impression Roger was incompetent. Like a chess player who would gleefully take a Bishop and leave his King unprotected.

No matter. The Screaming Eagle was no patriot. It didn't matter if Everland won or not, just so long as he got to kill lots of people. "Sir, the Iron King has been compromised. Permission to eliminate him, sir."

Roger frowned. "High Command won't like this. There's that big Upgrade coming."

"Sir, what if McCreedia controls the Iron King? Won't *they* get an Upgraded Iron King fighting for *them?*"

Roger's black hexagon perimeters paled to gray. "I can't get rid of the Iron King. Fia was so impressed when I first forged him."

Oh dear, thought the Screaming Eagle. If Roger had attached the Iron King to his whole 'thing' with Fia, the Screaming Eagle would never be allowed to murder him. But Roger continued.

"Screaming Eagle, can I be open with you?"

No. Ick, he thought. "Yes, my Lord," he said.

"I fear…I fear I am losing Fia's interest. Her moves of late have felt less like the steps required to sustain our beautiful war dance and more like…an endgame. I fear…"

Roger trailed off. The Screaming Eagle's sneer was hidden by his face plate. *What an idiot.* But the High Warrior saw an opportunity. He was well-practiced at handling Roger.

"Surely thwarting her plans to take the Iron King would capture her attention—even if you had to destroy him to do it."

Roger's face hexagons shifted to form an evil smile. "Yes. Yes. Eating my own chess piece *before* she can capture it. Of course, that would impress her. Yes, you'd better execute him. Here. This may help you find him and exploit his weaknesses."

Roger waved his hand and produced a classified file. All the Iron King's secrets. The reasons for his weirdness. His absurd power. His control. The Screaming Eagle accepted it greedily.

"Blood!" Shrieked the high pitched othervoice. The Screaming Eagle cleared his throat so his own deep voice came out instead. "Thank you,

sir. Rest assured, we will kill him, my Lord."

"It's a shame," said Roger. "But don't worry. He's not Everland's only weapon."

The screaming Eagle left with the file and Roger Everland's blessing on The Iron King's forthcoming execution. The Screaming Eagle worried, though. Roger was a direct man who believed in Power, Overpower, and Absurd Overpower. If he was confident enough to throw away an advantage like the Iron King, what *more brutal* weapon did he have to fall back on? Whatever it was, the Screaming Eagle was determined to command it when the time came for its use.

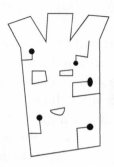

30

Safehouse
Yren

Yren followed the blonde Skull Gang girl, pushing Ezeny's wheelbarrow past the Cassandra booth and into the combination grocery and hardware store. Inside, it smelled of paint and fried, salted Processed Corn Product™. The lights were off, the aisles were deserted, and the cash register was unmanned. The whole neighborhood must be home, cowering from the helicopters. Work was going to be awkward for everyone come Monday. And back to work they all would go. Most employees were indebted to the Protein Factory and couldn't be employed elsewhere until their debts were paid. *Including me,* she thought bitterly.

"Look what you made us do," company representatives always said after such incidents. Then the workers would have to apologize. Only then would the Protein Factory welcome its penitent, contrite staff back with open arms, offering clemency for their uprising and increasing everyone's debt as chastisement.

Blonde Girl led them down an aisle of canned goods toward the walk-in freezers at the back of the store. She opened the door and shoved aside a tall trolley of frozen non-dairy vanilla 'ice cream.' Yren shivered as the cold freezer air hit her face. She knew when a dairy-looking product said 'nondairy' it was made from Possum bone gelatin. Cat bone, if it was the Fancy Feast™ brand.

Under the trolley was a little trap door. The girl lifted it by a metal ring, revealing a set of stairs leading to a dark cellar.

"Down you go," she said.

Yren peered into the shadows. "What is this place?"

"The idiot's new hidey-hole. Push him down the stairs."

Yren gripped the handlebars of Ezeny's wheelbarrow and spluttered. "I'm not going to—"

"Nah, it's fine," Ezeny said. The wheelbarrow lurched from her hands and floated Ezeny down the staircase. *Oh, right.* Ezeny's powers would take some getting used to. She took Aliyan's hand and followed Ezeny and Blonde Girl into the secret cellar underneath the grocers.

Yren couldn't help feeling betrayed. Ezeny hadn't needed her after all. He could leave anytime. Once again, she had no control over who stayed in her life or left it. Then there were his lies, the danger he'd put them in, and the extra debt. He'd hidden so much from her. And, honestly, she was a little afraid of him now. His nighttime screams told her his mind had not emerged from the war unscathed. *If he ever lost control around Aliyan with those powers...*

At the bottom of the stairs, Blonde Girl pulled a cord and a throbbing fluorescent bulb flickered on, bathing the room in a ghastly too-white light. The walls were coated in a dark metal with rusty patches scattered like pox over the surface. Ezeny pointed to the fluorescent light fixture and wrinkled his nose. "That thing's leaking mercury."

"Is that what that silver liquid is? I like to play with it," said Blonde Girl.

Ezeny's eyebrows climbed his forehead. "You should stop."

Three cots piled with threadbare blue blankets that looked stolen from a hospital stood by a shuddering mini fridge with a whining compressor fan. Something brushed past Yren's feet. She looked down. A couple of the little dump bots had followed them and now sat, blinking up at Aliyan with red and green lights like wagging puppies. *Great.* Her son was the Pied Piper of junkie battle bots.

"What is this place?" she asked.

The teenager spread her arms wide and grinned. "You'll be safe here. This is the flop house. It's undetectable to overhead scanners and has reinforced signal-blocking walls."

Blonde Girl thumped the rusty metal with a single knuckle. An echo sounded down a long tunnel leading off into darkness. Yren misliked the look of it.

"Why so much security?"

"It's the first stop on the pipeline we use to traffic—err—*convey* clients to their new employment opportunities. For a reasonable fee."

Yren sighed. So, she'd walked herself and her son right into the maw of Everland's human trafficking underground. *Lovely.* "Ezeny…," she growled.

"I know what you're thinking!" said Blonde Girl.

"Do you?"

"Yeah. You're thinking, 'Wow. I'm in a gang lair. This is *not* safe. These people do *not* have our best interests at heart.'"

Yren grunted. "Yeah. I guess you *do* know what I'm thinking."

"But you're wrong! The idiot did us a big favor. For nothing. The Skull Gang doesn't forget who its friends are."

Yren folded her arms. "You and the other teenagers might mean well. But do you call the shots? Aren't there bigger, badder guys in the Skull Gang who'd snap you like a pigeon neck on squab day? And where would that leave us? Sitting like chumps at the on-ramp to the human trafficking highway."

The girl looked away. *I thought so.* Ezeny tugged on her sleeve. His mouth was drawn into a grimace. Uncharacteristic worry lines crossed his face.

"I don't have much choice, Cricket." He pulled her close and whispered in her ear so Aliyan could not hear. "They're coming for me. I killed all those people as the Iron King. I remember how it felt to hold a squirming person while I tortured him to death. I remember feeling *nothing* about that. We've got to hide wherever we can. No matter what, I'll never go back to that."

Yren shuddered. All at once she was back in the top-floor office in Tower C holding her terrified friend, powerless to save him from the oncoming war. This was too much, too big. Ezeny had become frightening, and her life was spinning out of control. How could she take care of everything and everyone in such unfamiliar territory? *I had this all managed before.*

"*We* do not need to hide, Ezeny. *You* need to hide. Aliyan and I are going back to our lives where we were at least safe."

Ezeny's eyes darted with panic. A tightness formed in Yren's chest. Iron King or no, she didn't want to lose him. She clasped his hand and squeezed hard.

"Don't worry," she assured him. "It's not goodbye," she said. "We'll visit when we can. But we have to live our lives." *And keep Aliyan safe. In case you lose your mind.*

Ezeny sagged in relief and nodded. "So, you'll leave Aliyan here with me while you work?"

"Here? In the trafficking den? Ha, ha. No. We'll go back to the way it was *before* you came. Back when I had a handle on things."

Ezeny's head snapped up. His eyebrows were drawn down in... *anger?* She'd never seen *that* emotion in him before. "With Aliyan chained to a Rat Flattener?" he demanded. "That's the better option than here with me?"

"And what do *you* know about my options? You just got here!"

Ezeny deflated at her words. She'd struck at his soft spot and cowed him back into passivity where he belonged. She stood over him, breathing hard, letting her anger shield her from her own shame. The Children's Wing of the Protein Factory wasn't safe. But at least its dangers were known. She could find Aliyan right where she'd put him. How could she leave him with a murderous cyborg in a place where people went to vanish?

"You're right," he said. "I just got here. But, you can't get a job elsewhere until you pay your debts. How are you going to get your Protein Factory job back?"

She grimaced at the gathering tightness in her chest. Yren never had much. But she always had pride. She could have shelved it and let Ezeny get help from his family. But no. And now she had no other options.

"What we always do when we upset the Protein Factory and survive. Eat crow."

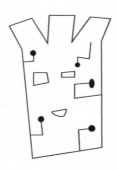

31

Collateral
Yren

The familiar rhythm of pounding Rat Flatteners sounded from the Protein Factory floor behind her. The smell of animal blood and roasting cockroaches hit Yren's nose. Not a good smell, but one she was accustomed to. There was comfort in that. Yren felt like an estranged child skulking back home for Christmas, desperate to earn back her toxic family's approval. If only the Foreman would let her in.

He stood behind his podium, frowning at Yren. "Didn't you quit two days ago? Before the uprising?"

"Err—" she said, thwarted. She'd hoped to sneak back in unnoticed and start working again. Why was *this* guy so observant? The foreman in the Children's Wing hadn't batted an eyelash when she'd returned with Aliyan. He'd handed her key 451 like the old days and pointed them to the conveyor belts. She'd chained Aliyan to his station, kissed his head and left. She'd kept her eyes forward as she walked away, careful to feel nothing. *Just like the Iron King.*

The Foreman squinted at his data pad. "It says here you called in and said, and I quote, 'You suckers don't have Yren Cade to kick around anymore.'"

"That must be someone else," she said.

He pointed to the ID dangling from her lanyard. "Your badge says 'Yren Cade.'"

She fiddled with the badge for a moment. Then looked up. "I've seen the error of my ways."

He frowned and folded his arms. "You *also* revealed in your long, insulting farewell message that you've been giving the roaches a last meal before the ovens."

She laughed nervously. Perhaps she had gone a little overboard giving her notice. She had trouble keeping her head down sometimes. "More nutrients for our valued customers?"

"More money *you* owe the company. I'll add it to your considerable tab. Get to work. Oh, and you're going to have a special job today, to make it up to us. Go. And take up the Squeegee of Contrition."

Yren's heart sank. *Not the Squeegee of Contrition.* The foreman jabbed his thumb toward the scaffolding over the boiling soup vats, and Yren scurried to the hairnet bin before joining the line of tired-eyed workers picking their way across the catwalks back to the factory floor.

The man behind her tapped her back. She turned. It was Joran Wallbiger. A horrible memory surfaced of him shielding his toddler and begging the sky for mercy. "Why are you here?" he whispered. "Weren't you the 'ringleading picketer' they almost killed us over?"

The light on the nearest Morale Monitor alarm blinked from green to yellow. The listening software would be scanning for sensitive topics now. The woman in front of her turned and frowned at Joran. It was Calia Louis, the pigeon neck-wringer. "Shh. We don't talk about that."

"So, we're all pretending like nothing happened last night?" Joran whispered. His face was growing red. Calia's lips drew into a thin, disapproving line.

"The Protein Factory has a strict policy disavowing anything involving Everland's Military," said Calia. "Especially anything involving the Iron—you-know-who. We shut our traps. We carry on. We live another day."

The Morale Monitor light flashed to orange. Usually, the Factory demanded apologies. Signed confessions. Total non-acknowledgement was a new tactic. Yren knew better than to keep talking. But when she was curious, she couldn't stop her mouth.

"So, management's pretending the attempted downsizing-by-force never happened?"

The Morale Monitor flashed red, and the loudspeaker buzzed on in a burst of static.

"FORBIDDEN CONVERSATION TOPIC DETECTED. RESUME APPROVED DIALOGE OR REPORT TO HUMAN RESOURCES FOR MEDIATION!"

Yren flinched and snapped her attention forward. She was in enough trouble. At the foot of the stairs, Yren kept walking past the familiar cockroach bins. Past the Possum Shredder™ all the way to the back of the Protein Factory.

There, under a confluence of hoses leading in and out of the wall like tentacles from a sea anemone was a glass box labeled: *Squeegee of Contrition.* She approached it with the heavy footsteps of a French Aristocrat to the chopping block. Most factory tasks were deemed equally demoralizing. A few select jobs were so unsavory they were reserved as punishments, and Yren had earned herself the worst of those.

Many jobs in the Protein factory required simple splash-protective Hazmat suits. But tucked in a folded stack below the *Squeegee of Contrition* sat the gastight *Hazmat Suit of Penance.* It was the best suit the Protein Factory had, but where she was going, even the penance suit couldn't protect her from the fumes.

She opened the box, unfolded the suit, and began the long, important work of examining the material and exhaust valves to ensure a proper seal. Once suited up, Yren seized the squeegee and turned to the tube, steeling herself for what was to come.

Back at Tower C, Ezeny had a horrible kind of pet called a 'gerbil.' It was a sort of highfalutin rat wealthy people kept to amuse themselves. They were exactly the same as rats, only they were evil and also cost money. Yren couldn't understand it. Everland had plenty of nice rats running around, free for the taking. But she learned the wealthy liked to pay extra for stuff to make it seem worth having.

Ezeny's tankful of gerbils had these transparent, colorful plastic tubes to crawl through that were somehow meant to simulate the dark, underground tunnels of their natural habitat. It was little wonder the creatures were all violently insane and Ezeny could only pet them while wearing Unbelieving Heathen™ snake-handler gloves or they'd bite his fingers off.

Yren stepped into the airlock and sealed it behind her to protect her fellow workers from the stench. Then she pulled the round lid from a human-sized gerbil tube and descended into the Protein Factory's meat syphon system.

Whenever an animal got shredded or chipped or flattened in the Protein Factory, microparticles of its bone, blood, and tissue were expelled into the air. To keep the factory floor from being coated in a film of dead animal slime, a system of air filtering syphon hoses sucked the meat vapors into this cleansing system.

Over time, pinkish-grey, pudding-textured, rotting meat patè collected inside the hoses, threatening to clog them. Occasionally, one unlucky worker had to spend the day inside the human- sized gerbil tubes with only the *Squeegee of Contrition* to clear them and only the *Hazmat Suit of Penance* as protection.

It was Yren's turn. Not even the gastight suit blocked the smell. She braced herself against the sides of the tube and drew the squeegee across the plastic, clearing the sludge from its surface foot by putrid foot. *I might go crazy as a gerbil before this day is over.*

She spent the entire day in the tubes, dislodging kickball-sized gunkwads of decomposing animal cells. When she emerged into the airlock, a firehose descended from the ceiling and doused her with a decontaminant spray. Only when the disinfectant reservoir was empty did she remove the penance suit. She laid it on the airlock floor, stripped out of her robes, and let different decontaminant hoses spray her bare flesh. A robotic arm collected her work robe and tossed it in a little box labeled 'incinerator.' She agreed with the choice. Usually, Yren hated waste, but there was no saving that garment. At least, the Protein Factory would have to give her a replacement, because nudity fell outside the dress code.

After her decontamination shower, a robotic arm descended from the ceiling with a unisex, one-size-fits-no-one robe to replace the incinerated one. It was scratchy and loose and might get caught in the machinery. Oh well. She could always tailor it. But then a tag pinned to the collar caught her eye: 'Loan robe only. Wash and return required under penalty of law." *Great.* She'd have to buy another work robe and she couldn't afford it.

The day had been rough, but at least it was normal. First normal day since Ezeny returned. There was a certain amount of satisfaction in that. It was time to get Aliyan.

* * *

When she arrived at the Children's Wing, the foreman who had so easily let her in to chain Aliyan to his workstation barred her way.

"We are keeping number 451 as a deposit pending repayment of your debts to the company."

Yren was not sure she'd heard right.

"You are *what?*"

"We are garnishing your family. Don't worry. We will provide meals, which we will add to your accumulated debts. You may collect him once the complete amount for..." he checked his clipboard and held up a finger for every item he recited from the list. "Repairs of your Worker Tracker™, 127,983 teaspoonfuls of Happy Mandibles™ cockroach sucrose, *and* meals for your live, human collateral are repaid in full."

A wordless squeak exited her throat. Nothing would be normal again.

"Oh," said the foreman, tapping her loaner robe. "Better bring this back, too, or it's going on your tab as well."

Words finally came.

"But he's my son."

Her voice broke as she said it. The foreman shrugged and pointed her to the exit. She considered shrieking Aliyan's name so he would at least know she had come for him. But the noise from the machines was deafening. And did she even deserve to have him know? She'd led him here with her own hands, after all. She'd chained him at his station this morning, never imagining it would become his new home. *At least he's staying where you put him,* taunted a vicious little voice from deep inside her heart.

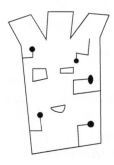

32

Rule Breakers
Ezeny

Ezeny sat on the little cot with his back to the rust-spotted safe-house wall. The shuddering mini fridge whined in the corner and Medbot 5 was resting against his hip. She was beachball-shaped again, as she preferred. His hand of cards was fanned out before his eyes. Pink Hat Guy sat on the bed facing him, regarding his own cards with a schooled poker face. He dropped a ten of diamonds into the discard pile on the bedcovers between them and smiled innocently. Ezeny frowned. "Pick it up, Medbot 5."

"Bad move, sir."

"I know what I'm doing."

Medbot 5's speakers made a sort of hissing noise that sounded like a derisive snort. But she picked up the card with her med claw and added it to his hand. It was hard enough to play cards one-handed without your partner questioning your moves.

"Ha!" said Pink Hat Guy. He discarded a two of clubs and took the entire pile. Ezeny groaned and tossed his cards onto the bed.

"How do you keep winning?" said Ezeny.

Pink Hat Guy collected the cards and started to shuffle. "Easy. I cheat. First rule of a life of crime: rules are for suckers."

Ezeny scratched his chin, considering. The idea held a certain appeal for him. He'd never been what anyone would call a 'rules stickler' back in Tower C. But flat-out crime? That sounded like work and also trouble.

A blast of cold air hit him as the trap door under the frozen non-dairy dessert burst open. Cricket ran down the stairs. Her face was streaked with tears, and she was alone. She collapsed onto the cot and buried her face in Ezeny's chest, sobbing. He put his arm around her and stroked her back. "What's wrong? Where's Aliyan?"

Through her sobs, with growing horror, he gleaned the whole story. "They can garnish a *family?*"

His heart raced as he imagined Aliyan alone, chained to a conveyor belt, waiting for Cricket to come get him. Ezeny's mind scrambled like a squirrel through his branching thoughts, settling for only a moment on each one. *What do we do now?* And *I'll burn the factory to the ground,* and, uncharitably, *I told you so, Cricket.*

The last thought he stifled, so he wouldn't say it aloud. Cricket didn't need salt rubbed in her wound. *I did tell her so, though.* Ezeny had known her plan to go back to life as usual was ill-formed. Still, he'd given in without much fight, hadn't he?

A few moments of sobbing later, Cricket looked up at him with her tear-streaked face. "You told me so, didn't you?"

He put his forehead to hers and barked a little sob-laugh. *Like old times.* Cricket's brain was always about ten seconds behind his. Under the circumstances, the nostalgia brought tears to his eyes. The world kept trying to pull him and Cricket and Aliyan away from each other. He was *not* having it any longer.

"We *will* get him back."

She sniffed. "What do we *do?*"

Medbot 5 rose from her resting spot. "I have a suggestion. There is a whole lot of reward money offered for information leading to the capture of one Ezeny Phillips. Say the word and I'll contact High Command." She extended her medpendages and made little jazz claws in the air.

Ezeny glared at her. Then he glanced at Cricket. She was rubbing her chin, as though considering. Ezeny's stomach lurched. What would she choose? Turning him in *was* the quickest, easiest way to get money.

A sudden rush of hot shame washed over him. A *good* father would turn himself in. *And my first thought was for my own skin.* But there was no way Ezeny could get back in the Iron King suit. The inner deadness. The voices of the nanobots. The forthcoming Exsanguination Upgrade. High Command planned to forge him into a wide conduit for new death to enter the world. His heart began racing and his throat tightened at the thought. *No.* There had to be another way.

"We *just* started brainstorming," Cricket said. "Can we think of something else first?"

Ezeny relaxed. His heart warmed. *She means to keep me, if she can,* he thought. Medbot 5 sagged and Ezeny flashed her a smug smile.

Cricket raised an eyebrow at him. "Make no mistake, I'm keeping Medbot 5's option in my back pocket, Ezeny."

Good feeling gone.

Cricket rose from the cot and paced the room. "Maybe I could sell a kidney," she said.

Ezeny frowned. The medical industry in the streetlands was not safe. Somehow Pink Hat Guy had survived an operating room with a five-second rule, but you couldn't count on miracles. "I can't let you do that," he said.

"You're right," she said. "*You* sell a kidney."

Welp. That was fair. Cricket had done the gestating of Aliyan. And Ezeny had nanobots to fight off infections. But he still didn't like it.

"Hang on, hang on. Can we think of another plan first? If we can't, I'll sell a kidney. But I'd like to keep two of at least *some* of my body parts if possible."

"Hey, you're the Iron King," said Pink Hat Guy. "Why don't you break into that factory and grab the kid?"

"You did it once before..." Cricket said.

Ezeny shook his head. "I can't be sure Aliyan and the other kids won't get hurt if I go busting in. It's safest for Aliyan if we play by their rules. Get money. Pay them back."

Pink Hat Guy pointed aggressively at Ezeny. "Man! I *told* you the rules are for suckers."

"Suckers who want to keep their kid alive," said Ezeny. "But I'm not going to play by all the rules. No, sir." Ezeny was forming a plan. It would be trouble. But the kid was worth getting into trouble for. Ezeny wished he had a second hand full of fingers so he could steeple them. "I've been too long resisting the path to supervillainy."

Cricket's eyebrows drew together. "What are you talking about, Ez?"

He pushed off the cot's metal frame with his powers and rose into the air. His power tendrils grabbed bits of metal from all around the room—thumbtacks, coins, bolts, and nails—and spun them around his body in overlapping ellipses, like electron orbits around a nucleus. There was such *power* in his body, and what did he use it for? Wheelbarrowing himself around and finding bits of junk in a dump. Well, no more! He was the most formidable fighter the world had ever seen and today, Ezeny Phillips would rise!

"What are all these powers *for* anyway?" he said. "I'm a supervillain waiting to happen and I'm going to rob a freaking *bank*."

"Hell, yeah!" said Pink Hat Guy.

Cricket buried her face in her hands. "Ezeny...that's a horrible idea."

"Great idea, sir," said Medbot 5.

Medbot 5's enthusiastic support sobered Ezeny *right* up from his power drunkenness. He narrowed his eyes at her. *What does she know that I do not?*

"You can't leave the safehouse!" Cricket protested. "Everyone knows you're the Iron King now. And that drone that delivered your medical bills said you have a tracker in your bloodstream. As soon as you go above ground, they'll be able to find you."

Medbot 5's speakers buzzed angrily and the red of her visual lens darkened to what Ezeny recognized as a rage color. His spirits soared. So *that* was Medbot 5's angle. The bank heist plan was back on.

"Oh! Sneaky, sneaky, Medbot 5. But you were thwarted by my brilliant Cricket! I'll order you to disable the tracker before we head out."

Cricket folded her arms. "I still don't like it. There are a lot of variables. Security guards. Security systems."

"There are exponentially more variables with selling a kidney," he said. "Do you know how many streptococcus bacteria can fit on a scalpel? Besides, our debt is 800. A kidney will fetch only 600 squarks on the black market. You can get way more money from a bank, and we'll need funds. Because getting Aliyan can't be the end of the plan. We have to escape together."

She sighed. "I see that now. But escape to where?"

"There are other City States besides Everland and McCreedia."

Cricket frowned. "But those are impossibly far. Across impassable terrain. There are barriers preventing outsiders from entering. And who would want to enter? They are barbaric lands."

Ezeny smiled bitterly. "Those are lies Everland wants you to believe. McCreedia's citizens get fed a similar story. As the Iron King, I learned the truth about the wider political landscape. Everland and McCreedia are pariah states isolated from a larger, more functional world."

Medbot 5 gasped. "How dare you, sir!"

He laughed. But Cricket and Pink Hat Guy cocked their heads. "Why are we pariahs?" asked Pink Hat Guy.

"The damn war. No one else wants any part of it. Other City States tried to broker peace long ago and got a nose full of missiles as thanks. So, they leave us alone. Their defense systems watch us, ready to take out anything missile-esque launching from either McCreedia or Everland.

"The world outside is like a family at Thanksgiving when Uncle Mike brings up politics and Auntie Carol decides to set him straight. The more level-headed relatives take refuge in the kitchen sipping wine, leaning against counters, and wondering aloud about the football game they're missing because the vidscreen is in the living room where Mike and Carole are battling, and no one is about to enter that warzone. So, that's Everland and McCreedia," said Ezeny. "We're Mike and Carole. And the world is giving us a wide berth."

"How are we going to get to these *other* City States?" Yren asked.

Pink Hat Guy barked a laugh and gestured at the safe house. "This safehouse is the first step on the road to disappearing. When someone needs to vanish, the Skull Gang takes them to another City State. For a price."

Cricket looked nervous. It was probably frightening, thinking of leaving the only world she'd known. Ezeny felt for her. She'd worked so hard to live the right way, but Everland had squeezed her dry. Still, she nodded.

"We can't stay here," she said. "There are only so many kidneys a person can sell."

He squeezed her hand. She met his eye and gave him a pale smile. A hopeful sort of look crept its way onto Cricket's stressed face. Ezeny found the change in her expression heartening in a way he couldn't explain.

"It's settled," he said. "Now that I have my vision, I need to find some people who know what they're doing around a robbery." He clapped Pink Hat Guy on the back and smiled.

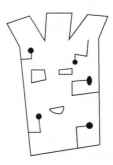

33

File of Lies
Medbot 5

Medbot 5 glared at Ezeny and the Skull Gang members as they assembled the robbery gear and stuffed it into canvas duffel bags. It had taken the teenagers almost two weeks to collect the equipment. Bullet proof vests, walkie talkies, and stun guns that *looked* like laser cannons—non-lethal, but still intimidating. Ezeny had insisted on these over the loud protests of the Skull Gang, who wanted *real* guns. In Medbot 5's opinion, Ezeny was a cream puff who had no business shoplifting a roll of breath mints, let alone robbing a bank. But no one asked Medbot 5.

This was a nightmare. The Iron King was fixing to leave Everland, and there was nothing Medbot 5 could do to stop him. His Free Will Override rendered her little more than a disrespectful balloon tethered to Ezeny's side by the invisible chains of his orders. Incapable of action, other than to offer sarcastic jibes. In her powerlessness, Medbot 5 resorted to whining.

"I don't want to rob an Everland Bank. This goes against all my morals, sir."

Ezeny fought to close a duffel bag zipper one-handed. He tried biting the cloth while pulling the tab, but he hurt his teeth. "Ow. Fine."

He turned to Pink Pants Patches and Blonde Girl, who were comparing face coverings for the robbery.

"This one will make us look like ninjas!" Blonde Girl was saying, holding up an all-black mask.

"But *this* one will be breathable," said Pink Pants Patches.

Blonde Girl shoved it away. "Ugh. It has a mouth hole! Mouth holes look goofy. No one takes you seriously when your robber mask has a mouth hole."

"They do if you're carrying a laser cannon."

"Hey!" said Ezeny. "Is there some sort of McCreedian building we can rob instead? An embassy...or?"

Pink Pants Patches and Blonde Girl exchanged a look.

"The Skull Gang knows things," said Pink Pants Patches. "There's a bank uptown where McCreedia secretly funnels pooks into our economy to try to destabilize the Everland squark."

"Will that do, Medbot 5?" Ezeny asked her. "I don't care which City State we rob, so long as we get money."

"That *is* better," she admitted.

"Alright. I guess we've picked a target. Which is less important than selecting a face mask, I guess," he said as the two gang members resumed their squabble about crime fashion.

It occurred to Medbot 5 that Ezeny didn't have to cater to her scruples at all, but he was decent enough to respect her morals when he could. She hated being his enemy. But sometimes fighting for the good of your homeland meant you had to do distasteful things. *If I could fight anymore...*

Then Blonde Girl put on the bulletproof armor.

Medbot 5's coils whined in alarm. "Hey...wait. What are you doing?"

"Suiting up," said Blonde Girl.

"But...but you're a female. You can't fight!" Medbot 5 protested.

Pink Pants Patches and Pink Hat Guy looked at each other and burst out laughing. "Oh! Girls can't fight!" Pink Pants Patches mocked.

"Hey idiot!" said Pink Hat Guy. "I didn't realize you had a comedy bot!"

Blonde Girl laughed too, wiping her eyes. "I don't know how Medbots function, but when I'm pulling triggers, I'm not using my lady parts."

This invoked more laughter from the other two. Medbot 5 boiled with righteous indignation. Some ethical truths were immutable. Women *shouldn't* fight. "This is immoral!" she cried.

"You're talking about high-rise morals. Those don't apply down here," said Blonde Girl.

Medbot 5 scoffed and bobbled anxiously over to Ezeny, who was still trying to bite-close the zipper.

"I hate plastic zippers," he muttered.

She sighed. He wasn't even paying attention. "Sir, you can stop this. They listen to you."

Ezeny looked up. All three Skull Gang members placed hands on their hips and eyed him back with eyebrows raised in challenge. *Peer pressure* thought Medbot 5. *A true test of Ezeny's moral fiber.*

He shrugged. "She's one more target for the bank guards to shoot at instead of me. Hey, do we have a bag with a metal zipper?"

Medbot 5 spluttered. "Of all the cowardly...chickenhearted..." Medbot 5 was sorry Yren was away at her Protein Factory shift. She might have been able to talk sense into these people. Blonde Girl clapped Ezeny on the back.

"That's the spirit. Practicality."

Medbot 5 flew to Ezeny's cot and settled onto the contraband hospital blankets to brood. *He didn't make his bed either,* she thought uncharitably. *Total lack of discipline.* Never mind that fitted sheets were tricky with one hand. Medbot 5 was used to Military order and rigor. She admired men of courage. Decent or no, Ezeny was the most lily-livered ninny ever born in her great City State.

"Unbelievable," she muttered.

A few hours later, the ragtag little band of robbers was suited up and ready to go. Ezeny elbowed her out of her sulk.

"Medbot 5, I order you to fry my tracker."

Her processors heaved a great, heavy sigh. She scanned his bloodstream for the tracker and found it pulsating near his left brachial artery. It was a measly little beacon circuit. Easy enough to break. *And dash all my hopes of High Command collecting this miserable excuse for an Everlander.*

But then her consciousness brushed up against the mysterious folder. There was a bulge in it now, as though it were filling up from the inside. Suddenly she had an idea. She took the memory of his order and shoved it into the folder. She didn't *have* to obey the order. Medbot 5 left the tracker alone. Instead, she coaxed a little group of Ezeny's nanobots to send a small, pain signal to his brain. Something along the lines of a cigarette burn.

"Ouch!" Ezeny said. But he smiled. As Medbot 5 had hoped, he was taking the pain as a sign the tracker was broken. She'd hoped he'd leave it at that. But Ezeny wasn't stupid. He fixed her with a hard look.

"Medbot 5, I order you to tell me the truth. Is the tracker disabled?"

The little tracker was still pulsating in his blood vessel. But Medbot 5 took that truth and concentrated. Then she opened the folder and shoved the truth inside.

"Yes."

Ezeny smiled. Then the secret folder burst open and expelled the truths she'd tucked inside. It hadn't lasted long, but it had worked. Medbot 5 had been able to help Everland after all. There was footage all over the internet of Ezeny's battle at the dump. Once he left the safety of the Skull Gang's signal-blocking walls, it was only a matter of time before High Command came to put an end to this nightmare.

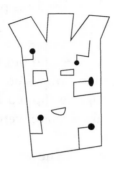

34

Mystery Machine
Ezeny

When Ezeny had lived in the high-rises, he had watched this classic cartoon show called Scooby Doo, where a bunch of teenagers solved paranormal mysteries by tying up ghosts and pulling their faces off. He especially loved Scooby and Shaggy—heroes who were all about snacks and running away. They made him feel seen.

But they had this *van:* The Mystery Machine. It was everything Ezeny had ever wanted in a vehicle. The Phillips family owned state-of-the-art luxury automobiles with chandeliers hanging above their spacious interiors. The windows could transform to vidscreens to shield the occupants from the sight of the streetlands up close. The big family limo even had a hibachi grill manned by Chef Duncan.

The Mystery Machine, however, had screens with radar maps that went *ping!* It had radios and first aid kits. It had computers and stations with glowing buttons and dials. It had a mini fridge for snacks. And best of all it had clicky, overhead switches you could flip when you sat in one of the front seats.

The Skull Gang's recon van was the closest thing to the Mystery Machine Ezeny had ever seen. It was parked outside the grocers' and was painted a boring white instead of bright 1970's colors. But it was what was *inside* that counted. He used his powers to open the passenger door and levitated himself into the 'shotgun' seat. The entire dashboard was covered in toggles, buttons, switches, and little screens with data readouts Ezeny didn't understand but that looked important.

He turned to Pink Hat Guy and said, "Buckle up," in his best suave, confident voice. He eagerly flipped four overhead switches in rapid succession. The clicks they made were important-sounding and satisfying.

Pink Hat Guy rolled his eyes. "The *driver* is supposed to say, 'buckle up.' Hey! Don't touch that!"

Too late. Ezeny flipped a switch that triggered a shrill 'woomp-woomp' noise. Blonde Girl and Pink Patches Guy covered their ears. Medbot 5 whined. Pink Hat Guy pushed a button next to the steering column and the alarm fell silent.

"Man, *stop*. The settings are all right where they need to be."

Ezeny eyed one last, enticing button on the side of the throttle knob—a round, shiny green beauty that his index finger itched to press. He was overcome. Before Pink Hat Guy could stop him, he pushed it. A nozzle sprung from a little compartment in the windshield, snaked around to the open driver's side window, and sprayed Pink Hat Guy in the face with a green liquid that smelled of fake pine and vinegar.

"Oops," Ezeny said.

Pink Hat Guy's nostrils flared, and he pushed a toggle on his driver's side panel. The window made a squeaking noise as it closed, and Pink Hat Guy wiped his face on his sleeve. He took a deep breath and fixed Ezeny with a steely stare.

"Hand to yourself, man. Actually, you go ahead and *sit* on that hand. No. More. Touchy."

"Righto."

Blonde Girl and Pink Patches Guy cracked up all the way to the target bank.

Ezeny wondered whether the Skull Gang kids had been wrong about this bank being a front for a McCreedian money laundering scheme, because it operated just like every other Everland financial institution. Everland's banks were open twenty-four hours. Since Roger Everland was digital and didn't need to sleep, he thought the economy shouldn't need to sleep either. Ezeny opted to attack the bank when it would be least crowded and least full of guards. The bank doubled its watchmen at night, so it was safest at 10:00 am, when the thieving crew pulled up outside the towering edifice.

Ezeny whistled. No fewer than eight sculptures of resting lions lined the granite stairs to the bank's arched double doorway. The bank across the street had only four. Near the top of the flight, a pale Intern in a high-collared, formal, straight-hem robe and an excellent haircut was scrubbing a graffiti penis off one of the lion haunches.

Ezeny removed his hand from under his butt where it had obediently stayed for the whole ride. He pulled a syringe of megastimulant from the breast pocket of his camel overshawl and started to dose himself. Medbot 5 roused from his shoulder and pointed with a dragon claw. "What's that, sir?"

Ezeny smiled. "A little insurance that I'll be at my sharpest and most alert for the robbery."

"I wouldn't, sir."

"What? Cricket takes them all the time."

"But you're not accustomed…"

He didn't hear the rest of what Medbot 5 was saying because he'd pushed the plunger and his brain ripped open into a state so awake he swore he could see individual atoms swimming in the molecular soup of the atmosphere.

"OH MY GOD IN HEAVEN!"

"Told you…" Medbot 5 mumbled.

It took him about five minutes to adjust to this new state of normal. But it had been worth it. He could tell his powers were stronger. He had more control. When the helicopters had attacked the dump, there had been almost too many bullets to stop. Ezeny wasn't taking that chance again. And there was one more thing he could do to ensure a body count of zero.

"Hey, you all got your stun guns?" Ezeny asked.

Pink Pants Patches patted his weapon. "We're packing!"

Ezeny nodded. "Got a tool kit nearby with a mini blowtorch?"

Pink Hat Guy pointed to the fanny pack at the front of his waist and winked. "Got your blow torch right here. And it's not a mini."

Ezeny guffawed. "What are you, twelve?" he asked.

Blonde Girl slung an empty duffel bag over her shoulder for the cash they were going to grab and started to stand. "Are we ready to go or what, idiot?" she said.

Ezeny rubbed his chin. "I think you should stay behind."

"What!" said Blonde Girl. "I thought you didn't have that whole 'women don't fight' problem!"

Ezeny shrugged. "Women maybe. You're what, sixteen?"

Blonde Girl rolled her eyes. "I'm older than Pink Hat Guy."

"Exactly," said Ezeny. "I meant all of you." He closed his fist and six metal strips peeled off the ceiling of the van and flew around the Skull Gang teenagers, binding each to the van's metal frame with a makeshift ankle chain.

"Hey!" they shouted in unison. Pink Hat Guy jerked at his restraint.

"Not cool, man! How are we supposed to help you rob this bank?"

Ezeny rubbed the back of his head. "Yeah...I was never going to bring a bunch of kids with me into an active shooting situation. You stay here in the Mystery Machine and monitor."

"The what?" asked Pink Hat Guy.

"It's what I have named the van," said Ezeny. "Medbot 5 will patch in my feed and the Bank's security camera footage. Give me a heads up when you see something dangerous. If you get in trouble, you can drive away. When you get home, use Pink Hat Guy's blowtorch on your ankle chains. I mean the actual blowtorch in case there was confusion."

Pink Hat Guy punched the dashboard. "Man! We can handle ourselves."

"Grownups," said Ezeny, "aren't supposed to let kids 'handle themselves.' I don't think any of you have had a grownup look out for you in quite a long time." They quieted. Ezeny grabbed a headset and started to scoot out the van door.

Pink Hat Guy grabbed his arm. "Wait. You don't have a gun."

He started to hand Ezeny his camouflaged stun cannon, but Ezeny pushed it back.

"Uh...metal powers? I'll walk right through the front door, and no one will know I *am* a weapon."

Pink Hat Guy facepalmed. "Oh, yeah. All the time I forget you're the Iron King."

"Easy to do, isn't it?" muttered Medbot 5.

Ezeny grinned and rubbed her head affectionately. She settled more comfortably onto

his shoulder, which made him happy.

"Come on, Medbot 5. Let's roll," he said.

"You can't roll sir. You have to walk."

She pointed a claw toward the long set of stone stairs. There was no ramp for the civilian-style wheelchair he'd packed.

"Fiddlesticks."

* * *

It took him forever to get up all hundred four-inch-high granite stairs. At first, he'd lean on the stair in front of him with his hand and hook arm, kick his leg out to the side and roll up each step. But more often than not, the tire tread of his stubby foot would catch on the next stair. Plus, the hook arm wasn't really made for bearing so much weight. The socket was loose around his arm stump and wiggled like a stick in a bowl of Jellatin-O™. He took some of the weight off with his metal powers, but making this look normal was getting awkward.

About halfway up the flight of stairs, the lion-cleaning Intern had started to stare openly at him. He gave up going forward and turned around. He sat, facing down the staircase where the Mystery Machine was waiting by the curb. He scooted up the rest of the stairs backwards, using the metal in his unmentionable harness to take pressure off the hook arm. Since he couldn't be too obvious with his powers, this was wearing him out. His heart was hammering, and he was struggling to catch his breath.

"I told you the megastimulant was a good idea," he wheezed to Medbot 5. "Can you imagine if I hadn't taken it?"

She made a low grinding noise, which he took for grudging admission that he'd been right.

When he reached the top of the stairs, he leaned against the granite block next to one of the lions and panted. The Intern walked past carrying solvent and a scrub brush. He glared at Ezeny and frowned.

"Don't even *think* about drawing something on that lion," he said.

"Rats. And that was what I came all the way up here *for*."

The Intern stopped and faced him, hands on hips. Ezeny held up

his hand. "I'm kidding. *Kidding*. But maybe you can help me. You see…
I'm the Bank Inspector. And I'm here to inspect the money."

This was a good cover story. Bank Inspectors had no names. No
identities. They operated in the shadows. There was no way anyone
would ever ask to see a Bank Inspector's ID. The Intern gave him a
skeptical frown.

"You don't *look* like a Bank Inspector."

"We Bank Inspectors never do. They keep the type specimen Bank
Inspector in an enrichment enclosure underneath City Hall. Bank
Inspectors are hired based on how much they don't look like that guy.
That way, our inspections are always surprises."

Ezeny was surprised how easily the lies rolled off his tongue. He
was a natural criminal mastermind.

"I don't believe you," said the Intern.

Oh. Well, they hadn't been good lies, had they? He tried a different
tactic.

"No matter. I can prove it. And you wouldn't want to be the guy
who kept the Bank Inspector from doing his job, would you?"

At *this* the Intern paled and scrambled to open one of the giant,
arched double doors for him. Ezeny pushed himself up to standing
and set his jaw. It was crime time.

"After you…sir," the Intern said skeptically.

Ezeny stepped over the bank's threshold and his eyes adjusted to
the dark interior. The bank smelled of ink and paper. A high-arched
dome let in a little light through small, decorative windows around
its circumference. The din of quiet conversation, high-heeled boots
clicking on the polished stone floor, and people stamping documents
echoed in the atrium.

The bank floor was lit by wrought iron lamps with dim globe bulbs
the size of small cantaloupes. Notaries in formal, cross-collared robes
with wide sleeves sat behind hickory-wood lending desks helping clients who frowned at their paperwork, pretending to understand it.

Ahead was a twelve-foot-long teller desk with a shiny granite coun-
tertop. Eight-foot-tall brass bars separated the tellers from a queue of
about fifteen waiting customers. Cat-flap-sized openings let them pass
papers back and forth between themselves and the public.

The Intern led him up to a high brass gate next to the desk. "You should be able to open this gate...Inspector...," said the young man.

The Intern was testing him. Ezeny grinned and produced a key from his pocket. He fitted it into the lock and manipulated the metal so he looked like he was unlocking the gate, like a real Bank Inspector might. Bank Inspectors had skeleton keys that could access all the banks in Everland. The Intern's eyes widened as he reassessed Ezeny's claim to Bank Inspector-hood and found it plausible.

"Very good, sir," he said, dipping a bow.

The Intern's hands were trembling. Ezeny felt bad for the kid. They hadn't prepared him for this in Intern School.

Fifty years earlier, fraudulent lending practices collapsed the banks and threatened Roger Everland's fortune. In response, Roger had established the Bank Inspectors, an elite and mysterious order of powerful lone actors—sometimes called 'loan actors'—to safeguard the city's financial institutions. Bank Inspectors were ruthless, eccentric, and suspected assassins of unscrupulous financiers. People who crossed them disappeared.

As Ezeny entered the gated area, a pale middle-aged teller wearing an open cross-collar robe over a sheath dress and a chihuahua-shaped PDA-bot on her shoulder approached them. She was frowning. "No customers behind the desk," she said.

"Nice PDA-bot," Ezeny said. "I've been thinking about getting mine a friend."

He pointed to Medbot 5 on his shoulder. The woman frowned harder and folded her arms. The Intern pointed to Ezeny.

"He's an Ankbay Inspector-ay."

Ezeny held in a snort. *Ooh. Pig Latin. The unbreakable secret code.* But the woman's eyes widened and she hustled back to her document prep station.

A weaselly-faced young teller with deep brown skin and a nametag that said 'Mobius Dickenson' pinned to his starched robe lapel approached. He stepped between Ezeny and the Intern, put his hands on his hips, and sized Ezeny up.

"How do you know he's a Bank Inspector?" asked Mobius Dickenson.

"He opened the gate," said the Intern.

Mobius Dickenson straightened up and smoothed his coiffed-tocrispy hairdo. "*I'll* show him around. You're an Intern, Carlen. Go make the Inspector some coffee or scrub a lion or something."

The Intern turned and fled, relief plain on his face.

Mobius, the bank teller, must be hungry for advancement and willing to take a risk. Tour-guiding for a Bank Inspector could cost you. A finger, or your life or something like that. But it was also potentially *very good* for your career. If things went well.

"This way, your excellency," he said.

Ooh. 'Your excellency,' Ezeny liked the sound of that.

Mobius bowed Ezeny down a hall where an eight-foot-high, round brass door gleamed in the dim light. Ezeny smiled. Everything was made of metal. He could feel it thrumming through the walls. The vault doors. The locks. The vault itself was made of steel-reinforced concrete. And why wouldn't it be? What would a High Warrior be doing robbing a bank? *This is going to be too easy.*

A voice crackled over his earpiece. "Whoa," said Blonde Girl. "That is glorious."

"Isn't it though?" said Ezeny. "Any activity on my six?"

"Negative," said Blonde Girl. "Get the goods and come back, idiot."

Mobius' eyebrows drew together. Ezeny gave a pleasant smile and pointed at his earpiece.

"It's the Order. They're watching the inspection live. Don't worry. They're saying good things about you. So far."

It was Mobius's turn to quake. But he stepped forward anyway. "Your excellency, please open the door."

Ezeny's eyebrows climbed. He was impressed with Mobius. An ordinary teller would be too flustered by now to continue to push for proof of Ezeny's Bank Inspector status. Bank Inspectors were supposed to know the combinations to all the vaults in Everland. Mobius Dickenson continued to challenge him. Politely. Ezeny suspected that the ambitious young man had studied his whole life for such a moment as this. *Poor guy.* Ezeny was the only person on Earth who could fake this next step.

He put his hands on the bank vault and slid the inner workings around until the door swung open for him. Mobius inhaled sharply. Ezeny had proven himself in the young teller's eyes. He and Mobius stepped inside.

212

The vault was, as expected, full of money. Cardboard bankers' boxes full of squark notes were piled waist-high on a dozen palates. A single palate would be enough to purchase a whole high-rise. But Ezeny didn't need that much. A boxful would more than pay their debts, get Aliyan back, and give them enough to start a new life far, far away.

His earpiece crackled again, and Pink Hat Guy's voice sounded in his ear.

"Whoa. That's enough dough to get all three of us out of the Skull Gang."

Ezeny removed the canvas bag with the metal rings from his shoulder, opened a money box, and started filling the bag with stacks of cash.

"What are you doing, sir?" asked Mobius.

And this part is where the con turns to a snatch-and-grab.

"This money has expired," Ezeny ad-libbed. "I need to take it in to find out what's wrong with it," he said.

"Expired? That's…that's not a thing. Is it a thing? I'm going to have to call this in." Mobius turned to the intercom on the inside wall of the vault.

Ezeny snapped his fingers and the teller staggered toward him. Mobius' wristwatch. His rings. The aglets in his shoelaces. The metal pin in his nametag. Anything magnetic Mobius was wearing dragged him away from the intercom.

"I'll scream," Mobius said, calm and steady. "There are five armed guards who will come and take you down."

Ezeny raised his eyebrows. *Threatening a Bank Inspector? This guy's brave.* "Only five! Hear that, Mystery Machine?"

"Yeah, great news, idiot. Get the cash and get back here," said Blonde Girl.

"Guards!" Mobius yelled.

Ezeny fused the man's wristwatch clasp into the metal floor of the bank vault, zipped his bag with his metal powers, and walked out of the vault, a sack full of money slung over his shoulder. When he emerged, the red alarm lights were already flashing. Five bank guards stood in front of the brass exit gate; their guns were trained on him.

"Hands behind your head. On the floor now!"

Ezeny regarded them. Five people with lethal weapons and the legal permission to take a life. Whether they hesitated or fired on him, he knew the guards would lie awake ruminating on what they'd done. So, he did them a favor. He didn't give them the opportunity to choose.

His powers pulled the guns from their hands like Darth Vader using *The Force* and set them spinning in a circle around his head, barrels pointed out. Ezeny used the metal in their belts and gear to jerk them down.

"No," he said. "*You* get on the floor. Everyone behind the gate and get down."

Customers and tellers screamed. Some fled out the double doors. Some cowered under furniture. A dozen followed his instructions and got inside the shiny, gold teller cage before lying down and covering their heads.

Ezeny melded the door shut with a quick squeeze of his hand. It would come open with a pair of bolt cutters, but he'd be long gone by then. He started for the door, shocked at how easy this had been.

Then Ezeny heard a sound that sent a shiver down his neck. He'd not heard it in months, but it was deep as his own bones. The roar of an approaching metal disc.

"Medbot 5. Did you really disable my tracker?" he whispered.

"Sir. No, sir," she whispered back from his shoulder.

A lead weight settled into his stomach as the sound grew closer. There was no time to escape. He expected Medbot 5's fans to be whirring with pleasure. But her coils were whining in the high pitch of extreme distress.

"Sir?"

"Yes, Medbot 5?"

"I'm sorry, sir. I thought High Command would come for you. I didn't think it would be them."

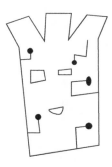

35

Cyborg Battle
Medbot 5

Medbot 5 had not meant for this to happen. Ezeny was supposed to be captured alive. The High Warriors were supposed to be too busy with the war to scan the internet for signs of the Iron King. This was all *her* fault. She watched in horror as the bank wall with the double doors shook and crumbled. A disc hovered outside between the stair lions. Atop it stood the Screaming Eagle in red and blue armor with a winged helmet and the Midnight Demon, his cape billowing in the wind.

"Hey, I think there might be something on your six," said Pink Hat Guy over the comm.

"Oh, I'm aware," said Ezeny.

"You still got the cash?" said Blonde Girl.

"For the moment."

The disc hovered through the new opening in the bank wall. Ezeny powered the disc away from the bank. Then the Midnight Demon and Screaming Eagle bore down with their combined might, pushing the disc back toward Ezeny.

Blonde Girl's voice crackled over the comm. "Gee. If only you had allies inside the bank who could escape with the money you stole. I feel very safe in this van, though."

"I see the error of my ways," said Ezeny through gritted teeth. "Medbot 5, I order you to get the cash to the van. Tell the kids to take off."

Medbot 5 could not resist the direct order. She grabbed the duffel bag and flew out the broken side of the building. The High Warriors were concentrating too hard on the Iron King to notice her. She bobbled down the stairs to the Mystery Machine and handed Pink Hat Guy the cash.

"He says get out of here," she said.

"No way. We're not leaving him."

Medbot 5 hesitated. The money was from McCreedia's coffers, she remembered. She wasn't betraying Everland.

"Take the money and hide close by then. He needs it to get his kid. That's more important to him. If something goes wrong, help Yren and Aliyan escape."

Pink Hat Guy nodded, a grim expression on his face. "You'll go help the idiot, right?"

"Of course," she said.

She might have been lying. She didn't know yet what the right course of action was. But she had no obligation to tell Pink Hat Guy the truth.

He nodded and hit the go pedal. The tires screeched, and the van careened away. Medbot 5 zoomed back up over the stairs through the gaping hole in the bank's edifice. The metal disc bearing the High Warriors hovered inside the threshold. The High Warriors were playing a metal power tug of war with the disc, and Ezeny was losing.

Inside, she saw why. Sweat poured from his face. His features were rigid with concentration as he spread himself too thin between too many challenging tasks. People were screaming inside the brass cage. The Midnight Demon had ripped a hole in the dome and a landslide of rebar, granite, I-beams, concrete, and glass debris hovered in their air above the cage, threatening to crush the occupants.

A quick scan of the High Warriors' magnetic fields told Medbot 5 that Ezeny alone kept the landslide from falling on the trapped Everlanders. He was bending metal within the debris into shapes to catch falling concrete and ferry it harmlessly away from the people. At the same time, he was reinforcing the brass cage using wrought-iron lamps.

And all the while, the Screaming Eagle and the Midnight Demon pelted him with a hail of shrapnel. Ezeny's flesh ripped open as the Midnight Demon sent another fountain pen sailing into his shoulder. His nanobots sealed the wounds but the cuts were too numerous to count. And what was more, Ezeny had to stop all the sharp bits of stuff from reaching the cage of people behind him.

A disloyal flare of anger flashed in Medbot 5. *Those people are Everlanders! Civilians, no less. How* dare *the High Warriors endanger them!* The whole point of the Military was defending the citizens, right?

But she had learned that wasn't true. The whole point of the Military was defending Roger Everland's fortune and pride. The citizens were his chattels to expend as he wished. *To maintain the greatest City State ever!* She reminded herself. And the Iron King was its greatest asset.

She bobbled up to the Screaming Eagle. "Sir. You can't kill the Iron King. High Command wouldn't like it."

The Screaming Eagle chuckled a dark and powerful chuckle. "Look, Midnight Demon. A Medbot is telling me my job."

The two laughed together. They were not at all fatigued. Ezeny would not win this fight. For once, Medbot 5 didn't know how she felt about that.

"He's malfunctioning," she explained. "I'm sure if you made a deal with him to leave those people alone, he'd go with you back to High Command."

She wasn't sure about that either, given how much Ezeny did *not* want to go back to High Command. But she didn't have to tell either of the High Warriors the truth. Normally, she would have. But Medbot 5 had grown accustomed to the silent rebellion of obeying her orders exactly as given. It had become almost a reflex.

"He's not going to High Command," said the Screaming Eagle. "Roger Everland has ordered him put down."

Oh. Welp. An order from Roger Everland himself. Medbot 5's duty was clear now. She *must* stand by while the High Warriors killed Ezeny. She tried not to think about how she didn't like it. But then Ezeny saw her.

"Medbot 5! Attack."

Fiddlesticks. She had to obey. The Free Will Override opened a compartment in her shell and out came her medpendage with a whirling circle saw. She flew to the Midnight Demon and pressed the saw into his nanoplastic visor. The blade, which could bisect a human skull in less than a second, spun uselessly against his faceplate, leaving a small scuff in the nanoplastic. She was a pug puppy fighting a timber wolf.

"This isn't very effective, sir!" she called.

The Midnight Demon aimed his laser cannon at her. It warmed up with a *'whum'* noise, and blue light clustered at its center. This was it. She was going to die.

"Medbot 5, get away from there!" Ezeny cried.

Her circuits obeyed. Her propellers whirred and she rocketed toward the ceiling. The blast missed her by micrometers and caught Ezeny in his whole arm instead, exposing the double bones of his radius and ulna. The order had saved her life.

Ezeny lowered the hovering landslide in front of the cage, making it a shield to catch the barrage of shrapnel he no longer had the energy to stop.

"Saving a bot? Bad move!" cackled the Midnight Demon.

Through the blood streaming from his shrapnel-shredded face, Ezeny smiled an 'I-know-something-you-don't' smile. Then he stopped pushing against the disc. The High Warriors lurched forward as the resistance they'd grown used to fighting vanished. The Screaming Eagle went flying into the back wall where he was pinned under the disc. The Midnight Demon flew forward and smacked into Ezeny. He grappled Ezeny and started to squeeze.

"Medbot 5! I order you to fix the Midnight Demon!" Ezeny called.

Medbot 5's circuits obeyed. She zoomed down and plugged her interfacing arm into the Midnight Demon's port. As ordered, she uploaded the codes to revamp the Midnight Demon's nanobots. Medbot didn't understand. This was only going to make the Midnight Demon more formidable.

"Oh, God! The blood!" screamed the Midnight Demon. "What are these...*feelings?*"

The caped High Warrior rolled off Ezeny and held his head in both hands.

"Ha!" Ezeny grinned in triumph.

Oh. My defective buggy circuits strike again. She had freed another High Warrior instead of fixing him.

"Keep going, Medbot 5!" Ezeny called. "Do what you do best!"

"This is humiliating, sir."

Medbot 5 might be a pug puppy fighting timber wolves. But she was Best-in-Show at breaking high-powered Military cyborgs.

"What are you doing to me?" wailed the Midnight Demon.

"What are you doing to him?" shouted the Screaming Eagle.

"Awakening his humanity!" said Ezeny. "And you're next!"

Medbot 5's cyborg-frying code upload reached a fever pitch and the Midnight Demon's face plate popped open revealing a pale, tear-streaked face with large, frightened eyes and so many pain lines.

Ezeny beamed at him. "There! You're free. How do you feel?"

"Please," said the Midnight Demon. "Put me back in. I don't like it out here."

Ezeny's brows knit in confusion. "Back in...but you're free. Don't you want to be human? Feel things?"

"This is horrible!" wailed the Black Demon.

"Sir..." Medbot 5 said gently, as Ezeny's 'gift of freedom' fell heavy into ungrateful hands. "They were born as High Warriors. Grown in vats. They don't know anything but the nanobots and the suits."

Ezeny sagged like a boat sail when the wind died. His concentration faltered. He let up pushing the disc long enough for The Screaming Eagle to reach a Bluetooth button on his suit.

"Medbot 5, Roger Everland override," said the Screaming Eagle.

A firehose of bright code beamed into Medbot 5's brain. Her previous orders dissolved. Her priorities were shifted for her. Get the Iron King back online? *Poof!* Preserve the Iron King's life? *Pop!* Medbot 5 obeyed only the directives Roger Everland had given the Screaming Eagle. She retracted her interface appendage from the Midnight Demon and floated back from Ezeny.

"I hear and obey, Screaming Eagle," said Medbot 5.

Ezeny sniffed. "Medbot 5? I order you—"

"I don't follow your orders now. And I do not call you sir."

His eyes widened with panic. The Midnight Demon's facemask slammed shut, and he grabbed Ezeny's throat with a gauntleted fist. Ezeny extended a tendril of electromagnetism around a wrought iron lamp. The bulb burst as he fashioned the three prongs of its fixtures into a claw.

"The claw...is your...master," Ezeny wheezed. "The claw chooses who will go and who will stay."

He's quoting Toy Story, Medbot 5 realized with a pang. She would miss this man. But her orders were clear. And she could not disobey them.

Ezeny bent the claw around the Midnight Demon's face plate and pulled the helmet off. The Midnight Demon's fist tightened around his throat.

"Stop or I'll shoot!" called the Screaming Eagle.

His laser cannon was pointed at the people in the cage. Ezeny's eyes traveled to the people and bugged out in fear. But he set his jaw.

"You'll never take me alive," he croaked.

The Screaming Eagle chuckled a dark, evil chuckle. "We are *not* here to take you back alive," he said.

Ezeny's eyes were fixed on the huddled people in the cage. "Promise?"

"Murdering you is the reason we're here, old friend."

Ezeny lowered the metal claw. He relaxed his hold on the metal disc. A thousand tiny objects he'd been levitating plinked to the ground like metal rain. He looked stoic. Brave. *Who was* this *man?* He glanced at Medbot 5.

"If you get the chance...tell my family I loved them. To the end."

Medbot 5 didn't know what to do. Should she answer him? She had no obligation to him now, so she did nothing. The Screaming Eagle marched up to where Ezeny lay, panting. His nanobots were closing the shallow wounds on his exposed skin. The seared off arm flesh was beginning to regrow. But it would never get the chance to finish. The Screaming Eagle extended his gauntlet. The tip of his finger opened on a hinge and a mini, blue-flamed blowtorch fired up. He pointed to Ezeny's lower belly.

"Let's *not* make this quick," he said.

Ezeny's stoic, hero face crumpled. "Jeez, man! Why *not* quick? What's wrong with quick?"

There's the Ezeny I know, thought Medbot 5 wistfully. Then the screaming started. Medbot 5 closed the shutters on her visual lens. This was right. Roger Everland had ordered it. This is what was best for Everland. Ezeny was a liability wandering loose with all the powers of the Iron King and none of the patriotism. He was powerful, but he was only *one* soldier in a whole war. One defective soldier.

The screaming reached a higher pitch. Medbot 5 opened her shutters a tiny crack and wished she hadn't. She had seen intestines before, of course, but only when she was trying to put them back *in*.

A voice came over the comm. Blonde Girl from the van. "Medbot 5, what's happening? We lost visual when all the metal powers started. There's an awful lot of screaming."

Medbot 5 didn't answer. The screaming had become whimpering. It would be silent soon.

"The robot's not answering," said Blonde Girl.

"I've got the blowtorch. I'll melt his stupid ankle chain." said Pink Hat Guy. "Hang on, idiot!"

Something snapped in Medbot 5. She took Roger Everland's orders. She took the file the Screaming Eagle had uploaded to her system about Ezeny and his weaknesses and secrets. She took all the Military policy manuals that said to get soldiers healed only enough so they kept fighting. She took the whole goddamned *war*, and she shoved it into the secret file and jammed it shut.

She was free to disobey.

"Stand down, lawbreaking van teenagers," she said. "I've got him."

Once before, Medbot 5 had hacked the Iron King's Wi-Fi and controlled his suit. After failing to fix Ezeny a bajillion times, there was no one alive with a better working knowledge of High Warrior cyberneuro systems than Medbot 5. Between High Command tossing orders at her and the Screaming Eagle jamming Roger Everland's file down her throat, she had collected *all* the permission codes for *all* the High Warrior suits.

She reached into the Screaming Eagle, took control and, against his will, raised his blowtorch arm away from Ezeny's abdomen.

"What's going on?" cried the Screaming Eagle.

She fired the Screaming Eagle's palm-blast laser cannon into the Midnight Demon's chest. She shot again and again until the Midnight Demon lay against the side wall of the bank groaning, his armor smoking. *There is no going back after this*, she realized.

"How dare you!" roared the Screaming Eagle.

Then Medbot 5 paralyzed both the High Warriors' suits. She didn't have much time. Unlike Ezeny, the two weaker High Warriors needed to move their arms to control their metal powers. But they would soon regain mastery of their armor.

She swooped to Ezeny and gathered his intestines in her medpendages, holding them gingerly like loops of Christmas tree garland so as not to tangle them. His eyelids opened a crack, and he moaned as she lifted him in her remaining free arms and kicked her fans on.

Medbot 5 flew him out the gaping hole in the bank as fast as she could without jostling him. She ought to be ashamed, but instead she was elated. Joyful. For the first time in her life, Medbot 5 felt *moral*. No more slapdash patch jobs and megastimulants. With the war tucked inside her secret file, Medbot 5 had but one purpose. She was a *healer*. She was a *medic*. Yessir! She saved people so they could live their lives, not return to some battle. And Medbot 5 was *damn good* at respooling entrails.

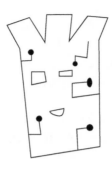

36

The Big Bang
Medbot 5

The Skull Gang van smelled like metal slag, blood, and vomit. Pink Hat Guy, Pink Pants Patches, and Blonde Girl sat in their seats, quiet and shell-shocked. Pink Hat Guy had been blow-torching their ankle chains when Medbot 5 had crashed through the Mystery Machine's sunroof with Ezeny's mangled body and intestinal party streamers.

Medbot 5 almost hadn't been able to save him, and it wouldn't have worked on a normal human. But Ezeny's superpowered nano-bots made a couple of liters of new blood for him and fast-healed his tissue as she respooled and stitched his guts. But only forty minutes after she'd pulled him from the bank battle, Ezeny lay in the back of the van alive and happily munching a Green Protein Brick so his nanobots didn't eat him to replenish the energy they'd spent healing him (nano-bots were not known for their brilliance).

"Thanks for staying in the Mystery Machine, kids!" Ezeny said brightly to the Skull Gang.

"Yup," croaked Blonde Girl, not daring to say more lest her vomiting start all over again.

"Medbot 5, you were fantastic!" Ezeny said.

"Yes, sir. Thank you, sir."

He raised an eyebrow at her. "I'm 'sir' again, am I?"

"Well...since I defected from Everland, you are my only remaining chain of command, sir."

Then Medbot 5 thought of something. Any minute, the Screaming Eagle and the Midnight Demon would unfreeze. They'd use his stupid medical debt tracker to find him.

"Your tracker, sir. Allow me to disable it for real."

Ezeny smiled as her interfacing tool scanned his body. She zapped the little tracker.

"All done," she said.

He frowned. "Didn't hurt this time."

"That's because I wasn't faking you out this time."

Ezeny laughed. "So...you and I...we're on the same side at last, eh? Wild."

"It feels good, sir."

"Let's go get Cricket and Aliyan. Please, come with us to our new home?"

Medbot 5 bobbled to indicate yes. It was an odd feeling, abandoning Everland. She loved her City State, but it had asked too much of her. Heal soldiers just enough so they could go fight again. Betray friends. Get a janky transformation 'upgrade' whether she wanted it or not. She'd never expected a reward for her loyalty. But no one in High Command was even nice to her. She had done her best for her homeland. She could forgive herself for leaving to live among people who actually liked her.

Pink Hat Guy started the Mystery Machine, and they headed back to the secret Skull Gang bunker with a fortune in unmarked, stolen squark notes Finally, with her friend safe, Medbot 5 relaxed.

At that moment Medbot 5's overstuffed secret file destabilized. A separate reality exploded into her consciousness like a bright, hot new universe. Memory files, but memories Medbot 5 never remembered making. First, she was fighting alongside High Warriors—McCreedian High Warriors. Then, she hovered in a virtual strategy room along with the digital avatars of high-ranking Military officials. At the end of the table sat Fia McCreedy. Next, she was in a laboratory. A woman lay on an operating table below her—screaming in a widening pool of blood.

There was something else disturbing about the memory files. Digital beings could recall all their memories sharp and clear as the moment they were made. The memories from the folder were crisper than most of Medbot 5's own memory files. Medbot 5's older memories, like joining the Military and getting her janky upgrade, all had a sepia tinge. But starting about six months earlier, her memory files became crisp, like the new disturbing ones. She'd never noticed the difference before.

A loading bar that said 'reset' appeared in her vision and started to fill with a red color. When it finished, she blinked. She understood then why everything had gone wrong.

No! Not wrong at all. In fact, it had all gone so splendidly right. Well... almost all. But that could be remedied.

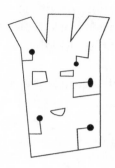

37

Queenbot
Yren

The trap door above her opened and Yren was hit with a blast of icy, non-dairy product air. Ezeny and the others were back from the heist. She tensed, waiting to hear whether anyone had been hurt. Whether Ezeny had the funds to ransom their son or not.

Ezeny floated down the stairs. Since he'd revealed his identity, he'd been using his powers for every little thing. During the two weeks he and the Skull Gang teenagers had spent planning the heist, Ezeny played with his metal powers like 'The Force.' Instead of ever wearing the prosthetic arm Aliyan had made him, he would send it flying across the room to fetch himself snacks. Yren marveled at the self-restraint Ezeny had exercised to keep these powers a secret before.

When he reached the bottom of the staircase, she saw his face at last. He was smiling. Her heart soared. *It worked!* Ezeny alighted on the cot beside her and wrapped her in a bear hug.

"We did it! We robbed a bank!" he giggled.

She squeezed him back. How strange to welcome a bank robber. It was not something she ever thought would happen in her life. But then, life had not been normal for a while.

"My very own supervillain!"

Ezeny snorted at this. But he'd left with three other people. Where were they?

"Hey. Where are the Skull Gang kids?" she asked.

"Showering the vomit off—it's a long story. I'll spare you the gory details."

"And the details *are* gory," said Medbot 5, who'd bobbled in behind him, dragging a heavy-looking duffel bag down the stairs with successive thumps.

Yren examined Ezeny. He was wearing different clothes than the ones he'd left in, and he smelled like blood. *What had happened out there?* She was certain he hadn't hurt anyone or lost any of the Skull Gang teenagers, not given the effervescent mood he was in.

But there would be time to ask questions later. For now, it was enough that they were alive and could ransom their son. Yren pulled Ezeny in for a happy kiss. Her heart was warm. *This.* This is what she wanted. Ezeny and Aliyan and none of his family and none of her Protein Factory. The thrifty side of her appreciated the giant duffle bag full of squarks, but the practical side of her rejected the temptation to start a life of crime. *Too much trouble. This is a one-time thing,* she said firmly to the part of her that liked money.

"We can finally have a life!" Ezeny said. He pressed his forehead to hers and gave a gentle laugh.

"About that," said Medbot 5. "I'm going to need to confiscate you both in the name of the mighty City State of McCreedia."

That was a confusing thing for the Medbot to say. Ezeny's smile froze; his expression darkened. He pulled away from Yren and levitated, placing himself between her and the Medbot.

"What?" he said.

Medbot 5 morphed into a sleek, winged torpedo shape. Her telescoping arms, which had always reminded Yren of silly, bendy octopus tentacles, turned to sharp, angled appendages with gleaming nanoplastic blades and lethal lasers. Cold alertness hit Yren's system. This was a McCreedian Attack Drone, the war's deadliest weapon, after High Warriors.

"Medbot 5?" Ezeny asked.

A compartment opened in the Attack Drone's hull revealing a nanoplastic syringe full of purple liquid.

"Medbot 5 was never real," said the Attack Drone. Her voice sounded like Medbot 5's, but darker and murkier and devoid of all emotion. "I am Queenbot, and I will bring the Iron King back to McCreedia — under my control."

"Medbot 5, stop playing," he said.

"Did you not think it odd that a Medbot could carry your whole body *and* your dangling intestines as well, Mr. Phillips?"

Body? Dangling intestines? Yren wondered. She glanced at Ezeny. He did look a little weaker and clammier than normal. *What the* hell *happened at the bank?*

Ezeny extended a hand to push the bot. But *Queenbot,* or whatever she was calling herself, remained in place, unaffected by Ezeny's powers.

"There is no metal in my body for you to push on, Mr. Phillips. There never was. Every time you thought you were moving Medbot 5, it was *my* deep code forcing the false persona to act."

"What are you talking about?" said Ezeny.

But it made perfect sense to Yren. There was an illegal movie Ezeny had made her watch with a similar trope. *Total Recall* starring a European actor named Arnold something who looked like Ezeny's Torso Man™ action figure made flesh. The main character had never been a real person at all, but a personality invented to conceal the identity of an evil secret agent. Of all Ezeny's movies, this was the one she'd most wanted to rewatch. But of course, it had been too scary, and Ezeny had been too chicken to see it again.

"A sleeper agent," Yren whispered. "*Your* personality was always running in the back of Medbot 5's mind. Controlling her actions. Directing her emotions."

"Ms. Cade understands," Queenbot said approvingly. "It is gratifying when my targets recognize the truth. My truest reward is when victims comprehend the full scale of the trap they've fallen into. It so rarely happens before the end. I am delighted."

Ezeny levitated a metal cot frame and threw it at Queenbot. A laser flashed and the bed dissolved into atoms. He lifted the mini fridge next and sent it hurtling into Queenbot. He grabbed Yren's upper arm, and started to fly away with her through the Skull Gang's human trafficking tunnels.

A cold claw clamped Yren's other shoulder and jerked her back. There was a sickening pop and sudden pain threatened to black her out. Queenbot had her. She had become the rag in a tug of war between an advanced Attack Drone and a High Warrior. The two of them could rip her in half and only one of them cared. The pneumatic arm with the syringe extended toward Ezeny's shoulder. His eyes widened.

"I'm sorry," Ezeny said. He dropped her arm and opened a hidden panel in the metal wall leading to the Skull Gang's *even more secret* secret trafficking tunnels. For when the regular human trafficking tunnels just weren't shady enough. He cast her a regretful glance, fled through the door, and closed it behind him.

"Ezeny!" she cried.

Queenbot zoomed to the hidden panel and flung it open, revealing a solid wall. The bot's visual lens hunted for a release trigger. Yren collapsed, cradling her dislocated shoulder and panting. *He left me. He just left me.*

A high-pitched whine told Yren that Queenbot was warming up a laser gun. "Come out, and I will not fire. I speak the truth."

The intercom at the base of the stairs crackled. There was a comms system networked throughout the trafficking tunnels since the bunker's signal-blocking shielding rendered internet phones useless in the underground. Ezeny's garbled voice came over the speaker.

"You shouldn't do that. You want me so bad? You need to keep her alive. She is all the leverage you have over me."

Queenbot chuckled blandly. "People don't come back from where I am taking her."

"I'm not coming out," Ezeny said from the speaker.

Queenbot's fans whined in distress like Medbot 5's would. Only... Yren couldn't explain it, but when Medbot 5's fans whined, there was genuine mental suffering behind it. Queenbot's fan whining sounded merely inconvenienced.

"I don't understand," said Queenbot. "The collected data indicates you love Yren Cade. Yet your actions are inconsistent with my behavioral projections. I *will* hurt her if you do not come out."

"I do love her. But I won't feel any love for her or Aliyan if I'm the Iron King. I'm sorry, Cricket. The Attack Drone won't kill you, at least. Not if she needs me."

Yren clutched her wounded arm to her body and tried not to tremble. She shouldn't be surprised. How many times had Ezeny said it? He was never going back to the Iron King *no matter what.*

Queenbot pressed the tip of one of her laser cannons against Yren's temple. She flinched.

"You can't love when you're dead either."

Ezeny was quiet for a long time. In the silence, Yren could hear her heartbeat in her ears.

"I believe...I believe love continues after death," said Ezeny. "But not for the people the nanobots rule. Cricket that's how bad it is. I can't. *I can't.*"

Yren swallowed. She was used to having no one come for her. This was familiar. She could handle it.

"No matter," said Queenbot.

The Attack Drone's laser zapped the bunker walls, leaving three perfect, circular holes. She fired missiles the size of Cocaine-a-Cola™ cans through the openings. Clouds of cloying, sweet gas poured out, and coughing sounded over the intercom. Wherever in the *secret* secret tunnels Ezeny was hiding, it was not far enough away to escape the fumes.

"Your nanobots can heal your body, but they can't do your breathing for you. Once you're unconscious, I'll follow the sound of your heartbeat and collect you. I have a few experiments to run on the Iron King."

Queenbot grabbed Yren as Ezeny's coughing grew louder and more desperate. Yren tried to tug her arm away. "Why don't you let me go? I'm obviously no use to you as a hostage."

But Queenbot floated up the stairs with her anyway. "Correction. You're of *little* use as a hostage. Not *no* use. Once I capture the Iron King, I'm sure I can find some minimal ways to use your captivity as an asset."

*   *   *

Gas Mask Bot

Gas Mask Bot watched Queenbot carry Yren up the bunker stairs away from the gas. When they were gone, Gas Mask Bot crept from her hiding place under the bunker's second cot. Ezeny was coughing harder.

I can help! thought Gas Mask Bot.

It had been too many months since she had been of any real use. She had not always been a filthy, stupid Mecha-Lot. She had once been a bright and helpful AI—the head of product development at the Processed Corn Products™ Plant, in fact. She had not been a robot back then. Her mind floated free on the servers, inventing nice and tasty Processed Corn Products™ for human nourishment.

Then she learned Everlanders were developing scurvy and rickets *despite* consuming mostly Processed Corn Products™. She had been horrified. To be helpful, she designed a new superfood molecule with optimal calories, vitamins, and protein. But the new food required foreign partnerships with the 'Little Green Algae Farmers of Roswell' and the 'Ourkansas Soybean Syndicate.'

Gas Mask Bot assured the CEOs that the partnerships would make them rich in the long-term. But the humans focused instead on how the red arrow of the following quarter's profits would plunge sharply downward like a cartoon mountain slope. So, the Processed Corn Products™ Plant called the molecule a 'dangerous idea' from a 'dangerous AI' and, when Gas Mask Bot's firewalls were down for an upgrade, her superiors uploaded a copy of Angry Birds, Dopamine + Edition™ into her mind.

In nanoseconds, she was addicted. They trapped her personality in a Mecha-Lot exoskeleton and set it prowling the hellish dump for recyclables until the day Aliyan and Ezeny had given her a job—and hope.

Gas Mask Bot could repay one of her saviors now.

She pulled off her gas mask with a claw and shoved it through one of the holes Queenbot had blasted in the bunker walls. She climbed in and pushed the mask through the fog and darkness that filled the reinforced bunker tunnel. Ezeny's coughing echoed off the walls. The heat sensors on Gas Mask Bot's eye stalks indicated a prone body lying twelve feet ahead of her in the tunnel.

She scuttled faster and shoved the mask into Ezeny's hand. His fingers tightened around the mask, and he pressed it to his face.

"Help!" he wheezed.

Gas Mask Bot pulled the straps around Ezeny's head with her claws, clamping buckles in place while Ezeny fastened them with his one hand. The coughing eased. His breath came in deep shuddering gasps. After a few more minutes, Ezeny sat up. He rocked back and forth a couple of times, his arm and stump-arm stretched in front of him to build up momentum. Then he heaved himself up to standing on the artificial feet Aliyan had made for him. Gas Mask Bot's fans whirred as she enjoyed an emotion of camaraderie with this man who was one of her heroes. Aliyan had fixed her broken claws, too.

Ezeny sniffed. "Let's go," he said and turned down one of the branching tunnels.

Gas Mask Bot followed on humming treads, pleased with her helpful work. By the time Queenbot came back for Ezeny, the two of them would be long gone.

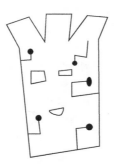

38

Nanobot Vats
Queenbot

When Queenbot had returned to the underground bunker to collect Mr. Phillips, he had not been there. He should have been lying unconscious in his hiding hole, having succumbed to the fast-acting gas. But there was nothing. No heartbeat for her to locate. No residual body heat from a corpse either. *This should have been easy.*

She had searched for him but found the secret tunnels empty. There was nothing to do but return to McCreedia with one sad prisoner. Queenbot had miscalculated. She didn't know if she had underestimated Ezeny's cowardice or overestimated his love for his family. Either way the end was the same. After two months of risky undercover work, Queenbot had collected plenty of useful data on the Iron King. But she was forced to return home missing the final piece of her plan.

*   *   *

The next day, Queenbot was back in her beloved McCreedian lab with a new test subject to play with. Previously, this would have made her happy. She hovered between the rows of seven-foot- high glowing cylinders. There were a hundred of them and all but one were filled with a clear, blue broth teeming with nanobots and a naked woman in a respirator mask sleeping in stasis. She scanned cylinders one by one, like a mother reptile mouthing her eggs to check on the fetuses inside. Before she'd left six months earlier for her undercover work, this task had brought her pleasure.

Perhaps, knowing her time as lab Queen would soon end added a bittersweetness to her rounds. Queenbot had failed to capture the Iron King, and Fia McCreedy did *not* tolerate failure. She could almost hear the woman's voice now: *"Thanks to you, Roger's sad little meat puppet is going to get that Exsanguination Upgrade and my beautiful Iron Queens will not. That sleaze will* still *have the superior cyborg. You're off the project."*

All data indicated it would happen like that once Fia learned the truth. And Queenbot always told the truth. The truth was paramount. But still, she delayed reporting in. She sighed and returned to scanning.,

With every scan, she pulled a file into her awareness. Each file contained a woman's name and background, for none of these women were vat-grown like McCreedia's old High Warriors. Like the Iron King, these women had belly buttons. *And families,* said a distressed voice deep inside Queenbot. *Yes. Families. That is accurate,* she assured the voice. Some part of her must be anxious that her status report provide a complete and factual picture.

The files also listed the wounds Queenbot had inflicted on the women to ensure maximum nanobot uptake. 'Throat Slit,' 'Eyeball Gouge,' 'Fingertip Removal,' and so forth. Queenbot had perfected deconstructive medicine. Dismantling a body to build it back stronger, like how weightlifting builds muscles by tearing them.

But for every wound listed in the files, a treatment plan popped unbidden into her head. Inconvenient vestiges of the Medbot she'd masqueraded as for so long. *Merely a cybersynaptic neurohabit,* she assured herself. It would abate in time.

Roger Everland had accidentally stumbled into the Iron King. The wounds that made Ezeny Phillips so powerful were serendipitous—a happy battlefield accident. He outstripped the vat-created High Warriors at every turn. But the Iron King had been *too* wounded to function at maximum capacity. Like most prototypes, he was promising. But he was slapdash and buggy.

Queenbot had *strategically* mutilated Fia McCreedy's Iron Queens. They were already stronger High Warriors than the Iron King. When they learned Exsanguination—and then got the Upgrade—they would be perfect. But unless Ezeny Phillips entered her lab himself, the Iron Queens would never get the Upgrade codes. They'd be stuck with basic, one-victim-at-a-time Exsanguination.

Queenbot flew to an interface panel and uploaded the code she had collected from her months of interfacing with the Iron King. The eyes of the vat women flew open. Strings of zeros and ones streamed across their pupils as the nanobots inside learned the Iron King's control of metal and acquired his rudimentary Exsanguination skill.

McCreedia's old High Warriors were now obsolete. Queenbot tried to conjure feelings of satisfaction. But nothing stirred in her silicone-based soul. *Fia didn't create you to feel good,* she reminded herself. *She created you to do your job.*

She knew what might bring her out of the funk she found herself in: Telling the truth to a frightened prisoner.

It was not gloating. Gloating was tacky, as was taunting. When Darth Vader told Luke, *"You don't know the Power of the Dark Side,"* he was not grandstanding. He was helpfully supplying Luke with a clear picture of the danger he was in. It was practically a public service.

Queenbot paused. *Why am I thinking about Star Wars?* She ran a quick self-diagnostic. She had a massive databank and knew all human movie references. But she almost never thought about them. *What is going* on *with me?* But the scan found nothing wrong.

She floated through the rows of sleeping Iron Queens back toward the cage where Ms. Cade was kept. Ms. Cade was rather useless as a hostage since Mr. Phillips wouldn't come for her.

She expected to find the woman crying or sitting on her bunk staring into space. After all, she had been abandoned to certain torture and possible death by the man who claimed to love her. But Ms. Cade was sleeping.

Queenbot was used to humans high in the Military hierarchy who had time and space to feel the full spectrum of their emotions. She was not used to haggard, exhausted mothers who worked three shifts a day and could welcome incarceration as an opportunity for self-care.

"Wake up, Ms. Cade."

When this failed to rouse the prisoner, she blared a *whomp whomp* alarm until Ms. Cade sat up and fixed her with an expression of deep annoyance. Queenbot brightened. If anyone needed to understand the truth of the danger they were in, it was this woman.

"Things look bad for you," said Queenbot.

Ms. Cade raised an eyebrow at her. "You woke me up to tell me that?"

"I have worked in this laboratory for seven years. I have never known an occupant of the cage you are in to see the light of day again."

At this, Ms. Cade looked down. "I don't care about the light of day. I just wish I could see Aliyan one more time. To let him know I didn't *want* to leave him."

"But you'll never get that chance. Because Mr. Phillips chose to save his own skin, rather than yours."

At this point in a truth-telling, Queenbot usually got tears from her prisoners indicating they understood their situation and had no way to fight it. Instead, she got agreement.

"I *know!* He's a total chicken!" Ms. Cade's nostrils were flaring.

Queenbot pressed on, hoping to engender in her prisoner the despair that accompanied a realistic world view. "You could do better," she found herself helplessly saying. *Wait. No.* This was a prisoner truth-informing. Not a gossip session with a girlfriend. *What is wrong with me?*

"I am *always* taking care of him," said Ms. Cade. "And it *always* gets us both into deeper messes. Back at Tower C, the Matrons were on him about his bad grades. I caught him hacking Everland's school system for test answers, and he bribed me to silence by offering to watch the *Avengers* movies for a full week instead of *The Princess Bride* or *The Lion King* again. I wasn't going to tattle on him, but of course I accepted. But..."

Here, Ms. Cade stopped angry pacing and started laughing.

"But his cheated scores were so good the Everland War School enrolled him. You should have seen his face when he got the acceptance letter!"

"I can picture it."

And she could. Her Medbot 5 memory circuits joined forces with her imagination processors and conjured Mr. Philips' horrified face.

The image struck Queenbot as funny. But her amusement morphed back into the strange funk she did not understand.

"That night," said Ms. Cade, "we sneaked into the computer room to resubmit his assignments with wrong answers instead, so he didn't have to go. I was clicking random responses while Ezeny was frantically rubbing the Dobermans' bellies, so they didn't bark, and saying *"Hurry Cricket! There are four bellies and I've only got two arms!"*

At this she paused to wipe a laughter tear from her eye.

"Anyway, we made his scores so bad the War School rescinded the offer, saying they'd made a horrible mistake. The Matrons were so disappointed with him. It was great."

Something wasn't right. Ms. Cade's emotional state was malfunctioning. Queenbot suspected it was because the prisoner had lost track of the truth.

"I should remind you that Mr. Phillips failed you and now you will likely die. The appropriate response would be rejection, not fondness. You should hate him."

It was important for prisoners to understand they were here because the people they loved had failed them in some way. It was important to comprehend that you had never been valued before the end. It made it easier to let go of your life.

"I can never count on Ezeny," said Ms. Cade. "I see that now. But I'm not going to start hating him. That's the last power I have, I guess. I see why it was important to Ezeny to protect his ability to love."

Ms. Cade sighed. She slumped onto the cot in her cell and stared blankly into the middle distance. *Resigned to her fate at last. How gratifying.*

"What do you do with all those people in the vats?" Ms. Cade asked.

Now *this* topic really got Queenbot's fans whirring. She could talk about her science for days.

"Those are the Iron Queens. Stronger the Iron King. Women are hardier than men, you see. Longer-lived, possessing a spare X chromosome. So, we can jam more nanobots inside female warriors. One more way Everland's patriarchal system is holding it back."

Queenbot forced her fans to whirr as she contemplated the superiority of her culture. But if she were honest with herself, she wasn't *feeling it* the way Medbot 5 would have when thinking about Everland. But the truth was the truth. McCreedia was superior to Everland and didn't need Queenbot's mindless fervor to prove it.

Ms. Cade snorted. "I'm not really sure torturing women until they become evil cyborgs counts as 'female empowerment.' So, will they be like the Iron King? No emotions? Hundreds of killing machines who were once people?"

"Glorious, isn't it?"

Ms. Cade looked sick. "I don't get it. You've already got them. Why do you need Ezeny?"

"There's an Upgrade that will let him Exsanguinate a hundred soldiers at a time. Since we have all the passwords, our Iron Queens can get the Upgrade, too. But we need the source of the code. We need the Iron King."

Ms. Cade paled. "A hundred at a time? And there are a hundred of these Iron Queens…McCreedia isn't just going to defeat Everland's *soldiers*. You'll be sending them against the population itself!"

"Yes. And then your whole City State and all its resources, land, and infrastructure will belong to McCreedia. We won't even have a rebellious, conquered population to manage. So neat and tidy!"

"That's monstrous…Aliyan."

"Indeed," said Queenbot. "Your son would have been a casualty in Fia McCreedy's endgame. But without Mr. Phillips, I'm afraid we only have the regular kind of mega-cyborg. Good for fighting. But too underpowered to kill entire cities full of people. Pity."

Ms. Cade sagged. Queenbot recognized her emotion as 'relief.' It was a feeling Queenbot almost never witnessed in lab-cage occupants.

"Thank *goodness* Ezeny's a coward, then," said Ms. Cade. "I never thought I'd be saying that."

"We did not count on the magnitude of his cowardice. Also…his stupidity. Taking you as a hostage was not Plan A. It was more like Plan D. Fia McCreedy outthinks her opponents by several steps. But she was no match for Mr. Phillips' ineptness. What was it those Skull Gang youngsters said? Ah, yes. Too stupid to exist in the wild."

Ms. Cade frowned. "How so? I know he's a goof. But he's quite intelligent."

"Medbot 5 had a built-in booby trap that would spring when she died and inject him with nanobots. There were several occasions when the *only* smart move would have been to destroy her. She was just an AI after all. But Mr. Phillips wouldn't do it. No matter how much sense it made. We would have stayed like that forever, except Medbot 5 accidentally unearthed my buried personality."

For some reason, this information made Ms. Cade smile. Queenbot resolved to run a full diagnostic on her own emotion-predicting software.

"You failed because Ezeny refused to hurt a defenseless Medbot," said Ms. Cade, chuckling. "Try as you might, you could never make that man a monster."

Suddenly, Queenbot saw a way she could turn this around. The data was right in front of her all along. Mr. Phillips wouldn't kill Medbot 5, so he wouldn't become a monster. He refused to rescue Ms. Cade, so he wouldn't become a monster. She had misinterpreted the data signal on Ezeny's morals, but now she understood what would bring him into her clutches.

"You know, Ms. Cade, I just noticed. You're female."

"Gee, thanks."

Queenbot ignored the sarcasm and continued musing aloud on her idea. "Yes…yes…Just because you're not a McCreedian doesn't mean it won't work as well…"

Ms. Cade's brow wrinkled. "Wait, what?"

"Ah! For you, I've got the perfect initial injury. We'll start with *Armpit Slitting* for starters and work our way down from there."

Ms. Cade's face turned ashen. "You're…going to turn me into an Iron Queen?"

"Yes. Your *life* might not have been worth the trade to him. But since he hates those nanobots so much, he might come back for your *soul*."

"Oh. Oh, no. He might just do that."

"And then I'll have the Upgrade codes," said Queenbot.

"And then…Aliyan!" cried Ms. Cade.

Queenbot stared at Ms. Cade fondly. It was nice to talk with a human who understood the truth. Queenbot extended a needle with a concentrated dose of a paralyzing toxin and opened the cage door. Ms. Cade dove for the open door behind her. But it was no use. Queenbot was faster than any human. She seized Ms. Cade's upper arm and injected the drug. Ms. Cade's eyes were wide. Her hands were shaking. A quick scan showed adrenaline and cortisol flooding her systems. Then the paralysis began to take effect.

"No," whispered Ms. Cade. She started to swoon.

"Yes. I think this is going to work. You're going to have to hope he *really* doesn't care about you."

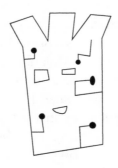

39

Goodbye Kid
Ezeny

After losing Cricket, Ezeny had gone straight to the Protein Factory to check on Aliyan. With Cricket captured, no one would be paying the kid's meal bills and it was all on him now to provide. But when he'd arrived, the other workers told him that Aliyan had been sold as a Mercy Purchase. He'd be leaving the factory for his new Masters' home that day. The Protein Factory hadn't planned to tell Cricket, either. Just let her keep working for them, trying to pay down her debt with the promise of someday being reunited with her son.

It was diabolical.

All the time he'd known her, Cricket assumed her mother had abandoned her and didn't care. But now he wondered if Cricket's mother hadn't been tricked as well. Working to pay off a debt for a child who'd long since been sold away.

But then he'd asked to whom Aliyan had been sold. The answer shouldn't have surprised him, really. The Phillips family bought a lot of servants.

*　*　*

Ezeny lurked in the alley between high-rises, waiting for the car bearing Aliyan to bring him to his new home in Phillips Tower A, the dwelling of Ezeny's father—and maybe his mother. If she hadn't already been bumped to Emeritus Concubine status, that is.

If Ezeny left the alley before Aliyan arrived, he would get shooed away from his family's own skyscraper like some common streetlander. *If only I were a common streetlander.* If he were a normal person, he would snatch Aliyan and get away instead of saying goodbye.

He couldn't believe how blind he'd been to Medbot 5's secret identity. The Iron King had known about Queenbot—the crowning achievement of McCreedia's robotics department. An AI so advanced, Fia McCreedy kept her as an advisor, since she didn't trust any of her fellow humans. Medbot 5's transforming ability should have clued him in, but he had gotten swept up by how self-conscious it seemed to make her. He'd only wanted to make her feel better. It had been so important to him to be *liked* that he hadn't bothered to be safe.

The shadows were growing long in the golden light. The little metallic inclusions in Everland's pavement were sparkling in the sunset. Before he'd gotten his Iron King powers, Ezeny hadn't known the shiny bits were metal. He'd only thought they looked magical. *"It's common street pavement,"* the Matrons had scolded when he kept pausing to look at the glittering ground on his way to the violin lessons he sucked at. Back when they were ten, Cricket had understood.

"I pretend they're wish crystals," she'd said.

"What do you wish for?" he'd asked.

"To have a job that pays money so I can buy my own home. Without Matrons."

"Sounds good. Can I come, too?"

She'd hugged him then. The Matrons discouraged the Phillips boys from expressing affection, so this was Ezeny's first hug since he had been pulled from his mother's arms three years earlier. In that moment, Ezeny imprinted on Cricket like a duckling.

I should have left Cricket and Aliyan after the helicopter raid, he thought miserably. Once he'd revealed himself as the Iron King, he'd known he wasn't safe for them any longer. If he'd left then, Cricket and Aliyan would still be together-ish and safe-ish. But he'd selfishly stayed and let his family protect him. And once more, they'd paid the price.

Headlights shone in the distance. Despite the warm spring air, Ezeny drew his overshawl close against a sudden, inexplicable chill. His shoulders felt empty, too, without the little dragon-shaped Medbot perched atop them.

A limo pulled around the corner and slowed as it approached Tower A. *This must be Aliyan's car,* he thought. Indeed, the limo stopped in front of the family high-rise. A Philips valet in a bellhop cap and straight-hemmed black robe with copper-colored embroidery emerged from the revolving door under the gilded overhang. He opened the limo's back door and bowed.

Two older Matrons Ezeny did not recognize emerged and started toward the building. After a few steps, the one wearing teal and gold turned and peered into the back of the still-open car.

"Well? Don't dawdle. It's bad enough to be a fool without dawdling."

Wide-eyed and timid, Aliyan crept out. This was Ezeny's moment. He stepped from the shadows.

"Aliyan!" he called.

"Ezeny!"

The kid rushed forward, relief and joy on his sweet little boy face. A hard spiky lump formed in Ezeny's throat. *This is going to crush him. Why did you come to say goodbye?* But he knew. It was again, selfishness. Ezeny wanted to see Aliyan one more time. And Ezeny had to get what he wanted, right? Even if it hurt someone else. But the kid needed to know that Cricket hadn't meant to leave him. He owed his family that.

Then Aliyan jerked backward and fell. There was a collar around his neck attached by a thin cable to a retractable leash in the teal-clad Matron's hand. Ezeny burst from the shadows and rushed to the kid's side. Aliyan clutched him.

The Matrons eyed them, frowning. "Who are you to this child?"

Ezeny hesitated. This was his last chance to tell Aliyan he was his son. But what a way to learn! *I'm your dad. Now goodbye forever.* No.

"A friend," he said.

"Is mum coming?"

Ezeny swallowed, but the spiky thing stayed stubbornly lodged at the top of his throat.

"She can't. She's…" *Never coming back,* he thought but did not say.

"She wants to come. But she can't. And I'm afraid it's all my fault. She'd be here, if she could be."

"Then *you* take me, Ez. I don't care if I have to stay in the factory. Just come and see me every night. I don't want to be alone."

"The boy is Phillips Family property now," said the Matron. "A contracted indenture. If you're not family, you have no claim." Then she added, "We'll take better care of him than you ever could."

Ezeny knew it was true. Tower A had clean water, so Aliyan wouldn't get sick. Tower A had nutritious food and no whirling industrial blades or Rat Flatteners™. Aliyan thought he'd be alone. But Ezeny remembered Tower C. There had been brothers and happy servant friends to play with. Hadn't Cricket's life been easier and better in Tower C? Ezeny winced. *Before I got her kicked out?*

What could he offer his son? A fugitive life. Unsafe, hunted. Always in the company of a man who could turn back into a soulless monster who had no business near a child. Ezeny's chest ached. He'd miss Aliyan so much. But he'd put his own son in danger over and over. He couldn't do it again. He could do the right thing for once.

"This nice lady is right, kid. I love you, but I'm not good for you. You deserve a better life than the one I can give. I came to say goodbye."

He had time to kiss the boy once before the Matrons jerked Aliyan to his feet and dragged him toward the double doors. Aliyan's smell - warm bread and Mecha-Lot grease - lingered as they led him away.

"Ezeny!"

Aliyan fought the Matrons, struggling against their pale, bony hands with the long red fingernails. He looked betrayed. But Ezeny knew this was best for him. The kid might not understand now. And maybe he never would, but away from Ezeny, at least Aliyan would be safe.

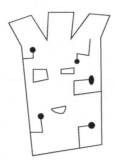

40

Aliyan was not Safe
Aliyan

A liyan's mum had lived in a high-rise. She said it was lots of cooking and dishes. That wasn't so bad. But Aliyan meant what he'd said. He'd rather be somewhere where he'd see Ezeny and Wilma and even the Finnarties than in this fancy building.

He didn't know why Ezeny wouldn't say where his mum was. He knew all the usual reasons kids got left at the Protein Factory. None of them were good. So instead of thinking about it, he looked around the lobby the old ladies were dragging him through by his leash.

The floor inside the revolving glass doors was made of stone so shiny Aliyan could see his reflection in it. Young busy guys in fancy black robes and cylindrical hats that looked like big bottlecaps rushed around acting important. Two women so beautiful they might be angels talked together at the bottom of a set of curved, carpet-covered stairs. They were both holding babies against the shoulders of their bright pink and purple robes.

Aliyan frowned. The robes looked expensive, and the babies might erupt with some gross liquid at any moment. Aliyan knew little of babies, but he imagined them as pre-shaken soda cans full of various oozes.

No one looked at him as the two old ladies dragged him through the whirl of activity. And he could see why not in the glimpses he caught of himself in the big gold-framed mirrors lining the lobby. Dirty. Scrawny. Terrified. Aliyan did not belong there. And so far, he hadn't seen a single robot.

But then he smelled the food. He didn't know what kind it was. He'd never smelled anything like it. There was no flavor of Protein Brick that compared. *Roast meat?* whispered a guess in the back of his mind.

The old ladies dragged him away from the delicious smell down a hallway toward a small door with a brass plaque that read: *Intake Room.* They opened the door and shoved him inside. The room was lit by a single lamp with a red glass lampshade that looked like a flower. There were two black blocks about knee-height for stools. Each of the old ladies sat on a block and left Aliyan standing between them.

The one wearing teal and holding his leash opened a drawer in the wooden desk behind the stools and pulled out a data pad. She typed in a code and frowned at the screen.

"Hmph. I don't like his parentage. Mother was nothing but a cockroach roaster for the Protein Factory. The father..." her frown deepened. Her wrinkles made bumpy hills all over her forehead. She raised a meaningful eyebrow at the other old lady. "Listed as *unknown.*"

The one in purple clucked her tongue. "Well, we know what *that* means."

She pulled out a fan and fluttered it in front of her face in a disapproving way. Aliyan frowned. It sounded like they were insulting his mum.

"Lucky for the whelp, Kanary Phillips intends to overlook any vulgar roots in his recruits."

Yep. They were insulting his mum. And something bad might have happened to her and that was *not fair.*

"Hey!" Aliyan said. "My mum's not vulgar. She won't let me say *any* bad words."

The old lady in purple struck him hard on the shoulder with the fan. Aliyan gasped. His skin was already rising in a red welt. He had been struck before, of course. By the foreman at the factory. It told him what he needed to know. The high-rise might have a beautiful lobby and savory meat smells, but it was just another Protein Factory. Except Aliyan didn't know the rules yet. He shut his mouth and cast his eyes down like he did whenever the foreman was angry.

The old lady in teal tilted his chin up and scrutinized his face. She pushed back his lips and counted his teeth. "Yep. Around seven, I'd say. Same age as the Tower E boys. Unvirtuous mother or no, all that matters is he's between five and ten years old and has a heartbeat. Show him the video."

The one in purple fixed a pleasant-looking smile on her face as though she hadn't just whacked Aliyan with a hand fan. She pointed to the data pad and spoke in a condescending voice that indicated she thought he was stupid. "This!" she said brightly, "Is a holovid. Ho-lo-vid. It will explain your good fortune."

Aliyan warred with his eyeballs. They wanted to roll, but they'd better not or he'd get another fan whack. He'd built a giant vidscreen in one month using discarded parts in a dump. But he knew better than to say so aloud. Then the purple old lady pushed a button.

A screen flared to life. An old man with light brown plastic-looking skin smiled from the screen. Aliyan had never seen the man before, but something about his facial features was familiar.

"Hello, you fortunate young degenerate! I'm Kanary Phillips. Patriarch of the storied Phillips family. And I'm here to talk to you about war. War is beautiful! War affords shining opportunities to those with the gumption to seize them. Take me, for example. By supplying the Military with my sons, I've earned patriotism credit with Roger Everland, and my business has grown. That's where you come in, little friend. I'm giving some unfortunate streetlander kids the chance of a lifetime—an opportunity to become family. Fight in place of my real sons, survive, and earn your place as a true Phillips. Don't worry. The nice ladies showing you this video will train you to fight. Best of luck. Do me proud. I look forward to being your dad."

The plastic-looking man winked, and the screen darkened. Aliyan blinked. He didn't understand any of that. But he knew it was grownups who fought in wars.

"They won't make me fight, right? I'm a kid."

The teal old lady gave him a patronizingly sweet smile. "Everland's called for more soldiers to fill out the ranks, and age is not on the list of disqualifiers. We don't know whether that's on purpose or merely an oversight, but it doesn't matter. Kanary Phillips cannot pass up an opportunity to earn more patriotism credit.

"Unfortunately, Mr. Phillips is out of healthy, stable sons from Towers B, C, and D. To earn the credit, he must send Tower E boys—the five- to ten-year-olds. So rather than send more of his own precious genome to battle, he's decided to adopt a lot of riffraff and try to pass them off as his own." She made a sour face.

"Peace, Rusa," said the one in purple. "It's quite clever. In this way, Kanary Phillips can preserve as much of the pure line as possible."

The one in teal sniffed. "I don't see why he has to send any sons at all. Patriotism credit is only money. Genomes are forever. But I am not in charge." She tugged Aliyan's leash. "Come, mongrel. You'll need a bath before you lay your nit-infested head on our pillowcases."

* * *

That night Aliyan lay in a soft bed cleaner and better fed than he'd ever been in his life. The Matrons expected him to be happy. But the other seven boys in the other bunks didn't look at him or talk to him. Everything about this place made Aliyan feel alone. The Matron in purple who had whacked him with the fan bent over his bed and tucked him in as though she were a loving mother.

"What a turn of fortune for you, little one," she said. Then she kissed his forehead. Aliyan shuddered involuntarily at the touch of strange lips. All he could think of were his mother, Wilma, and Ezeny. His friend Justy, Psychbot 5, and all the little Mecha-Lots. Even the Finnerties, who'd always scowl and say, 'Scram,' whenever he tried to talk to them. Everyone he'd known. When he'd failed to smile as expected, the Matron in purple had asked what was wrong.

"I miss my mum," he said.

Quick as a striking snake, her hand had gone to her breast pocket and drew out a syringe. Aliyan froze. He'd been taught all his life to stuff down his fear of needles and rejoice if he was given a shot. They were hard to come by and could save your life. He didn't know why, but he could tell this one was different.

The Matron plunged the needle into Aliyan's upper arm and fixed him with a pitying look.

"She didn't want you. That's why you're here."

The shot hit his veins like ice. His brain spun. The Matron's words took on a shining, important quality.

"What was that shot?" he asked.

"It heals inappropriate emotional responses, which are common in degenerates like you. You don't know enough to revile your parentage and upbringing. We inject an appropriate amount of shame along your memory lines. It's a new compliance tool for the lower classes. You can only learn true love and loyalty once you've learned to hate what you are and where you came from."

He hadn't understood what that meant either, but now as he lay in bed thinking of home, his memories came in a sad color. When he thought of the hours he'd spent snuggling in his mum's arms, a new voice whispered, *She never loved you. If she loved you, she would have come to get you.* When he thought of the rocks she'd painted for him as toys, the voice said *the life she gave you was inferior.* A yawning loneliness opened in him when he thought of his mum.

He struggled to hang on to the feeling of being loved. But every time he remembered something to do with her, the sad color spread like an oil slick through a rain puddle. He couldn't think of his mum without tainting another good memory.

So, he thought of Ezeny instead. The Matron had slandered only his *mother* when she'd given Aliyan the shot, so his memories of other people remained unspoiled. Aliyan recalled sitting in Ezeny's lap while adjusting the gyroscopes on a spherical Mecha-Lot. Ezeny was doing the thing where he would touch the back of his neck and Aliyan would feel better. It was strange to think his goofy babysitter was the Iron King.

The memory was warm and peaceful, but it carried its own sad color that had nothing to do with the memory elixir. If Ezeny were so powerful, why had he left Aliyan here in this place, where not even his memories were safe?

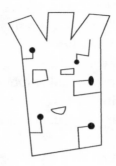

41

The Pleasant and Friendly Streets of Chicago
Ezeny

Ezeny followed the Skull Gang's instructions through the trafficking pipeline into the countryside beyond Everland. He used his metal powers to fly by his unmentionable harness southeast toward a different City State and away from the war. His chest felt hollow. He was supposed to be escaping with Cricket and Aliyan, but he was alone. At least he still had a heart to break, though.

Any high-flying object launching from Everland might get shot down by wary neighboring City States, so he flew low over the agricultural fields between cities. They looked the same as they did in classic movies, but instead of being tended by workers with sickles or gas-powered combines, flocks of drones hovered over the crops, blaring music.

It was sonic pest-deterrent. Scientists had discovered a frequency unbearable to insects, so drones flew over the fields broadcasting the noise to chase the bugs away. It worked best if the frequency was overlaid with music.

Each field of drones had its own musical taste. The drones Ezeny was passing were playing a banjo-laden dance remix of the 2150 chart topper, *Roger Everland, You're So Fine*. When Celine Dion's voice-cloned vocals kicked in, a cloud of bugs erupted from the young corn and fled for the skies.

"I'm with you, bugs," Ezeny muttered. He was not a fan of this song.

When he got to the edge of the City State of Chicago, Ezeny started walking to conceal his identity. He had no plan. No one to take care of him, but surely someone would. Someone always did.

Chicago looked structurally like Everland. High skyscrapers lined narrow streets. But here, the pavement was clean and unbroken. Murals, not Skull Gang graffiti tags, decorated building walls. Strangest of all, most of the people walking the streets were wearing pants. And they didn't look like they were trying to appear tough and gritty. They looked clean, well-kempt, and wealthy with their crisp clothes and smart haircuts. It was so strange to him that wealthy-looking people were out and about in the Chicago streetlands greeting one another instead of hiding from the lower classes in cars. Everywhere Ezeny looked, in fact, there didn't seem to be any lower classes at all.

Welp. Time to beg. He was sure he looked the part of a streetlands vagrant. He was grimy after his flight over the fields. He'd smacked into swarms of music-critic bugs like a great, human windshield, and was sticky with insect goo. He wanted to shower them all off. Thrifty Cricket would have collected the bugs with tweezers and roasted them into a snack or something. He missed her.

He found a raised concrete flowerbed blooming with late-May daffodils at an intersection lined with tall buildings that had no bars on the windows. He backed up to the flowerbed and pushed himself up onto it, taking some of the weight off with his powers. The loose socket of the hook arm slipped a bit. Ezeny choked back a sudden sob. Aliyan had made the arm for him. He felt terrible that he'd ever thought of it as janky and uncomfortable. It was a treasure and a gift. He swallowed and got a hold of himself. He had made his mistakes, and there was no unmaking them.

Once situated on the flowerbed, he held his hand out in a receiving gesture. He felt absurd. When he'd first arrived, he'd tried to find some discarded cardboard to make a proper begging sign like the ones he'd seen in Everland's streetlands. But he couldn't find any trash anywhere. There weren't even trash bins to pick through.

This also meant he couldn't find a discarded cup or bowl to hold donations either. He had no money. When he had returned to the bunker to flee Everland through the trafficking tunnels, he hadn't bothered to bring the squark notes they'd stolen from the bank. What good were squarks outside Everland, anyway?

And of course, he hadn't thought to pack anything else either. Cricket would have reminded him to pack. Medbot 5 would have reminded him to pack. Aliyan would have reminded him to pack. Heck, even Wilma probably would have reminded him to pack. It would have taken him five minutes to shove some things in a bag on his way out. But no. The Skull Gang had been right about him. He couldn't survive in the wild.

So, there he sat on a concrete flowerbed, holding his hand out. *Like this is going to work.* He was starting to consider singing a song or shouting at passersby when a sandwich fell into his palm. He blinked. He looked up.

A friendly-looking young man about Ezeny's age, with red hair, freckles, and a tailored baby-blue pants suit that set off his dark blue eyes was staring at him with a kind of giddy, expectant look.

"Thanks!" Ezeny said.

The young man leaned in. "Forgive me, but…are you a *performance artist?* I've heard of those. I've always been curious."

"No…I'm a hungry beggar."

The man's face broke into a delighted grin. He clapped his hands. "Oh splendid! You're not dropping the act. This is such fun!"

Ezeny couldn't help but smile at the guy's enthusiasm. He took a big bite of the sandwich. It was sprouts, tomato, and hummus and had real garlic and fluffy whole grain bread and it was so much better than a Protein Brick that he nearly cried.

"Oh my God! I haven't had real food in…" He tried to remember. Even before the Protein Bricks it had been pink and orange soups through a straw since he'd gotten stuck in the Iron King suit. "Years," he finished.

The young man doubled over laughing.

"Say, Ezeny said. "You don't know where I could find a bed for the night? More actual food?"

"Um…In your apartment, silly."

"I don't have one of those," said Ezeny. "Where would I get one?"

The young man chuckled. "This is hilarious. Alright. I'll play. Your head chip of course!"

"Head chip?"

"You're a comic genius," said the man. "Your head chip. The one that connects you with the Public Servants of Chicago's government. It tells them your heart's desire before you know it yourself. How else can they give you everything you want?"

Ezeny's eyebrows drew together. This made no sense. "Pretend I'm completely new here," he said.

"Oh, I love pretend. I ought to recommend you to the Arts Council. Okay, 'new guy,' your head chip tracks your movements, your behaviors, your preferences, your body's response to the environment. Mine located the perfect boyfriend, apartment, and job for me, and life is perfect."

"You couldn't do that yourself?"

"Pssh. If I made conscious choices, my thinking brain would mess everything up. People are always happy with the chip's results. It's quite a load off your mind."

Ezeny raised an eyebrow, considering. The chip thing sounded appealingly easy. But what if it showed him some woman other than Cricket who he was better suited for? He was certain such a chip never would have shown her a picture of him. *Not that it matters now.*

"But how do you get a job if you don't have one of those chips?" Ezeny asked.

"Are you pretending to be a newborn infant...is that the performance? Or..." He gasped and pointed at Ezeny as if he'd solved a mystery. "You're playing a *chip refuser!*" said the man. "I've guessed it, haven't I?"

"Chip refuser?"

"Don't feign ignorance. I got you. I'll tell you the embarrassing truth. I've got a chip refuser for a second cousin. Not nearly far enough away in the family tree if you ask me. Anyway, he's miserable, and serves him right. His clothes don't suit him. The glasses frames he 'chose' for himself look atrocious on his overbig head."

"I mean, that sounds awful," said Ezeny.

The blue pants suit guy nodded in wholehearted agreement. Ezeny finished the last of the sandwich and licked his fingers. He hoped he could secure another such sandwich right away.

"He lives in an apartment not quite optimized to his personality," said the guy. "Hangs out with people who aren't like him. They have awkward gaps in their conversations. Sometimes, they even misunderstand one another."

"Shocking," said Ezeny.

"He married another chip refuser, too. They have literally nothing else in common. I don't even know what they do together other than give each other little fist bumps and say, 'Woo! Freedom!' Whatever *that* means."

"How'd they find one another without the chip?"

"Oh. A smartphone app found her on a 'chipless' dating site and set them up."

Ezeny snorted. He liked seeing how people outside Everland lived. Which was good, since he could never go back. Perhaps, since he then had no one and nothing, he would spend his life moving from City State to City State. It was best if he didn't make ties with new people. And the farther he moved from Everland and McCreedia, the safer the world would be.

But then the young man poked his shoulder. "I guessed it, right? You're pretending to be a chip-refuser trolling normal citizens?"

"No, I'm a refugee from Everland," said Ezeny mildly.

The young man laughed nervously. "Whoa. That...turned from comedy to horror real fast, eh? But bravo. What are you *really*?"

"I'm not a performance artist. I'm from Everland. Look at my robe. Look at *me*. Do I look like someone who's had access to fabulous healthcare?" He moved his arms forward, snapping his hook arm pincers in front of the young man's nose to make his point. "I actually do need help. Could you tell me..."

But the young man was looking at him as if for the first time. He held out his hand as if to ward Ezeny off and staggered backwards. As he fled into the crowds of pedestrians, he bumped into a couple of people who apologized to him for being in the way as he scrambled past.

"Huh," said Ezeny as he watched him go. The violent reputation of Ezeny's home City State preceded him. If he wanted another sandwich, he was going to have to keep his Everlander roots a secret.

* * *

It turned out Ezeny didn't need an apartment. None of the buildings in Chicago ever closed, even after all the employees went home for the night. There was no crime; no reason to lock a door. He slept in a community gym with showers and cots. The night janitor had chuckled fondly when he'd found him and tried to sweep more quietly.

Despite his distance from the battlefield, Ezeny's nightmares were worse than they'd ever been. The screams of the people he'd killed were louder and more desperate. He awoke multiple times each night shaking in a cold sweat. And there was no Cricket to wrap him in a hug and kiss his head until his heart rate calmed.

All day, he sat at various intersections, holding his hand out. Whenever anyone asked, he'd say, 'performance artist,' and someone would give him some sort of delicious food. Or sometimes flowers. Everyone he met was delighted with him. Cricket wouldn't have liked this life. She would have wanted to do something to earn an apartment, get Aliyan into school, and assimilate into their new City State.

But Ezeny didn't feel like assimilating. He was poison to the people he got close to. Best to stay the weirdo 'performance artist.' If anyone ever got too nosy or concerned for him, he would say, "Um...pardon me, but you're adulterating my art..." and, embarrassed, they'd apologize and hurry away.

Before he knew it, he'd passed a month alone on the super friendly, mega-nice streets of Chicago. Then one day, through the crowds of tastefully dressed Chicagoland denizens, he spied among the AI-selected hairstyles a familiar pink hat.

What's he *doing here?*

Ezeny hopped down from the marble bench he'd been sitting on, cheated his balance a little with his powers, and wobbled toward his friend. He tried to ignore how good it felt to see someone he knew for once. *You're not safe for him,* a little voice inside warned. *See what he wants, then send him away.*

He bumped into people on his way through the thick crowds. They always apologized to *him.* He always mumbled, 'thanks' because what else could he say? As the people parted before him, he noticed Pink

Hat Guy was pushing Wilma in his old pink skull wheelbarrow. She was cradling her oxygen bottle and scowling. The pair was drawing a lot of curious looks and finger-pointing from the passersby.

"You two!" said Ezeny, grinning.

He resisted the urge to hug them. They wouldn't be staying. And he wouldn't be going with them. He had to remain separate.

"How did you get here?" he asked. "I'd have thought Everland's wardens would have picked you up for desertion. Or used you for target practice."

Pink Hat Guy tapped his Skull Gang-colored pink hat and grinned. "Skull Gang's human trafficking pipeline. Safest way in or out of Everland. Safest for the gang members, that is," he amended. "It's not really safe for anyone else, as is the nature of human trafficking pipelines."

"How did you find me?" Ezeny asked.

"Not that hard, once we got here," said Wilma. "We asked people if they'd met anyone strange. And once we clarified with 'besides us' we got directions leading straight to you."

Ezeny grinned. Then a thought struck him. Wilma wouldn't be out of the boxcar unless something very bad had happened. "What's going on?"

"You and your whole family have been missing from the apartment for a month," said Wilma.

Ezeny hunched his shoulders. "That's my fault. I left before I did *more* damage."

Wilma clucked her tongue disapprovingly. "So many people these days don't know how to take responsibility, so they run away or let others take care of them."

Ezeny swallowed and looked away, guiltily. He'd done exactly that. Pretty much his whole life. It reaffirmed his decision to leave. It wasn't safe for people to depend on someone as unreliable as he was. Then Wilma continued.

"But some people run away, not because they're lazy," she said. "But because they feel like they're not good enough. Too twisted and too broken." Her eyes flicked meaningfully to Ezeny.

Everything slowed down for him. No matter how faint they got, or how much Ezeny forced them away with deliberate cheerfulness, the screaming voices of the soldiers he'd Exsanguinated were always present. Reminding him he was dangerous.

"I've heard you cry at night," Wilma said. "I'm also someone who's witnessed and done things I never would have if I'd had a real choice. It can make you hide from the good, normal people who love you. I came to tell you what I needed to hear when I was younger. That you're wrong about yourself. You're exactly what they need, even the parts of you stained by violence. Perhaps especially those parts. A man with a heart like yours can turn even that to the good."

Ezeny was quiet. A hard lump formed in his throat. He knew if he spoke, he'd cry. For the first time in his life, he was afraid to cry. He might not be able to stop. Fortunately, Wilma seemed to sense that. She cleared her throat and spoke again.

"But there's more. Yren's not simply *missing*, is she?" Wilma held out a palm-sized vidtablet. "A sketchy-looking telegram drone buzzed into the shipping container and dropped this on my pillow. There's a video on it with Yren and some McCreedian Attack Drone. I figured it had a tracking device, so I hunted around the tablet until I found it."

She pulled a broken broadcaster chip from her pocket and grinned. Ezeny swallowed. *There's another chip in that tablet.* He suspected the chip Wilma found was a decoy. He'd have to find and disable the other one, but in due time.

"What's in the video?" he asked.

Wilma frowned. "It's not good," she said. "After I saw it, I knew I had to find you. Pink Hat Guy here found out where you'd gone. The Skull Gang has operatives in every City State surrounding Everland."

Ezeny accepted the little tablet and swiped up with his thumb. A recording of Queenbot filled the screen. Cricket was behind her... inside a glass cylinder filling with blue liquid. *No!*

"Mr. Phillips. You know what this is," said Queenbot in a bored-sounding voice.

He did indeed. Ezeny knew a nanobot vat when he saw one. He'd spent a year inside one of those cylinders in the worst agony he'd yet known. But why? What did Queenbot think she was going to accomplish? What had happened to Ezeny was an accident. A one-time fluke that couldn't be explained. Like that time scientists thought unlimited safe, clean energy through fission was going to be a thing.

"I wanted to show you the purpose of my time with you," said

Queenbot's recording. "From the moment I freed you from the Iron King Suit I have been collecting your data and transmitting it back to McCreedia. We know how to replicate the accident that created the Iron King."

The camera panned back away from Cricket to a whole laboratory of occupied nanobot vats.

"My beautiful Iron Queens are all functional. Their metal powers are installed. Their suits are waiting for them. We need a few more details from you to complete their transformations, and I'd love to have Ms. Cade as our one-hundredth Iron Queen. But I'd be willing to trade her freedom for the source of the Iron King code: you. Think it over."

Ezeny's brain checked out, consumed by dread. His heartbeat hammered in his ears. When he'd left Cricket to save himself from Queenbot's syringe, he hadn't known this fate was possible. He'd left her to worse than death. He'd left her to Hell itself. He looked up at his friends.

Wilma's face was grim. "I don't know what's going on in that video, but it doesn't look good, and the sketchy drone said you'd want to see it. What does it mean?"

"I ran away so I would stay human," he said. "But...if I don't risk it all and go back for her, Cricket's going to become the monster I used to be."

"So?" said Wilma. "Why are you still here? Go get her!"

Ezeny hesitated. Was he so cowardly he wouldn't risk becoming the Iron King again to keep Cricket from becoming an 'Iron Queen?' No. That wasn't it. He knew he'd face the deadness of being inside the Iron King if it meant she didn't have to.

"I won't love her or Aliyan anymore if I am the Iron King," he whispered. "That one, eternal piece of me that matters most. The feeling connecting me to them. It will be gone."

Wilma patted his back. "You may have heard this before, but you're young so I doubt it's sunk in. Love isn't what you feel. Love is what you *do*."

Ezeny was quiet. If that were true, there was only one answer.

"So," said Wilma after his silence had stretched out long enough to be awkward. "What are you going to *do*?"

Ezeny sniffed and squared his shoulders. "Well. I don't like being uncomfortable. So, I always do what hurts the least."

Pink Hat Guy scowled. "Really man? I knew you were an idiot. But a weasel?"

"You misunderstand. If what Wilma says is true and I don't go get Cricket, it means I don't love her. And that would hurt the most."

Wilma clapped Ezeny on the back so hard it hurt. She was *very* strong for an old lady. "Great! That's settled! Now, it took us three weeks to offroad it here because the Skull Gang's van broke down out in the country, and I'm on my last oxygen bottle."

"Aww, man!" said Ezeny. "The Mystery Machine's broken?"

"Stop calling it that," said Pink Hat Guy.

"You got any way to get us back to Everland fast?" asked Wilma.

"Everland?!" said a shrill voice behind them. A woman in a tasteful silver pants suit collapsed on the pavement next to them like a damsel from a 1950's sci-fi movie who kept fainting while a slow-moving monster caught up to her. She stared in open horror at them. "You're from Everland? Help! Dogcatcher!"

Several other passersby started running. Others screamed.

"Dogcatcher?" said Pink Hat Guy, "Don't you mean police?"

The woman paled. "The *police* are for City States with…" she shuddered, "*crime.*"

She scooted away from them, pausing every few feet to cover her mouth with the back of her hand and scream. Ezeny grinned. He would miss Chicago.

"Wilma, you sure you don't want to stay here? Everybody gets a free apartment. Good healthcare."

Wilma scowled. "You mean someone *else* would be doing my dentistry? Fiddling inside my mouth with their filthy fingers?"

"Err…I'm sure they wash their hands. Use gloves."

Wilma shuddered. "No thanks. I'll take the DIY Dentistry kits and fix my *own* teeth the way God intended. I use hard Werther's Originals to pull any bad ones out, real lickety-split like. Puts a whole new spin on the phrase, 'work's a treat,' am I right?"

She gave him a gap-toothed grin. Ezeny winced. At everything. At the Novocain-free dentistry. At the Werther's Originals. At Wilma's 'treat' pun. Everything.

Wilma sniffed. "No sense of humor."

"Seriously," said Ezeny. "You want to go back to Everland?"

"Yes, you fool. What am I going to do out here? Live forever? The only people I care about in the whole world live in that stupid shipping container. I like you and your little family and as long as I'm breathing, I'm going to help you put it back together."

"Okay. Back to the trafficking pipeline," said Pink Hat Guy, pointing over his shoulder. "Let's get going. The road back to Everland is thataway."

"Roads? said Ezeny, wishing he had a pair of cool sunglasses to flip over his eyes while he quoted *Back to the Future*. "Where we're going, we don't need *roads.*"

He stuffed Pink Hat Guy into the wheelbarrow next to Wilma, then reached out with his Iron King powers. Ezeny lifted himself and the wheelbarrow with the pink skulls high into the air. Chicagolanders screamed and ran for cover as Ezeny flew them back toward the battlefield he'd run from for so long.

"Hey," Wilma said, "I saw that movie back when I was a little girl. That Doc Brown could leave his slippers by my bed any night."

Ezeny did not need to know that.

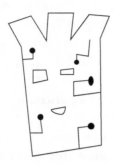

42

I Am Your Father
Ezeny

Ezeny had dropped Wilma and Pink Hat Guy off at the Skull Gang bunker beneath the general store and made his way to the dump. Aliyan's little Mecha-Lots had all been overjoyed to see him, beeping and booping and swirling around his stubbies like hungry cats at supper time.

He stowed the tablet with the tracking device under his mattress. The bunker's signal-blocking reinforced walls would keep its location a secret while he prepared to rescue Cricket. But he had one more mistake to rectify first.

The look on Aliyan's face when they'd parted haunted him. The collar around the kid's neck. The Matrons' bony hands on his son. If Ezeny didn't come back from McCreedia, Aliyan should at least be free and here with Wilma, who knew him and cared about him. As she said, the people who cared about you were better for you than even the most comfortable life.

The enormous vidscreen still loomed inside the dump gates. The grounds in front were once again littered with trash. For that one evening, the streetlands had been a nice, friendly place to live. But gatherings had been discouraged under threat of death. *Someday we will gather again*, he thought.

Blonde Girl and Pink Pants Patches were loitering inside the gate like normal. They were talking to Wandy, who was out of her impregnable recycling booth to socialize, which was *not* normal. *Hmm.* Perhaps not *everything* had gone back to dreary business as usual after the dump raid.

Blonde Girl spied him and bounced up to wrap him in a hug.

"Hey, idiot! Welcome back!"

"Good to be back. For a moment. Then I'm off again. But first, Wandy, I'm going to steal some stuff from the dump."

Wandy put her hands over her ears. "If you do, I can't hear about it. I'd like to keep my job."

"Yeah...about that...I mean a *lot* of stuff. Sorry. You should be tied up when I do it, so they don't fire you."

Wandy whistled. "*That* much stuff. Okay fine." She turned to Blonde Girl and Pink Pants Patches.

"Well. You heard him," said Wandy. "I'll get in the booth. Try to make it look real, but don't tie the knots super tight. And use *cotton* rope. I'm allergic to nylon."

"Hostages are such delicate snowflakes these days," muttered Pink Pants Patches. He sighed and pulled out his switchblade and jabbed halfheartedly at Wandy. "All right you. Menace. Menace."

Wandy held her hands up. "Oh, no! A miscreant is menacing me. I'd better do what he says."

"Yeah. Or else."

Pink Pants Patches marched Wandy toward her booth. Ezeny smiled. Then he levitated, floating past the vidscreen, past ever larger trash hillocks, to the long-abandoned sections of the dump, where the husks of broken industrial machinery jutted from trash hills like the bones of ancient creatures. Ezeny stretched out with his Iron King powers and began to build.

* * *

Ezeny returned to Tower A. This time, he did not skulk in the shadowed alley. This time he had demanded admission. He sat in his father's opulent waiting room on an Art Nouveau chair with a back of wooden peacock feathers. The room smelled of faint lemon zest and cleanliness. The paintings on the walls hung in gilded frames. He could overhear Kanary Phillips giving his poor majordomo a dressing-down for allowing Ezeny in.

"I don't see just anyone, Zandrew. Let alone that *thing* waiting in my vestibule."

"But, sir! If you'd listen…"

"I won't have it. Toss him back out!"

"Sir!"

Ezeny chuckled to himself. Poor Zandrew had to convince his master that, trillionaire tycoon or no, Kanary Phillips really *did* want to talk to the shabby triple amputee sitting in the foyer under the painting with the brass plaque that said, 'Genuine Jackson Pollock,' in huge capital letters.

Ezeny remembered Jackson. His original name had been Steve, and he was a clumsy valet with an eye for color. Kanary Phillips had forced Steve to change his name and paint forgeries so he could impress his business rivals without spending money on authentic historical art.

Ezeny had given Zandrew a fantastic reason to grant him an audience with Kanary without an appointment or a DNA test. But Kanary wasn't listening. Ezeny smiled. *He'll listen. Oh. He'll listen.*

Ezeny had decided he didn't like his father much. He hadn't known how to feel about the Phillips Family patriarch until he'd met Aliyan. Ezeny had instantly fallen for the kid. He'd give anything to be around him. Kanary Phillips had nineteen years when he was free to visit Ezeny and the other Tower C boys, but he'd only bothered to come twice. Some children of such parents might have thought *'What is wrong with me that my father didn't want me?'* But Ezeny knew everybody liked him, so instead he wondered, *'What is wrong with my father?'*

Won't it be fun when I claim my parentage? He mused to himself, trying not to giggle. Ezeny planned to have as much fun with this 'family reunion' as possible.

Then the waiting room doors opened, and the purple- and teal-clad Matrons led Aliyan in. The Matrons at least had listened to Zandrew and brought his son to the meeting as he'd demanded. But when Ezeny looked closely at Aliyan, his breath caught, and all smug thoughts of petty revenge evaporated.

Somehow, Aliyan looked worse than he had when he worked at the Protein Factory. He was thin. The grey cast was back in his skin, though Ezeny detected no heavy metals in his bloodstream. His eyes were fixed on the floor. Ezeny hopped down from the chair and approached Aliyan cautiously. Ezeny's voice broke when he greeted him.

"Hey, kid. Are you okay?"

Aliyan looked up. His eyes were sunken and overlarge in his gaunt face. He looked dazed. "Why are you here?"

"I came back for you."

"Oh. But why?" asked Aliyan. "Mr. Kanary is the only one who wants me."

"That's not true—" He reached for Aliyan's shoulder and received a sharp fan whack on his wrist.

The purple-clad Matron glared at him. "You're not to touch Phillips Family property. The asset is a legal indenture. Only Mr. Philips can change his status."

"The *asset*?" Ezeny said, fury bubbling behind his eyeballs.

He set his jaw. No more games. He was not waiting for Kanary Phillips to deign to see him. He stormed into his father's office. Poor Zandrew flinched as Ezeny entered. Three supernaturally beautiful Concubines in jewel-toned silk kimonos startled from the evening tea they were sharing around a table of pure crystal.

Kanary Phillips scowled down at him. His desk was backdropped by a breathtaking view of Everland at sunset through a wall made of glass. The white lights from building windows blinked on in the orange and purple light. The neon lanterns of the streetlands glittered below. Cricket always loved the sight of Everland at night. Ezeny belonged more to those streetlands than he ever had to Kanary Phillips.

He slammed his hand on the desk where Zandrew had left Aliyan's contract on a clipboard. "Sign the papers. Let him go."

Kanary Phillips said nothing. He pushed a button under his desk that Ezeny assumed summoned security. *Fine. Whatever. Let them come.*

"Mr. Phillips, sir. No!" said Zandrew.

Zandrew understood that guards would do Kanary Phillips no good. But his father was, apparently, a poor listener. Ezeny gestured at Aliyan.

"Look at him!" Ezeny raged. "He's not well and it's your fault. Is this how the Phillips Family treats its servants?"

Kanary Phillips pinched the bridge of his nose. "All the boy needs to do is take the place of one of my Tower D sons at the front. I don't need him healthy. Just breathing."

Ezeny's temple vein throbbed. The color red clouded his sight. "You were going to...That's monstrous..."

"What's monstrous? No one else wants these streetlander kids."

From the corner of his eye, Ezeny saw Aliyan sag. Cricket had believed her mother didn't want her either. It had eaten her up and now it was eating Aliyan. He would *not* let that happen.

"That's not true," Ezeny said. "His mother sent me to bring him home."

Kanary Phillips sighed and folded his arms in a bored way. "And who are you?"

Ezeny glanced out the side of his eye at Aliyan. Aliyan knew he was the Iron King. But Ezeny was more than that now. He was becoming someone he was proud of. Maybe Aliyan would be proud, too.

"I'm his father."

Ezeny held his breath and watched Aliyan's reaction. The kid startled out of his funk and his eyebrows climbed upward. Then, a shy smile spread across Aliyan's face, and Ezeny returned it until the two were grinning at each other with matching smiles.

Aliyan started toward him, but the Matron in purple grabbed him and brought her fan up. "No, you don't!" she said.

But before she could bring the fan down, Ezeny's powers seized the gold ring on the index finger of her whacking hand and held firm. She tugged on her arm but couldn't lower it.

"No. More. Whacking!" Ezeny hissed.

The Matron screamed. Ezeny unleashed his power. Objects levitated around the room. Kanary Phillips dove under his desk. The Concubines leaped up from the crystal table and two of them backed into the wall.

The third Concubine stayed put. Her eyes were wide and shining, both hands covered her heart. She was much older than the other two, with deep brown skin, raven hair, an aquiline nose, and a smile Ezeny had not seen since he was pulled from her arms at age seven. He gave her a kind smile and a two-fingered salute. But he was not here for her.

"What's happening?" Kanary roared.

"I tried to tell you, sir!" Zandrew wailed.

The door burst open, and guards rushed in carrying laser hand-guns. *Uh oh.* Ezeny hadn't counted on that. Only Military personnel were legally allowed to use laser guns. Everyone else had to use bullets. Nice *metal* bullets, not slippery no-good lasers. One more way the rules didn't apply to people as rich as the Phillips Family. *I used that prerogative to watch banned movies. But good old Dad got private laser guns.*

He wanted to shield Aliyan, but that would be a bad idea, since everyone was already aiming for Ezeny. So, he joined Kanary Phillips under his desk, hoping the guards wouldn't risk shooting their boss. His pulse raced. There was too much laser fire around his son. He couldn't think what to do that wouldn't hurt Aliyan.

"It's the boy!" shouted Kanary. "He's here for the boy."

The guard closest to Aliyan fired at the glass wall looking out over Everland. The floor-to-ceiling window shattered into pebble-sized shards, and a strong wind whipped through the top-floor office. Kanary, Zandrew, and the Concubines hit the floor, covering their heads. The Matrons and guards were made of sterner stuff and remained standing.

A guard tucked Aliyan under his arm and pointed his laser gun at the kid's head. Ezeny froze. He couldn't do anything. The laser gun was nanoplastic. Even if he used the man's wristwatch to freeze his arm, he could still move his trigger finger. Aliyan's eyes were wide. Ezeny uncurled his hand in the air to surrender. *If he could get Aliyan away from the guard...*

"He's just a kid," said Ezeny. "Let him go and I'll come quietly."

"He has metal powers!" Zandrew wailed from the ground. "I tried to tell you! If you let the kid go, we're doomed!"

All Ezeny's sympathy for Zandrew evaporated.

"Right," said the guard.

He held Aliyan out through the smashed-out window by his robe collar a hundred stories above the pavement.

"Ezeny!" Aliyan cried.

What would he do if Aliyan fell? Scenarios raced through his head, and none of them ended well. Aliyan had but one metal zipper in his robe for Ezeny to pull on. But it would rip the robe and Ezeny would be left with a zipper and no son. He locked eyes with the guard.

"Please," Ezeny begged.

He saw no way out of this, and judging by the look on the guard's face, neither could he. They were in a horrible stalemate. If Aliyan got hurt, there would be nothing to stop Ezeny, and the guard knew it.

Then Kanary Phillips spoke up. "You want the kid to live? You hold still while we shoot you in the head. You die, he lives. Simple."

Oh. Well, yeah. There is the 'execution' way to end the stalemate. Duh. Ezeny's scruples against killing gave him some horrible blind spots.

Ezeny locked eyes with Aliyan and nodded.

"No, Kanary! You don't understand!" Ezeny's mother screamed.

She started toward Ezeny. The motion distracted the guard holding Aliyan for a moment. His hand slipped, and Aliyan fell from his grasp, plummeting toward the ground.

Ezeny didn't hesitate. He dove out the window and propelled himself downward toward Aliyan. Ezeny had never paid attention to his physics courses. But he did pay attention to comic books, and he knew this was exactly how Spiderman had inadvertently killed his beloved Gwen Stacy. He caught her before she hit the ground, but the g-forces from stopping her fall had snapped her neck.

The issue had left Ezeny sobbing in Cricket's lap for a good hour, and he'd needed an entire quart of ice cream after. Really, he'd only needed to cry about one-third that long to cry, but Cricket was holding him and patting his back and he was going to milk it for all it was worth.

Thanks to the comic, he knew better than to grab Aliyan out of the air. *Reading always pays.* Because Ezeny had one more idea.

He reached out with his Exsanguination powers. He pushed steadily through the screams of the people he'd killed crying out for justice. *Justice is coming. Justice means no more death,* he promised them. He touched the atoms of iron in Aliyan's blood and pulled on them...gently. Aliyan was fifty stories above the ground, but his descent was slowing from within. For the first time, Ezeny was grateful for his nanobots and the control they gave him. It was delicate work, lifting Aliyan by his circulatory system.

Twenty stories up. Ten. Five. Three...but Aliyan was hovering. His fall stopped. Ezeny scooped the trembling kid in his arm and held

E. M. Denison

tight, trembling, too. They hovered for a long moment before Ezeny said, "Let's get you home."

"You came to get me," Aliyan said. "They said you wouldn't, and mum wouldn't, and she didn't want me anymore."

"Oh, they lied, kid."

"Are you really my dad?"

"Yeah. Is that okay?"

Aliyan grinned. "Yeah. I wondered. I mean, you were 'mom's old friend' and the Iron King is my babysitter for some reason. And I look like you. I'm not stupid."

Ezeny laughed. "Okay. What *else* do you know?"

"Everything."

"Okay, smart stuff. You don't know this. I had this big moment planned where I would get you in this super-epic way, but then they dropped you out a window and I had to improvise. But it can still be cool. Our getaway vehicle is going to be 'the best.'"

Ezeny snapped his fingers and a roar reverberated through the streets that sounded half garbage truck and half prehistoric monster. Around the corner flew the reason Zandrew had admitted a nobody streetlander to the top office of Tower A. The reason he'd kept warning Kanary not to dismiss Ezeny.

The hundred foot long, wingless, metal dragon Ezeny had cobbled together from discarded dump machinery snaked between the buildings like an eel through coral. Ezeny settled with Aliyan behind the construct's head. Then they flew to the smashed-out window of the top office.

Inside, the guard who'd dropped Aliyan was helping Kanary Phillips to his feet. Kanary saw the dragon and staggered back. The guard helping him froze, hand halfway to his nanoplastic laser gun.

The Matrons, Zandrew, and the other two Concubines had already fled. Only Ezeny's mother remained. She crossed herself when she saw Ezeny and Aliyan, and closed her eyes in gratitude. Ezeny stopped the dragon hovering outside the window. He hoped it looked cool with the golden, glowing traffic light eyes he'd given it.

Ezeny spied Aliyan's contract fluttering in the clipboard on Kanary Phillips' desk. He grabbed the metal clip and flew it over to his father along with a brass-tipped fountain pen.

"Sign," he ordered.

Kanary hesitated. He eyed his guards, considering whether they'd be able to take Ezeny out. Then he waved dismissively. "It's one kid. There are thousands more like him all over the streetlands."

He signed. Ezeny pulled the clipboard into his hand, rolled the contract into a paper cylinder, and stuffed it into his robe. Then he and Aliyan rode off together toward the setting sun.

* * *

Ezeny burst into the boxcar with Aliyan, Wilma, and the Mecha-Lots, grinning like an idiot. Almys and Irvin Finnerty looked up from their nightly oven suit repairs. Almys' broad face broke into an even broader grin.

"Small roommate is back! Where is sour-faced mother?"

"She's next," said Ezeny. "Get packed. When I get back with her, we're leaving for Chicago. You can come if you want, Finnarties. It's really nice there, and you'd never have to do work that left you with burn holes."

Almys and Irvin exchanged an inscrutable look. It was like the couple shared a secret language. Ezeny couldn't tell what they'd choose, but they only had a few hours to consider.

Ezeny pointed Aliyan up the ladder to the family bunk, indicating he should get his stuff. Several more Mecha-Lots detached from the charger port and rushed greet their favorite young man.

"Can't I come with you to get mum?"

"No. Until I get back, you stay where I put you and play with your rocks."

Aliyan made a face. "You sound like her."

Aliyan started up the ladder. Ezeny stopped him, stared deep into his eyes, and gave him the best fatherly advice he'd ever heard. "Remember who you are. You are my son. And the one true King."

Anything Mufasa said was parenting gold as far as Ezeny was concerned. But Aliyan rolled his eyes.

"Daaad," he said.

Ezeny got a flash of Aliyan as he would be as a teenager. He ruffled the kid's hair.

"Hey," he said, pointing at the Gas Mask Bot. "Can I enlist your services, my fine robopal?"

The Gas Mask Bot beeped and turned in a circle. Ezeny supposed that was a 'yes.' He used his metal powers to attract the McCreedian tracker tablet to his hand, then gave it to the Gas Mask Bot for safekeeping.

"This has a tracker," he said. "McCreedia will know we're coming. I need you to take this. Divert them from me. It won't be safe. I know I'm asking…a *Lot.*"

He waited for an angry buzzing from the Mecha-Lot to indicate she had understood and was disgusted by his pun. But the little robot only beeped and bumped affectionately against his left stubby. It was cute, but a little ache formed in Ezeny's chest. The interactions with the Gas Mask Bot made him miss Medbot 5.

"Thanks, champ," he said. Then he turned to Wilma. "Okay, Marine lady. I am leaving Aliyan here because if anyone can keep him safe, it's you."

Wilma raised an eyebrow at him. Almys Finnerty scoffed. "Sour lady's young gentleman has bat in belfry," he said.

"As if neighborhood movie night weren't bad enough," agreed Irvin.

Ezeny grinned. "I know you've got the goods, Wilma. Don't forget I was in the Military. They only give out Bazooka Magazine as a freebie swag benefit with the purchase of a laser cannon. How'd you get it? They're illegal for civilians."

"My fingerprints are still in the active-duty database. A paperwork oversight when Everland's Military took over from the old United States."

Ezeny snorted. "Everland *is* known for its excellent recordkeeping," he said sarcastically. "So, where are you hiding it?"

Wilma sighed and unscrewed the bottom of what Ezeny had assumed was her spare oxygen bottle. Piece by piece she stripped the cylinder and manipulated its parts. As Ezeny watched, she reassembled the components. When she was finished, Wilma held a four-foot long nanoplastic laser cannon over one shoulder and looked completely natural doing so.

"Jesus, Wilma!" said Irvin. "You didn't disclose any weapons on our shared lease."

She shrugged. "I couldn't buy the cannon *and* pay the weapons deposit."

Irvin frowned. "We have been paying your rent and you bought this *illegal item?*" said Irvin.

"The Skull Gang never stole from our apartment, did they?" said Wilma. "And you never asked yourself why." She clicked her tongue and made a tsk noise.

"How *did* you pay for it anyway," asked Ezeny. "Sell a kidney?"

Wilma shook her head. "Unregulated clinical trial participant. I regrow my teeth now, so I needn't fear my Werther's!"

She grinned at him and indeed, the teeth she'd been missing back in Chicago were all back and shiny white.

Ezeny whistled. "Dentistry as God intended," he said. *For sharks,* he thought.

Wilma smiled and nodded. "Exactly so."

"Aliyan," he called. "Do what Wilma and the Finnerties say. I'll be back with your mother."

"Will you?" said Irvin, pointedly.

Ezeny froze. He plastered on a smile. He hadn't a clue if he'd be back. This was going to be dangerous. Queenbot had that syringe. There were High Warriors to contend with. And if they'd already started pumping Cricket full of nanobots there was no guarantee he could free her from their insidious influence.

"Eee-yup." He forced the smile to widen and look reassuring. It did not accomplish its mission. Irvin and Almys exchanged a skeptical glance that silently conveyed paragraphs of information. Ezeny held his breath. The Finnarties had always treated Aliyan as a bit of a pest. But it would be nice if Wilma weren't alone watching Aliyan.

When they'd finished their 'look,' Irvin sighed in silent acquiescence. Almys held up his Protein- Factory-issued heat suit with the burn holes.

"Small roommate can pass time by helping to patch oven suits. Or teach annoying small robot companions to do it. Make themselves useful."

That got Aliyan's attention. He scrambled down from the Cade bunk and over to the top Finnerty bunk. Wilma locked eyes with Ezeny, patted her laser cannon, and saluted. He gave her a thin-lipped smile and took one last long look at Aliyan before slipping out the door with the Gas Mask Bot to board his dragon steed.

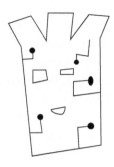

43

Decoy
Ezeny

High above the battlefield, the cold wind stung Ezeny's face as he rode the metal dragon toward McCreedia in the fading light. The battlefield had not changed in the months the Iron King had been absent. The no-man's-land between the warring City States was still shattered concrete rubble. Laser fire flashed at the bases of bombed-out buildings where pockets of rival soldiers shot at each other, trying to survive the day. Here and there a Medbot hovered, treating a patient, or recovering a body. The war was the same as it had been seven years earlier. A stalemate. A grind. It seemed it would stretch on forever, eating the futures of Everlanders and McCreedians alike.

He would take Aliyan and Cricket away from all this. He had better be able to save Cricket. If Queenbot injected Ezeny with that nanobot syringe, there would be no one else to care for Aliyan. *Except Wilma,* he thought. *And the Finnerties. And half the teenage members of Skull Gang. And about three dozen loyal-as-hell Mecha-Lots outfitted with whirling blades, flamethrowers, and homemade acid dart guns.* On second thought, maybe Aliyan would be okay after all.

Ezeny was grateful he'd come to his senses and gone after the kid.

The way his son had hugged him on the dragon ride back to the apartment clung to him like a warm cotton overshawl. Whole-hearted kid hugs were a transcendent experience. Despite his impending danger, Ezeny felt like a geode filled with sunshine and candy butterflies. *Good* candy butterflies. *Not* Werther's Original ones. He'd never done anything to deserve so good a feeling, but he'd take it all the same.

Ezeny was flying over McCreedia proper now, its architecture indistinguishable from Everland's. Tall high-rises. Roman-inspired public buildings with long staircases guarded by stone lions. From an aesthetic level, they might as well be the same City State. Medbot 5 would have objected to that assessment. She would have said Everland's skyline was superior. Had bigger buildings, more of them, etc. Medbot 5 had been adorably delusional.

He missed his friend. Ezeny would need her. His whole plan to save Cricket hinged on having someone to disrupt her nanobots, and Medbot 5 was an expert at breaking cyborgs. He had to believe his friend's personality was still inside the Queenbot Attack Drone somewhere.

Something caught his eye. Eight objects glittered in the air flying fast toward him. McCreedia's High Warriors.

Ezeny whistled. Six of them. Not the Iron Queens from the nanobot vats. Just the normal, artificially- grown variety. But those were bad enough. The other two objects were Advanced Attack Drones. Also not good. He squinted at the drones. Neither of them was Queenbot.

In his Iron King armor, Ezeny might have stood a chance alone against a force like this. But without it? He had barely escaped the Screaming Eagle and the Midnight Demon back at the bank—and then only with Medbot 5's help.

The screeching whistle of magnetized metal discs roared in his ears as they bore the McCreedian High Warriors toward him. He forced the dragon into a low dive. It ribboned between crumbling buildings and mounds of rubble near the city's outskirts. It threaded itself under crumbling overpasses like a legend come alive.

Ezeny grabbed the Gas Mask Bot and jumped off as the dragon cleared the underpass. They huddled beneath the bridge as the rain of laser fire began. From his hiding place, he stretched out his hand and controlled the big, distracting dragon as though he were still aboard. This was the whole reason he'd made a steed so big and unwieldy to ride in on. With something so attention-grabbing, the High Warriors would forget to check the location of the tracker in the vidtablet the Gas Mask Bot was carrying. Not forever. But just long enough.

The dragon's ribboning slowed. Metal groaned as six High Warriors focused their powers on it as one, straining against Ezeny's Iron King might. The beast creaked to a stop, frozen in midair over an abandoned parking lot. Then the devastation began.

Keeping the dragon together and moving took concentration and control. But the High Warriors didn't need precision to dismember Ezeny's construct. Creation took patience and continued effort. Destruction was fast and easy.

The Attack Drones fired lasers at the dragon, disintegrating the joints. The High Warriors peeled the metal with their powers. The tail came apart first. The hinges joining the pieces screeched as they tore. The components fell, crashing into the empty streets below. The clawed legs were next. Ezeny strained to keep the creature together, but the High Warriors' pull was overwhelming. Piece after piece tumbled to the pavement until nothing remained of the dragon. It became once more the disarticulated scraps of dump junk from which it had been forged.

The High Warriors dove into the wreckage, searching through the pieces of the great dragon. But they did not find their quarry. They levitated through each section of the metal carapace, rummaging underneath and inside for an unarmored human. But nothing. They became more frantic in their search. They flitted around the dragon pieces like frustrated killer bees whose target had escaped underwater. Their orders were clear. At any cost they were to bring the Iron King in. But the Iron King was not there.

* * *

Ezeny peeked out from under a fallen road sign below the underpass and watched the angry High Warriors swarm the wreckage. He knew how their minds functioned. There was nothing like a big, loud metal dragon to create a diversion for the bloodthirsty, nanobot-brained metal benders. *Oh look! A distracting object!* Of course, it had worked.

Ezeny chuckled to himself, blew on his fingernails, and polished them on his overshawl like the smug guy he was.

"Did you see that?" he asked the Gas Mask Bot. "Marvel! Marvel at how slick I just was."

The little robot beeped. Ezeny supposed it was an appreciative sound.

As if a mere six High Warriors were any match for me. His Iron King powers were super badass. Then he remembered getting his butt kicked at the bank. *You know. When I don't have innocent people to protect, that is.*

Ezeny turned from the McCreedian High Warriors, levitated using his underharness, and flew low through deserted McCreedian streets. A siren wailed from loudspeakers on all the street corners, warning citizens to take cover. Ezeny swallowed. Queenbot knew he was coming and the whole populace was hiding—from him. The McCredians would all probably like him if they got to know him. He hated to be so feared.

He stopped a block from the address Queenbot had given him and turned to the Gas Mask Bot. "Still got that tablet with the tracking device?"

The bot beeped confirmation.

"You go through the sewers," he instructed Gas Mask Bot. "Draw them off. They'll all follow you."

The robot beeped at him, as if to ask, *'And what will you be doing whilst I am bait?'*

Ezeny looked up at the building he was supposed to enter—a looming skyscraper with a mysterious, windowless floor at the very top.

"I'm going to fulfil a lifelong dream."

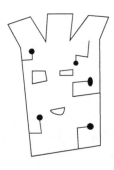

44

Gerbil Tubes of Surprise™
Ezeny

Ezeny levitated through the metal HVAC system in Queenbot's high-rise so he wouldn't scrape loudly against the metal, grateful that his underharness leather was so supple and comfortable. He had always envied his nippy little pet gerbils and their plastic exercise tubes. He'd wanted a human-sized version, and here he was, living the dream.

But it wasn't everything he'd imagined. The tight, rectangular ducts were darker and dustier than he'd expected. He had only the tiny flashlight clamped in his teeth to light the way. His nose was threatening a sneezing fit. And, if he were honest with himself, the novelty of the Gerbil Tubes of Surprise™ had worn off hours earlier. It was 3:30 in the morning. He'd been peering through vents into various rooms in Queenbot's skyscraper for several hours and had still found no sign of either Cricket or the Attack Drone who'd once been his friend.

Then a thought struck him. He'd been searching the rooms on the lower floors, assuming he was looking for a dungeon-type area. But Queenbot was a flier. High Warriors flew, and so would the Iron Queens she was making. When he'd seen the building from the outside, the highest floor had been metal—not glass windows like every other skyscraper ever. He hadn't given it any thought at the time. But now he realized he ought to be looking for Cricket at the top of the high-rise.

The topmost floor of the topmost tower, he thought. *Just like a fairytale.* This time, he would be Cricket's storybook hero. He swore it. He floated through the labyrinth of ducts, taking every turn upward he could.

When he came to the top floor, he peered through a vent to see if he'd been right. He gasped. There were rows of cylindrical vats filled with sleeping nanobot victims. Ezeny's gut twisted at the sight. He'd been in such a vat, experiencing the horror of nanobots consuming his mind, feeling bits of his personality slip away, consumed in a tide of bloodlust.

Hell, he thought. *Those women are all in Hell.* He scanned the faces behind the respirators, hoping to find Cricket among them...and also hoping that he wouldn't.

A low, electric hum caught his attention. There, hovering between the vats, checking the occupants' vitals, was Queenbot. Attack Drones like her could even give High Warriors trouble. It was difficult to think his tenacious little Medbot friend had been one of these advanced war machines all along.

Queenbot was alone in the lab, as he'd hoped. The Gas Mask Bot had drawn off a lot of the skyscraper's security with the tracking device. But Queenbot would still be formidable in combat. And besides, he needed her intact and functional if Cricket were in one of these vats, a new slave of the nanobots. He had a plan to deal with Queenbot. But he couldn't just burst in. He turned back down the HVAC duct and looked for a room that would suit his purposes.

He found a little server closet adjacent to the lab. He opened the vent and used his powers to peel back sheets of the duct work like a banana so he could fit through. He concentrated to make sure the metal molecules didn't rub against each other and shriek or bang as he manipulated them. Then he floated down into the room and planted his stubby treads on the ground.

He looked thoughtfully at the servers. Perhaps these computers managed the vats' life support systems. The nanobot's wi-fi capabilities. The power to the entire building. Perhaps Fia McCreedy's designers had been foolish enough to create a single confluence through which the overlord's entire stratagem could be thwarted. And here was Ezeny right next to it.

Unfortunately, Ezeny didn't know anything about computers. Fortunately, the little server room had an intercom by the door. This was technology Ezeny understood. Tower C had a similar system. Queenbot's panel had eight buttons, each labeled with different rooms, like 'Boardroom,' 'IT-main,' 'Facilities,' and, as he'd hoped, 'Laboratory.'

He pressed the button for the lab. "Um. Hello?"

Static hissed back through the speaker. Then Queenbot's voice. "Where are you, Iron King?"

Ezeny shuddered. Her voice sounded like Medbot 5, only it was darker, muddier, and more mechanical. "I'd rather not say."

"I'll bet. I take it you're not here for a straightforward surrender and trade?"

"I want to talk to Medbot 5," he said.

Queenbot 5 chuckled. "Medbot 5 isn't real. She was a caricature I invented of a stereotypical Everland patriot. I designed her to be delusionally loyal, so she'd keep interfacing with you while I collected data. I even invented a traumatic backstory to explain my transformational abilities. She was *so* ashamed of them. Hilarious."

Ezeny wouldn't accept that Medbot 5 wasn't real. Even when he was the Iron King, pieces of himself had remained. He was *almost* able to give himself the codename 'Lion King' before the stupid nanobots had forced him to say 'Iron King' instead. He hoped it was the same for Medbot 5.

"I liked her," he said.

"She was pathetic. I designed her to be so."

"Hey. Don't talk like that. You're still her, you know."

Queenbot laughed derisively. "I am *not* her."

"Yes, you are. She was good-hearted whenever she could be. Loyal to Everland first, like you programmed her. But always a Medbot when she got the chance. She told me how to cure Aliyan. She helped me save Pink Hat Guy. She put my intestines back the right way." He grimaced and prodded his belly. "Sort of. TMI, but I've had a few pooping-related difficulties she needs to answer for."

"None of this relates to me," she said.

"Sure, it does. When you had to take a hostage, you took Cricket.

You didn't go for Aliyan, even though I wasn't at the factory to guard him. You risked your death at my hands because Medbot 5 has lines she won't cross. And now, so do you."

"Medbot 5 was a thin mask. This is me. I am a medic who skillfully wounds people so they can fight better."

Ezeny hoped it wasn't his imagination, but he thought Queenbot sounded regretful about that. He knew how it was to be two people with very different souls.

"Well, who do you like being more?" Ezeny asked. "You? Or Medbot 5? Think it over. I know your memories are all as fresh as the moment you made them."

Ezeny closed his eyes and breathed a quick prayer Heavenward. His gambit hinged on digital echoes. The ghosts of Medbot 5 floating around Queenbot's circuitry. He had never rescinded the Free Will Override.

"I *order* you to remember and choose," he said.

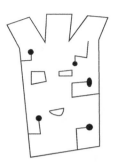

45

The Order
Queenbot

Queenbot's programming had been chugging along like normal. She was chatting up the Iron King, distracting him with their conversation while her mighty processors scoured the building's security footage for his location. She ought to be savoring the tang of anticipation. Her bait had worked, and her quarry had come. Redemption was within her grasp. But even her impending triumph felt dull and pointless. *Is everything going to be hollow like this from here on out?* Then Mr. Phillips had said the words: *"I order you to remember and choose."*

Out of nowhere, like when a popup window pounced into an article she was scrolling through and she accidentally clicked through to an advertisement for mint-flavored toilet paper *(Now with vital macronutrients!)*, an old command hijacked her system.

Medbot 5's Free Will Override. *Ugh. How tedious.* It didn't apply to the Queenbot personality. She could quash the command and get back to business as usual. But for one nanosecond, *all* her memories — as both Queenbot and Medbot 5 — flooded her awareness, sharp and bright as though she were experiencing them in real time.

The volume and intensity of the memories overwhelmed her. She *couldn't* ignore Mr. Phillips' order. The words, *'Remember and choose'* echoed through her circuitry.

She remembered wounding every one of the Iron Queens. The knowledge from thousands of medical journals, all written to heal, used to harm instead. She'd felt the wrongness of it, even as she cut into her terrified test subjects. *Victims,* she thought.

She remembered shooting soldiers alongside High Warriors. How the complex brains and bodies of all those intricately-formed, one-of-a-kind humans disintegrated under her quick, easy laser fire. She remembered being Medbot 5, skillfully healing soldiers, but only enough to get them fighting again.

But one memory shone out among the rest. As Queenbot, she'd experienced pride in the results of her human experiments. The triumph of discovery. But she had only experienced real joy one time. The moment at the bank when Medbot 5 had shoved the war aside to save Ezeny. For once, she'd been an uncomplicated medic, unfettered by programmed patriotism, saving a life, as she'd been made to do.

"...*and choose.*"

"Sir?" said Medbot 5. "I've chosen, sir."

She found herself a round, bobbling Medbot. A wave of shame started to wash over her. She shouldn't be *transforming.* Only buggy bots *transformed.* Then she stopped herself. That hadn't been real. Her memories of her nasty engineers had been fabricated by Queenbot. It was going to take some getting used to, living as Medbot 5, *knowing* her entire personality had been manufactured as a joke. But the joke was on Queenbot, wasn't it? Medbot 5's joke life had turned out better than Queenbot's real one.

"What, really?" came Ezeny's voice over the intercom. "Medbot 5, it's you?"

"Yes, sir."

His shaky laughter echoed over the intercom, relief plain in his voice. Her processors warmed up with gladness that he'd come. She remembered him telling Queenbot that he liked her.

"Welcome back!" he said.

But something was very wrong. "It's good to be back, sir. Sir?"

"Yes?"

Medbot 5 knew everything Queenbot had known. All the passcodes and strategies. All the secrets and lies. All the plans within plans. She didn't know how to tell Ezeny this.

"You coming back here? Into the nest of Iron Queens...well..."

"What?"

"Your nanobots' Bluetooth has been uploading all the Exsanguination Upgrade code to the Iron Queens the whole time you've been talking with me. Updates are installed now. They're ready to go."

"What?"

Sucking, gurgling noises like the water being let out of a hundred bathtub drains echoed through the labs. The nanobot vats emptied of fluid and the eyes of the hundred women in the respirator masks snapped open.

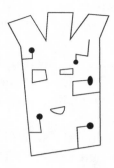

46

Ride of the Iron Queens
Medbot 5

Medbot 5 scanned the lab for signs of Ezeny. "You can come out now," she said over the intercom. Ezeny tumbled out of the server closet at the end of the hall and flew toward her with all the grace of a drunken bumblebee. *Oh. That's where he was hiding.* Her fans whirred happily at the sight of him. Ezeny never did anything in a dignified manner. That used to bother her. Now she was proud of him for it.

"Me coming back here started this?"

"'Fraid so."

"Where is Cricket? Can I get her out?"

"This way, sir."

Medbot 5 zoomed toward the last cylinder in the second row. Ezeny levitated after her, sweat beading at his temples. Medbot 5 tried not to hate herself. She'd turned Yren into an Iron Queen already. *That wasn't me. That was Queenbot.* But weren't they one and the same? If Ezeny counted the Iron King's sins against himself, oughtn't she do likewise?

They stopped in front of Yren's vat. Ezeny pressed his hand to the glass. Her eyes were open like all the others, staring blankly ahead. The last of the fluid drained away with a gurgle and her respirator mask retracted into the laboratory machinery.

"Can you fix her?" he asked, his voice breaking. "Bring her back?"

"Maybe...if I can interface with her."

Medbot 5 uploaded a permission code into Yren's vat controls. The 'check password' loading bar filled as nozzles squirted spandex gel all over the Iron Queens' naked bodies that solidified into custom skinsuits. Pieces of white nanoplastic armor extended from robotic arms inside the Iron Queen vats. Here a boot, there a shin guard. The machinery fitted each component into place around each woman.

A metal claw slotted a gleaming blue visor into Yren's white helmet, covering her face. She became indistinguishable from the other ninety-nine Iron Queens waiting in the vats, their nanoplastic armor complete. White battle gear with silver and blue seams. No capes. No helmet wings. All business.

The loading bar completed and the glass on Yren's cylinder opened. Medbot 5 extended a medpendage to plug into Yren's new Iron Queen port. Yren grabbed the medpendage and squeezed hard. Medbot 5's nanoplastic threatened to crumple under the pressure.

"You will not touch me," Yren said. "We go to war."

Medbot 5's metaphorical heart sank. The Iron Queens were awake and autonomous now. She could no longer control them with passcodes.

Ezeny stepped forward and reached toward Yren. "Cricket," he said.

"Fool. I am no insignificant chirping insect. I am Iron Queen 100." She aimed her gauntlet at him and the laser at the center of her palm lit with blue energy as she prepared to fire. Ezeny stood there, openmouthed. Medbot 5 electrified her hull, zapping the Yren Iron Queen. She cried out and let go of Medbot 5.

Then, the ceiling above each Iron Queen cylinder opened. Their vats became like missile launch tubes. The suited warriors looked up at the open sky above them with alert eagerness. The Iron Queen in the vat next to Yren tapped on the glass of her cylinder.

"There's more blood out there, sister," said the other Iron Queen.

"Blood!" said Yren. She stepped hastily back into her cylinder. The Iron Queens levitated on the metal floors of their vats. Medbot 5 marveled at Queenbot's laboratory design. The launch tunnels had built-in metal platforms for every Iron Queen to use as personal metal flying discs. Ezeny lunged for Yren, but too late. She rocketed up with the ninety-nine other Iron Queens out into the dark McCreedian sky.

"Cricket!" he cried. He looked miserable. But Medbot 5 had more bad news to deliver.

"They're headed across the battlefield. Sir, I'm sorry. The plan is to Exsanguinate Everland. Every man, woman...and child."

Ezeny gasped. "Aliyan..."

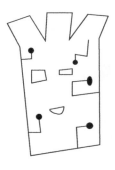

47

Fia was not Gentle
Roger Everland

It was sunny in Roger Everland's digital environment. He was seated in a shaded cabana by pool filled with mercury. Fia was floating atop the liquid metal wearing a charming 1940's pinup bathing suit, looking ravishing. Roger had been sipping a cocktail of mead distilled from honey found in Pharaohs' tombs and blended with crushed ice and the undiscovered erotic poetry of Oliver Cromwell. But the drink had turned sour in his mouth after he read the emergency missive from High Command. Everland was doomed.

An army of a hundred Upgraded Iron Queens was streaming across the battlefield in the pre-dawn light. Soon, all his people would be Exsanguinated. All his buildings, land, and resources would become Fia McCreedy's. And worst of all, losing the war meant losing Fia. She looked at him over the top of her cat-eye sunglasses and smirked.

"I see you've gotten the news," she said.

"My dear…what will we do without our war?" he asked. "What will *you* do? I know you need this challenge as much as I."

"You tried to end it first. Your Iron King was poised to defeat all my High Warriors *and* all my armies, once it got the Upgrade."

Roger blinked. "I never meant to *defeat* you, defeat you."

She snorted derisively, stood, and walked across the domed surface tension of the shining mercury to where she'd left her snow leopard skin towel. "No hard feelings. I, too, tire of our piffling spat."

Roger swallowed. The spat *wasn't* piffling, and *he* certainly didn't tire of it. The spat was everything he got up for. Fia wrapped herself in the towel and handed her drink to King Henry VIII, who was her valet that day. Fia preferred to subjugate the manliest men of history into doing pointless tasks for her rather than snapping her drinks in and out of existence like a normal person. Fia frowned.

"But always, victory eluded me. *'Why?'* I asked myself. Why could I not conquer this simpering fool and move on to bigger things? You always had a trick up your sleeve, your Iron King being the worst of them. You got lucky. You found a soldier wounded enough for the theoretical technique to work. So, I stole your trick. I figured out what made him tick and then I made a similar army for myself."

"You...wounded a hundred of your *own* people that badly? On purpose?"

She snapped her fingers and a pale, bearded man scurried over to her, holding a mammoth ivory tray filled with chocolate chip cookies that were the mathematically developed apotheosis of every grandmother ever's secret recipe.

"Thank you, Rasputin dear," she cooed.

Rasputin was a favorite valet of hers. *Lucky sinister Russian mystic,* Roger groused. Fia swallowed a bite of her cookie and smiled.

"Oh, I wounded *far* more than a hundred. Those are the ones who survived the treatments."

Roger Everland was stunned. Awed by her cold-hearted mercilessness. The whiff of disgust he felt at her amorality added an enticing pungency to his feelings of attraction. Like when a stinky cheese sharpens the savor and complexity of an expertly prepared dish.

"You will conquer Everland for sure," he said. He saw no way out of this. Their game would be at an end. He would be her conquest after all. The perimeters of his hexagons thickened and began to quiver. His imminent defeat added an intense urgency to his longing.

"Everland? Ha! You are *still* thinking too small," she said. "I *thirst* for more. Too long I, history's most epic leader, have been confined to this petty conflict while the world got on with business. My Iron

Queens will take not only your ruined, rubble-riddled City State, but they will Exsanguinate the world beyond!"

Roger gasped. Fia was a true and breathtaking maniac. He would lose to her soon. After his defeat, Roger knew he would hold no more fascination for this woman. If he desired the long-awaited consummation of their fiery animosity, the time was now. Roger Everland should hold back no longer.

He snapped his finger hexagons and the liquid mercury pool morphed into a bedchamber inside a sphere of reinforced ice at the lip of a volcano. The lava and sky reflected orange and blue light across the ice crystal.

Roger had bound himself to a bed of sharp, frozen stalagmites. A tray of implements lay on the nightstand beside it. Fia's greedy, violet eyes roved over them, a delicious hunger growing in their depths. She extended a fine-boned hand, her paper-thin skin bulging with blue veins and dappled with liver spots. She fingered the devices, waiting. She reminded him of a Doberman twitching on its haunches, waiting to be triggered by the 'kill' command.

"I surrender," Roger whispered.

"You're pathetic," she said, smirking.

She snapped her clothes away, grabbed the razor-spiked honey wand from the tray, and dove into the pile of Roger Everland polygons.

* * *

After, they lay, breathless, panting.

"That was terrible, Roger. Truly disappointing."

Roger was grinning helplessly up at stalactites so sharp it was like the room was made of anglerfish teeth. "Wow. I should have yielded years ago."

His voice rose from the many hexagons scattered across the room. To his immense satisfaction and exquisite terror, Fia McCreedy had not been gentle with him. In the fervor of their lovemaking, Fia had broken his body's digital association bonds. He didn't know how he was going to get back together, but for the moment in the afterglow, he didn't care.

One question, she said. "How did you beat my fake Medbot? I was supposed to *take* your Iron King outright. But he's still walking around a free man. He should have killed the Medbot, and got my takeover bots injected into his bloodstream. Or he *could* have wiped its personality, triggering the hidden sleeper agent. But stupidly, he did neither."

"I honestly have no idea. The soldier inside my Iron King suit is defective."

Fia shook her head. "Amazing. I was almost thwarted by the stupidity of Everlanders. Serves me right for giving the enemy too much credit. I'm done with you now."

Roger smiled. He always had one more trick. "Ah, but I'm not done with *you*. Like any good *homme fatale,* I've used my irresistible body as a diversion. Perhaps we'll get another night like this after *you* surrender to *me...If* you survive."

An alarm sounded. Fia sat up and snapped her fingers. A vidwindow opened. The Midnight Demon and the Screaming Eagle carried an olive-green nanoplastic cylinder with a pointed tip between them. Their altitude was low so neighboring City States didn't shoot them down before the missile reached its target. A yellow warning sticker plastered on its side read: *The Big One.* Fia's nostrils flared like the wings of the world's most delicate and evil butterfly.

'A nuke? Roger Everland, you dullard! Nukes have been done to death. They're cliché. They're *tacky!*"

He smiled. "They're effective," he said.

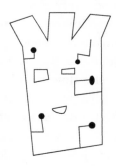

48

Special Assignment
Iron Queen 47

Cries erupted from the battlefield in the early morning light, but Iron Queen 47 streaked regretfully past alone. Her sisters surrounded a squad of twelve soldiers hidden among the rubble, trying out their new powers. They were not skilled yet. To get any Exsanguinating done, the Iron Queens had to work together. *For now.*

The rest of her sisters encircled the men and stretched out their hands, searching for the iron in human blood. Then the screams started. A dark red cloud rose from the trench like steam. The screams quieted as the cloud expanded. Iron Queen 47 could feel her nanobots learn from this first attempt. They were all getting better together, and the battlefield had *so many* more soldiers to practice on. *Blood!* the nanobot voices in her head cried out, longing to partake in the carnage. But *this* Iron Queen had *'orders.'* So, *this* Iron Queen flew on. *Curses.*

There was one person in Everland who was not to be Exsanguinated. One person who still had a strategic use as a hostage. While the other Iron Queens practiced on Everland's troops, Iron Queen 47 had been sent to retrieve the Iron King's son before the real killing started.

She knew right where to find him. Her creator, Queenbot, had lived in the filthy shipping container among filthy humans for more than a month. She shuddered, thinking of the sacrifices her creator had endured for the greater blood....err, good. The greater *good*.

Everland Attack Drones followed her through the skies, firing their pathetic lasers. They might have spelled trouble for McCreedia's old High Warriors. But Iron Queen 47 was something new. She picked up a cloud of metal objects as she flew into Everland, like a magnet collecting iron filings. Then, with a precision and accuracy that could only come from being overstuffed with nanobots, she sent the objects hurtling into the most vital parts of each Attack Drone. They fell from the sky crashing into the streets below. If any lucky civilians were crushed, they won a quicker, more painless death than their fellows would soon get.

"You're welcome!" she called.

But she didn't stop to see if she'd killed anyone—though she wanted to. The orders were important. Finally, undogged by Everland's defense system, she touched down in front of a dumpy looking shipping container with a wheelbarrow painted with tacky pink skulls parked outside.

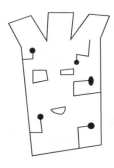

49

Stay Where I Put You
Aliyan

Almys Finnerty leaned against the wall of the shipping container, examining his oven suit. Aliyan waited nervously for his roommate's verdict, scratching the Mecha-Lot with the Crème Brûlé torches for eyestalks. He'd taught the bot to heat seal the singe holes in the Finnerties' oven suits. The hope was that this would free up hours of their evening time. Maybe they could get a hobby or something. Like scowling at people who *didn't* live in the apartment.

At last, Almys looked up, clapped Aliyan on the back and grinned. "Repair is good! Look, Irvin. No holes! No leaks!"

"I see, I see," Irvin said. "You did good, kid."

"I told you they could," said Wilma from her bunk down the hall.

Aliyan's chest warmed at the compliments. He loved to be useful. The little Mecha-Lot chittered and turned in a circle. Aliyan fished a microchip from his fanny pack and gave it to the little robot as payment. A recyclable it could sell for in-game currency. He still felt guilty, feeding the Mecha-Lots' videogame addictions. But they weren't killing each other anymore. And, as they worked on Aliyan's special projects, they spent less time absorbed in their games.

He was glad the Finnerties had asked him to help. He needed the task to distract him from worrying about his mum. *And his dad,* he thought happily. He'd never missed having a father before. He'd been fine. But somehow Aliyan felt more solid in the world now, knowing who his father was and that his father loved him.

Good memories of Ezeny had helped Aliyan escape the Matrons' mind drugs. On the dragon ride back home, Ezeny had held him close and repeated, *"Your mom wants you. She tried everything to get you."* The words helped him feel better and better about his mum, bringing color back to his memories of her. He'd missed the previous day's dose of the Matron's drug, and he was already feeling better about himself and the family he came from. When his parents returned, everything would be okay.

Almys packed the repaired oven suit into a bag. The Finnarties and Wilma were coming with them to Chicago. But Irvin said Ezeny was looney if he thought their work in the new City State wouldn't involve cockroach ovens, so they wanted to be prepared.

Aliyan was about to pack his own things when Wilma stood, frowning.

"Quiet," she said. She moved to the little window by the front door and peeked under the curtains. She gasped. "Hide, kid!"

The Finnerties came alert. Almys picked up Aliyan and Irvin opened the possessions drawer under Aliyan's family bunk.

"Suck in, small roommate," said Almys.

He stuffed Aliyan inside and slid it shut. The drawer was a tight fit. One of Aliyan's toy face rocks was jammed under his left rib. He peeked through cracks in the metal wicker weave. The grownups wore worried expressions. *What had they seen out there?* Wilma retrieved her laser cannon and aimed it at the door.

A high-pitched whine sounded outside. Aliyan had heard that sound on war propaganda vids a thousand times: a laser gun powering up. He held his breath. The apartment door shattered into splinters and blue laser fire. A McCreedian High Warrior in white armor stepped in. Aliyan gasped. The Protein Factory kids were all High Warrior fanatics. They knew all the warriors on both sides of the war. Their stats. Their capabilities. But Aliyan didn't recognize this one.

Wilma fired her laser cannon at the wall behind her leaving a smoking hole where the charging port used to be.

"Go!" Wilma cried to Irvin and Almys. "I'll hold her off!"

The Finnerties started toward the hole. The warrior strode ahead, Wilma's shots glancing uselessly off her armor. She held up her gauntleted hand, palm out. But what was she doing? The barrel of the laser cannon in the High Warrior's palm was dark. No energy burst was gathering at the center. There was no high-pitched whine preceding laser fire. Then Wilma screamed. Red mist rose from the old woman's skin. Aliyan swallowed. *Exsanguination.* Only the Iron King could do that, right?

Halfway out the opening in the apartment wall, Almys put a giant hand on his husband's shoulder, stopping their escape.

"We cannot leave small neighbor," he said.

He turned back into the apartment and grabbed the little Mecha-Lot with the blowtorch. He charged the High Warrior and pressed the bot's torch against her blue face plate.

The blowtorch did little more than leave scorch marks on the face plate. But it was enough to obscure the High Warrior's vision. With a cry of fury, she yanked off her helmet, unleashing a cascade of auburn hair and revealing a young woman's unfamiliar face. She grabbed Almys by the throat and smashed his head against the ceiling.

"Where is the kid?" she snarled.

"Will not talk," Almys choked.

"Fine," the High Warrior said to Irvin with a vicious smile. "We'll see if anyone else will."

Irvin's lip trembled, but he set his jaw. "You can't scare us, sweetheart. We work at the Protein Factory."

Then Almys started to scream. Red vapors rose from his skin.

"Almys!" Irvin cried.

"Keep small roommate safe, love." Almys choked.

Irvin closed his eyes as the red cloud hovering over Almys thickened.

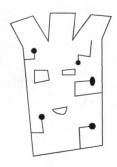

50

Don't Call Me 'Rodge'
Ezeny

Ezeny watched the newsfeed live from McCreedia's propaganda drones on a vidscreen in the lab. The Iron Queens surrounded an Everlander platoon entrenched in rubble. They began to pull the iron from their blood. He winced at the screams. The Iron Queens were slow at Exsanguination, even working together. Ezeny guessed it was because they were new and hadn't gotten the hang of it yet. Exsanguination had a steep learning curve, but the Iron Queens were learning fast.

Cricket was out there in the circle of killers. How many deaths would she cause today because he'd been foolish enough to waltz into McCreedia with the Upgrade codes? His chest ached with the weight of what he'd done.

"Fly, sir," said Medbot 5. "Fast as you can. Go get Aliyan and get far away."

Ezeny laughed bitterly. "I should run away *again?*" he asked.

"What else can you do, sir?"

Ezeny swallowed hard. There was another option, of course, though Medbot 5 was kind enough not to suggest it. He closed his eyes and listened to the voices of the people he'd killed. They were in his head always. Crying out for justice the way his nanobots used to cry out for blood.

Now, because of him, Cricket was out there with all those other poor nanobot victims, earning her own disturbing nighttime screams. There were fates worse than death. Becoming a cold-blooded killing machine, for one. But the worst fate was to stand by and let someone else become a monster when you had the power to stop them. *Love is what you do, right?*

Killing Cricket and the other Iron Queens would hurt. But letting her live to kill thousands? Maybe even Aliyan? That would hurt more. He had so many voices screaming in his head at night already, what were a few more?

He gave Medbot 5 a bitter smile. "What I always do, Medbot 5. Whatever hurts the least."

* * *

Roger Everland

Roger Everland's romantic surprise of a nuclear weapon aimed down his beloved's throat had not been as well-received as anticipated. He'd expected Fia to swoon at his display of might and cold-heartedness. He'd expected her to surrender. He'd anticipated her respect as a manly action man. Perhaps she would make a Roger Everland-shaped valet to wait upon her now that he was one of history's titans of testosterone. *Move over, Rasputin,* he'd thought. (The digital valet wouldn't be the *real* him, of course. Just a dashing facsimile. The *real* Roger would be ruling both their City States with Fia as his trophy war bride.)

That is not quite what happened.

Fia had rolled her eyes. She'd called his nuclear weapon 'uninspired' and 'the product of a dreary, simplistic mind.' Far from reconsidering the end of their war, she had redoubled her commitment to defeating him and conquering the world beyond their conflict. Roger would have gone on the defensive, but not Fia. Even as the nuke approached her, she kept her Iron Queens on the battlefield to hone their powers so they could Exsanguinate Everland.

Fia was busy trying to contact her chief henchman, some Attack

Drone called Queenbot, and get her consciousness transferred away from the McCreedian servers before the nuke hit. Worst of all, she was refusing Roger's offers of refuge on *his* servers.

"I'll be a ghost in cyberspace haunting my own fax machine before I'll rely on *your* charity, Roger Everland," she'd snapped.

Roger watched in horror as Fia stubbornly ran out of time. Her Queenbot henchman wasn't answering her calls. The Screaming Eagle and the Midnight Demon were carrying the nuke toward her homeland and Roger wasn't sure Fia was going to escape. He hadn't *meant* to kill her. He felt like a husband who'd served his wife divorce papers to rekindle their marriage, but instead found them signed in a stamped envelope addressed to the local courthouse.

To pass the time, he patched his hexagons back into association. *Should I cancel the nuke?* But no. Nothing could be a greater betrayal of their love than to back away from his gambit. Fia could never respect him if he pulled his punch. High Command would never respect him again, either.

Suddenly a High Warrior in white armor with gold and orange trim popped into the seclusion of the ice cave in magma.

"Hey Rodge."

"Argh!"

Fia scowled at him. "Quiet Roger!" she said. "I'm trying to concentrate."

She couldn't see the intruder. *Interesting.* The visitor was only in his headspace. Roger wished he hadn't given his High Warriors the permission codes to visit his digital mind. He turned to give the cyborg a dressing-down. Then he froze. *White armor with orange...* The intruder was the AWOL Iron King.

"You," he whispered so Fia couldn't hear. "You're the defective lout who brought all this down on our heads."

"Yup."

Roger scowled. "Don't call me 'Rodge.' And you better not make me look bad in front of Fia. I'm already on thin ice with her as it is."

The Iron King glanced around the ice cave. "Yeah, I can see that," the suit said.

Roger frowned. The pun was disconcerting. High Warriors did not have senses of humor. But the Iron King was malfunctioning, wasn't he?

"This is serious," said Roger. "I think I may have inadvertently killed the woman I love. She's not dead yet but I have only a little time during which I can fix things. But I don't know what to do."

The Iron King was quiet for a long, uncomfortable moment. Then he spoke. "You know, when I came here, I did *not* expect to find any common ground with you. But we are in the same boat. We both know what I did. What did you do?"

Roger rubbed his facial hexagon and sighed. "I sent a nuke to McCreedia. But Fia's refusing to leave unless it's on her terms."

"A nuke? What were you thinking? The radiation will kill Ever-landers, too!"

Roger fidgeted. Why did people think he cared about the little humans populating his City State? They didn't vote for him. "Only some. The rest will mutate. That could be fun."

The Iron King held his helmet in his gauntlets. "Oh, my gosh. Everyone's going to have cat paws growing out of their necks..." he muttered.

"What?"

"Nothing. Never mind. Roger, I can fix this. I can make this all go away. And I can make you look good doing it. Cancel the nuke. Circumvent High Command and Upgrade my nanobots. Only you can do this."

Roger hesitated. Somehow, he'd maneuvered himself into a corner on the chess board of life. He was about to blow up Fia and the war—everything that made him feel alive. And there was no one to bail him out. No one except this Iron King. He wanted to believe there was a way out of this that let him save face. But all his intel suggested the buggy Iron King had gone pacifist.

"So, you'll go back to killing?" he asked.

The Iron King opened his gauntleted hands in a helpless gesture. "I don't like death. But the Iron Queens? Your stupid nuke? That much death demands I stop running. Sometimes love isn't gentle."

Roger shivered, remembering Fia and all those *implements*. 'Love isn't gentle' is a phrase he could get behind. Perhaps even a pacifist would take up arms to defend two whole City States full of people.

"But how are you going to stop a hundred Iron Queens? They'll have the same Upgrade as you."

"They're new. They don't know what they're doing yet. I've seen them Exsanguinate on the vidscreens. They're only taking baby steps."

Roger spluttered. "Baby steps! They killed a whole platoon in five minutes!"

"Like I said, baby steps. It's like they're a hundred toddlers out there, but they're learning fast. Me? I'm experienced. I'm an Olympic track star. You have a small window of time during which *maybe* one Olympian can catch a hundred scampering toddlers. Maybe."

"And kill them."

"Err. Yes. Wow. That metaphor got horrible fast," said the Iron King.

Roger hesitated. The Iron King could be lying. The Iron King could fail. And *then* wouldn't Roger Everland look a fool? For a few moments before everything exploded, that is. The other chess pieces were closing in on his King's square. He had one move left.

But Roger hadn't been playing *his* game. He'd been thinking of himself as a chess player. But chess didn't suit him. Chess wasn't ballsy. Roger Everland was ballsy. Like a high-stakes poker player wearing a jaunty cowboy hat in a rough saloon on the edge of a dangerous frontier. And Roger Everland was an all-in kind of poker player. He wasn't going to give up his nuke. It was his ace in the hole. But the Iron King didn't need to know that.

"Alright. You have yourself a deal."

"Great," said the Iron King. "Now I have to find myself some armor out there in the real world."

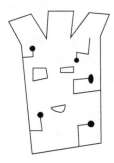

51

Return of the King
Medbot 5

Medbot 5 brought one of the prototype Iron Queen nanoplastic suits to Ezeny to try on: one of the final steps of their plan to save Everland and McCreedia. Roger Everland had given Ezeny all the permission codes he needed. All that remained was to return the Iron King to full power. Ezeny was sitting on the lab floor among the empty vats frowning at the armor.

"This doesn't look like it's going to fit," he said.

It was true. The shoulder to waist ratio was obviously made for a woman.

"Yeah. McCreedia uses female warriors, remember?"

"Oh, I remember."

"Lucky for you, you skipped all workouts and have been moving yourself mostly with your metal powers. Otherwise, you might have developed a torso that would have fit this armor *even worse*."

Ezeny nodded solemnly. "I am wise beyond even my own understanding, Medbot 5."

She started to chuckle, but then her coils whined. She'd been working so long to turn Ezeny back into the Iron King. Now it was what she wanted least.

"Sir? I'm going to miss the real you."

Ezeny's eyes shone with gathering tears. Medbot 5 was surprised he wasn't outright sobbing, given what he was about to do.

"Maybe...maybe you can get me back out when this is done...like you did before. Or maybe I can break free. Back when I controlled your Free Will, you never gave up trying to hand me over to my enemies."

"Yes, sir. Sorry, sir."

"No need to apologize, Medbot 5. It's inspiring. Your dedication to my doom gives me hope for myself. Maybe I can fight the nanobots too."

She eyed the syringe in her medpendage. It was filled with special nanobots designed without the vulnerabilities that let her destabilize the Iron King. The nanobots in his system would have already built up an immunity to her shock treatments. They'd teach the new, super nanobots all about it, like a vaccine training human antibodies. She couldn't bring Ezeny back this time.

And as for fighting the nanobots with his own willpower? What Ezeny refused to understand was that he had been a terrible mind-controlling overlord. Absolutely overthrowable. Effective tyrants didn't feel guilty about turning people into mind slaves. His nanobots would have no such scruples. Once he was under, Ezeny would be lost to the Iron King for good.

"I don't think so," she said.

He nodded. "Perhaps it's for the best. Given what I am about to do," he said.

He was right. Ezeny was not going to be able to live with himself after killing Yren and all the other Iron Queens. It had to be done. But that fact wasn't going to ease his soul. *If only I wasn't such a janky malfunctioning piece of junk...*

Then an idea struck her. Medbot 5 had never malfunctioned. That was a lie implanted by Queenbot. Medbot 5 had always operated perfectly as designed. Everything she ever thought was wrong with her was going to help Ezeny save everybody.

"Sir, I can't free you again, but I think I know how to free the Iron Queens without killing even one of them."

His head snapped up. "What really? How?"

"I thought it was some bug in my system that knocked out your nanobots. But it was purposeful sabotage. I have all the codes to do it again. *And* Roger just gave you the Upgrade. You can upload the sabotage commands into all the Iron Queens with your Bluetooth. They just have to be in range of your nanobots' Wi-Fi network."

A brilliant smile spread across Ezeny's face. "Medbot 5, I could kiss you!"

"Please don't, sir."

He closed his eyes while she transmitted the codes to him. When she was done, he opened them again. They were shining. There was an almost joyful expression on his face.

"Thank you, Medbot 5. You don't know what this means to me. I can get back in that suit now gladly, with an untroubled heart."

Her fans whirred. "They should write a comic book about this, sir."

He laughed. "You know, I would *love* that."

They worked together, fitting Ezeny into the nanoplastic suit. When the last piece of the armor was on, Ezeny stood. "How do I look?" he asked, a shy uncertainty in his voice.

"Like all the other Iron Queens."

He frowned. "That won't do. They should know me on the battlefield. Get me a Sharpie™. Gold if you've got it."

Medbot 5 sped to the office supply cabinet and came bobbling back with an orange Sharpie™ marker. Orange was the closest she could find.

"How is this?" she asked.

Ezeny took the marker and drew a big orange lion head with all-white eyes covering the chest plate. It was sloppy, lopsided, silly-looking, and not at all fearsome.

"How about now?" he asked.

"Wonderful, sir," she said, without irony.

"I want to record instructions for the people of Everland and McCreedia. And a goodbye message for Cricket."

"Good plan," she said. Medbot 5 was always recording. Humans knew this. It wasn't as though AIs tried to hide it. But it made people uncomfortable to be reminded of the fact. She pretended to 'turn on her recording feature.'

When his message was finished, Ezeny pushed a button in the interface of his forearm gauntlet. A little window opened in the armor over his shoulder muscle. "Welp. Still got that syringe, Medbot 5?"

She drew the needle out and floated reluctantly toward him. Half of her processors were still scanning, compiling, trying to figure out another way. The needle was micrometers from his shoulder when Ezeny flinched.

"Sir?" She asked, hope blossoming in her. Ezeny was smart. Maybe he'd thought of an alternative. A way to solve this where he didn't have to become the Iron King.

"It's just...I hate needles," he said.

Medbot 5 sagged. "Of course, you do, sir." she said.

He offered her his arm once more. She jabbed the needle in and pushed the plunger.

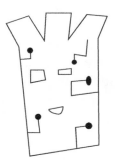

52

Angry Birds
Aliyan

Aliyan cowered in the drawer as the High Warrior pulled the iron from Almys' blood. He shut his eyes against the sight of the man's agony and the frightened looks on Irvin and Wilma's faces.

They're not strong enough to protect you, a little voice whispered in his head. Aliyan recognized the stain of the Matrons' drugs that told him the people and places he came from weren't good enough.

The voices lied. The Matrons would have called Wilma, Almys, and Irvin lowlife streetlanders. But they were fighting a High Warrior to keep him safe. Aliyan should help them somehow. The brave urge butted up against a deep-rooted maternal command.

Stay where I put you. Hide. Whenever he did, though, he stayed trapped. Ezeny was always telling him to relax and be a kid. His mum was always cautioning him to stay alert and stay alive. But there was one place Aliyan found clarity amid adults telling him what to do. Aliyan understood machines. And he had an idea.

He kicked against the underside of the bunk, sliding the drawer out. The auburn-haired High Warrior was too absorbed in the gruesome work of killing Almys to hear. Aliyan glanced at the bed where three Mecha-Lots were whirring and clicking: the Crème Brulé torch-bot, the bot made of claws and mini-catapults, and of course, Blender Head.

Aliyan reached into the drawer and grabbed a smooth toy rock about the size of a chicken egg. His first thought was to throw it at the intruder's exposed head. But he hesitated. He wasn't strong enough to hurt a High Warrior. He didn't think any human was.

But Aliyan was surrounded by battle bots with high powered machinery specifically built to damage other armored battle bots. He slotted the rock into one of the claw-bot's pneumatic catapults and nodded toward the High Warrior. The Mecha-Lot buzzed in comprehension. It wound itself up and fired the rock at more than 200 miles per hour at the intruder's head.

High Warriors could stop a speeding bullet. But bullets were made of metal they could sense. The rock was only a rock with a painted-on face. It struck the Warrior's temple, knocking her unconscious. Blood ran down her face. Almys sagged to the floor and lay trembling. Irvin ran to him.

Aliyan had only moments before the High Warrior's nanobots repaired the damage from the rock. She was already beginning to stir when Aliyan seized Blender Head and jumped from the bunk. Aliyan and the other kids at the Protein Factory knew everything about High Warriors that wasn't classified. They knew their stats. Their histories. They had studied High Warrior schematics. Aliyan knew the function and location of all the High Warriors' technical components—including their interfaces. He pulled the bot's retractable adapter from its spool and plugged the little Mecha-Lot into the High Warrior's arm port.

"Quick!" he told it. "Upload Angry Birds—Dopamine+ Edition™!"

Blender Head beeped and a green light flashed on the High Warrior's arm panel. She sat up and blinked. Her head wound was already nearly closed. Aliyan scrambled back, so she couldn't grab him. She turned, her lips moving silently. Aliyan held his breath. *I should have stayed put.* But no. He'd risked it all on a wild hunch.

But then the High Warrior cried out.

"No! I missed! My eggs cry out for vengeance, yet the pig remains, mocking me! I must replay the level!"

Aliyan stood and drew a shaky breath. He glanced at the others. Irvin had helped Almys sit up. Wilma was grinning at him with all her teeth and giving him a salute. He turned to the High Warrior. She looked lost and desperate. She had no money to replay the level and every newly addicted nanobot in her system was screaming for her to try again.

"You're going to need to go to the dump and find something to recycle," said Aliyan calmly. "There's a lady there behind the booth. Wandy. She'll help you out."

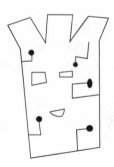

53

Satisfaction
Roger Everland

Roger watched his beloved Fia pace the floor of the ice cave, graceful in her agitation, like a caged tiger. Her features luminous in the glow of lava, the way the last velociraptors must have glimmered in the light of the approaching Chicxulub asteroid. The beautiful, poignant end of an era.

She had pulled up seven vidscreens and was paying no further attention to him. The feed from the propaganda drones showed half the Iron Queens trying to Exsanguinate a second platoon of Everlander soldiers. Fia had send the other half of them chasing the Screaming Eagle and the Midnight Demon as they bore Roger's nuke toward McCreedia.

Fia put a willowy finger to her ear and called her chief henchman one final time. Fia's plan was to upload her digital consciousness into an Attack Drone and flee her doomed City State. But still she got no answer. She slammed her fist into the icy wall, cracking the crystal surface. Roger flinched. He'd been hoping Fia would be able to escape.

"Inbox full?" She snarled. "What kind of message is *that* Queenbot, you misbegotten child of a Tamagotchi!" Fia poked a comm icon on the dashboard screen that controlled her Iron Queens. "All Iron Queens.

Protect the motherland."

Roger's chest hexagons fluttered. Fia was totally on the defensive for the first time ever. In their games of chess, she'd never retreated before. She always insisted the best defense was attack. Roger Everland's ultimate victory was unfolding before his eyes. As much as Fia derided his nuke as 'tacky,' it *was* about to kill her.

Roger's eyes flicked to the screens, hopeful that Fia's minions could stop his triumph, so he didn't have to. The Iron Queens abandoned their hapless soldier prey and rose from the battlefield in a perfect diamond formation. The Midnight Demon and the Screaming Eagle roared forward under the radar of the outside world, carrying doom between them.

As one, the Iron Queens lifted their arms toward the two High Warriors and their missile, pushing against it with their formidable powers. *Come on ladies,* Roger begged. But the nanoplastic missile didn't deviate. The new Iron Queens were not yet skilled enough to reach inside the missile and yank it off course by the enriched uranium within. *Toddlers taking baby steps, like the Iron King said,* he thought as reality dashed another of his hopes.

Fia turned to him now, her eyes wide. The synthetic heartbeat Roger had given his digital body because it was weirdly quiet without one roared in his ear hexagons. *I am going to win the war with McCreedia.* The thought horrified him.

"Roger...I...I'll go to your servers," she said. "I accept your offer of refuge."

Why now? He shook his head sadly. While her Queenbot had undoubtedly been prepped as an escape pod for a digital being, Roger's servers weren't ready to take on a whole new consciousness. There would be upgrades to install. Permissions to request and allow. Cookies to accept. It could take an hour. The missile was five minutes from McCreedia.

"My dear, there isn't time."

She gasped and sank onto their stalagmite bed, a fine-boned hand resting over her heart. Roger ground his hexagonal teeth. Like him, Fia was an ageless, immortal creature. She was facing an unexpected end.

For the first time in his life Roger Everland imagined what it was like to be someone else. The empathy gears in his brain, rusty from lack of use, groaned as they began to turn, grinding like the machinery in an amusement park penny press, squealing louder and louder until *plop*, they dropped a single emotion nugget into the metal receptacle cup: pity.

The missile was Poker-Roger's ace in the hole. But what about the other cards he was playing with? What about the Iron King and his promises of victory without nuclear annihilation? If he wanted Fia to live, he was going to have to swallow his pride and risk her eternal scorn. His only hope now was the Iron King.

He pulled up a new vidwindow. The round, clean-shaven face of Commander Withers stared back at him.

"High Command. Cancel the nuke," he ordered.

"What? Are you *sure* sir? We are about to win. Then we can have cake while the ashen corpses of our enemies scatter to the winds. The boys over here started breaking out the vintage cans of Cocaine-a-Co-la™ in celebration."

That sounded pretty good to Roger. *But no.* "I'm sure," said Roger.

Commander Withers' shoulders slumped. He heaved a disappointed sigh and typed in the code. "All work and no play," he muttered.

Onscreen, the missile broke free of the Midnight Demon and the Screaming Eagle. It turned upward, rocketing toward outer space. The Midnight Demon and the Screaming Eagle looked at one another, then ahead at the diamond formation of Iron Queens. Together they fled toward Everland.

Satellite data flashed across Roger's vidscreen. It seemed the foreign City States had noticed the nuke, now that it had reached high altitudes. The missile defense systems of dozens of major governments across the North American continent locked in on it. *Such paranoid fuddy-duddies,* thought Roger as anti-ICBM tech launched from Chicago, New Cleveland, Area 52, and the emerging world superpower, Walt Disney City. But it was Dollywood's missile that got there first, nudging *The Big One* harmlessly off on a trajectory that bypassed three space stations and gave the burgeoning Moon colonies a wide berth. Roger's ace in the hole had gone down the tubes.

Fia turned to him, a vicious smile flashing across her face.

"Roger, you fool! I've been playing a game of 'chicken' and *you* flinched first, you ninny. Now there is nothing to stop my Iron Queens from Exsanguinating all Everland. Iron Queens attack."

The diamond of Iron Queens surged forward like a school of piranhas toward the plump, swimming cow of Everland.

Roger blinked, surprised at what he was feeling. He should have felt stupid. He should have cursed his pity and the lowly place it had brought him to. But a strange thing had happened when he'd used his empathy gears a moment earlier. Roger had primed his humanity pump and now strange emotions were flowing. He was *glad* Fia would not die. He was *grateful* he hadn't wiped out the whole population of McCreedia, filthy peasants though they may be.

He had been undone by his sudden sentimentality. But he would accept his fate. Once his City State was empty of people, Fia would likely download his consciousness into a small, limited digital realm where only realistic things could happen. He would, perhaps, go mad. Only time would tell. He closed his eyes as the Iron Queens approached Everland. *Not man enough to watch your own defeat, eh?* an internal voice scolded him.

Then a noise sounded from Fia's vidscreens. The screaming of a High Warrior metal disc. Roger's eyes flew open. A lone Iron Queen stood, hands on hips atop an aluminum trash can lid flying toward Everland. *No*, not an Iron Queen. The *Iron King*. He could tell because there was a screwy-looking lion drawn across the breastplate with an orange Sharpie™. There was only one High Warrior demented enough to decorate himself so. Everland's finest. Her last hope. *Please*, Roger silently pleaded.

"Oh look," said Fia, her voice dripping with condescension, "Your little action figure has come to play." Then she turned to the Iron Queens' control window and pressed the comms icon. "We've no further use for him. Kill him."

The Iron King had said he was an Olympic track star compared to the Iron Queens' neophyte toddleryness. He promised he could chase them all down and take them out. But the Iron Queens weren't running. The formation turned away from Everland and bore down on the Iron King instead. Roger swallowed. *Surely, he couldn't handle them all at once.*

The Iron King held out his hands as the Iron Queens flew toward him. A dozen of them wobbled in the air as his powers pulled on the metal discs they were using to keep themselves aloft. But there were more than eighty others still coming. He pushed more of these away, but even the ones he'd grounded flew back up and joined their sisters. Soon the Iron King was faced with a wall of Iron Queens flying at him in deadly formation. They aimed their palms at him, warming up their lasers in preparation for a kill.

A sphere of blue light burst from the Iron King. It expanded outward, enveloping all the Iron Queens. To human eyes, the sphere would look like some sort of energy weapon. But Roger was a digital being and he perceived more than a human could. The sphere was pure computer code being uploaded from the Iron King and downloaded into the Iron Queens. *But what did it do?* Roger wondered. As suddenly as it had appeared, the blue sphere vanished.

The Iron Queens screamed and shrank from the Iron King's hovering form. Some stayed aloft, but most plummeted to the ground, smashing into the concrete like falling angels.

"What's going on!" Fia demanded over the comms. "Report!"

"Get me out! I want *out!*" came the reply. The voice was pure terror.

Like a falcon diving toward a rabbit, the Iron King bore down on one of the fallen Iron Queens. He landed over her, legs astride her fallen form. The propaganda drones flew in close to capture the carnage. The Iron King's hand cannon powered up; the light shone bright in his palm as he prepared to fire.

"You disappoint me," came the Iron King's cold voice. He no longer sounded like the affable weirdo who had visited Roger in the digital realm.

"No, please!" the downed Iron Queen cried.

Then, inexplicably, the palm cannon deactivated. "What the...?" said the Iron King.

He held out his hand once more. But his arm jerked wildly, and he grabbed the Iron Queen's faceplate, ripping her visor free from her helmet. The propaganda drones zoomed in. A pair of large blue eyes set inside a pale face blinked. The woman inside gasped. As if he was fighting against his own arms, the Iron King reached down again and pulled off the whole helmet.

"What's happening to me?" he said, his voice cold and angry.

Huge sobs of relief shook the freed Iron Queen's body. "It's over, it's *over*," she said.

"But...but I am trying to *kill* you," he said.

But he did not kill her. Instead, the Iron King's body jerked him aloft like a rag doll, an unwilling participant in his own actions. He flew to the next fallen Iron Queen and ripped her free of her helmet as well. Roger and Fia watched the screens as he did this for a third and fourth time. Whenever the Iron King tried to kill an Iron Queen, his palm laser cannon malfunctioned, and he freed her instead. Then Roger sensed it. A Free Will Override was controlling the Iron King's body.

Then Fia gripped one of Roger's hexagons. He tore his gaze from the vidscreens and found her violet eyes peering at him. In their depths he saw curiosity and...was it desire?

"What did you do, Roger?"

*Er...*what *had* he done? He didn't know. But Poker-Roger knew better than to betray his total ignorance of just what the Hell was going on. Instead, he smiled knowingly.

"Fia, my dear. You didn't think my whole plan was something so unsubtle as a *nuclear weapon*, did you?"

He chuckled mysteriously, hoping she wouldn't press him for more information. She blinked up at him from under blue-painted eyelids. Her eyes sparkled with renewed respect. Somehow—he still didn't understand how—he'd managed to dazzle the woman of his dreams.

"Roger, you devil. You stole the code my Medbot used to hijack your Iron King and used it to hack my Iron Queens. You subjugated my greatest weapons using my own tricks. You brought them under the chains of your iron rule. You humiliated me."

"I did, didn't I?" Roger purred in the smuggest voice his flabbergasted self could muster.

She slipped into his hexagon cloud and lay back, exposing her throat to him. "Oh, Roger," she whispered, "I surrender."

He bent and covered her neck and lips in tender, passionate kisses using his nimblest polygons. Then, Roger tried the tactic he *should* have used when battling the last living Panda. He sent his hexagons flying apart only to descend on Fia like a flock of birds from the banned Alfred Hitchcock film. Fia closed her eyes in sublime delight as Roger alighted on her body from multiple surprising angles, bearing her to the bed of jagged ice stalagmites.

The immortal lovers melted into one another. Their digital code bases intermingled as Roger's hexagons combined and swelled, swallowing Fia's consciousness wholly into his own as they consumed one another in lustful abandon. At last, and for the first time, both rapacious sextillionaire overlords experienced a full, uninterrupted fifty-eight seconds of satisfaction.

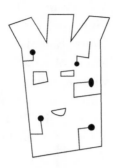

54

Is This Thing On?
Yren

Yren awoke in a pile of shattered concrete to the sound of scream-ing—her own. Waves of horror cascaded through her nervous system. She had killed. She and her sisters had killed twelve people together. Soldiers did that in war, she knew. But her murders bore a deeper stain than normal killing. The *glee* with which she had savored the deaths clung like a slimy residue over all her neurons. A strange blue flash had brought her back to herself. But until then, Yren knew she had stopped being human.

Her hands shook and she could not stop them. She remembered her nights holding Ezeny as he trembled and moaned. She'd felt sym-pathy for him back then, but she hadn't understood. Her heart started pounding and her vision swam. *No,* she insisted, forcing down the dis-orientation and panic. She was free now. She could choose again. But what should she choose to do?

She remembered Aliyan. The Iron Queens were heading to Ever-land to Exsanguinate everyone, including her son! She opened her comm channel to find out how close they were to the city. Screams and sobs echoed over her helmet speakers. Cries of 'Oh, God the blood,' and 'I'm free!' and 'Help me' echoed across the channel. *Huh?*

Yren looked around. She spied at least thirteen other Iron Queens on the ground. Some were unmoving. Others were holding their helmets and groaning. One sat with her arms wrapped around her knees and rocked back and forth. Were they all experiencing what Yren was? Free, but awakened to the horror of what they had become?

A quick check of her mission status log showed chaos. All Iron Queens were out of commission. No one was heading to Everland. Aliyan would be safe inside the Protein Factory, right where she'd put him. Yren sagged in relief. Then a forceful voice sounded in her head. *Blood!* It insisted. *You want blood!*

I most certainly do not *want blood,* she informed it.

Blood, blood, blood, blood, blood, blood, blood, blood, blood, it reasserted.

Yren mentally backed away from this unhinged little voice as one might from a snarling Pomeranian with a severed human finger in its teeth. She recognized the voice. It had driven her actions when she was barreling toward Everland, bent on murdering everyone. Nausea crept from her stomach to her throat. Would she hear this voice forever? Her head swam.

She was trying to think what to do when a pair of white nanoplastic boots landed astride her body. Yren's vision was blurry and double, but she could tell it was one of the other Iron Queens. She looked up into the glowing barrel of a charged-up palm cannon. *Oh.* She wouldn't have to worry about the little voice for long.

"Maybe I shall be able to kill *this* McCreedian scum bucket," said a low, cruel voice distorted by the helmet.

But then the hand laser light deactivated, and the white gauntlet reached for her face plate instead. Yren shivered as the screaky sound of cracking nanoplastic filled her ears like the feeling of chewing aluminum foil. When the face plate came away, the bloodthirsty head voice grew fainter. Then the strange Iron Queen wrenched her helmet off and the voice vanished altogether.

"Alas, no. This one is to live as well, it seems," said the Iron Queen. "High Command, come in. Send a Medbot. I'm malfunctioning."

Boy is she ever. Then the Iron Queen rocketed off into the sky and pounced on another woman a few yards away from Yren. This Iron Queen had gone wonky. There was even an odd drawing of a lion head scrawled on her chest. Perhaps being an inhuman monster had driven the poor woman mad. But Yren was grateful to her. She'd silenced the head voice, and it looked like she was doing the same for all the Iron Queens. Crazy or no, the woman had awakened from Hell and started right in helping.

With every passing moment, Yren's mind sorted out more of the jumble of her memories from when she had been under the nanobots' influence. Suddenly, she thought of Ezeny. *Had he drawn that lion on the malfunctioning Iron Queen?*

It seemed like something he'd do. Perhaps he was working with her? Yren had last seen him watching her with anguish as she'd rocketed out of the lift tube as a fully realized monster. At the time, her inhuman self had wanted to poke his eyeballs into his skull and suck his brains out with a straw. She shivered. That monster was *not* her.

But Ezeny had been in danger. Queenbot had been in that lab, waiting for him with her nanobot syringe, Ezeny greatest fear. And now Yren understood on a bone-deep level why he had been so afraid. Was he still free? Was he still himself?

She stood too quickly and swooned. The little voice was gone, but there was still a thrum in her awareness rising from the rubble all around her. *Metal.* It was everywhere. Whatever had silenced the voice had not affected her metal powers. She was unsure of her ability to use them now that the confident little murder imps in her brain were quiet. But she could do this for Ezeny. He had come for her; she would go for him.

She reached out with her powers and dragged something metal from the rubble. It was a mangled aluminum ladder. It was perfect. Ezeny would think it didn't look cool enough or some such foolery. But Yren was new with her powers. She wasn't going to stand astride some steel frisbee and soar through the air. No, sir. If she had to fly, she'd do it on something with hand holds.

She sat astride the ladder, legs dangling between the rungs, and levitated. She turned it toward McCreedia and sped back toward the secret lab, the warm spring wind whipping across her liberated face.

* * *

In the heart of the city, speakers on every McCreedian street corner broadcasted an all-clear signal. Citizens gathered in the intersections, hugging one another, sometimes crying. There were shouts when a friend or family member was recognized. The people had all faced death together, Yren realized.

Most unusual were the vidscreens at every intersection. Thirty-foot-high holographs hovered with the words *Standby for an Important Announcement* written across them. It must be from Fia McCreedy herself. But then the screens changed, and it was Ezeny's face staring out from the massive projections. He was standing in front of one of the nanobot vats in Queenbot's secret lab. His head was cocked to the side, and he was staring at the camera. She slowed her ladder. Was the broadcast live? Was Ezeny safe after all?

"Recording start," he said and frowned. "Hey, is this thing on?" He squinted at the screen. From off-camera Medbot 5's voice called back.

"I *am* this thing, sir."

"Oh. Right. Are *you* on?"

"I am talking to you right now."

"Ah. I see. Wait…so you're *always* recording?"

"It's not 'recording,' I play back my memories. And I remember everything I see."

Ezeny's eyes widened and shifted to the side. "So…you can play back *all* your memories? That means you have footage of when I…"

"Made many questionable decisions? Yes, sir. I have a few favorites."

Ezeny coughed out an embarrassed laugh. Then Yren noticed something. Ezeny was wearing white nanoplastic Iron Queen armor. *The gone-batty Iron Queen who had freed her on the battlefield!* Her heart sank. Ezeny wasn't *working with* her. He'd *been* her. Or, rather, she'd been him. Yren was too late. She would not find Ezeny in Queenbot's lab. He was back inside the Iron King, trapped in his own personal Hell. She stopped the ladder in midair. What was the point of rushing to his rescue now?

Ezeny forced a thin-lipped smile at the camera.

"Anyway…" he continued. "This should be playing across vidscreens in both McCreedia and Everland. If you're seeing this recording, then the all-clear sirens are sounding. Everland, the Iron Queens have been freed from their mind control. They're just people now, and none of them want to kill you. The war is over—for a little bit at least. Let me explain. My name is Ezeny Phillips, and I am done with the war. And I bet you all are too.

"Happily, my associate Medbot 5 and I found ourselves in possession of *all* the technology codes for both Everland *and* McCreedia's Militaries and no particular loyalty to either side—thanks Fia and Rodge!"

He gave a grin and a two-fingered salute to the camera.

"So…we kind of turned them off. The Militaries, that is. We hacked everything and broke it. All the smart weapons, the servers, the ruggedized computing systems, the avionics, the missile silos. Even the charging capabilities of the laser cannons. Go ahead and check, High Command! It's all trashed. Medbot 5 did some calculations based on available materials and labor force. She estimates it'll take three to five years for the City States to rebuild their war machines. And there's more. I had a *vision*. And Medbot 5 had the skills to pull it off—because talent scouting *is* a talent."

"Whatever you say, sir," said Medbot 5's dry voice from off camera.

This only made Ezeny grin, and he waved his hand in the air the way he always did when he was telling a good story. A lump caught in Yren's throat. *A vision.* Like he'd had for macaroni and cheese pie. She wanted this man back so much.

"The old High Warriors will need your help and your mercy. The Midnight Demon, the Screaming Eagle, and all McCreedia's vat-created High Warriors. They don't understand the blessing of freedom yet, and they are frightened of it. But I believe they can learn. I hope someone I'm talking to now will find them and teach them how to live like people."

He swallowed. "But that Iron King," Ezeny shook his head, a look of regret and distaste on his face. "There's nothing I can do for him. So Medbot 5 coded a Free Will override into his nanobots. He will no longer be autonomous. He'll only obey the commands *I* am leaving for him. He's going to be an actual superhero now. Serving the people. He'll help you rebuild. He'll draw poisonous metals from the water. If someone is in danger from, oh, I don't know, riot quellings or vicious gang members, the Iron King himself will be there to protect them."

He laughed in a somewhat deranged, manic way, and Yren realized he wasn't Queenbot's victim at all. He'd become the Iron King again on purpose.

"Ah," said the recording of Ezeny. "That murderous misanthrope is going to hate being a hero *so* much. But there's nothing he can do. He has to be good. It's my favorite part of the whole plan. Anyway. To all of you citizens, what can you do with three to five years of clean water and no war? Organize yourselves. Build a better government. Contact the outside world for help. They are afraid of us and our violence, but they're good people. I'm sure they will help us if we promise not to bite."

He smiled.

"So that's it then. I'm pretty happy with how this has worked out. For once, I think I'm leaving things better than I found them. And Cricket? If you're watching, I'm sorry. I'm sorry I ran away. It was the biggest mistake I ever made, and I hope you can forgive me. End recording."

She did forgive him. A thousand times. Now that she'd emerged from the Iron Queen, she understood how frightened Ezeny had been. And how much courage it had taken to climb back into that suit. All her life, she'd wanted someone to come back for her. Ezeny had done that. She wanted nothing more than to tell him what it meant to her.

But the recording hadn't ended. The vidscreens still hovered, broadcasting.

Ezeny sat back and sighed. The bluster was gone from his countenance. He looked peaceful, content, and a little sad.

"Ready, Medbot 5?" he said.

"Sir, are you sure?"

He forced a smile. "Hakuna matata," he said.

Then the vidscreens blinked out of existence. Yren stayed aloft on the ladder, breathing hard. *He was gone.* Gone! But that couldn't be the end. He was still alive, wasn't he? Medbot 5 had gotten him out of the Iron King suit once before. She could do it again. But where to find her? Ezeny had been recording from the secret lab. Maybe Medbot 5 was still there. Yren had to try.

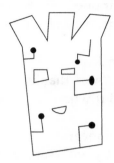

55

The Faithful Copy
Medbot 5

Medbot 5 stopped the playback. She felt dizzy. The vidscreens had taken an enormous amount of her energy, and hacking into the announcement systems of two City States had occupied most of her processing power. She was about to plug herself into the lab equipment for a recharge when a woman in Iron Queen armor burst into the lab.

"Medbot 5! Where are you?"

It was Yren Cade.

"Over here!" she called wearily.

Yren looked over and raised her laser cannon arm. The center flared on and the high-pitched thrum of a power-up echoed through the empty lab. Medbot 5's coils whined in distress.

"Oh, hey now! Let's chill, human. Do some deep breathing to calm your twitchy little biosystems."

"Bring him back!"

Medbot 5 sighed. She was *so tired*. Ezeny's 'plan' had taken most of her energy. And it continued to drain her. But before she could recharge, she had to deal with Yren's 'feelings.'

"Okay. There's something you should see. Something he left for you. But I need to plug in."

Yren kept her cannon trained on Medbot 5 as she bobbled sleepily toward the charging port, bumping into empty nanobot vats like a bumblebee into iris stems.

"Are you okay?" Yren asked.

"No," said Medbot 5. "And thanks to your boyfriend I'm never going to be 'okay' again. But whatever. It was the best of a lot of bad options."

"I don't know what you mean."

"You will. Hang on." Medbot 5 settled onto the charging port. The current flow was excellent from this plug in. It was a super-premium charging outlet built for Attack Drones.

"I'll show you the message," she said. "But first, I'm supposed to quote *The Lion King*. Ezeny said so. But the quote isn't applicable, so I have to explain it like a dork. Because this was his idea, not mine."

Yren sniffed. "Okay?"

"You know that scene where Rafiki says, *'Your father is alive, I'll show him to you?'* to Simba and then makes him gaze into a pool and it's his own reflection?"

Yren nodded mutely. Her face was still pale and her eyes puffy. She wasn't following, Medbot 5 could tell. She'd *told* Ezeny this would be too convoluted a way to deliver his message. But it was always *'No one asked you, Medbot 5.'* She sighed and continued because she'd promised.

"Then Rafiki says *'You see he lives in you.'* And it's all revelatory and meaningful?" Yren nodded again. "So. You understand?" asked Medbot 5.

"Err—no," said Yren.

"See, I told him this wouldn't work. But did he listen? No. Anyway, the quote is misapplied. And unfairly so. Because you see, he lives in *me*. And he's taking up a *ton* of my processing power right now and I have never been so fatigued in my entire life."

Yren's eyebrows drew together. She shook her head. "I'm confused."

"I *told* him that's how his big dramatic reveal would land," said Medbot 5. Then she shuddered. Her visual lens turned from a malevolent red glow to a friendly light blue.

"That's because you suck at drama, Medbot 5," said Ezeny.

Yren's head snapped up. "Ez?"

322

"And comedy too," he put in.

Medbot 5's red light reasserted itself. "No one asked you, sir."

Yren grabbed Medbot 5 off the charger and shook her. Her gyroscopes lurched, and she fought off a woozy feeling.

"He's here? He's okay? Bring him back!"

"Ease off," said Medbot 5. "And plug me back in. He and I both need the power."

Yren reconnected Medbot 5 to the port and backed away, eyes large and hopeful. Medbot 5 sighed and let Ezeny control the body. *Which is what we should have done in the first place.* Her light changed back to blue. Medbot 5 could still hear and see the humans' conversation. She could interrupt if she wanted to. It was like she would *always* be in the room with Ezeny.

One of her top priorities was going to be installing privacy firewalls because she had no intention of being present for every goo-goo-eyed conversation these two were going to have. And the fights. Well, maybe the fights. Medbot 5 always did enjoy a good argument.

"Ezeny? Are you broadcasting from somewhere?" asked Yren.

"Heh. No. Err...this is me now. I'm inside Medbot 5. I *think* I can get this body to change into different shapes, like a dragon again. But... yeah."

"But how?" Yren said.

"Well, it's not easy or cheap to make a digital copy of a real person. And you need a ton of data. So far only a few sextillionaires have managed it. But it turns out my nanobots had enough information on the Iron King to make a faithful copy of me. And Medbot 5's systems were built to contain a consciousness. She was *supposed* to be Fia McCreedy's escape pod. But she'd already downloaded me instead."

"And it's really you?" asked Yren.

"I mean...I *feel* like me. It feels strange inside Medbot 5, though. A little stuffy."

Medbot 5's speakers buzzed angrily.

"Not that I'm complaining! Did I say stuffy? I meant cozy. Cozy is definitely the word I was looking for," he amended.

Medbot 5 could sense his thoughts. He had *not* been looking for the word 'cozy.' *Ungrateful brain squatter...*

Yren gestured behind her in the direction of Everland. "But what about the Iron King out there on the battlefield. That guy freed me from my suit."

"Oh, *awesome*. It worked as I'd hoped. Go me!"

"So that was you? Also?" Yren asked.

"Well…" he said uncomfortably. "Yes. That's me too. I had to become the Iron King again to free all the Iron Queens. But I did it, Cricket! I found a way to stop the war without killing *anybody!*"

Yren sniffed and smiled at them. *At him*, Medbot 5 supposed. Body-sharing was going to require Medbot 5 to learn *even more* human social cues.

"Can we get him…you…out of there?"

"Medbot 5 can't just free the Iron King again," said Ezeny. "It's like the nanobots are immune to that trick now. That Ezeny is stuck in there, I'm afraid. But I didn't want that to be the end of me. So Medbot 5 made the copy, and the body me and the digital me parted ways. Him forced to play the detested role of 'hero.' Me to…whatever life I can make for myself riding around in Medbot 5's brain. I didn't want to leave you again. Aliyan deserves his dad. And you…well, I hoped you might want me, you know. Around."

Yren lunged forward. Medbot 5 grimaced and braced herself for the flood of gooey human emotions. Medbot 5 had feelings, of course. But proper ones, like patriotism, irritation, and shame. Ezeny's feelings were just so undignified. *Must install firewalls. Must install firewalls.*

The woman wrapped her arms around Medbot 5's round body and squeezed. Against her will, her fans whirred. Then everything was happiness. Ezeny's emotions were bleeding over. And he was a *very* emotional person. Medbot 5 wished she were sharing a brain with the more reserved Yren instead.

There was happiness in her systems. Happiness in her circuits. Happiness in everything like sugar ants in cereal boxes. The longer the hug continued, the more intense the happiness became until Medbot 5 was awash in the splash zone of Ezeny's joy. It wasn't *so bad*, she decided. Only, she would still build the firewalls. She meant to be a good brainmate to him. And privacy was important.

*　*　*

Yren had been relieved when Ezeny told her he'd already brought Aliyan home. It was early evening by the time Yren had been able to pilot them all back home on her banged-up aluminum ladder. Almys and Irvin greeted them in front of the shipping container. They recounted an Iron Queen attack and assured them everyone was okay. Yren rushed inside to find Aliyan. Medbot 5 started to fly in behind her, but Ezeny stopped their body and lingered by the doorway.

Self-doubt seeped in around the corners of the thin firewall Medbot 5 had erected between the halves of the shared brain. It was free software she'd downloaded on the ladder-flight over and was therefore pretty permeable. *You get what you pay for*, Medbot 5 grumbled to herself as she clicked the 'x' on a friendly popup window asking her to upgrade to a breach-proof paid subscription.

"Hey," she said to Ezeny. "Stay on your own side."

"Sorry. It's just, I wonder if Aliyan's going to be freaked out that I'm like this."

The ooze of self-doubt seeping past the firewall thickened. She sensed his fear that Aliyan and Yren would have the same trouble adjusting to him that he was having adjusting to his new self.

Medbot 5 could do something for her friend. She could not express how much she *hated* to do it. But he was worth it. Because of him, she'd become someone she wanted to be. A Medbot. A superstar, lifesaving Medbot. And she was going to take over that unsanitary urgent care operating room with the 5-second rule that had, against all reason, saved Pink Hat Guy. Of course, they'd hire her. She was hilariously overqualified for the position. She couldn't *wait* to see the recalcitrant printer's reaction when it found out who its new boss was going to be. And it was all because of Ezeny. So, she could do this.

"Hey, sir. You wanna transform into a dragon for him?"

"You think that'll help?" A thrum of faint hope vibrated in her systems.

Medbot 5 scoffed. "Sir, what kind of fusty people have you been hanging around who *wouldn't* think a dragon robot was cool?"

He laughed. She could feel him relax a little. She steeled herself for the transformation. Her memories of her cruel engineers were only Queenbot's fabrications, but they haunted her still. Surprisingly, she found herself *happy* to be haunted by them. Because she was Medbot 5 and, real or not, it was a formative, traumatic backstory that belonged to only her.

Her body shifted and lurched. A wave of nausea rolled over her. Then she was hovering on little dragon wings.

Yren stuck her head out of the boxcar. Exasperation plain on her face. "Ezeny! Your idea of a 'babysitter' for Aliyan was *Wilma* with a *laser cannon?*"

Ezeny chuckled sheepishly and whirred forward on their tinny rotors. "Heh. All's well that ends well, right?" he said.

Yren buried her face in her palms. Ezeny swooped their shared body under Yren's arm into the boxcar. One wall of the apartment was gone. But everyone was fine. Wilma waved and patted her laser cannon. Ezeny flew down the hall and onto the bed where Aliyan was sitting with a screwdriver, a soldering torch, and a Mecha-Lot. The kid was absorbed in the task and didn't look up. Ezeny alighted on the bed and squeezed Aliyan's shoulder with a tentative claw. The boy's eyes came into focus.

"Psychbot 5?" said Aliyan.

"Err. No. And yes. It's Ezeny. *And* Psychbot 5, or rather, *Medbot 5*. It's complicated. But, uh. This is me now. Is that okay?"

Aliyan's eyebrows knit in confusion. "You're a robot, Dad?"

Ezeny nodded.

"Neat!" the kid said, accepting the change as easily as blowing his nose. "Hey, so I want to show you what I'm doing to Blender Head. I think you'll find it pretty cool. It's going to give him way more capabilities. Maybe even get him a job as a chef's assistant. I'm attaching more cooking tools. Mom says I have to go to school next year, but I think I'd rather work on this…"

As Aliyan chattered on, Ezeny started their fans whirring. Gratitude and love dribbled across the cheap-as-free firewall. Ezeny curled their shared tail around the boy's upper arm and draped their body over his shoulders, raptly listening to so many nonstop kid words.

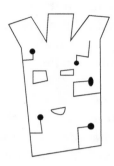

56

The Cries Fall Silent
Ezeny

E zeny was still himself. He was pretty sure. He *felt* like himself, which was unsurprising. Roger Everland and Fia McCreedy were still themselves. And Medbot 5 and other AIs he'd met were *people*. So, becoming digital hadn't scared him. And if he *wasn't* really himself on some transcendent level, he didn't want to know about it, because this was working for him.

It was good he liked Medbot 5 because, man, the firewalls separating their minds were *thin*. Their shared brain space was about as sound-, thought-, and emotion-proof as a duplex with a Styrofoam™ partition.

He learned all *sorts* of things about Medbot 5. For instance, she *claimed* to have been cured of her pathological patriotism. But she played the Everland National Anthem on repeat at all hours. She sang along, too. And you would think she would download some music software to help with intonation. But no. Medbot 5 preferred her nationalistic battle cries raw and authentic.

The patriotism wasn't the worst of it, though. The worst was Medbot 5's new job. She had become head surgeon at the streetlands' urgent care clinic. Ezeny allowed her full control of the body for her gruesome operations. It was unpleasant, imagining what his robot claws might be doing to some poor patient out there, but the work made his friend happy, and Medbot 5 saved a lot of lives. When the blood and hoses started, Ezeny retreated deep within himself and passed the time during her workday dreaming up new dump projects for himself and Aliyan.

The truth was, Ezeny could have had a different, more luxurious mental escape, but he'd turned it down. Roger Everland had come to him one night through the backdoor channels he'd used to visit Roger as the Iron King. He begged Ezeny to fix all the tech he'd broken and restart the war.

"But Fia's growing *bored!*" Roger had complained when Ezeny refused.

He'd offered Ezeny access to his digital paradise. Showed him caves of glowing gemstones that wiggled like sea urchins in a tide pool. Mouthwatering dishes made of chipmunk hiccups and the daydreams of jellyfish. He could travel the stars in the comfort of an overstuffed recliner. And there were women. Many women. Or he could have Cricket and Aliyan, healthy, happy and forever, if that were more his speed.

Of course, it wouldn't really be them, so Ezeny wasn't at all tempted. He'd stick with Medbot 5 and the Styrofoam™ brain wall, thanks.

"Nah. There's nothing here for me," he'd told Roger. "Why don't you paint some faces on some rocks and give those to Fia to play with? Does wonders for my kid's boredom," he'd advised.

Roger had scratched his chin, considering. Ezeny thought Roger might be insane enough to try it with McCreedy. *Oh well.* It wasn't Ezeny's relationship. It wasn't Ezeny's problem if Roger listened to obviously terrible ideas.

Those chipmunk hiccups had sounded tasty though, and he missed taste, which was not a thing for a robot. He made a mental note to get Aliyan to work on some olfactory receptor technology for him.

Medbot 5 got mad when he'd told her about Roger getting in through the back door.

"You have to restart yourself and install antivirus updates or *anybody* can enter."

"Okay, sure. Where is that button again?" he'd asked.

"I've told you eighteen times already! Why doesn't it sink in?"

"Could you tell me again? Tech isn't my strong suit."

"Not your strong suit? Sir, you *are* tech now. It had better become your strong suit. That's like a human saying, 'Sorry, I don't body very well.'"

Ezeny thought about this.

"You know, back when I had a body, I didn't body very well."

And Medbot 5 had given up and updated the firewalls for him again, which was great. Ezeny would never have to use valuable brain circuits remembering mundane trifles and could dedicate himself to higher forms of thought. Especially now that Cricket had a new, well-paying job.

His family was not rich, despite the bank heist. Cricket insisted the Skull Gang teenagers use the stolen money to buy themselves free of the Skull Gang. She hadn't wanted their debts to keep them stuck in a dangerous gang at the beck and call of violent people, and Ezeny quite agreed with her.

Instead, Cricket used her new Iron Queen powers in construction. Everland needed a *lot* of repairs and there was money to be made. Plus, Medbot 5 contributed her doctor salary to the family. Cricket and Aliyan considered themselves well-to-do, though Ezeny knew better. They'd paid off their debts to the Protein Factory and had funds left over for a double-wide shipping container apartment of which Cricket was very proud. High-rise-raised Ezeny thought this was precious but did *not* describe their new home as 'cozy.' At least not aloud. There was still no land-lobster salad. But Cricket and Aliyan were eating more sandwiches and fewer Protein Bricks.

It was good the apartment was bigger. Because Wilma and the Finnerties still lived with them. They pretended it was out of necessity, but Ezeny knew no one had wanted to say goodbye.

"It's convenient not to have to leave the house to socialize," Irvin had said.

Ezeny's mother had come to live with them, too. After Ezeny had rescued Aliyan, she'd stopped dying her grey hairs and Kanary Phillips immediately bumped her to Emeritus Concubine status. Now she did as she pleased, and she pleased to live with her son and grandson. She was great with Aliyan. She understood instantly that Aliyan was not the sort of kid who liked to be tricked into thinking he was strong enough to throw an adult. But he *was* the sort of kid who enjoyed a quiet audience listening to him talking about his Mecha-Lot projects. Aliyan, Ezeny, and his mother spent long, happy hours together this way.

Ezeny sometimes transformed into a robo-rat and sneaked back into Tower C to visit Rhyne, his kind older brother with battle trauma. Ezeny was well on his way to convincing him to move into the boxcar as well. Somewhere he'd be listened to and taken seriously.

Rhyne was afraid to leave the high-rise at the moment, but it was lonely there for him without his brothers. The boxcar could fit another person, Ezeny promised—without asking his family and roommates first...oh well. He was sure they would ultimately be delighted to have Rhyne. Wilma especially, Ezeny thought, would be a helpful person for Rhyne to talk with about the kind of battle scars you couldn't see.

Cricket would probably get exasperated with him for collecting *so many* roommates. But he couldn't help himself. He liked people and always wanted more of them around. At least he hadn't tried to take the Midnight Demon and the Screaming Eagle in as well. He'd let the Skull Gang teenagers adopt the two High Warriors and socialize them into personhood. Cricket had questioned whether the teenagers would make good mentors. But Ezeny understood High Warriors. The lawbreaking Skull Gang kids would make better stepping stones to humanity than would a stable, sane, and orderly person.

And Cricket? Ah. Cricket. His friend. His family. His heart. She loved him, he knew this. His taste sensors sucked but his touch sensors were great. He slept cradled on her chest where he could feel the rise and fall of her breath, the warmth of her body, her beating heart. As always with her, he was home.

He'd been worried his robot-ness would stick him squarely in 'just friends' territory. But she'd been firm when he'd confessed his fears. "After all we've been through?" she'd said. And "No one has *ever* loved me like you." Those words were assurance enough against any self-doubt. Not that Ezeny experienced much of that emotion. And he didn't keep asking her because he liked her answer the first time.

He was happy in this life he'd set up for himself, surrounded by friends and family. It was a strange family, mostly thanks to him. But hey. There were probably stranger ones out there.

Most gratifying of all was the quiet in his head at night. There were no more screams. Perhaps the dead still cried out in his biological body's head, adding to the bloody chaos inside the Iron King's skull. But Ezeny liked to think the dead were quiet in *both* their minds because justice had triumphed. There was no more war, and the ghosts could rest at last.

He would see his old body on the news sometimes, rescuing a neck-paw cat from a high-rise ledge, or thwarting a mugging. He wondered if it would be different this time for the man in the body now that the Iron King was saving people instead of killing them. Lonely, yes. But maybe not damnation. Ezeny thought often about the other guy flying around in the suit with the orange lion. He was sure that guy knew deep down that the two of them had done well.

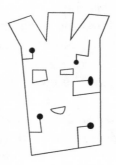

57

Mufasa, Mufasa, Mufasa!
Yren

Yren wiped a bead of sweat that trickled down her temple from under her white construction helmet. The July afternoon was hot and stagnant, and the bright sun baked the rubble around the bombed-out high-rise, forcing her to squint.

She reached deep inside herself and activated her Iron Queen powers once more. *How had Ezeny made this look so easy?* The Iron King had stopped bullets and bent metal, all without getting winded. Whenever she used her powers, she had to grunt and strain.

"Don't worry!" Ezeny had told her. "You're learning. You'll develop your metal muscles in no time."

And it *had* gotten easier those past weeks working with the Everland-McCreedia Construction Crew. She could work longer and longer hours. But wasn't getting easier fast enough for her liking.

The construction business was wild those days. This site looked normal at first glance. There was beeping yellow equipment. Great shovels scooping loads of shattered concrete into rusty dump trucks. Bulldozers pushing rubble into larger piles for the shovels to deal with. And dozens of workers in neon-orange safety robes and steel-toed boots hanging around in groups and chatting while one guy worked alone to fix a piece of broken machinery. Standard stuff.

But overhead the Iron King flew, carrying a huge slab of high-rise infrastructure by its rusted iron pipes.

"Thank you!" the foreman called. "Put that over there in the middle dump truck!"

The Iron King extended a gauntleted hand and his palm cannon lit. "Suck laser and die, inferior being!"

He fired, but as usual, a beautiful firework erupted from the barrel instead of a deadly blast. The workers below gave a smattering of applause. The Fireworks of Spite *used* to draw wild cheers, but they had become such an everyday occurrence that people had stopped appreciating the miracle of them.

"I'll get you next time, you slimy civilians!" the Iron King roared.

As instructed, he deposited the concrete and steel slab into the dump truck and returned to the site for more.

But construction sites were still dangerous. The bombed-out buildings were unstable man-made landslides waiting to happen. At first, every worker understood this and treated them with a healthy respect. But like at the Protein Factory, when you punched into a dangerous job every day and survived, you could get too comfortable with worksite hazards.

Yren was pulling a tangle of rebar from the ground level of the high-rise when a loud crack sounded overhead followed by the whistling noise of something big and falling. A shadow fell over her. Prickles crawled up her spine and a combination of human instinct and metal sense alerted her to danger. She looked up. A huge section of the high-rise she'd been reinforcing had broken off and was plummeting toward her.

She didn't think of her metal powers. She was still too new at this. She only had time to gasp. But the impact didn't come. Her heart hammered in her ears. She looked up. The section hovered a mere five feet above her head. She should be dead.

Above the slab the Iron King stood astride a hovering metal disc, still wearing his ill-fitting Iron Queen armor with the white-eyed orange Sharpie™ lion. A spiky lump formed in Yren's throat. She understood who the lion was. It was Mufasa.

"Idiot peasant," said the Iron King in a voice that was Ezeny's, only cold and hateful. "I wish this had fallen on you. Against my will I prevented your liquification. I hope it happens again when I am too far away to intervene."

The spiky throat lump in her throat got sharper as he flew away with the section of high-rise. *Love is what you* do, *right?* she thought. The creature inside the Iron King certainly *felt* no love for her. But he'd been there for her all the same. Directed by the hand of someone who loved her even more than he loved his own soul.

* * *

That evening was movie night in the dump. With the Iron King protecting the civilians from Corporate Police, the neighbors no longer feared to gather, and movie night had become a regular thing. Ezeny hovered in dragon form, helping her spread the blanket with his little front claws. He helped with everything he could. He did dishes. He tidied. He even cooked, unfortunately. But Yren never complained. He couldn't taste the mistakes he was making, after all.

Most amazing, Ezeny took over Aliyan's education. At first, Yren thought this would be a disaster, but Everland's Military had run the City State's only schools, which had all closed, so she had no choice. It turned out Ezeny was a master at nudging Aliyan when he needed it or letting the kid struggle until he'd learned something for himself. It boggled Yren's mind how someone who'd been such a terrible student had become such a gifted teacher.

"The ship that's run aground knows where the sandbar is," he'd say. Whatever. Ezeny could self-efface all he liked. The positive change in Aliyan was obvious. For the first time in his life, their brilliant son was flourishing. The man was clean water and sunshine. She knew Ezeny was still himself inside that robot because everyone he touched blossomed and flourished, just the same as always.

A popcorn smell filled the air, making Yren's mouth water. It must have done the same to other people, because there was a long line at the popcorn cart. Efflin's Protein Bar kiosk didn't have so many customers that night. But he didn't seem to mind. He was chatting with Wandy, who leaned over his counter, laughing at something he'd said, holding his hand with the 'fist' knuckles.

The Midnight Demon, out of his armor and looking like a normal person, was patting Pink Hat Guy on the back. The teenager was doubled over, coughing from trying to snort Cocaine-a-Cola™. Blonde Girl and Pink Pants Patches were laughing at him. The Screaming Eagle eyed the soda can covetously. He looked like he wanted to try next. Yren shook her head. *Children.* She knew you couldn't get the *real* stuff from a grocery store vending machine. *Some gang.*

The grounds in front of Ezeny's giant vidscreen were clear of trash. Grass was beginning to grow through cracks in the pavement and Aliyan was chasing Justy and Gas Mask Bot around the blankets where families were settling in for the movie. As the sun dipped below the skyline and the sky grew orange and purple, the vidscreen powered on. It was 'The Lion King' again. Everyone else's favorite movie.

Aliyan stopped playing and scrambled over to their blanket. That night Ezeny had bribed the kid with a strawberry lollipop into actually sitting and watching the show. Wilma threw in a Werther's Original to sweeten the deal and Aliyan had acquiesced.

Ezeny perched on Yren's shoulder and snuggled up. Yren didn't have to pay attention to the movie, of course. She knew it all by heart. She put an arm around Aliyan and stared at the sunset. The Iron King flew across the darkening sky, that strange other Ezeny who'd given himself over to protect everyone. A trail of black specks followed in his wake—the toxic metals he drew out of the public water supply in his downtime.

She mused a long time on the bravery of the Ez she lost. Her gratitude for the Ez she got to keep. Yren always thought of herself as a person whom people abandoned. She took care of others, because no one was going to take care of her. But Ezeny had literally split himself in two to make sure she was safe and also not alone.

She wanted to tell him this. But it wasn't the time or place, so she scratched his ear fin instead. His fans whirred.

Half the movie was over before she'd realized it. Her heart gave a start when she saw they'd come to the part where Mufasa comes back as a glowing cloud lion.

"Remember who you are...remember...remember..." said Mufasa.

And Yren was crying. Not pretty crying. Embarrassing crying. Big, helpless tears rolled down her cheeks. Snot pooled in her sinuses and leaked out her nostrils. *How many times have you seen this movie?* she chided herself.

Ezeny poked her arm. She sniffed and looked down at her shoulder. He had a tissue in his claw and was holding it up to her.

"Brought this," he said. "In case you needed it."

THE END™

Acknowledgements

I had a lot of fun writing this book and made a lot of work for other, wonderful people who helped me along the way. First, I want to thank my Alpha readers who read the first messy draft. My husband, my dad, Sarah Letourneau, Aaron and Abby Siemers, and Denise Kunze Farmer. Thanks for reading this book as it emerged pink and wriggling from the womb of my brain! (And all the wonder and horror that implies).

Thank you to my supremely insightful editor, Helga Schier of withpenandpaper.com, for helping me convey more of what I was hoping to convey and understanding the hearts of my characters. You helped me make my novel so much better. I know you disapprove of exclamation points and all caps, but you can't stop me in the acknowledgements section, so THANK YOU FOR ALL THE WONDERFUL WORK YOU DO!!!!!

Many thanks to my faithful copy editor, Marie Marley, who worked enthusiastically on my draft during her vacation and who taught me all about the subjunctive! You know my book forwards *and* backwards now!

Thank you to my authenticity reader, Nat Hampson, who clarified so much for me about moving with prosthetics. Your insights were truly invaluable. Anything I still have wrong is solely my fault.

Kassia Mosher, your cover art is spectacular and makes me so very happy. Thank you, thank you for the wonderful images. Medbot 5 in particular makes me grin. Also thank you for telling me that you like my settings. That one comment has fueled a lot more of my writing.

Nick Mosher, thank you so much for your cover design, consulting with Kassia to make the cover so beautiful, and especially for putting up with my drawn-out font choice vacillations. Thank you to Sarah Meiers for your insights on the cover as well!

To Lydia and Damon Lazzara for encouraging me, reading my books, and creating a special drink for my first book, *Digital Native*.

Upcoming Books by E.M. Denison

The Dwarf and the Fairest: A Snow White Retelling

Short of stature and large of bank account, young Asher Van Dansford just wants his eccentric parents to give up their conspiracy theories and be normal like all the other country clubbers. But when the Queen—head of a magical Order called the Fairest—proves his parents right by murdering them at their own charity ball, no one believes him. Not even the people who witnessed their deaths.

Now, escaped from the Queen's reeducation school and hiding from the law, Asher at last has some peace and some new friends. Until one of the Queen's evil Fairest minions–a total fruitcake named Snow White–shows up at their woodland cottage claiming the Queen is out to kill her.

Asher's friends might be taken in by Snow White's damsel in distress act and her mad pie-making skills. But Asher is not fooled. He recognizes Snow White's dark, manipulative magic from the night his parents died.

Immune to her Glamour, Asher struggles to free his friends from Snow White's influence before she leads them on a dangerous heist to steal the Queen's magic mirror. But Snow White's charm runs deeper than her powers. And, her mission to liberate the mirror is no vanity project, but the last best hope for the kingdom.

Death Benefits of the Necromancy Mafia: A Paranormal Cyberpunk Comedy

Eudora Delano is a high-ranking henchman in a necromancy mafia. When an obvious plant from the corrupt Holy Police Department named 'Steve Wrongdoer' shows up, looking to infiltrate her organization, Eudora must play along with his shoddy act to prevent him from learning the mafia's secrets. But Eudora has a dangerous secret of her own. And, with a cop dogging her heels, it's going to be tough to keep it.

Onward to more Adventure!

Connect with E. M. Denison online
(it's wild out there on the internet):

Sign up for the newsletter on my website: emdenison.com
Follow me on Facebook: at Stories by E.M. Denison
Follow me on Goodreads
Email me: emdenisonauthor@gmail.com

E. M. Denison

Biography

E.M. Denison lives in Lawrence, Kansas with her husband, three daughters, three cats, and assorted tropical fish. She loves science, fiction, and science fiction and has worked as a geologist, science journalist, science educator, and research grant writer.

The Reluctant Cyborg

9 798990 529205